December 2007

Madeleine x

# LINE
# DANCING

# LINE
# DANCING

## Stories from East Anglia

Chosen by
Peter Tolhurst

Foreword by
## Julie Myerson

Black Dog Books

First published in England 2003
by Black Dog Books
104 Trinity Street, Norwich, Norfolk, NR2 2BJ.

Foreword © Julie Myerson 2003.
Stories © Individual Authors/Authors' estates.

A CIP record of this book is available from the British Library.

ISBN  0-9528839-7-X

Typeset in 11 point Berkely Book.


Printed in Great Britain
by Biddles Ltd., *www.biddles.co.uk*.

# Contents

# Acknowledgements

I would like to thank the following for permission to reproduce copyright material:

For *Never Ending Rainbow* by Tessa Newcomb, the artist and David Messum Fine Art; for *Hilda's Letter* from *The Complete Short Stories of L P Hartley* (1973) published by Hamish Hamilton, the Society of Authors; for *Summer People* from *After Bathing at Baxters* (1997), D J Taylor; for *Water* by Henry Sutton, Rogers Coleridge & White; for *Two Children* from *The Innocent and the Guilty* (1971) and *Elphenor and Weasel* from *Kingdoms of Elphin* (1977), both published by the Random House Group, Susanna Pinney©; for *Negative Equity* from *Evangelista's Fan* (1995) by Rose Tremain, published by Vintage, Sheil Land Associates; for *The Custodian* from *A Bit of Singing and Dancing* (1973) by Susan Hill, published by Penguin, Sheil Land Associates; for *The Storm* from *Regeneration* (1991) by Pat Barker, published by Viking, Gillon Aitkin Associates; for *Oh Whistle and I'll Come to you my Lad* from *Collected Ghost Stories* (1931) by M R James, Nick James; for *Sea Lavender* from *Phosphorescence* (2003), Raffaella Barker; for *Funeral in the Fens* by Edward Storey, David Higham Associates; for *What The Sky Sees*, Jon McGregor; for *Gap Kids*, Julia Bell; for *The Journal Of Miss Joan Martyn* in *The Complete Shorter Fiction Of Virginia Woolf* (1985), published by the Hogarth Press, the Random House Group; for *Weeds* from *The Copper Peacock* (1991) published by Hutchinson, Ruth Rendell; for *Master of None* and *Arnulf and Esther*, Ronald Blythe; for *The Shield* from *Acky* (1973) by George Ewart Evans, published by Faber and Faber, Mathew Evans on behalf of the author's estate; for *A Clean Death* from *Pack of Cards* (1986) by Penelope Lively, published by Heinemann, David Higham Associates, for *Home Win*, Marilyn Tolhurst; for *Cyd's Cafe*, Bernadine Coverley.

My thanks also to Lesley Kershaw for tea and techno.

Peter Tolhurst
Black Dog Books
2003

# *Foreword*

## JULIE MYERSON

Of this collection of 22 stories you're about to read – some of them very new, others much older – a startling number share a common thread: they're spooky and the fact that they're published by Black Dog Books is no coincidence. Even if not openly concerned with actual ghosts, many contain elements of haunting sadness, lost souls, emotional bleakness.

Or maybe it's not so startling. Because there undoubtedly is something unnerving about East Anglia. Whether it's those huge skies, that almost aggressively flat landscape – or the sheer, slightly agoraphobic sense that the world could at any moment tilt and swallow you up – it's a place that makes the heart race, the blood quicken. It's a landscape that makes you tread cautiously, glance behind you, check your tracks. In fact, if it weren't for its windswept, eerily unsteadying beauty I would have run from it long ago.

About two years ago, I began researching my novel *Something Might Happen*. I didn't know exactly what I was going to write – only that it would be set in Suffolk, a place I've had a passion for since I first went there on holiday when I was eight. I say I was researching, but mostly – as writers tend to – I just used the smokescreen of writing a novel as an excuse to spend more time there. So my three children and I did all the things we'd always done – crabbing at Walberswick, sandwiches from the fish man in Southwold, tennis-ball cricket up on Gun Hill, long walks on the beach at dusk as a pink liquid sun slips down behind the dunes.

It wasn't all play. I did set myself to some proper research and I determinedly read through as many creepy tales of East Anglia as I could find. You know the kind of thing – thin shiny stapled books of ghost stories and local legends, stocked by the newsagents on the High Streets of Southwold, Aldeburgh, Reydon.

It was while staying in my friend Esther Freud's cottage on Walberswick

Green, that I first read the story of Old Shock (aka Black Shuck). He is the huge black dog 'with a matted shaggy coat and green eyes' said to have appeared to poor souls just about everywhere from Bungay to – yes – Walberswick. It was a hair-raising tale – if only because of the sheer apparent number of sightings – and I decided not to alert my kids to it (Jake was then twelve, Chloë ten and Raphael nine). In fact, like any good parent, I hid the book.

Anyway, dusk fell. Jake and Chloë went as usual to walk Betty, our reliably enthusiastic Border Collie. They hurried off, chatting – relishing the independence of swerving away down the darkening lane and out of my sight, something rarely allowed in London. I poured myself a glass of wine and enjoyed the peace.

It was short-lived. Less than ten minutes later they came rushing back, panicky excitement on their faces. By now it was almost dark: the light had drained suddenly, the way it can in East Anglia. A moment previously you could see right across The Green, but now all I could hear was the distant sound of kids being called in to bed or bath; all you could make out was the white of Jake's T shirt, the sudden pallor of Chloë's face.

'We were chased!' she announced breathlessly.

'Well, followed,' said Jake, shuddering, 'We thought we should get back.'

I was concerned. 'What do you mean followed? Who followed you?'

They looked at each other. 'An animal.'

'Like a dog – kind of. But bigger than a dog.'

'A black dog the size of a lion!' said Chloë, 'It was on the other side of the hedge. We could hear it breathing. It was awful. We ran.'

'But it kept going,' said Jake, 'Every time we moved, it moved!'

I said I was sure it was nothing. We retraced their steps, to the hole in the hedge where they'd first glimpsed it. Only the sly rustle of leaves in the evening wind. Jake then added that Betty hadn't seemed to notice the animal - hadn't even barked or pulled at the lead. This, we knew, was hugely out of character.

'It must be someone's pet,' I said, 'A Great Dane or something.' I sounded convinced but I wasn't. If they'd read and memorised the tale I'd just read, my kids couldn't have described Black Shuck better. Had I somehow summoned their vision, just by reading the story? Even the hyper-imaginative novelist in me knew this was a ludicrous idea. Meanwhile the Mum in me put the kids to bed, locked all the doors and watched some comfortingly inane TV.

And no, I never told them. And no, I can't explain it. But I do know one thing. This area has always unnerved and haunted me. In the Sixties we'd drive every August from Nottingham to spend a summer fortnight at Henstead Hall – a huge, dilapidated (and spooky) country house hotel, where peacocks screamed on the lawns and bats swooped under the cedars at dusk. Every year we tried to catch the bats with our fishing nets (we never succeeded).

And then, every morning we'd take a packed lunch – hard-boiled eggs and floppy ham sandwiches wrapped in greaseproof paper – to what I now know is probably the loneliest beach in all England. Benacre was a desolate place – unreachable except by an hour's walk through cornfields, with its Second World War pillboxes sliding down into the saltwater lake and its dangerously shelved shingle beach. It still is desolate. Even the groynes seem to point black, accusing fingers up at the sky.

No wonder, then, that this unforgiving coastline has inspired so many uneasy stories, so many sombre insights of loss, madness and woe. The deadpan, landlocked claustrophobia of Jon McGregor's *What The Sky Sees*, for instance, could only take root in East Anglia. 'People don't come here because they've been drawn by the romantic sound of the place,' states his disturbed narrator, '. . . the poetry of this place is not in the names but in the shapes, the flatness, the bigness, the completeness of the landscape. Only what is beneath the surface of the earth is hidden, everything else between you and the landscape is visible.'

This theme of 'bigness' that McGregor pins down so chillingly lingers in many of these stories. *The Lost Housen* by Mary Mann is a devastating, century-old tale of ruin and waste, of suicide and madness that – you feel - has somehow been wrought by the landscape itself. The same is true in a differently coloured way in the strikingly modern *Water* by Henry Sutton. Here our narrator perceives himself somehow altered by the 'shockingly sunny days' and the sudden thunderstorms. He is driven to act out of character by . . . what? Is it the landscape, is it the weather? Who knows, it's an East Anglia thing.

Meanwhile, in *Negative Equity*, Rose Tremain's anxious coast watcher is drawn to his fate as if to a kind of sickness. He has premonitions that something might happen to him and his final progress into darkness seems to have a nauseating inevitability, a terrible contrast to the sparkling brightness above the water.

There are lighter, funnier stories here too. In *Summer People*, D J Taylor perfectly captures the quirky, pent-up comedy of this coast – the rules, the gossip, the snobbery and ritual. And Bernardine Coverley's *Cyd's Cafe* is somehow refreshingly down to earth and urban. It goes against the spooked grain – showing Suffolk small-town life in all its gentle mundanity.

And then there's the one story that I realised I already knew. I say 'realised' because M R James's unashamedly terrifying *Oh Whistle My Lad And I'll Come To You* was all but lost from my memory. What I didn't know was that it had settled like dark sediment somewhere deep in my consciousness. I think I devoured it as a teenager under the bedclothes (and no doubt had to sleep with the light on after). This story contains a dream where a man is being chased along the shoreline by a 'figure in pale, fluttering draperies, ill-defined . . . it would stop, raise arms, bow itself towards the sand, then run stooping across the beach to the water-edge and back again; and then, rising upright, once more continue its course forward at a speed that was startling and terrifying.' Finally, in a movement that I still find inexplicably chilling, the phantom (or whatever it is) seems to stop and consider a moment before darting deliberately 'straight forward towards the groyne'.

I don't quote this dream to spoil the story for you – trust me, I haven't. I quote it because I find, to my surprise and shock, that it's been with me all these years. That collision of beach, night, groyne and pursuit, that moment of deliberation and then sudden speed on the part of the pursuer amounts to one of the most frightening things I've ever read.

I thought I'd forgotten it but I hadn't. Old tales make their mark on you, they leave their scars. It may even be why I found myself writing my very own scary novel set in East Anglia. It's almost certainly why I still catch myself glancing back over my shoulder when I'm there.

*Coastlines*

**L P Hartley** never lived in Norfolk but it is no coincidence that his two best known works, the *Eustace and Hilda* trilogy (1944-47) and *The Go Between* (1954), are both set in the county during the years of his Edwardian childhood. Brought up in the fens, it is clear from his depiction of Hunstanton (Anchorstone) in *The Shrimp and the Anemone* that Hartley was familiar with the resort from family holidays. Chronologically *Hilda's Letter*, published in his short story collection *The White Wand* (1954), appears in the 1958 omnibus edition of the trilogy between volumes one (*The Shrimp and the Anemone*) and two (*The Sixth Heaven*)

# Hilda's Letter

## L P HARTLEY

It may take time to get over an obsession, even after the roots have been pulled out. Eustace was satisfied that 'going away' did not mean that he was going to die; but at moments the fiery chariot still cast its glare across his mind, and he was thankful to shield himself behind the prosaic fact that going away meant nothing worse than going to school. In other circumstances the thought of going to school would have alarmed him; but as an alternative to death it was almost welcome.

Unconsciously he tried to inoculate himself against the future by aping the demeanour of the schoolboys he saw about the streets or playing on the beach at Anchorstone. He whistled, put his hands in his pockets, swayed as he walked, and assumed the serious but detached air of someone who owes fealty to a masculine corporation beyond the ken of his womenfolk: a secret society demanding tribal peculiarities of speech and manner. As to the thoughts and habits of mind which should inspire these outward gestures, he found them in school stories; and if they were sometimes rather lurid they were much less distressing than the fiery chariot.

His family was puzzled by his almost eager acceptance of the trials in store. His aunt explained it as yet another instance of Eustace's indifference to home-ties, and an inevitable consequence of the money he had inherited from Miss Fothergill. She had to remind herself to be fair to him whenever she thought of this undeserved success. But to his father the very fact that it was undeserved made Eustace something of a hero. His son was a dark horse who had romped home, and the sight of Eustace often gave him a pleasurable tingling, an impulse to laugh and make merry, such as may greet the evening paper when it brings news of a win. A lad of such mettle would naturally want to go to school.

To Minney her one time charge was now more than ever 'Master' Eustace; in other ways her feeling for him remained unchanged by anything that happened to him. He was just her little boy who was

3

obeying the natural order of things by growing up. Barbara was too young to realize that the hair she sometimes pulled belonged to an embryo schoolboy. In any case, she was an egotist, and had she been older she would have regarded her brother's translation to another sphere from the angle of how it affected her. She would have set about finding other strings to pull now that she was denied his hair.

Thus, the grown-ups, though they did not want to lose him, viewed Eustace's metamorphosis without too much misgiving; and moreover they felt that he must be shown the forbearance and accorded the special privileges of one who has an ordeal before him. Even Aunt Sarah, who did not like the whistling or the hands in the pockets or the slang, only rebuked them half-heartedly.

But Hilda, beautiful, unapproachable Hilda, could not reconcile herself to the turn events had taken. Was she not and would she not always be nearly four years older than her brother Eustace? Was she not his spiritual adviser, pledged to make him a credit to her and to himself and to his family?

He was her care, her task in life. Indeed, he was much more than that; her strongest feelings centred in him and at the thought of losing him she felt as if her heart was being torn out of her body.

So while Eustace grew more perky, Hilda pined. She had never carried herself well, but now she slouched along, hurrying past people she knew as if she had important business to attend to, and her beauty, had she been aware of it, might have been a pursuer she was trying to shake off.

Eustace must not go to school, he must not. She knew he would not want to, when the time came; but then it would be too late. She had rescued him from Anchorstone Hall, the lair of the highwayman, Dick Staveley, his hero and her *bête noire*; and she would rescue him again. But she must act, and act at once.

It was easy to find arguments. School would be bad for him. It would bring out the qualities he shared with other little boys, qualities which could be kept in check if he remained at home.

'What are little boys made of?' she demanded, and looked round in triumph when Eustace ruefully but dutifully answered:

> 'Snips and snails and puppy-dogs' tails
> And that's what they are made of.'

He would grow rude and unruly and start being cruel to animals. Schoolboys always were. And he would fall ill; he would have a return of his bronchitis. Anchorstone was a health-resort. Eustace (who loved statistics and had a passion for records) had told her that Anchorstone had the ninth lowest death-rate in England. (This thought had brought him some fleeting comfort in the darkest hours of his obsession.) If he went away from Anchorstone he might die. They did not want him to die, did they?

Her father and her aunt listened respectfully to Hilda. Since her mother's death they had treated her as if she was half grown up, and they often told each other that she had an old head on young shoulders.

Hilda saw that she had impressed them and went on to say how much better Eustace was looking, which was quite true, and how much better behaved he was, except when he was pretending to be a schoolboy (Eustace reddened at this). And, above all, what a lot he knew; far more than most boys of his age, she said. Why, besides knowing that Anchorstone had the ninth lowest death-rate in England, he knew that Cairo had the highest death-rate in the world, and would speedily have been wiped out had it not also had the highest birth-rate. (This double pre-eminence made the record-breaking city one of Eustace's favourite subjects of contemplation.) And all this he owed to Aunt Sarah's teaching.

Aunt Sarah couldn't help being pleased; she was well-educated herself and knew that Eustace was quick at his lessons.

'I shouldn't be surprised if he gets into quite a high class,' his father said; 'you'll see, he'll be bringing home a prize or two, won't you, Eustace?'

'Oh, but boys don't always learn much at school,' objected Hilda.

'How do you know they don't?' said Mr. Cherrington teasingly. 'She never speaks to any other boys, does she, Eustace?'

But before Eustace had time to answer, Hilda surprised them all by saying: 'Well, I do, so there! I spoke to Gerald Steptoe!'

Everyone was thunderstruck to hear this, particularly Eustace, because Hilda had always had a special dislike for Gerald Steptoe, who was a sturdy, round-faced, knockabout boy with rather off-hand manners.

'I met him near the post office,' Hilda said, 'and he took off his cap, so I had to speak to him, hadn't I?'

Eustace said nothing. Half the boys in Anchorstone, which was only a small place, knew Hilda by sight and took their caps off when they passed her in the street, she was so pretty; and grown-up people used to stare at her, too, with a smile dawning on their faces. Eustace had often seen Gerald Steptoe take off his cap to Hilda, but she never spoke to him if she could help it, and would not let Eustace either.

Aunt Sarah knew this.

'You were quite right, Hilda. I don't care much for Gerald Steptoe, but we don't want to be rude to anyone, do we?'

Hilda looked doubtful.

'Well, you know he goes to a school near the one – St Ninian's – that you want to send Eustace to.'

'Want to! That's good,' said Mr. Cherrington. 'He is going, poor chap, on the seventeenth of January – that's a month from today – aren't you, Eustace? Now don't you try to unsettle him, Hilda.'

Eustace looked nervously at Hilda and saw the tears standing in her eyes.

'Don't say that to her, Alfred,' said Miss Cherrington. 'You can see she minds much more than he does.'

Hilda didn't try to hide her tears, as some girls would have; she just brushed them away and gave a loud sniff.

'It isn't Eustace's feelings I'm thinking about. If he wants to leave us all, let him. I'm thinking of his – his education.' She paused, and noticed that at the word education their faces grew grave. 'Do you know what Gerald told me?'

'Well, what did he tell you?' asked Mr. Cherrington airily, but Hilda saw he wasn't quite at his ease.

'He told me they didn't teach the boys *anything* at St Ninian's,' said Hilda. 'They just play games all the time. They're very good at games, he said, better than his school – I can't remember what it's called.'

'St. Cyprian's,' put in Eustace. Any reference to a school made him feel self-important.

'I knew it was another saint. But the boys at St. Ninian's aren't saints at all, Gerald said. They're all the sons of rich swanky people who go there to do nothing. Gerald said that what they don't know would fill books.'

There was a pause. No one spoke, and Mr. Cherrington and his sister exchanged uneasy glances.

'I expect he exaggerated, Hilda,' said Aunt Sarah. 'Boys do exaggerate sometimes. It's a way of showing off. I hope Eustace won't learn to. As you know, Hilda, we went into the whole thing very thoroughly. We looked through twenty-nine prospectuses before we decided, and your father thought Mr Waghorn a very gentlemanly, understanding sort of man.'

'The boys call him "Old Foghorn",' said Hilda, and was rewarded by seeing Miss Cherrington stiffen in distaste. 'And they imitate him blowing his nose, and take bets about how many times he'll clear his throat during prayers. I don't like having to tell you this,' she added virtuously, 'but I thought I ought to.'

'What are bets, Daddy?' asked Eustace, hoping to lead the conversation into safer channels.

'Bets, my boy?' said Mr. Cherrington. 'Well, if you think something will happen and another fellow doesn't, and you bet him sixpence that it will, then if it does he pays you sixpence, and if it doesn't you pay him sixpence.

Eustace was thinking that this was a very fair arrangement when Miss Cherrington said, 'Please don't say "you", Alfred, or Eustace might imagine that you were in the habit of making bets yourself.

'Well – ' began Mr. Cherrington.

'Betting is a very bad habit,' said Miss Cherrington firmly, 'and I'm sorry to hear that the boys of St. Ninian's practise it – if they do: again, Gerald may have been exaggerating, and it is quite usual, I imagine, for the boys of one school to run down another. But there is no reason that Eustace should learn to. To be exposed to temptation is one thing, to give way is another, and resistance to temptation is a valuable form of self-discipline.'

'Oh, but they don't resist!' said Hilda. 'And Eustace wouldn't either. You know how he likes to do the same as everyone else. And if any boy, especially any new boy, tries to be good and different from the rest they tease him and call him some horrid name (Gerald wouldn't tell me what it was), and sometimes punch him, too.'

Eustace, who had always been told he must try to be good in all circumstances, turned rather pale and looked down at the floor.

'Now, now, Hilda,' said her father, impatiently. 'You've said quite enough. You sound as if you didn't want Eustace to go to school.'

But Hilda was unabashed. She knew she had made an impression on the grown-ups.

'Oh, it's only that I want him to go to the right school, isn't it, Aunt Sarah?' she said. 'We shouldn't like him to go to a school where he learned bad habits and – and nothing else, should we? He would be much better off as he is now, with you teaching him and me helping. Gerald said they really knew *nothing*; he said he knew more than the oldest boys at St. Ninian's, and he's only twelve.'

'But he does boast, doesn't he?' put in Eustace timidly. 'You used to say so yourself, Hilda.' Hilda had never had a good word for Gerald Steptoe before today.

'Oh, yes, you all boast,' said Hilda sweepingly. 'But I don't think he was boasting. I asked him how much he knew, and he said, The Kings and Queens of England, so I told him to repeat them and he broke down at Richard II. Eustace can say them perfectly, and he's only ten, so you see for the next four years he wouldn't be learning anything, he'd just be forgetting everything, wouldn't he, Aunt Sarah? Don't let him go, I'm sure it would be a mistake.'

Minney, Barbara's nurse, came bustling in. She was rather short and had soft hair and gentle eyes. 'Excuse me, Miss Cherrington,' she said, 'but it's Master Eustace's bedtime.'

Eustace said goodnight. Hilda walked with him to the door and when they were just outside she said in a whisper:

'I think I shall be able to persuade them.'

'But I think I want to go, Hilda!' muttered Eustace.

'It isn't what you want, it's what's good for you,' exclaimed Hilda, looking at him with affectionate fierceness. As she turned the handle of the drawing-room door she overhead her father saying to Miss Cherrington: 'I shouldn't pay too much attention to all that, Sarah. If the boy didn't want to go it would be different. As the money's his, he ought to be allowed to please himself. But he'll be all right, you'll see.'

The day passed and Hilda wept in secret. Sometimes she wept openly, for she knew how it hurt Eustace to see her cry. When he asked her why she was crying she wouldn't tell him at first, but just shook her head. Later on she said, 'You know quite well: why do you ask me?' and, of course, Eustace did know. It made him unhappy to know he was making her unhappy and besides, as the time to leave home drew nearer, he became much less sure that he liked the prospect. Hilda saw that he was weakening and she played upon his fears and gave him *Eric or Little by Little* as a Christmas present, to warn him of what he might expect when he went to school. Eustace read it and was extremely worried; he didn't see how he could possibly succeed where a boy as clever, and handsome, and good as Eric had been before he went to school, had failed. But it did not make him want to turn back, for he now felt that if school was going to be an unpleasant business, all the more must he go through with it – especially as it was going to be unpleasant for him, and not for anyone else; which would have been an excuse for backing out. 'You see it won't really matter,' he explained to Hilda, 'they can't kill me – Daddy said so – and he said they don't even roast boys at preparatory schools, only at public schools, and I shan't be going to a public school for a long time, if ever. I expect they will just do a few things to me like pulling my hair and twisting my arm and perhaps kicking me a little, but I shan't really mind that. It was much worse all that time after Miss Fothergill died, because then I didn't know what was going to happen and now I do know, so I shall be prepared.' Hilda was nonplussed by this argument, all the more so because it was she who had told Eustace that it was always good for you to do something you didn't like. 'You say so now,' she said, 'but you won't say so on the seventeenth of January.' And when Eustace said nothing but only looked rather sad and worried she burst into tears. 'You're so selfish,' she sobbed. 'You only think about being good – as if that mattered – you don't think about me at all. I shan't eat or drink anything while you are away, and I shall probably die.'

Eustace was growing older and he did not really believe that Hilda would do this, but the sight of her unhappiness and the tears (which sometimes started to her eyes unbidden the moment he came into the room where she was) distressed him very much. Already, he thought, she was growing thinner, there were hollows in her cheeks, she was silent, or spoke in snatches, very fast and with far more vehemence and emphasis than the occasion called for; she came in late for meals and never apologized, she had never been interested in clothes, but now she was positively untidy. The grown-ups, to his surprise, did not seem to notice.

He felt he must consult someone and thought at once of Minney, because she was the easiest to talk to. But he knew she would counsel patience; that was her idea, that people would come to themselves if they were left alone. Action was needed and she wouldn't take any action. Besides, Hilda had outgrown Minney's influence; Minney wasn't drastic enough to cut any ice with her. Aunt Sarah would be far more helpful because she understood Hilda. But she didn't understand Eustace and would make him feel that he was making a fuss about nothing, or if he did manage to persuade her that Hilda was unhappy she would somehow lay the blame on him. There remained his father. Eustace was nervous of consulting his father, because he never knew what mood he would find him in. Mr Cherrington could be very jolly and treat Eustace almost as an equal; then something Eustace said would upset him and he would get angry and make Eustace wish he had never spoken. But since Miss Fothergill's death his attitude to Eustace had changed. His outbursts of irritation were much less frequent and he often asked Eustace his opinion and drew him out and made him feel more self-confident. It all depended on finding him in a good mood.

Of late Mr. Cherrington had taken to drinking a whisky and soda and smoking a cigar when he came back from his office in Ousemouth; this was at about six o'clock, and he was always alone then, in the drawing-room, because Miss Cherrington did not approve of this new habit. When he had finished she would go in and throw open the windows, but she never went in while he was there.

Eustace found him with his feet up enveloped in the fumes of whisky and cigar smoke, which seemed to Eustace the very being and breath of manliness. Mr. Cherrington stirred. The fragrant cloud rolled away and his face grew more distinct.

"Hullo,' he said, 'here's the Wild Man.' The Wild Man from Borneo was in those days an object of affection with the general public. 'Sit down and make yourself comfortable. Now, what can I do for you?'

The armchair was too big for Eustace: his feet hardly touched the floor. 'It's about Hilda,' he said.

'Well, Hilda's a nice girl, what about her?' said Mr. Cherrington, his voice still jovial. Eustace hesitated and then said with a rush:

'You see, she doesn't want me to go to school.'

Mr. Cherrington frowned, and sipped at his glass.

'I know, we've heard her more than once on that subject. She thinks you'll get into all sorts of bad ways.' His voice sharpened; it was too bad that his quiet hour should be interrupted by these nursery politics. 'Have you been putting your heads together? Have you come to tell me you don't want to go either?'

Eustace's face showed the alarm he felt at his father's change of tone.

'Oh, *no* Daddy. At least – well – I . . . '

'You *dont* want to go. That's clear,' his father snapped.

'Yes, I do. But you see . . . 'Eustace searched for a form of words which wouldn't lay the blame too much on Hilda and at the same time excuse him for seeming to shelter behind her. 'You see, though she's older than me she's only a *girl* and she doesn't understand that men have to do certain things' – Mr. Cherrington smiled, and Eustace took heart - 'well, like going to school.'

'Girls go to school, too,' Mr. Cherrington said. Eustace tried to meet this argument. 'Yes, but it's not the same for them. You see, girls are always nice to each other; why, they always call each other by their Christian names even when they're at school. Fancy that! And they never bet or (Eustace looked nervously at the whisky decanter) or drink, or use bad language, or kick each other, or roast each other in front of a slow fire.' Thinking of the things that girls did not do to each other, Eustace began to grow quite pale.

'All the better for them, then,' said Mr. Cherrington robustly. 'School seems to be the place for girls. But what's all this leading you to?'

'I don't mind about those things,' said Eustace eagerly. 'I . . . I should quite enjoy them. And I shouldn't even mind, well, you know, not being so good for a change, if it was only for a time. But Hilda thinks it might make me ill as well. Of course, she's quite mistaken, but she says she'll miss me so much and worry about me, that she'll never have a peaceful moment, and she'll lose her appetite and perhaps pine away and . . . ' He

10

paused, unable to complete the picture. 'She doesn't know I'm telling you all this, and she wouldn't like me to, and at school they would say it was telling tales, but I'm not at school yet, am I? Only I felt I must tell you because then perhaps you'd say I'd better not go to school, though I hope you won't.'

Exhausted by the effort of saying so many things that should (he felt) have remained locked in his bosom, and dreading an angry reply, Eustace closed his eyes. When he opened them his father was standing up with his back to the fireplace. He took the cigar from his mouth and puffed out an expanding cone of rich blue smoke.

'Thanks, old chap,' he said. 'I'm very glad you told me, and I'm not going to say you shan't go to school. Miss Fothergill left you the money for that purpose, so we chose the best school we could find; and why Hilda should want to put her oar in I can't imagine – at least, I can, but I call it confounded cheek. The very idea!' his father went on, working himself up and looking at Eustace as fiercely as if it was his fault, while Eustace trembled to hear Hilda criticized. 'What she needs is to go to school herself. Yes, that's what she needs.' He took a good swig at the whisky, his eyes brightened and his voice dropped. 'Now I'm going to tell you something, Eustace, only you must keep it under your hat.'

'Under my hat?' repeated Eustace, mystified. 'My hat's in the hall. Shall I go and get it?'

His father laughed. 'No, I mean you must keep it to yourself. You mustn't tell anyone, because nothing's decided yet.'

'Shall I cross my heart and swear?' asked Eustace anxiously. 'Of course, I'd rather not.'

'You can do anything you like with yourself as long as you don't tell Hilda,' his father remarked, 'but just see the door's shut.'

Eustace tiptoed to the door and cautiously turned the handle several times, after each turn giving the handle a strong but surreptitious tug. Coming back still more stealthily, he whispered, 'It's quite shut.'

'Very well, then.' said Mr. Cherrington. 'Now give me your best ear.'

'My best ear, Daddy?' said Eustace, turning his head from side to side. 'Oh, I see!' and he gave a loud laugh which he immediately stifled. 'You just want me to listen carefully.'

'You've hit it,' and between blue, fragrant puffs Mr. Cherrington began to outline his plan for Hilda.

While his father was speaking Eustace's face grew grave, and every now and then he nodded judicially. Though his feet still swung clear of the

11

floor, to be taken into his father's confidence seemed to add inches to his stature.

'Well, old man, that's what I wanted to tell you,' said his father at length. 'Only you mustn't let on, see? Mum's the word.'

'Wild horses won't drag it out of me, Daddy,' said Eustace earnestly.

'Well, don't you let them try. By the way, I hear your friend Dick Staveley's back.'

Eustace started. The expression of an elder statesman faded from his face and he suddenly looked younger than his years.

'Oh, is he? I expect he's just home for the holidays.'

'No, he's home for some time, he's cramming for Oxford or something.'

'Cramming?' repeated Eustace. His mind suddenly received a most disagreeable impression of Dick, his hero, transformed into a turkey strutting and gobbling round a farmyard.

'Being coached for the 'Varsity. It may happen to you one day. Somebody told me they'd seen him, and I thought you might be interested. You liked him, didn't you?'

'Oh, *yes*,' said Eustace. Intoxicating visions began to rise, only to be expelled by the turn events had taken. 'But it doesn't make much difference now, does it? I mean, I shouldn't be able to go there, even if he asked me.'

Meanwhile, Hilda on her side had not been idle. She turned over in her mind every stratagem and device she could think of that might keep Eustace at home. Since the evening when she so successfully launched her bombshell about the unsatisfactory state of education and morals at St. Ninian's, she felt she had been losing ground. Eustace did not respond, as he once used to, to the threat of terrors to come; he professed to be quite pleased at the thought of being torn limb from limb by older stronger boys. She didn't believe he was really unmoved by such a prospect, but he successfully pretended to be. When she said that it would make her ill he seemed to care a great deal more; for several days he looked as sad as she did, and he constantly, and rather tiresomely, begged her to eat more – requests which Hilda received with a droop of her long, heavy eyelids and a sad shake of her beautiful head. But lately Eustace hadn't seemed to care so much. When Christmas came he suddenly discovered the fun of pulling crackers. Before this year he wouldn't even stay in the room if crackers were going off; but now he revelled in them and made almost as much noise as they did, and his father even persuaded him to grasp the naked strip of cardboard with the explosive in the middle, which stung your fingers and made even grown-ups pull faces. Crackers bored Hilda;

12

the loudest report did not make her change her expression, and she would have liked to tell Eustace how silly he looked as, with an air of triumph, he clasped the smoking fragment; but she hadn't the heart to. He might be at school already, his behaviour was so unbridled. And he had a new way of looking at her, not unkind or cross or disobedient, but as if he was a gardener tending a flower and watching to see how it was going to turn out. This was a reversal of their roles; she felt as though a geranium had risen from its bed and was bending over her with a watering-can.

As usual, they were always together and if Hilda did not get the old satisfaction from the company of this polite but aloof little stranger (for so he seemed to her) the change in his attitude made her all the more determined to win him back, and the thought of losing him all the more desolating. She hated the places where they used to play together and wished that Eustace, who was sentimental about his old haunts, would not take her to them. 'I just want to see it once again,' he would plead, and she did not like to refuse him, though his new mantle of authority sat so precariously on him. Beneath her moods, which she expressed in so many ways, was a steadily increasing misery; the future stretched away featureless without landmarks; nothing beckoned, nothing drew her on.

Obscurely she realised that the change had been brought about by Miss Fothergill's money. It had made Eustace independent, not completely independent, not as independent as she was, but it had given a force to his wishes that they never possessed before. It was no good trying to make him not want to go to school: she must make him want to stay at home. In this new state of affairs she believed that if Eustace refused to go to school his father would not try to compel him. But how to go about it? How to make Anchorstone suddenly so attractive, so irresistibly magnetic, that Eustace would not be able to bring himself to leave?

When Eustace told her that Dick Staveley was coming to live at Anchorstone Hall he mentioned this (for him) momentous event as casually as possible. Hilda did not like Dick Staveley, she professed abhorrence of him; she would not go to Anchorstone Hall when Dick had invited her, promising he would teach her to ride. The whole idea of the place was distasteful to her; it chilled and shrivelled her thoughts, just as it warmed and expanded Eustace's. Even to hear it mentioned cast a shadow over her mind, and as to go there, she would rather die; and she had often told Eustace so.

It was a sign of emancipation that he let Dick's name cross his lips. He awaited the explosion, and it came.

'That man!' – she never spoke of him as a boy, though he was only a few

13

years older than she was. 'Well, *you* won't see him, will you?' she added almost vindictively. 'You'll be at school.'

'Oh,' said Eustace, 'that won't make any difference. I shouldn't see him anyhow. You see, he never wanted to be friends with me. It was you he liked. If you had gone, I dare say he would have asked me to go too, just as your – well, you know, to hold the horse, and so on.'

'You and your horses!' said Hilda, scornfully. 'You don't know one end of a horse from the other.' He expected she would let the subject drop, but her eyes grew thoughtful and to his astonishment she said, 'Suppose I *had* gone?' 'Oh, *well*,' said Eustace, 'that would have changed everything. I shouldn't have had time to go to tea with Miss Fothergill – you see we should always have been having tea at Anchorstone Hall. Then she wouldn't have died and left me her money – I mean, she would have died; but she wouldn't have left me any money because she wouldn't have known me well enough. You have to know someone well to do that. And then I shouldn't be going to school now, because Daddy says it's her money that pays for me – and now' (he glanced up, the clock on the Town Hall, with its white face and black hands, said four o'clock) 'you would be coming in from riding with Dick, and I should be sitting on one of those grand sofas in the drawing-room at Anchorstone Hall, perhaps talking to Lady Staveley.'

Involuntarily Hilda closed her eyes against this picture – let it be confounded! Let it be blotted out! But aloud she said:

'Wouldn't you have liked that?'

'Oh yes,' said Eustace fervently.

'Better than going to school?'

Eustace considered. The trussed boy was being carried towards a very large, but slow, fire; other boys, black demons with pitchfork, were scurrying about, piling on coals. His mood of heroism deserted him.

'Oh yes, much better.'

Hilda said nothing, and they continued to saunter down the hill, past the ruined cross, past the pierhead with its perpetual invitation, towards the glories of the Wolferton Hotel – winter-gardened, girt with iron fire-escapes – and the manifold exciting sounds, and heavy, sulphurous smells, of the railway station.

'Are we going to Mrs Wrench's?' Eustace asked.

'No, why should we? We had fish for dinner; you never notice. Oh, I know, you want to see the crocodile.'

'Well, just this once. You see, I may not see it again for a long time.'

Hilda sniffed. 'I wish you wouldn't keep on saying that,' she said. 'It seems the only thing you can say. Oh, very well, then, we'll go in and look round and come out.'

'Oh, but we must buy something. She would be disappointed if we didn't. Let's get some shrimps. Aunt Sarah won't mind just for once, and I don't suppose I shall have any at St. Ninian's. I expect the Fourth Form gets them, though.'

'Why should they?'

'Oh, didn't you know, they have all sorts of privileges.'

'I expect they have shrimps every day at Anchorstone Hall,' said Hilda, meaningly.

'Oh, I expect they do. What a pity you didn't want to go. We have missed such a lot.'

Cautiously they crossed the road, for the wheeled traffic was thick here and might include a motor car. Fat Mrs Wrench was standing at the door of the fish shop. She saw them coming, went in, and smiled expectantly from behind the counter.

'Well, Miss Hilda?'

'Eustace wants a fillet of the best end of the crocodile.'

'Oh, Hilda, I don't!'

They all laughed uproariously, Hilda loudest of all; while the stuffed crocodile (a small one) sprawling on the wall with tufts of bright green foliage glued round it, glared down on them malignantly. Eustace felt the tremor of delighted terror that he had been waiting for.

'I've got some lovely fresh shrimps,' said Mrs. Wrench.

'Turn round, Eustace,' said Miss Cherrington.

'Oh must I again, Aunt Sarah?'

'Yes, you must. You don't want the other boys to laugh at you, do you?'

Reluctantly, Eustace revolved. He hated having his clothes tried on. He felt it was he who was being criticized, not they. It gave him a feeling of being trapped, as though each of the three pairs of eyes fixed on him, impersonal, fault-finding, was attached to him by a silken cord that bound him to the spot. He tried to restrain his wriggles within himself but they broke out and rippled on the surface.

'Do try to stand still, Eustace.'

Aunt Sarah was operating; she had some pins in her mouth with which, here and there, she pinched grooves and ridges in his black jacket. Alas, it was rather too wide at the shoulders and not wide enough round the waist.

'Eustace is getting quite a corporation.' said his father.

'Corporation, Daddy?' Eustace was always interested in words.

'Well, I didn't like to say fat.'

15

'It's because you would make me feed up,' Eustace complained. 'I was quite thin before. Nancy Steptoe said I was just the right size for a boy.'

No one took this up; indeed, a slight chill fell on the company at the mention of Nancy's name.

'Never mind,' Minney soothed him, 'there's some who would give a lot to be so comfortable looking as Master Eustace is.'

'Would they, Minney?'

Eustace was encouraged.

'Yes, they would, nasty scraggy things. And I can make that quite all right.' She inserted two soft fingers beneath the tight line round his waist.

'Hilda hasn't said anything yet,' said Mr. Cherrington. 'What do you think of your brother now, Hilda?'

Hilda had not left her place at the luncheon table, nor had she taken her eyes off her plate. Without looking up she said:

'He'll soon get thin if he goes to school, if that's what you want.'

'*If* he goes, said Mr.Cherrington. 'Of course he's going. Why do you suppose we took him to London to Faith Brothers if he wasn't? All the same, I'm not sure we ought to have got his clothes off the peg . . . Now go and have a look at yourself, Eustace. Mind the glass doesn't break.'

Laughing, but half afraid of what he might see, Eustace tiptoed to the mirror. There stood his new personality, years older than a moment ago. The Eton collar, the black jacket cut like a man's, the dark grey trousers that he could feel through his stockings, caressing his calves, made a veritable mantle of manhood. A host of new sensations, adult, prideful, standing no nonsense, coursed through him. Involuntarily, he tilted his head back and frowned, as though he were considering a leg-break that might dismiss R. H. Spooner.

'What a pity he hasn't got the cap,' said Minney admiringly.

Eustace half turned his head. 'It's because of the crest, the White Horse of Kent. You see, if they let a common public tailor make that, anyone might wear it.'

'Don't call people common, please Eustace, even a tailor.'

'I didn't mean common in a nasty way, Aunt Sarah. Common just means anyone. It might mean me or even you.'

Hoping to change the subject, Minney dived into a cardboard box, noisily rustling the tissue paper.

'But we've got the straw hat. Put that on, Master Eustace . . . There, Mr. Cherrington, doesn't he look nice?'

'Not so much on the back of your head, Eustace, or you'll look like Ally Sloper. That's better.'

'I wish it had a guard,' sighed Eustace, longingly.

'Oh well, one thing at a time.'

'And of course it hasn't got the school band yet. It's blue, you know, with a white horse.'

'What, another?'

'Oh, no, the same one, Daddy. You are silly.'

'Don't call your father silly, please, Eustace.'

'Oh, let him, this once . . . Now take your hat off, Eustace, and bow.'

Eustace did so.

'Now say "Please sir, it wasn't my fault".'

Eustace did not quite catch what his father said.

'Please, sir, it was my fault.'

'No, no. *Wasn't* my fault.'

'Oh, I see, Daddy. Please, sir, it wasn't my fault. But I expect it would have been really. It nearly always is.'

'People will think it is, if you say so. Now say "That's all very well, old chap, but this time it's my turn".'

Eustace repeated the phrase, imitating his father's intonation and *dégagé* man-of-the-world air; then he said:

'What would it be my turn to do, Daddy?'

'Well, what do you think?' When Eustace couldn't think, his father said: 'Ask Minney.'

Minney was mystified but tried to carry it off.

'They do say one good turn deserves another,' she said, shaking her head wisely.

'That's the right answer as far as it goes. Your Aunt knows what I mean, Eustace, but she won't tell us.'

'I don't think you should teach the boy to say such things, Alfred, even in fun. It's an expression they use in a . . . in a public house, Eustace.'

Eustace gave his father a look of mingled admiration and reproach which Mr. Cherrington answered with a shrug of his shoulders.

'Between you you'll make an old woman of the boy. Good Lord, at his age, I . . .' he broke off, his tone implying that at ten years old he had little left to learn. 'Now stand up, Eustace, and don't stick your tummy out.'

Eustace obeyed.

'Shoulders back.'

'Head up.'

'Don't bend those knees.'

'Don't arch your back.'

Each command set up in Eustace a brief spasm ending in rigidity, and

17

soon his neck, back and shoulders were a network of wrinkles. Miss Cherrington and Minney rushed forward.

'Give me a pin, please Minney, the left shoulder still droops.'

'There's too much fullness at the neck now, Miss Cherrington. Wait a moment, I'll pin it.'

'It's the back that's the worst, Minney. I can get my hand and arm up it – stand still, Eustace, one pin won't be enough – Oh, he hasn't buttoned his coat in front, that's the reason – '

Hands and fingers were everywhere, pinching, patting, and pushing; Eustace swayed like a sapling in a gale. Struggling to keep his balance on the chair, he saw intent eyes flashing round him, leaving gleaming streaks like shooting stars in August. He tried first to resist, then to abandon himself to all the pressures. At last the quickened breathing subsided, there were gasps and sighs, and the ring of electric tension round Eustace suddenly dispersed, like an expiring thunderstorm.

'*That's* better.'

'Really, Minney, you've made quite a remarkable improvement.'

'He looks quite a man now, doesn't he, Miss Cherrington? Oh, I wish he could be photographed, just to remind us. If only Hilda would fetch her camera – '

'Hilda!'

There was no answer. They all looked round.

The tableau broke up; and they found themselves staring at an empty room.

'Can I get down now, Daddy?' asked Eustace.

'Yes, run and see if you can find her.'

'She can't get used to the idea of his going away,' said Minney when Eustace had gone.

'No, I'm afraid she'll suffer much more than he will,' Miss Cherrington said.

Mr. Cherrington straightened his tie and shot his cuffs. 'You forget, Sarah, that she's going to school herself.'

'It's not likely I should forget my right hand, Alfred.'

After her single contribution to the problems of Eustace's school outfit, Hilda continued to sit at the table, steadily refusing to look in his direction, and trying to make her disapproval felt throughout the room. Unlike Eustace, she had long ago ceased to think that grown-up people were always right, or that if she was angry with them they possessed some special armour of experience, like an extra skin, that made them unable to feel it. She thought they were just as fallible as she was, more so, indeed; and that in this instance they were making a particularly big mistake. Her father's high-spirited raillery, as if the whole thing was a joke, exasperated her. Again, she projected her resentment through the æther, but they all had their backs to her, they were absorbed with Eustace. Presently his father made him stand on a chair. How silly he looked, she thought, like a dummy, totally without the dignity that every human being should possess. All this flattery and attention was making him conceited, and infecting him with the lax standards of the world, which she despised and dreaded. Now he was chattering about his school crest, as if that was anything to be proud of, a device woven on a cap, such as every little boy wore. He was pluming and preening himself, just as if she had never brought him up to know what was truly serious and worthwhile. A wave of bitter feeling broke against her. She could not let this mutilation of a personality go on; she must stop it, and there was only one way, though that way was the hardest she could take and the thought of it filled her with loathing.

Her aunt and Minney were milling round Eustace like dogs over a bone; sticking their noses into him. It was almost disgusting. To get away unnoticed was easy; if she had fired a pistol they would not have heard her. Taking her pencil box which she had left on the sideboard she slouched out of the room. A moment in the drawing-room to collect some writing paper and then she was in the bedroom which she still shared with Eustace. She locked the door and, clearing a space at the corner of the dressing-table, she sat down to write. It never crossed Hilda's mind that her plan could miscarry; she measured its success entirely by the distaste it aroused in her, and that was absolute – the strongest of her many strong feelings. She no more doubted its success than she doubted that, if she threw herself off the cliff, she would be dashed to pieces on the rocks below. In her mind, as she wrote, consoling her, was the image of Eustace, stripped of all his foolish finery, his figure restored to its proper outlines, his mouth cleansed of the puerilities of attempted schoolboy speech, his mind soft and tractable – forever hers.

But the letter did not come easily, partly because Hilda never wrote letters, but chiefly because her inclination battled with her will, and her sense of her destiny warned her against what she was doing. More than once she was on the point of abandoning the letter, but in the pauses of her thoughts she heard the excited murmur of voices in the room below. This letter, if she posted it, would still those voices and send those silly clothes back to Messrs. Faith Brothers. It could do anything, this letter, stop the clock, put it back even, restore to her the Eustace of pre-Miss

Fothergill days. Then why did she hesitate? Was it an obscure presentiment that she would regain Eustace but lose herself?

DEAR MR. STAVELEY (she had written),

    Some time ago you asked me and Eustace to visit you, and we were not able to because . . . (Because why?)

    Because I didn't want to go, that was the real reason, and I don't want to now except that it's the only way of keeping Eustace at home.

Then he would see where he stood; she had sacrificed her pride by writing to him at all, she wouldn't throw away the rest by pretending she wanted to see him. Instinctively she knew that however rude and ungracious the letter, he would want to see her just the same.

    So we can come any time you like, and would you be quick and ask us because Eustace will go to school, so there's not time to lose.

Yours sincerely,<br>HILDA CHERRINGTON.

Hilda was staring at the letter when there came a knock on the door, repeated twice with growing imperiousness before she had time to answer.

'Yes?' she shouted.

'Oh, Hilda, can I come in?'

'No, you can't.'

'Why not?'

'I'm busy, that's why.'

Eustace's tone gathered urgency and became almost menacing as he said:

'Well, you've got to come down because Daddy said so. He wants you to take my snapshot.'

'I can't. I couldn't anyhow because the film's used up.'

'Shall I go out and buy some? You see, it's very important, it's like a change of life. They want a record of me.'

'They can go on wanting, for all I care.'

'Oh, Hilda, I shan't be here for you to photograph this time next Thursday week.'

'Yes, you will, you see if you're not.'

'Don't you want to remember what I look like?'

'No, I don't. Go away, go away, you're driving me mad.'

She heard his footsteps retreating from the door. Wretchedly she turned to the letter. It looked blurred and misty, and a tear fell on it. Hilda had

20

no blotting paper, and soon the tear-drop, absorbing the ink, began to turn blue at the edges.

'He mustn't see that,' she thought, and taking another sheet began to copy the letter out. 'Dear Mr Staveley . . .' But she did not like what she had written; it was out of key with her present mood. She took another sheet and began again:

'Dear Mr. Staveley, My brother Eustace and I are now free . . .' That wouldn't do. Recklessly she snatched another sheet, and then another. 'Dear Mr. Staveley, Dear Mr. Staveley. Strangely enough, with the repetition of the words he seemed to become almost dear; the warmth of dearness crept into her lonely, miserable heart and softly spread there – 'Dear Richard,' she wrote, and then, 'Dear Dick.' 'Dear' meant something to her now; it meant that Dick was someone of whom she could ask a favour without reserve.

DEAR DICK,

I do not know if you will remember me. I am the sister of Eustace Cherrington who was a little boy then and he was ill at your house and when you came to our house to ask after him you kindly invited us to go and see you. But we couldn't because Eustace was too delicate. And you saw us again last summer on the sands and told Eustace about the money Miss Fothergill had left him but it hasn't done him any good, I'm afraid, he still wants to go to school because other boys do but I would much rather he stayed at home and didn't get like them. If you haven't forgotten, you will remember you said I had been a good sister to him, much better than Nancy Steptoe is to Gerald. You said you would like to have me for a sister even when your own sister was there. You may not have heard but he is motherless and I have been a mother to him and it would be a great pity I'm sure you would agree if at this critical state of his development my influence was taken away. You may not remember but if you do you will recollect that you said you would pretend to be a cripple so that I could come and talk to you and play games with you like Eustace did with Miss Fothergill. There is no need for that because we can both walk over quite easily any day and the sooner the better otherwise Eustace will go to school. He is having his Sunday suit tried on at this moment so there is not time to lose. I shall be very pleased to come any time you want me and so will Eustace and we will do anything you want. I am quite brave Eustace says and do not mind strange experiences as long as they are for someone else's good. That is why I am writing to you now.

With my kind regards,

Yours sincerely,

HILDA CHERRINGTON

21

She sat for a moment looking at the letter, then with an angry and despairing sigh she crossed out 'sincerely' and wrote 'affectionately'. But the word 'sincerely' was still legible, even to a casual glance; so she again tried to delete it, this time with so much vehemence that her pen almost went through the paper.

Sitting back, she fell into a mood of bitter musing. She saw the letter piling up behind her like a huge cliff, unscalable, taking away the sunlight, cutting off retreat. She dared not read it through but thrust it into an envelope, addressed and stamped it in a daze, and ran downstairs.

Eustace and his father were sitting together; the others had gone. Eustace kept looking at his new suit and fingering it as though to make sure it was real. They both jumped as they heard the door bang, and exchanged man-to-man glances.

'She seems in a great hurry,' said Mr. Cherrington.

'Oh yes, Hilda's always like that. She never gives things time to settle.'

'You'll miss her, won't you?'

'Oh, of *course*,' said Eustace. 'I shall be quite unconscionable.' It was the new suit that said the word; Eustace knew the word was wrong and hurried on.

'Of course, it wouldn't do for her to be with me there, even if she could be, in a boys' school. I mean, because she would see me being, well, you know, tortured, and that would upset her terribly. Besides, the other fellows would think she was bossing me, though I don't.'

'You don't?'

'Oh no, it's quite right at her time of life, but, of course, it couldn't go on always. They would laugh at me, for one thing.'

'If they did,' said Mr. Cherrington, 'it's because they don't know Hilda. Perhaps it's a good thing she's going to school herself.'

'Oh, she *is*?' Eustace had been so wrapped up in his own concerns that he had forgotten the threat which hung over Hilda. But was it a threat or a promise? Ought he to feel glad for her sake or sorry? He couldn't decide, and as it was natural for his mind to feel things as either nice or nasty, which meant right or wrong, of course, but one didn't always know that at the time, he couldn't easily entertain a mixed emotion, and the question of Hilda's future wasn't very real to him.

'Yes,' his father was saying, 'we only got the letter this morning, telling us we could get her in. The school is very full but they are making an exception for her, as a favour to Dr. Waghorn, your head-master.'

'Then it must be a good school,' exclaimed Eustace, 'if it's at all like mine.'

'Yes, St. Willibald's is a pretty good school,' said his father carelessly. 'It isn't so far from yours, either; just round the North Foreland. I shouldn't be surprised if you couldn't see each other with a telescope.'

Eustace's eyes sparkled, then he looked anxious. 'Do you think they'll have a white horse on their hats?' Mr. Cherrington laughed. 'I'm afraid I couldn't tell you that.' Eustace shook his head, and said earnestly:

'I hope they won't try to copy us too much. Boys and girls should be kept separate, shouldn't they?' He thought for a moment and his brow cleared. 'Of course, there was Lady Godiva.'

'I'm afraid I don't see the connection,' said his father.

'Well, she rode on a white horse.' Eustace didn't like being called on to explain what he meant. 'But only with nothing on.' He paused. 'Hilda will have to get some new clothes now, won't she? She'll have to have them tried on.' His eyes brightened; he liked to see Hilda freshly adorned.

'Yes, and there's no time to lose. I've spoken to your aunt, Eustace, and she agrees with me that you're the right person to break the news to Hilda. We think it'll come better from you. Companions in adversity and all that, you know.'

Eustace's mouth fell open.

'Oh, Daddy, I couldn't. She'd – I don't know what she might not do. She's so funny with me now, anyway. She might almost go off her rocker.'

'Not if you approach her tactfully.'

'Well, I'll try,' said Eustace. 'Perhaps the day after to-morrow.'

'No, tell her this afternoon.'

'Fains I, Daddy. Couldn't *you*? It is your afternoon off.'

'Yes, and I want a little peace. Listen, isn't that Hilda coming in? Now run away and get your jumping-poles and go down on the beach.'

They heard the front door open and shut; it wasn't quite a slam but near enough to show that Hilda was in the state of mind in which things slipped easily from her fingers.

Each with grave news to tell the other, and neither knowing how, they started for the beach. Eustace's jumping-pole was a stout rod of bamboo, prettily ringed and patterned with spots like a leopard. By stretching his hand up he could nearly reach the top; he might have been a bear trying to climb up a ragged staff. As they walked across the green that sloped down to the cliff he planted the pole in front of him and took practice leaps over any obstacle that showed itself – a brick it might be, or a bit of fencing, or the cart-track which ran just below the square. Hilda's jumping-pole was made of wood, and much longer than Eustace's; near

23

to the end it tapered slightly and then swelled out again, like a broom-handle. It was the kind of pole used by real pole-jumpers at athletic events, and she did not play about with it but saved her energy for when it should be needed. The January sun still spread a pearly radiance round them; it hung over the sea, quite low down, and was already beginning to cast fiery reflections on the water. The day was not cold for January, and Eustace was well wrapped up, but his bare knees felt the chill rising from the ground, and he said to Hilda:

'Of course, trousers would be much warmer.'

She made no answer but quickened her pace so that Eustace had to run between his jumps. He had never known her so preoccupied before.

In silence they reached the edge of the cliff and the spiked railing at the head of the concrete staircase. A glance showed them the sea was coming in. It had that purposeful look and the sands were dry in front of it. A line of foam, like a border of white braid, was curling round the outermost rocks.

Except for an occasional crunch their black beach shoes made no sound on the sand-strewn steps. Eustace let his pole slide from one to the other, pleased with the rhythmic tapping.

'Oh, don't do that, Eustace. You have no pity on my poor nerves.'

'I'm so sorry, Hilda.'

But a moment later, changing her mind as visibly as if she were passing an apple from one hand to the other, she said, 'You can, if you like. I don't really mind.'

Obediently Eustace resumed his tapping but it now gave him the feeling of something done under sufferance and was not so much fun. He was quite glad when they came to the bottom of the steps and the tapping stopped.

Here, under the cliff, the sand was pale and fine and powdery; it lay in craters inches deep and was useless for jumping, for the pole could get no purchase on such a treacherous foundation; it turned in mid air and the jumper came down heavily on one side or the other. So they hurried down to the beach proper, where the sand was brown and close and firm, and were soon among the smooth, seaweed-coated rocks which bestrewed the shore like a vast colony of sleeping seals.

Eustace was rapidly and insensibly turning into a chamois or an ibex when he checked himself and remembered that, for the task that lay before him, some other pretence might be more helpful. An ibex *could* break the news to a sister-ibex that she was to go to boarding school in a few day's time, but there would be nothing tactful, subtle, or imaginative in such a method of disclosure; he might almost as well tell her himself.

24

They had reached their favourite jumping ground and he took his stand on a rock, wondering and perplexed.

'Let's begin with the Cliffs of Dover,' he said. The Cliffs of Dover, so called because a sprinkling of barnacles gave it a whitish look, was a somewhat craggy boulder about six feet away. Giving a good foothold it was their traditional first hole, and not only Hilda but Eustace could clear the distance easily. When he had alighted on it, feet together, with the soft springy pressure that was so intimately satisfying, he pulled his pole out of the sand and stepped down to let Hilda do her jump. Hilda landed on the Cliffs of Dover with the negligent grace of an alighting eagle; and, as always, Eustace, who had a feeling for style, had to fight back a twinge of envy.

'Now the Needles,' he said. 'You go first.' The Needles was both more precipitous and further away, and there was only one spot on it where you could safely make a landing. Eustace occasionally muffed it, but Hilda never; what was his consternation therefore to see her swerve in mid-leap, fumble for a foothold, and slide off on to the sand.

'Oh, hard luck, sir!' exclaimed Eustace. The remark fell flat. He followed her in silence and made a rather heavy-footed but successful landing.

'You're one up,' said Hilda. They scored as in golf over a course of eighteen jumps, and when Hilda had won usually played the bye before beginning another round on a different set of rocks. Thus, the miniature but exciting landscape of mountain, plain and lake (for many of the rocks stood in deep pools, starfish-haunted), was continually changing.

Eustace won the first round at the nineteenth rock. He could hardly believe it. Only once before had he beaten Hilda, and that occasion was so long ago that all he could remember of it was the faint, sweet feeling of triumph. In dreams, on the other hand, he was quite frequently victorious. The experience then was poignantly delightful, utterly beyond anything obtainable in daily life. But he got a whiff of it now. Muffled to a dull suggestion of itself, like some dainty eaten with a heavy cold, it was still the divine elixir.

Hilda did not seem to realize how momentous her defeat was, nor, happily, did she seem to mind. Could she have lost on purpose? Eustace wondered. She was thoughtful and abstracted. Eustace simply had to say something.

'Your sandshoes are very worn, Hilda,' he said. 'They slipped every time. You *must* get another pair.'

She gave him a rather sad smile, and he added tentatively:

'I expect the ibex sheds its hoofs like its antlers. You're just going through one of those times.'

25

'Oh, so *that's* what we're playing,' said Hilda, but there was a touch of languor in her manner, as well as scorn.

'Yes, but we can play something else,' said Eustace. Trying to think of a new pretence, he began to make scratches with his pole on the smooth sand. The words 'St. Ninian's' started to take shape. Quickly he obliterated them with his foot, but they had given him an idea. They had given Hilda an idea, too.

He remarked as they moved to their new course, 'I might be a boy going to school for the first time.'

'You might be,' replied Hilda, 'but you're not.'

Eustace was not unduly disconcerted.

'Well, let's pretend I am, and then we can change the names of the rocks, to suit.'

The incoming tide had reached their second centre, and its advancing ripples were curling round the bases of the rocks.

'Let's re-christen this one.' said Eustace, poised on the first tee. 'You kick off. It used to be "Aconcagua",' he reminded her.

'All right,' said Hilda, 'call it Cambo.'

Vaguely Eustace wondered why she had chosen the name of their house, but he was so intent on putting ideas into her head that he did not notice she was trying to put them into his.

'Bags I this one for St. Ninian's,' he ventured, naming a not too distant boulder. Hilda winced elaborately.

'Mind you don't fall off,' was all she said.

'Oh, no. It's my honour, isn't it?' asked Eustace diffidently. He jumped.

Perhaps it was the responsibility of having chosen a name unacceptable to Hilda, perhaps it was just the perversity of Fate; anyhow, he missed his aim. His feet skidded on the slippery seaweed and when he righted himself he was standing in water up to his ankles.

'Now we must go home,' said Hilda. In a flash Eustace saw his plan going to ruin. There would be no more rocks to name; he might have to tell her the news outright.

'Oh, please not, Hilda, please not. Let's have a few more jumps. They make my feet warm, they really do. Besides, there's something I want to say to you.'

To his astonishment Hilda agreed at once.

'I oughtn't to let you,' she said, 'but I'll put your feet into mustard and hot water, privately, in the bathroom.'

'Crikey! That would be fun.'

'And I have something to say to you, too.'

26

'Is it something nice?'

'You'll think so,' said Hilda darkly.

'Tell me now.'

'No, afterwards. Only you'll have to pretend to be a boy who isn't going to school. Now hurry up.'

They were both standing on Cambo with the water swirling round them.

'Say "Fains I" if you'd like me to christen the next one,' said Eustace hopefully. 'It used to be called the Inchcape Rock.'

'No,' said Hilda slowly, and in a voice so doom-laden that anyone less preoccupied than Eustace might have seen her drift. 'I'm going to call it "Anchorstone Hall".'

'Good egg!' said Eustace. 'Look, there's Dick standing on it. Mind you don't knock him off!'

Involuntarily Hilda closed her eyes against Dick's image. She missed her take-off and dropped a foot short of the rock, knee-deep in water.

'Oh, *poor* Hilda!' Eustace cried, aghast.

But wading back to the rock she turned to him an excited, radiant face.

'Now it will be mustard and water for us both.'

'How ripping!' Eustace wriggled with delight. 'That'll be something to tell them at St. Ninian's. I'm sure none of the other men have sisters who dare jump into the whole North Sea!'

'Quick, quick!' said Hilda. 'Your turn.'

Anchorstone Hall was by now awash, but Eustace landed easily. The fear of getting his feet wet being removed by the simple process of having got them wet, he felt gloriously free and ready to tell anyone anything.

'All square!' he announced. 'All square and one to play. Do you know what I am going to call this one?' He pointed to a forbiddingly bare, black rock, round which the water surged, and when Hilda quite graciously said she didn't, he added:

'But first you must pretend to be a girl who's going to school.'

'Anything to pacify you,' Hilda said.

'Now I'll tell you. It's St.Willibald's. Do you want to know why?'

'Not specially,' said Hilda. 'It sounds such a silly name. Why should Willie be bald?' When they had laughed their fill at this joke, Eustace said:

'It's got something to do with you. It's . . . well, you'll know all about it later on.'

'I hope I shan't,' said Hilda loftily. 'It isn't worth the trouble of a pretence. Was this all you were going to tell me?'

'Yes, you see it's the name of your school.'

Hilda stared at him. 'My school? What do you mean, my school? Me a school-mistress? You must be mad.'

Eustace had not foreseen this complication.

'Not a school-mistress, Hilda.' he gasped. 'You wouldn't be old enough yet. No, a schoolgirl, like I'm going to be a schoolboy.'

'A schoolgirl?' repeated Hilda. 'A schoolgirl?' she echoed in a still more tragic voice. 'Who said so?' she challenged him.

'Well, Daddy did. They all did, while you were upstairs. Daddy told me to tell you. It's quite settled.'

Thoughts chased each other across Hilda's face, thoughts that were incomprehensible to Eustace. They only told him that she was not as angry as he thought she would be, perhaps not angry at all. He couldn't imagine why she wasn't, but the relief was overwhelming.

'We shall go away almost on the same day,' he said. 'Won't that be fun? I mean it would be much worse if one of us didn't. And we shall be quite near to each other, in Kent. It's called the Garden of England. That's a nice name. You're glad, aren't you?'

Her eyes, swimming with happy tears, told him she was; but he could hardly believe it, and her trembling lips vouchsafed no word. He felt he must distract her.

'You were going to tell me something, Hilda. What was it?'

She looked at him enigmatically, and the smile playing on her lips restored them to speech.

'Oh, that? That was nothing.'

'But it must have been something,' Eustace persisted. 'You said it was something I should like. Please tell me.'

'It doesn't matter now, she said, 'now that I am going to school.'

Her voice deepened and took on its faraway tone. 'You will never know what I meant to do for you – how I nearly sacrificed *all* my happiness.'

'Will anyone know?' asked Eustace.

He saw he had made a false step. Hilda turned pale and a look of terror came into her eyes, all the more frightening because Hilda was never frightened. So absorbed had she been by the horrors that the letter would lead to, so thankful that the horrors were now removed, that she had forgotten the letter itself. Yes. Someone would know . . .

Timidly Eustace repeated his question.

The pole bent beneath Hilda's weight and her knuckles went as white as her face.

'Oh, don't nag me, Eustace! Can't you see? . . . What's the time?' she asked sharply. 'I've forgotten my watch.'

'But you never forget it, Hilda.'

'Fool, I tell you I *have* forgotten it! What's the time?'

Eustace's head bent towards the pocket in his waistline where his watch was lodged, and he answered with maddening slowness, anxious to get the time exactly right:

'One minute to four.'

'And when does the post go?'

'A quarter past, But you know that better than I do, Hilda.'

'Idiot, they might have changed it.' She stiffened. The skies might fall but Eustace must be given his instructions.

'Listen, I've got something to do. You go straight home, slowly, mind, and tell them to get the bath water hot and ask Minney for the mustard.'

'How topping, Hilda! What fun we shall have.'

'Yes, it must be boiling. I shall hurry on in front of you, and you mustn't look to see which way I go.'

'Ho, no, Hilda.'

'Here's my pole. You can jump with it if you're careful. I shan't be long.

'But, Hilda – '

There was no answer. She was gone, and he dared not turn round to call her.

A pole trailing from either hand, Eustace fixed his eyes on the waves and consciously walked backwards, so that he should not see her. Presently he stumbled against a stone and nearly fell. Righting himself he resume his crab-like progress, but more slowly than before. Why had Hilda gone off like that? He could not guess, and it was a secret into which he must not pry. His sense of the inviolability of Hilda's feelings was a *sine qua non* of their relationship.

The tracks traced by the two poles, his and Hilda's, made a pattern that began to fascinate him. Parallel straight lines, he knew, were such that even if they were produced to infinity they could not meet. The idea of infinity pleased Eustace, and he dwelt on it for some time. But these lines were not straight; they followed a serpentine course, bulging at times and then narrowing, like a boa-constrictor that has swallowed a donkey. Perhaps with a little manipulation they could be made to meet.

He drew the lines closer. Yes, it looked as though they might converge. But would it be safe to try to make them when a law of Euclid said they couldn't?

A backward glance satisfied Hilda that Eustace was following her instructions. Her heart warmed to him. How obedient he was, in spite of everything. The tumult in her feelings came back, disappointment, relief, and dread struggling with each other. Disappointment that her plan had

29

miscarried; relief that it had miscarried; dread that she would be too late to spare herself an unbearable humiliation.

She ran, taking a short cut across the sands, going by the promenade where the cliffs were lower. She flashed past the Bank with its polished granite pillars, so much admired by Eustace. Soon she was in the heart of the town.

The big hand of the post office clock was leaning on the quarter. Breathless, she went in. Behind the counter stood a girl she did not know.

'Please can you give me back the letter I posted this afternoon?'

'I'm afraid not, Miss. We're not allowed to.'

'Please do it this once. It's very important that the letter shouldn't go.'

The girl – she was not more than twenty herself – stared at the beautiful, agitated face, imperious, unused to pleading, the tall figure, the bosom that rose and fell, and it scarcely seemed to her that Hilda was a child.

'I could ask the postmaster.'

'No, please don't do that. I'd rather you didn't. It's a letter that I . . . regret having written.' A wild look came into Hilda's eye; she fumbled in her pocket.

'If I pay a fine may I have it back?'

How pretty she is, the girl thought. She seems thoroughly upset. Something stirred in her, and she moved towards the door of the letter box.

'I oughtn't to, you know. Who would the letter be to?'

'It's a gentleman.' Hilda spoke with an effort.

I thought so, the girl said to herself; and she unlocked the door of the letter box.

'What would the name be?'

The name was on Hilda's lips, but she checked it and stood speechless.

'Couldn't you let me look myself?' she said.

'Oh, I'm afraid that would be against regulations. They might give me the sack.'

'Oh, please, just this once. I . . . I shall never write to him again.'

The assistant's heart was touched. 'You made a mistake, then,' she said.

'Yes,' breathed Hilda. 'I don't know . . .' she left the sentence unfinished.

'You said something you didn't mean?'

'Yes,' said Hilda.

'And you think he might take it wrong?'

'Yes.'

The assistant dived into the box and brought out about twenty letters. She laid them on the counter in front of Hilda.

'Quick! Quick! she said. 'I'm not looking.'

Hilda knew the shape of the envelope. In a moment the letter was in her pocket. Looking at the assistant she panted; and the assistant panted slightly too. They didn't speak for a moment; then the assistant said:

'You're very young, dear, aren't you?'

Hilda drew herself up. 'Oh, no, I've turned fourteen.'

'You're sure you're doing the right thing? You're not acting impulsive-like? If you're really fond of him . . .'

'Oh, no,' said Hilda. 'I'm not . . . I'm not.' A tremor ran through her. 'I must go now.'

The assistant bundled the letters back into the box. There was a sound behind them: the postman had come in.

'Good evening, Miss.' he said.

'Good evening,' said the assistant languidly. 'I've been waiting about for you. You don't half keep people waiting, do you?'

'There's them that works, and them that waits.' said the postman.

The assistant tossed her head.

'There's some do neither.' she said tartly, and then, turning in a business-like way to Hilda:

'Is there anything else, Miss?'

'Nothing further today,' said Hilda, rather haughtily. 'Thank you very much,' she added .

Outside the post office, in the twilight, her dignity deserted her. She broke into a run, but her mind outstripped her, surging, exultant.

'I shall never see him now,' she thought, 'I shall never see him, now,' and the ecstasy, the relief, the load off her mind, were such as she might have felt had she loved Dick Staveley and been going to meet him.

Softly she let herself into the house. The dining-room was no use: it had a gas fire. She listened at the drawing-room door. No sound. She tiptoed into the fire-stained darkness, crossed the hearthrug and dropped the letter into the reddest cleft among the coals. It did not catch at once so she took the poker to it, driving it into the heart of the heat. A flame sprang up, and at the same moment she heard a movement, and turning, saw the fire reflected in her father's eyes.

'Hullo, Hilda – you startled me. I was having a nap. Burning something?'

'Yes,' said Hilda, poised for flight.

'A love letter, I expect.'

'Oh, no, Daddy; people don't write love letters at my age.'

'At your age – ' began Mr. Cherrington. But he couldn't remember, and anyhow it wouldn't do to tell his daughter at her age he had already written a love letter.

'Must be time for tea,' he said, yawning. 'Where's Eustace?'

As though in answer they heard a thud on the floor above, and the sound of water pouring into the bath.

'That's him,' cried Hilda. 'I promised him I would put his feet into mustard and water. He won't forgive me if I don't.'

She ran upstairs into the steam and blurred visibility, the warmth, the exciting sounds and comforting smells of the little bathroom. At first she couldn't see Eustace; the swirls of luminous vapour hid him; then they parted and disclosed him, sitting on the white curved edge of the bath with his back to the water and his legs bare to the knee, above which his combinations and his knickerbockers had been neatly folded back, no doubt by Minney's practised hand.

'Oh, there you are, Hilda!' he exclaimed. 'Isn't it absolutely spiffing! The water's quite boiling. I only turned it on when you came in. I wish it was as hot as boiling oil – boiling water isn't, you know.'

'How much mustard did you put in?' asked Hilda.

'Half a tin. Minney said she couldn't spare any more.'

'Well, turn round and put your feet in,' Hilda said.

'Yes. Do you think I ought to take off my knickers, too? You see I only got wet as far as my ankles. I should have to take off my combinations.'

Hilda considered. 'I don't think you need this time.'

Eustace swivelled round and tested the water with his toe.

'Ooo!'

'Come on, be brave.'

'Yes, but you must put your feet in too. It won't be half the fun if you don't. Besides, you said you would, Hilda.' In his anxiety to share the experience with her he turned round again. 'Please! You got much wetter than I did.'

'I got warm running. Besides, it's only salt water. Salt water doesn't give you a cold.'

'Oh, but my water was salt, too.'

'You're different,' said Hilda. Then, seeing the look of acute disappointment on his face, she added, 'Well, just to please you.'

Eustace wriggled delightedly, and, as far as he dared, bounced up and down on the bath edge.

'Take off your shoes and stockings, then.' It was delicious to give Hilda orders. Standing stork-like, first on one foot, then on the other, Hilda obeyed.

'Now come and sit by me. It isn't very safe, take care you don't lose

32

your balance.'

Soon they were sitting side by side, looking down into the water. The clouds of steam rising round them seemed to shut off the outside world. Eustace looked admiringly at Hilda's long slim legs.

'I didn't fill the bath any fuller,' he said, in a low voice, 'because of the marks. It might be dangerous, you know.'

Hilda looked at the bluish chips in the enamel, which spattered the sides of the bath. Eustace's superstitions about them, and his fears of submerging them, were well known to her.

'They won't let you do that at school,' she said.

'Oh, there won't be any marks at school. A new system of plumbing and sanitarization was installed last year. The prospectus said so. That would mean new baths, of course. New baths don't have marks. Your school may be the same, only the prospectus didn't say so. I expect baths don't matter so much for girls.'

'Why not?'

'They're cleaner, anyway. Besides, they wash.' Eustace thought of washing and having a bath as two quite different, almost unconnected things. 'And I don't suppose they'll let us put our feet in mustard and water.'

'Why not?' repeated Hilda.

'Oh, to harden us, you know. Boys have to be hard. If they did, it would be for a punishment, not fun like this . . . Just put your toe in, Hilda.'

Hilda flicked the water with her toe, far enough to start a ripple, and then withdrew it.

'It's still a bit hot. Let's wait a minute.'

'Yes,' said Eustace. 'It would spoil *everything* if we turned on the cold water.'

They sat for a moment in silence. Eustace examined Hilda's toes. They were really as pretty as fingers. His own were stunted and shapeless, meant to be decently covered.

'Now, both together!' he cried.

In went their feet. The concerted splash was magnificent, but the agony was almost unbearable.

'Put your arm round me, Hilda!'

'Then you put yours round me, Eustace!'

As they clung together their feet turned scarlet, and the red dye ran up far above the water-level almost to their knees. But they did not move, slowly the pain began to turn into another feeling, a smart still, but wholly blissful.

'Is'nt it wonderful?' cried Eustace. I could never have felt it without you!'

Hilda said nothing, and soon they were swishing their feet to and fro in the cooling water. The supreme moment of trial and triumph had gone by; other thoughts, not connected with their ordeal, began to slide into Eustace's mind.

'Were you in time to do it?' he asked.

'Do what?'

'Well, what you were going to do when you left me on the sands.'

'Oh, that,' said Hilda indifferently. 'Yes, I was just in time.' She thought a moment, and added: 'But don't ask me what it was, because I shan't ever tell you.'

\* \* \* \* \*

**D J Taylor** was born and educated firstly in Norwich to which he and his family have recently returned. His first, partly autobiographical, novel *English Settlement* (1996) won the Grinzane Cavour Award. He has also written several studies of modern British fiction and a biography of Thackeray. His most recent novel *The Comedy Man* (2001) is set partly in Great Yarmouth. Several short stories with an East Anglian setting, including *Summer People*, appeared in his collection *After Bathing At Baxter's* (1997). Taylor's centenary biography of George Orwell was published in 2003.

# Summer People

## D J TAYLOR

The Summer People began arriving in May. They came in small, rickety trains on the branch line from Cromer, in smoking cars, or were disgorged from charabancs and coaches in the marketplace. From his vantage point at an upstairs window Julian watched them toil to the crest of the hill, where the rows of holiday cottages began: framed by his moving hand they re-emerged as perspiring, red-faced men awkwardly manhandling cases, children in the skimpy clothing their parents had thought suitable for a Norfolk summer, frozen by the wind. There was a pattern to their migrations. May brought young, childless couples who loitered hand-in-hand along the front or turned over the bric-a-brac in the sixpenny arcade. In July came holidaying families who foraged over the rock-pools for crabs and crayfish; in late August a few pensioners who drowsed in the end-of-season sun. By September the town had reverted to its antique state: rain falling over the pebble-dash houses, sending the high street shoppers scurrying for cover beneath awnings or into the porch of St Peter's church. In the distance cloud hung over the long grey spar of the sea.

As the town's second-largest newsagent-cum-stationer, Mr Holroyd could not afford to despise the Summer People, but he allowed himself sardonic remarks over their choice of newspaper – which, for example, preferred the *Guardian* to *The Times* or the *Daily Telegraph*, or declined to place sixpences in the box held up by the imploring blind boy. Once, in distant days, a man had requested the *Morning Star*. Mr Holroyd had pushed it with his own hands through the narrow holiday-home letterbox, so great was his disgust. The Summer People irked Mr Holroyd. He disliked their grainy Midlands accents, the too-easily earned five-pound notes picked up in the engineering shops of Wolverhampton and Dudley which they flicked over the counter in exchange for cigarettes and ice-cream, and he suspected them of sexual irregularity, or what passed for

35

sexual irregularity in Sheringham in the 1960s. But he made an exception of Miss Hoare, who arrived in the town halfway through July, rented an expensive property on the cliff and spent fifty shillings on sketching pads on her first visit to the shop.

'A very personable woman,' he informed the silent breakfast table audience of wife and son. 'She was staying at the Saracen's Head, but apparently the light wasn't what she wanted.'

The Saracen's Head was the most expensive hotel in Sheringham. The town's masonic lodge met in its back parlour on alternate Thursdays. Mr and Mrs Holroyd occasionally took afternoon tea there in a rather ostentatious way on winter Saturdays.

Julian first caught sight of Miss Hoare two days later in the shop, where she was making a fuss about cartridge paper. She was a large, fat but undoubtedly stylish woman in early middle age, her clothes of a kind not generally seen in Sheringham: a billowing dirndl skirt, white blouse patterned with sunflowers, wide-brimmed Panama hat. Stepping suddenly from the street into the cool interior, Julian heard her say: 'Of course the A4 is no good at all. Would it be possible to get the A3 do you think?' Unexpectedly, Julian heard his mother agreeing to this request: similar demands, made by sun-cured old men for obscure angling magazines, had not been so kindly received. 'This is Julian,' she said in a slightly subdued way, as he moved further into the shop towards the counter. Miss Hoare gave him a frank, appraising stare of the kind that old farmers at the County Show bestowed on horses, 'Oh yes,' she said. 'You're the young man who's so keen on art,' and Julian smiled wretchedly, not wanting his private experiments with watercolours and charcoal to be known to a pale-faced woman of forty with cropped hair and scarlet lipstick. 'I'll call again then, about the paper,' Miss Hoare said briskly to his mother, gathering up a little pile of purchases that included three packets of Park Drive cigarettes and a sophisticated woman's magazine in which Mrs Holroyd made occasional scandalised forays.

When she had gone, mother and son sat on the low stools behind the counter in a space made smaller by her absence, as motes of dust danced in the sunlight of the open door and shadow fell over the rows of shrimping nets and water pistols. Eventually the silence was broken by a gang of children squabbling over the ice-cream chiller. 'I expect we can get the cartridge paper from Norwich,' Mrs Holroyd said vaguely. 'She needs it for her work, you see . . .' Mrs Holroyd added as an afterthought. 'That lipstick . . .'

It was a hot summer that year. Julian drew salmon-skinned children who romped on the worm-casted sand beneath the pier, or shrieked at the Punch and Judy. Old fat women swimming sedately like porpoises in the shallows. Mrs Holroyd chided him affectionately, small things and large things mixed: the condition of his room, the length of his hair, his self-absorption. Impending O-level results, she implied, were no excuse for sequestration. In the end he embarked on long, futile cycle rides out along the North Norfolk flat, towards Wells and Blakeney. These, too, had their Summer People: well-groomed schoolgirls playing tennis on windswept courts overlooking the sea; civil young men in boats. Miss Hoare turned up frequently on these excursions: seated, sketch pad on knee, in rock crannies on the cliff path or arranging her easel on the beach. Occasionally she smiled or waved a hand from which cigarette smoke trickled slowly into the dense air. Once Julian found the easel unattended halfway up the stone escarpment flanking the putting course. He had time to register an enticing impressionist's vista of frothing waves and shipwrecked mariners before the sound of footsteps from below drove him away.

Each night at supper Mr Holroyd uncovered the little cache of lore which the day's traffic had afforded him. 'I asked about that Miss Hoare. At the Saracen's Head.' They ate Cromer crabs, shrimps, salad, dyspeptic hunks of white bread. Mr Holroyd was an advocate of 'plain English food': a birthday dinner had once been ruined by the intrusion of alien sauces. 'Apparently she's made quite a name for herself. Exhibitions and so on. At any rate she seems to make a living out of it.' Julian bent his head at the implied rebuke, which was, he knew, intended to emphasise the distance between an Art sanctified by commerce and feckless bohemian daydreaming. Later that evening Mrs Holroyd sought him out in a bedroom lined with neatly-executed Airfix kits and pictures of the England World Cup squad. 'You musn't mind your dad,' she said. 'He just wants what's best for you.' The letter from Julian's headmaster pressing the claims of the sixth-form science course and stating the necessity of a speedy decision, lay on the sill next to the *Collected Drawings of Aubrey Beardsley*, which Mr Holroyd had looked through with tolerant disdain. 'And you could always keep up your drawing,' Mrs Holroyd suggested timorously, 'as a kind of *hobby* . . .'

Once, the summer before, Julian had disappeared on his bicycle for an entire day, returning only at dusk, an hour after Mr Holroyd had telephoned the police. 'Why did you do it?' his father had asked, shocked and puzzled out of his evening routine of checking the stock cupboard and bundling up unsold copies of the *Daily Mirror*. 'I did it to get away from you,' Julian had answered, which was honest but scarcely sensible. Memories of this incident still rankled.

The next evening his father said unexpectedly: 'I saw that Miss Hoare the other day.' 'Yes?' 'A very interesting woman, that. Who was it she was telling me about? Some artist chap or other that she knew . . . Anyway, the upshot of it was that she wondered if you'd like some help with your drawing.' 'Perhaps,' Julian heard himself saying, 'she could have asked me herself.' But Mr Holroyd was absorbed in the correspondence columns of the *Cromer Mercury*. 'I don't think there's any call for that kind of remark,' he said absently.

Julian had little experience of women in early middle age, let alone artistic ones. Mrs Arkwright, the school's art department, specialised in Norfolk landscapes populated by vast Stubbsian horses. A spinster friend of his mother's routinely dispensed faded, self-painted watercolours as Christmas presents. Miss Hoare, etching in the corners of her tumultuous seascapes, seemed infinitely removed from these pale exemplars. She painted putting courses filled with giant golfers waving their irons like weapons, a vortex of wind, debris and flailing black birds descending on the spire of St Peter's church. 'You can be honest with me,' she told Julian. 'Do you like them?' 'I don't *dis*like them,' Julian replied truthfully. 'But in the sea picture you've put the gulls in the wrong place. You see, they always alight on the highest point.' Miss Hoare was delighted. 'A very good answer,' she said. 'If you'd said you liked them, I wouldn't have believed you.'

Conscious of their roles of native and interloper, they strolled around the town in search of vantage points: the gallery of the church, the high ground to the north, the tiny station with its dozing porter. 'Why Sheringham?' Julian asked at one point. 'I mean . . .' He stopped for a second, crimson-faced. 'I thought artists went to the South of France, places like that.' 'So they do,' Miss Hoare said judiciously. 'But my dear, I've had enough of Menton and Nice to last me a lifetime. Full of hopeless Englishmen thinking they're Pierre Loti.' Reaching the front again, they turned into the high street. Here the characteristic high summer smells hung in the air: fried fish, candyfloss, oil, each mixed with the pervasive tang of salt. 'Do you suppose,' Miss Hoare wondered, 'there is anywhere we could get a drink? A proper drink, that is.' 'Not a chance,' Julian told her cheerfully. 'Everyone knows I've only just turned sixteen. If I went into a pub and ordered a half of cider they'd probably telephone my father.'

'Oh well, if *that's* the difficulty,' said Miss Hoare. At the bar of the Saracen's Head she loomed brazenly above a knot of Summer People in khaki shorts and sunhats and announced: 'Two glasses of white wine. And this young man is my nephew.' Later, as they sat in an alcove looking out over the humped keels of upended crab boats, she said: 'Will it matter? Saying you're my nephew, I mean.' 'I shouldn't think my father will be very pleased.' 'Will he find out?' 'Oh, I expect someone will tell him,' Julian told her, elated by the wine and not caring very much. 'They usually do.'

August came, with flaring skies. An old man had a heart attack on the beach, and an air-sea rescue helicopter came to ferry him away. The O-level results were due in a week. 'Exams,' Miss Hoare pronounced, 'are the curse of the educated classes.' They were in the Saracen's Head again, whose staff, curiously, had yet to complain to Mr Holroyd. 'Are you still set on Art?' She enunciated it as one would the name of a favourite relative or a honeymoon destination. 'I don't know,' Julian wondered, realising that for all his disparagement of mathematics, physics, chemistry and the dreary people who taught them, he really did not know. 'There's an art school at Norwich,' he explained. 'Or even Lowestoft. And then . . .' Miss Hoare beamed back at him. Reckoning up the number of glasses of white wine she had consumed, Julian calculated it at six or perhaps seven. 'You must lend me those sketchbooks of yours,' she said. 'Let me look at them and see what can be done. It may take a day or so because I've got a friend arriving, but then I'll have a look and we'll see what can be done.' And Julian, glimpsing his face suddenly in the glass of the window, felt the kind of wild excitement he had once experienced as a child watching the Lancaster bombers veer inland from the sea towards the RAF stations of the Norfolk plain.

Mr Castleton, Miss Hoare's friend, was a thin, red-haired man in an outsize purple blazer and a cravat, who made himself unpopular in the town within half-an-hour of his arrival by parking his car across a narrow street entrance and then remonstrating with the people who tried to remove it. Subsequently he antagonised Mr Holroyd by asking for a copy of *Health and Efficiency*. 'I told him,' Mr Holroyd reported testily, 'that if he wanted pornography he could go to Cromer for it.' He and Miss Hoare dined noisily at the Saracen's Head and were seen picnicking on the cliff. Once, passing them in the crowded market square, Julian was certain that they saw him, but the wave went unacknowledged. No word came about the sketchbooks.

The O-level results arrived on a grey Saturday morning. Julian felt his hand tremble a little as he turned over the brown, rectangular envelope he remembered addressing to himself six weeks before. He need not have worried. 'An excellent set of results,' Mr Holroyd crowed. 'And especially in Science. I must confess I'm gratified.' With some ceremony he presented Julian with a creased ten-shilling note. Knocking at the door of Miss Hoare's cottage, an hour later, Julian realised that he had still made no decision, that the tangle of contending paths still ran away before him. Some time later the door was opened, with bad grace, by Mr Castleton. He wore a pair of ancient, buttonless pyjamas and was smoking a cigarette. Mr Castleton examined Julian without interest. 'It's your artist friend,' he said over his shoulder. Back in the belly of the house came the noise of vague, indeterminate movement. 'She's sozzled,' Mr Castleton said ruthlessly. 'Pissed. You better take these while you're here.' Stooping to retrieve the sketchbooks in their brown wrapping, Julian saw, a room away, the lurching figure: nightdress awry, wild staring face, one eye blinking in confusion. 'Go on, piss off,' Mr Castleton said equably.

Towards lunchtime, as the wind whipped up, he stood on the low, rocky promontory overlooking the station, where Summer People with bags and suitcases laboured towards the waiting train. Then, with one of those sharp, decisive gestures that define our lives, he began to tear up the books, one by one, casting each fragment out on to the swelling breeze. Later the rain came on, noisily, across the long bar of the sea.

\* \* \* \* \*

**Henry Sutton** was born and brought up in Norfolk where he started work as a freelance journalist before moving to London. Most of his fiction draws on his knowledge of the county including *Gorleston* (1995), the east coast town where he spent his early years. *Bank Holiday Monday* (1996) was inspired by family holidays on the coast at Burnham Overy Staithe. *Water* is set in north Norfolk and scenes from his most recent novel *Kid's Stuff* together with his work in progress, *Notes For All The Family*, are also drawn from the locality Sutton knows so well.

# Water
## HENRY SUTTON

By July we came to believe that Robert was about as unconnected with the real world as most of the artists he represented. Still he had such a sense of wonder about him, a boyish innocence, a terrible vitality, that you couldn't help being drawn to him. Everyone was swept along on his mad dream. At least that is what I like to think now. Because the memory of the day when I began to see the darkness edging his dream still echoes deep in my mind.

June left the park hot and humid. The green in the woods seemed to drip and the deer park shimmered on the shockingly sunny days, that were broken now and then by sudden thunder storms that rolled in from the east only to shudder further inland some twenty minutes later leaving the place temporarily fresh and us feeling somehow reprieved. The deer like some pack of prehistoric beasts shifted silently across the horizons, always too far away to reveal their true, harmless selves. The wood pigeons and pheasants were rendered listless by the heat or were just too young and shy to make much of an appearance. Only the ducks and a few grubby swans made any effort, and that wasn't much, on the man-made lake, which had been thankfully deserted by fishermen since May, even though it wasn't until August that the algae really started to grow and make the big birds' lazy forays out into the shallow centre for food quite impossible. Many died, their bloated, stinking bodies piling up along the neon-green shoreline, and going dark and scarlet as their guts split open.

I suppose I remember that image more vividly because it reminded me of Sarah Bruce's installation which I saw a good month before. Indeed her work now seems like a precursor, a warning even of what was to come, not just of the park but of Robert's world, his explosion of self-belief, and our involvement with him. It was Sarah I took to the beach that day.

41

The sun as usual started to pour into our room at about seven and by seven thirty I knew I couldn't just lie there anymore, the sun making me sweat and hurting my sticky eyelids. My wife and I became pretty used to doing our own thing, as long as we prearranged who was to look after Rebecca. It was my day off from our daughter, so I slipped out of the bedroom leaving Victoria quite unaware of my movements. And I ignored the first stirrings of my daughter in the next door bedroom as I crept along the landing, an uncontrollable and quite unexpected surge of excitement welling up in me. The excesses of Robert's party the night before seemed to only enhance the morning. The gulls noisily and brightly larking outside, the sun glinting on the chrome taps in the kitchen, and the kettle rattling as if it were empty. I could see the roof of the hall from the kitchen window, the red tiles turning pink and mottled. I couldn't see the flag, but I knew it would be flying, or at least drooping in the windless morning, because it was always raised when Robert was in residence. An affectation he thought particularly funny given that the flag was in reality a glittering appliqued blanket known as The Queen's Rug, and made by an artist who was obsessed by royalty and who died of Aids shortly after he was visited in hospital by the Princess of Wales, or at least that was the story Robert associated with his lofty insignia. But like all the stories Robert related at one time or another to his works of art, and I suppose you could say the works of art themselves, the story and meaning varied according to the occasion and those present.

I finished my tea on the lawn, the dew drying as my tea cooled and feet made sharp imprints in the grass. And I wondered whether anybody would be up yet in the big house, my own cottage and small walled garden making me seem terribly cut off and lonely. For much of that summer many of the park's other residents admitted to similar feelings when they were not being entertained by Robert, or at least in his presence. We knew it was a pathetic, childish longing. But there was little we found we could do about it. A friend of my wife's who came to stay for a weekend told us much later that we behaved as if we were in a trance the whole time she was there, and it was not *that* bloody hot. I left the empty mug on the lawn and vaulted the vintage brick wall that swooped and slanted in various directions but was largely somehow still standing. I cut through the edge of the great wood, the route I had taken home not so many hours earlier, shortly before sunrise. The wood at twilight was an extraordinary place, the deep blue of the sky making the trees ink black and sly. It wasn't hard to imagine the trees were talking, plotting to each other, closing in, closing the way forward, particularly after a rich meal and much to drink. Earlier that morning my imagination had got the better of me and I had found myself running home, cracking twigs, branches scratching my arms and face. Now the wood was cool and still, except for an odd clanking sound that I took to be the taller trees rubbing together somewhere up by the thin canopy, the clanking reverberating deep into the wood and startling no one because no one was about except me. Shafts of sunlight made it to the forest floor, and speckled me as I progressed quietly, surreptitiously towards the hall.

Sarah's installation was called simply Water, though if you were not aware of that I don't think you would have understood what the piece was about. It was laid out in the library, Robert's favourite room. The floor was a bed of shredded green fabric, which I was reminded of when I saw the algae build-up on the lake a month later, and which was meant to represent seaweed. Actually Sarah told me that the next day, still I seem to remember it was pretty obvious. On top of the seaweed then, were mini-sand dunes of sand dyed dark scarlet. I suppose if you had looked at it one way the shredded green fabric could have represented the sea, the scarlet sand the beach. But that was not how you were meant to look at it, I was assured. No, the planet had dried up and the sea was missing which was why the seaweed had become fantastically green and mutant and why the sand had started to bleed dry.

Sarah was thin and pale and had dark brown hair and eyes which helped make her paler. She painted her lips a lush pink, and she didn't look like an artist everybody said at the party. Robert didn't have private views, he had parties, or dinners or balls. Events anyway which were often far grander than the work on view, or for that matter the people present. Everybody assumed Robert was sleeping with Sarah, so I was pretty surprised to find Sarah at the bottom of the formal lawn gazing up at the sky, or at least a flickering of a bird in the sky, at eight in the morning. She didn't seem at all startled to see me as I blundered out of the woods, dishevelled and barely dressed. Except for Robert most of us who lived on the park wandered about that summer in scruffy abandon. Robert always managed to look immaculate, without being fastidious. Nobody ever tried to emulate him, it would have been far to obvious.

'Hi,' she said, brightly.

'Hi,' I said. In the harsh morning light she looked tired. There were dark patches under her deep eyes, and she looked older than I had imagined the previous evening.

'I've been watching the birds,' she said. 'The way the light catches them, and the way they seem to fly in such an unpredictable manner. It's as if they dont know where they're going until they get to a particular patch of sky.'

'Yes, I suppose so,' I said not at all sure I knew what she was getting at. But there was something enormously attractive about her, and I didn't want her to disappear. I have often thought about her since but have never managed to quite pinpoint what I found so attractive. It wasn' t anything obvious like her eyes, or mouth, or complexion, it was something more innate than that, some essence that floated from her. In a way the same could be said of Robert. He wasn't obviously attractive, but people were immediately attracted to him.

'I wish I could do that,' she said. 'Just fly about without knowing or planning where I was going, stopping in the odd patch of sky until I found myself flying off somewhere else, unable to stop.'

She smiled at me and her teeth caught the sun and a sort of halo developed around her head, and for some reason the words of one of Robert's favourite dictums came to mind: *Conceptual artists are mystics rather than rationalists. They leap to conclusions that logic cannot reach.* He had another saying he used a lot: *The artist may not necessarily understand his own art. His perception is neither better or worse than that of others.* He often said the latter in front of me, I suspect because he knew I was looking in on a world that I didn't properly understand, or at least one I didn' t used to understand. I thought he had made them up, but recently I was browsing in an art book shop and I came across a manifesto, I suppose that's what it was, by Sol Lewitt. The above statements were there, verbatim, paragraphs one and twenty five.

'I like that idea of uncontrollable disorder,' she said, adding, 'coffee?'

'Yeah, I would love some.' I followed her across the lawn, past the kinetic fountain, which had been switched off because someone in a drunken, jealous rage had tried to smash it up, and the water instead of spurting upwards spurted outwards with a terrifying velocity. Robert refused to have it mended, saying it was just as important now, perhaps more so, because so much more passion and energy had gone into it. *A work is never finished, only in transition*, he also said on a number of occasions. This wasn' t Sol Lewitt, I checked, or by anyone else I've come across so far.

Sarah was wearing a simple summer dress, and her feet were bare. I could see the grass and dirt stains on the heels of her feet as she walked, her calves blanched in the sun, and the dress hugging then swaying around her slim frame. She slipped into a side door and for a moment I lost her in the sudden darkness. I felt my way forward and caught up with her in the massive kitchen. The maid must have been in already, the place was neat and clean, no debris from the night before. However, there was a staleness in the air. I noticed this before when the house was largely empty, and I was surprised because Robert was such a perfectionist I couldn't understand why he put up with it. It was almost as if the smell was the last legacy of the old house which Robert couldn't control. An aspect of the past he couldn't deny.

'Here,' she said passing me an espresso-sized amount of coffee. 'God, I'd like to get away from this place.' She rubbed her eyes, as if to emphasise her tiredness, her exasperation with it all. 'I feel I've just about had it.'

'But your show was a great success,' I said.

'They all are here. That's not the point.' She slurped her coffee loudly. 'Isn't there a beach or something near?'

I found my heart was pounding heavily and my hands were becoming moist with sweat, felt my coffee cup might slip out of my hand even, so I put the cup down and wiped them on my trousers. I believe I agreed to take her because she then said something that I didn't understand at the time but think I'm beginning to now.

'Sometimes I feel Robert's just laughing in the dark.'

I went to get my car and met her halfway down the drive. It was as if she couldn't wait to get away from the hall and was hoofing it alone, would've made it to the beach without me. It truly was a glorious day. A few puffy clouds hung to the corners of the troposphere, reminding us we were still on earth. The noon-time heat-haze would evaporate them, but there were a couple of hours before that would happen, and I drove slowly on narrow country lanes, deliberately taking the back way because the hedges were full of ripening wild wheat and strawberries and smelt sweet and of summer and of freedom. We made a number of family trips to the beach during the earlier part of the summer, but somehow as time progressed we seldom ventured out of the park, Rebecca enjoying Robert's swimming pool and playing with the numerous other children who lived in the park. My wife and I were happy to put it down to Rebecca, our resistance to explore the outside world, but as I look back now I know it was more to do with Robert, our feelings towards him. And I can still remember that strange sense of freedom and guilt I felt driving through the gate house and away from the park with Sarah.

I stopped to look at a map at one point, reaching across Sarah to the glove compartment. She didn't move out of my way. I knew then that I could still go back, it wasn't too late, but I found the route quickly and we moved off and I drove faster along the lanes with blind corners and humps. Sarah was pretty quiet for the forty minutes or so it took us to reach the beach, and I didn' t question her about Robert or her work for him. She smoked two cigarettes, the smoke swirling and lingering in the car, where I knew it would stay for longer than just that day. She brightened once we were there. The sand was hot on our feet as we started to walk across the beach dodging groups of people, young families, kids playing cricket or throwing frisbees. Sarah wondered what on earth time these people must have got there. Whether they were there when the sun had got up, which reminded me that I didn't have any sunscreen. My wife always took care of stuff like that, and as we moved further out, further away from the families and kids, I knew I was definitely making a mistake, but I couldn't turn round, even then.

'You know,' said Sarah, 'it was Robert's idea, to dye the sand scarlet. It was his idea to call the piece Water. He's got a thing about water. Why don't we stop in those dunes?' She pointed to a clump of dunes way in the distance. 'We might find some shade there.'

The sun had got to her as well, she was shading her eyes as she walked, sometimes covering her forehead with a pale hand. The sand was so fine sprays of it were kicked up by our feet and I let her walk ahead for a while, watching the spray, thinking of speedboats, things moving through water fast. The installation Robert put on before Sarah's involved a tank of water and a couple of naked mannequins, a gas mask and submarine echo-chamber noises. It was called Earth, and was executed by a Chinese American artist, who told everyone who would listen at the party that the piece represented the unreported, underwater war America was waging on China, in its bid to colonise the world. As we walked across the scorched sand Sarah told me she had bought the green fabric for her installation from a shop in the East End. And she told me how she had shredded it, how Robert had advised her to make it look like the fried seaweed you get in Chinese restaurants, only more vibrant, as if it had been fried by a nuclear oven. Then he had advised her on where exactly she should mound the scarlet sand. A dog came scampering up to us and Sarah sort of hid behind me as the dog, a mangy-looking mongrel, licked my legs and nestled up to me wanting to be stroked and patted. It stayed with us for nearly five minutes, the whole time Sarah seemed really quite frightened of it. At last it slunk off and Sarah told me that Robert had two more shows planned for the summer, on the themes of air and fire. She said he had numerous artists working on projects, but that he wouldn't decide whose he was going to use until the last minute, which she thought was pretty inconsiderate of him, actually.

'You see he's a control freak,' she said. 'No one gets to do their own work. It's always his ideas. He says he knows what sells, knows what his clients want. But it' s not right. It can't be.' She paused, sucked in air and it sounded as if she were using a snorkel and some water had got into the bendy, plastic tube. 'And how come most of his artists are women? Think about that. I don't ever want to work for him again.'

I remember thinking at the time that Robert and Sarah must have had some major argument, or bust up, or whatever, and that that was why she was having a go at him. It wasn't until much later that it seemed what she had told me was pretty well justified. I couldn't have just accepted it then, Robert was too real, too alive, too essential. Still, whether it was the heat or the glare on that day, I don't know, I sympathised with her, took her hand for a while. We reached the sand dunes, and climbed through thick grass that stung our legs, both of us puffing and sweat glistening our foreheads. On a crest we could see the sea ahead, water washing the shore, the smallest hint of wave-breaking white water. We found shade against a sand peak and sat huddled out of the sun in silence for a long while. Sarah shut her eyes and I wondered for a moment whether she had fallen asleep. She looked so young and peaceful she reminded me of my daughter. I wanted to hold her then, protect her. My daughter was six that summer and we had grown somewhat apart from each other.

'He' s not going to laugh at me anymore,' Sarah muttered, stood up and pulled her flimsy dress over her head. She set off for the sea in just her knickers, and I rushed after her, over stubbly mounds of sand and through tangled thickets of marram and the heavy heat. There was no one about in the dunes, and if it wasn't for the tick of insects and spacey bird calls, one might have imagined we were the only living things about. Sarah was all arms and legs, her elbows jutting accusingly. We reached the beach and Sarah started to run, the sand too hot to walk on here. But the sea was far and Sarah stopped eventually and I caught up with her, the odd shell sharp underfoot. She didn't look at me, but into the hazy blue distance, searching for birds, and their chaotic, unpredictable flight patterns, I imagined.

'You're really something of a mystic,' I said, and she was off again, running faster than before, limbs splaying, unable to stop herself. 'Hey, slow down,' I shouted. She kept running right into the sea, kicking up sea spray and a clump of dull seaweed.

* * * * *

**Sylvia Townsend Warner** lived most of her life in Dorset with her lover Valentine Ackland but came to know Norfolk well from the holidays they spent in or near Winterton where Valentine's mother had a house. As a result two of Warner' novels, *The Corner That Held Them* (1948) and *The Flint Anchor* (1954) are set in the county together with several short stories including *Two Children* that first appeared in the collection *The Innocent and the Guilty* (1971) .

# Two Children
## SYLVIA TOWNSEND WARNER

During the night the easterly gale had blown itself out. For three days it had screeched over the flint-built Norfolk fishing village. Now everything looked gentle and smiling, and the blown sand plastered on windows and seaward-facing tarred walls had an air of partaking in the general relief by adding a sparkle – as thought it were a cake decoration. Only the noise of the breakers perpetuated the force of the gale, filling the air with a sullen, continuous rumble. As the two children stood on the doorstep with the expanse of the school holiday before them, Johnnie said to his sister Bella, 'Listen to them waves. That sound more like a railway train.'

Their grandmother came out behind them. Her eye roved over the sagging fence, the sand plastered on everything, the puddle round the water-butt, a bit of wet sacking entangled in the gooseberry bush. She hadn't properly finished the spring cleaning and now there was all this outside work added to it. She fetched the children's outdoor clothes and tied a handkerchief over Bella's flaxen curls. 'Go you down to the beach.' she said. 'Tide's going out and now's the time to stock up woodhouse again.'

Johnnie had an idea. He had had it for some time, now it boiled up in him. 'Why can't we go on the heath? There's wood there, too.'

'Go on the heath? You'll do no such thing. Why, there's great old vipers on the heath, and if one of them bit you, you'd fare to die. No! Off with you to the beach. And I don't want you back till dinner-time.'

It is the unknown we fear. Ellen Hodds had lost at different times a husband, two sons, and an uncle by drowning. No member of the family had ever died of snakebite. She watched the children set off along the sandy track across the dunes, dragging the home-made cart behind them, and went indoors with a quiet mind.

49

They heard the door slam. Johnnie paused, and looked round cautiously. Then without a word he turned and set off inland for the heath.

'You'll catch it,' said his sister.

'She won't know.'

'That she will. She'll know by the wood. It will be different wood.'

'Shan't get any wood. We'll go on the beach after.'

Their father had been one of the drowned sons. Wearing heavy seaboots, he was tossed off the deck of a herring drifter by a sudden lurch of the boat over a sandbank, and the sea swallowed him within sight of his native village. The *Hopeful Star* put in at the nearest port to tell the news, and went on after the others, the crew depressed by a limping start and bad omen. The fishing fleet was making the long summer trip to Icelandic waters, they would not be back for several months. By then, the edge of his family's grief for Beauty Hodds would be blunted; it would be the accustomed, acquiescing grief of a fishing community, a traditional wearing like the black shawls the older women threw over their heads when they went out early in the morning to feed the hens.

Within a year of Beauty's death, his widow married again. She married an outsider, an engineer from Coventry, whom she had met while working at the Holiday Camp. He had been offered a job in Venezuela. She went with him, saying that when they were settled in a house she would come back and fetch the children. She sent money regularly and asked for photographs, but never re-appeared, and the children lived on with their grandmother. Bella was the elder. She could remember her father, and remembered him even when she had forgotten her mother; he had made a pet of her, and his long absences at sea had given him a rarity value. Johnnie, two years younger, remembered neither parent. He loved his grandmother, the dog at the village shop, and, from afar, Miss Worsley, the rector's sister.

Presently, Bella began to talk. 'I'm not afraid of the heath. I've often been there.'

'When?'

'Often and often. When you were a baby. My Daddy used to take me there. And there were ever so many vipers. But we weren't afraid. My Daddy said to them, "You just bugger off."'

'You oughtn't to say that.'

'I didn't neither. My Daddy did.'

She was a vexing companion, and he wished he had come without her. As though reading his thought, she said, 'Next year, I'll go to confirmation class, and be done in Yarmouth by a bishop. In a veil. And after that I'll go with the big girls, with Doreen Pitcher and Rowena Crask. And I won't have no kid brother tagging round after me, nor you won't catch me on the heath. *What's that?*'

'A bit of old rope.'

Having looked searchingly all round her, she said, 'I'm tired. Let's sit down.'

'Why, we aren't as much as on the heath yet.'

'We'll pretend we are. We'll pretend it's a very dark night, and that it's snowing, and that we've lost our way. I'm a princess, see, and you're a page, holding my train. And you say, 'I'm so frightened, I darsn't go on.' And I say . . .'

He sat staring at the heath, his desire probing into it, beyond the ungainly tufts of furze and the birch coppice glittering in the sunlight. A gull cried overhead, and behind Bella's scatter of words was the continuous harsh rumble of the waves. If only he could have come alone! If only she would leave off talking! He rolled over on his stomach. When you lie on your face, things sound different: the noise of the waves was now on top of him. He burrowed his forefinger into the sandy earth, delved a hole, put his nose to it and snuffed. The act reminded him of Bingo, the dog at the shop. Bingo would have dug a hole in no time, his front paws lashing, the earth flying up all round. Then he would sink his nose, give a long, exploring, ecstatic snuff, raise his head, his velvety muzzle all powdered with earth, take a firmer stance with his hind legs, and fall to digging again. Bingo's father was Mr Larter the gamekeeper's retriever, and he was a nice dog, too; but nothing to Bingo. When Bella was confirmed and going with the big girls he would go for long walks alone with Bingo. But it couldn't be yet. Bella was forever talking about the confirmation and how she would wear a veil and buy a pair of falsies with her savings-bank money, but it was all her romancing. She was eleven, no bishop would do a girl of eleven, they had to be over thirteen. If he were with Bingo now, they would be right on the heath, beyond the birch coppice, away from the noise of the sea and hearing the sounds of inland: the swish of bracken, the rattle of holly leaves, the quick flutter of small birds. He knew what it would be like because the stranger schoolmaster last summer had twice taken them there for nature walks.

51

But he had never managed to get there alone – and he wasn't alone now.

Bella was still talking. 'What I would really like would be a budgie. I would have a gold cage for it, with a swing and a looking glass, and I would teach it to say 'Bella,' and 'Hustle Up' and 'Pretty Budgie-Boy.' Things that Gran wouldn't be old-fashioned about, not like that parrot at The Three Mariners. And I would make it so fond of me that it would sit on my shoulder wherever I went, and come when I whistled.'

The sea was still resounding, though now it had a different voice for the tide was at the ebb and the waves fell on sand instead of on pebbles.

'Whatever are you doing, Johnnie? Digging for pignuts? Going to Australia? Sit up and say something, do. You'll catch cold, lying sprawled out on the ground. Then it'll all come out, where we've been. And I shall be blamed for it. I shouldn't wonder if I'm not catching a cold myself, sitting here all this time waiting for tomorrow to be yesterday. Then it'll be bronchitis. When I was a baby I nearly died of bronchitis. For three Sundays I was prayed for in a church and Reverend Worsley – What's that noise?'

'Larks.'

'Don't tell me it's larks.'

Listening, she was silent for at least a minute. Then she retied the handkerchief over her head more becomingly, to show her curls. 'Come on! Whatever it is, we aren't going to stay here any longer. Come on, hurry up! Johnnie, do you hear me? We're not going to stay in this God-Help-Us place another minute. Nor you won't catch me here again, I can tell you that. I only did it to please you. Come on down to the beach. We've got that wood to get.'

She set off, retracing the way they had come by. Passing the coil of old rope she paused and looked at it attentively. Then she gave it a kick, and quickened her pace to a run; he came after, trundling the little cart. It was not till they were among the dunes that she slowed down and began to talk about the lumps of amber which the sea might have cast up, and of what she would do with them. 'And mind you look too, instead of mooning. There'll still be lots of time for the wood.'

'Most of it will be toothbrushes and ketchup bottles,' he said, being more cognizant of what is cast up by a storm than she.

They clambered up from the shelter of the last sand hill. The roar of the waves, the smell of salt, assailed them. The gray pebble-bank, the sand beyond, the spray twirling like a rope along the line of the breakers, extended on either hand as far as the eye could reach.

'Look! Look, Johnnie!'

The austere beach was dotted with flecks of alien brilliant colour.

'Oranges,' he said.

'Yes. And there'll be folks after them. Hurry!'

They ran plungingly down the sand hill, the marram grass stinging their legs. Johnnie picked up an orange and bit into it. 'It's sour.'

'Of course it is. They're Seville oranges, for making marmalade. That'll keep Gran busy.'

He picked up another. It squelched between his fingers. 'This here's rotten.'

'Never mind if it is. It'll do for something. Oh for goodness' sake, child, don't stand there arguing. Pick them up, hurry before other folks get them all. They're at it already, farther along.'

He had seen the group of men, farther along the beach, and had seen that they were standing motionless. A deep-rooted recognition rose slowly into his mind. The dark, huddled object, prostrate among the standing men, was a body, was a drowned man whom the tossing sea had tired of and cast on shore.

'What are you staring at now? Get on with the oranges. Pile them up. Here's a beauty. Them as Gran don't want, we'll sell. We'll dress up as gypsies and cycle into Henham and sell them for a penny each. Johnnie! Do you hear me? What's come over you?'

'None of your business,' he said.

'None of my business?'

She reared up in astonishment, shook the curls out of her eyes, looked where he was looking. Her eyes darkened, her jaw dropped.

'Oh no! Oh, don't say it. It's just a seal they're looking at, just a dead seal.'

He began to walk toward the group of men. She ran after him, clutched his arm. 'Don't go! I won't have it. Gran wouldn't never allow it. And I'll tell her. Besides, they don't want you. They don't want a kid interfering, whatever it is.'

He drove his elbow into her and freed himself.

'And it's nothing but a seal, anyhow, a dead seal.'

'Then get you on with your oranges.'

He was astonished to hear himself speaking so harshly, and the dialect so strong in his voice.

'I won't. If you're going, I'm coming too. To look after you. I won't be left. Johnnie, Johnnie, I don't want to be left alone.'

He turned and saw her furious suppliant face, and how she glanced this way and that, as though at any moment more bodies might be cast up.

'I tell you, I won't have you go. You're to stay here with me, and do as I say. I'm two years older than you, I know what's best, I – '

'You bugger off,' he said. He saw her face contort for tears and walked on with a firm tread to join the men.

\* \* \* \* \*

**Rose Tremain** was one of the first to graduate from the creative writing course at the University of East Anglia. She is now a best selling author with novels such as *Restoration* (1989), shortlisted for the Booker Prize, and the highly acclaimed *Sacred Country* (1992), both set in East Anglia. Several early short stories are also set in the region including *Negative Equity* that first appeared in the collection *Evangelista's Fan* (1995). A more recent novel *Music And Silence* won the 1999 Whitbread Novel Award. Her latest novel *The Colour* was published earlier this year. Tremain lives near Norwich with the biographer Richard Holmes.

# Negative Equity

## ROSE TREMAIN

On the night of his fortieth birthday, Tom Harris dreams about a flotilla of white ships.

For a while, he enjoys this dream and feels safe in it. He's admiring the ships from a distance, from a dry cliff. He's wondering, lazily, if they're taking part in a race and looks past them for a fluorescent marker buoy.

The next moment, he realises he's no longer safe. He's in the water, in among the flotilla. He's trying to swim and call out at the same time, but he knows that his head's too small to be seen in the rough water and that his voice is too feeble to be heard. He dreams that he's about to die and so he wakes himself up and still feels frightened and says to his wife Karen: 'Actually, they weren't ships. They were dishwashers and ovens. They were kitchen appliances.'

Karen is Danish. She is forty-three. Her voice is as gentle as a nocturne. She says to Tom in this soft voice of hers: 'I think it's rather peculiar that they should be floating like ships. Would they do that? Is it their hollowness?'

'I don't know,' says Tom, holding onto Karen's hand. 'Perhaps they would float for a while, like empty oil drums, if their doors were shut.'

'But I can't imagine it,' says Karen. 'Ovens bobbing around on the waves. In my mind, they would certainly go down to the bottom.'

Tom and Karen lie silent for a while, just touching. It's a May morning, but their bedroom window is small and doesn't let in much sunshine. The house where they live has always been dark. Tom's mind has now let go of the dream and is concentrated on the realisation of being forty. But he notices that the figure 4 is ship-shaped, and he wonders whether somehow, at forty, a man loses ground and has to set sail for a new place. Karen listens to the noisy summer birds and says after a while: 'I dreamed

55

about the new house.'

'Did you?' says Tom. This house is their future. They refer to it as the Scanda-house because they're building it to a Danish design, with warm pine floors and solar heating.

Karen gets up and puts on her white dressing gown. 'I think I'm going to go and see how the builders are getting on today. Shall I?'

'Yes,' says Tom. 'Why not?'

Then they hear Rachel get up and start talking to her cat. Rachel is twelve and their only child. She has long, smooth limbs and long, smooth, bright hair, like Karen's. Tom, who is dark and small, often finds it strange that he lives his life in the company of these two tall women who are so beautiful and so fair. It's both wonderful and difficult. It's like living with two all-knowing angels.

Tom Harris is a diver. His official title is Coastwatcher. His territory is a ribbon of sea bed ten miles long and a mile wide and his task is to examine this area for signs of life and death. He knows his job is an important one. The periphery of every living thing can yield information about the health of the whole. He was told this at his interview. 'Consider the tail of the bison, Mr Harris,' they said, 'the fin of a whale and the extreme outer branches of a fir.' And Tom is happier in this job than in any he's had. His tools are those of the archaeologist – the trowel, the knife, the brush, the memory, the eye – but his site is infinitely more vast and changeful than any ruin or barrow. Anything on earth can be returned to the sea and found there.

He wonders what he will find today, the first day of his forty-first year. In Denmark, as a child, staying near Elsinore for the summer, Karen found a lapis lazuli brooch in a rock pool. She has been proud of this find, always. And in his nine years as a coastal diver Tom has found nothing as beautiful or as valuable as this. But his discoveries have a private value. Sometimes they're so odd that his mind starts work on a story to explain how they got to be there and this gives him a nervous kind of satisfaction. He used to tell the stories to Rachel, but now, for reason's he's unclear about, they have a harsher edge. And he no longer talks to Rachel at bedtime. She prefers talking to her blue-eyed cat. The cat's name is Viola. 'Viola,' says Rachel, 'quite soon we're going to live in a much more brilliant house.'

Tom drives an old Land Rover to the sea. He leaves early, while Rachel and Karen eat their muesli and talk softly together. This morning, as he drives away from the house, he thinks, suppose I never saw them again? Suppose I could never again wake up with Karen? Suppose Rachel's life were to be lived without me? He's never had any tragedy in his life. He can't imagine how certain kinds of tragedy can be borne.

He follows a similar routine each day. He meets his co-diver, Jason, and they put on their wet suits. They comb the beach for lumps of oil and plastic waste and dead things. Jason is a neat man with a lively smile and an old passion for Jane Fonda. In summer, they occasionally find the drowned body of a dune-nesting lark. Cod come into the shallow water and are stranded by the fierce ebb tide and bloat in death. Tom and Jason note the quantity of bladderwrack, the precise colour of the spume on the breakers and the presence or absence of sea birds. They breathe in the wind. Through binoculars, they examine the sea for trawlers and tugs. Sometimes, vast sections of an oil rig are pulled across the horizon, like a piece of scenery across a film location.

They return to Tom's Land Rover and make notes on their beach observation. Jason always brings a Thermos of coffee 'to keep up the body temperature.' (His idol, Jane, has taught him everything he wants to know about the body.) Then, they put on their masks and their lamps and their compressed air cylinders, strap on their instruments and walk to the water, carrying their flippers.

Crashing through the waves always troubles Tom – the bulkiness of them, their roar. They're a barrier to where he wants to be. He's not happy until he starts to dive and then he begins to feel it: the thrill of the sudden silence, of the long, beautiful downward flight into darkness. The light closes above his feet and the world is filleted away. He feels ardent, single-minded, like a man travelling to a longed-for rendezvous. He describes this feeling to Karen as happiness and instead of being offended she's amused. 'It's so *Nordic*, Tom!' she says, 'Really and truly.'

He moves slowly across the sea bed, his meanderings guided by the compass attached to his wrist. Steer north-east and the continental shelf will eventually drop away and leave him poised above the real depths he's never entered. So he goes in a westerly way, remembering to stay quite close to Jason, the sea grass just brushing his body, his lamp like a cartoon wand creating a pathway of colour in front of him. Clusters of tiny brownfish explode into sudden stillness, like spilt wild rice, petrified by its light.

57

He's hoping for some discovery today, for something man-made, trailing a thread of story. He remembers the megaphone and the thurible. The stories he made up around these have taken on substance in his mind, as if they were events and not inventions.

He keeps swimming west, then, signalling to Jason, north a little, out towards the deep. He finds a rusty camera and a bicycle wheel – nothing of interest. He and Jason measure the areas where the sea grass has died.

And so the day passes. He spends quite a lot of it thinking about his two demanding angels and the Scanda-house he's building for them, so that more light can fall on their hair and on their breakfast spoons.

When Rachel has done her homework and taken Viola upstairs ('I don't want her going out at night. She chases birds'), Karen makes strawberry tea and sits at the kitchen table opposite Tom. She warms and warms her hands on the tea mug. 'Tom,' she says, 'you know I went to the mortgage people today?'

'Did you? I thought you were going to see the builders.'

'First the builders. Then the mortgage people about the new loan.'

'And?'

'The Scanda-house can't be finished unless we take out another loan, can it?'

'No. But there shouldn't be a problem. This house is worth far more than we've borrowed, so when we sell it – '

'It isn't, Tom. Not any more.'

'What are you talking about, Karen?'

'They sent a young man back here with me. He looked at this house. Just *looked* at it. Barely came inside. Didn't even go upstairs. He said, "Mrs Harris, there's no question of any further loan. You already have negative equity on this property." '

'Negative equity?'

'It's a term. Nowadays, there's a term for everything you can't quite believe could ever happen. I suppose the term is meant to make it real to you.'

'It's not "real" to me. What does it mean?'

'You haven't heard it? I'd heard it somewhere. Out in the air somewhere. It means the house is worth less than the sum we've borrowed on it.'

'It's not, Karen. We had three valuations.'

'But they were a while ago and now all its value is gone. I mean, like water or something. Or into the same air where all these new terms come from. It has just gone heaven knows where. And so I don't see how the Scanda-house is ever going to be completed now.'

Tears start to fall into Karen's tea. Tom feels a hollow place open inside him and bloat with misery. He reaches out and takes Karen's hand and says weakly: 'You may have been misinformed. They may be quite wrong.' He wishes this moment were a story or a dream. 'I'll look into it, Karen,' he says. 'I'll go into it, love.'

He takes a day off. He talks to the builders, to the mortgage company, to the bank loans department. He is told that the gap between what his present house is worth and what he has borrowed to pay for the new one is now approximately £40,000. The only way the Scanda-house can be finished is by borrowing yet more. But nobody will lend him any more because he can't, now, repay the existing loan. His collateral is used up, suddenly, without any warning, like the compressed air in a cylinder that has no reserve valve. He can't move.

He tells Karen he will find a way. 'What way?' she says. 'Tell me what way.'

'I don't know,' he says, 'but I will.'

They say nothing to Rachel. One evening, she informs the cat: 'Our room in the Scanda-house is going to be right up in the roof, Viola, and we're going to be able to see the sea.'

Tom considers asking Karen to go back to work. She used to be an art teacher. One day, she said: 'I can't do this any more, Tom. These children are too savage for me. In Denmark, pupils are not like this.'

She got Tom's agreement. He could see that the children had no interest in the kind of knowledge that Karen could give. So Karen left the school and stayed at home and painted and now and then made a little money from drawings and watercolours. One of the things promised to her in the new house is a studio of her own. It would have a big, sliding window and a balcony made of steel. And Tom longs to see her in there, working quietly, in her own space at last. He can't ask her to return to teaching. He can't. She's forty-three. She wants a sunny house with a studio and her days alone with her painting. It's not unreasonable.

Back he goes, down into the deep, to think, to try to work it out. He moves more slowly than usual over the sea bed, barely noticing what appears in the beam of his lamp. He feels like the victims of his stories about the megaphone and the thurible, caught up in something they never intended, that no one intended, but which happened nevertheless. He retells the stories to himself, to see if they shed light on his predicament:

*One day, a Scouts decathlon is taking place on the beach. There are scarlet markers out at sea for the thousand metres freestyle. The Scoutmaster's name is Dawlish . . .*

*One winter's day, a Mass is said out at sea on a trawler for a drowned fisherman. The thurifer is a boy named Marcus Grice who is prone to sea-sickness . . .*

Tom stops and thinks, so much of our life is invention, so much the way we choose to see it. I see Karen and Rachel as my bossy angels. Karen sees the lost land of her childhood coming back to her in the guise of a house. The men I work for see this ribbon of water as the conscience of England. In both cases, I have inherited so much responsibility.

*And so. A boy named Pip (the fair-haired boy Dawlish loves single-handedly in his single bed night after night) is coming last in the thousand metres freestyle. Out at the scarlet marker, Pip starts to panic, to wave his arms, to signal that he's in trouble. Dawlish, wearing his Scoutmaster's heavy shoes, wades into the sea and calls to Pip through the megaphone . . .*

*And so. At a certain moment in the Mass for the dead fisherman, with twenty-foot waves hurling the trawler about, Marcus Grice realises he is about to vomit. Forgetting everything but his own nausea, he drops the thurible and staggers to the ship's rail. Burning incense falls onto the trawler's wooden deck . . .*

'Oh no,' said Karen, when Tom told her these stores, 'I see the endings. I see tragedy coming. Don't tell me, I hate tragedy, when it's so senseless.'

As Tom swims on, he realises a truth that he's never understood before: he wants, through the design of the new house, to remind Karen that England is only partly a dark place, that it can be calm, not savage, that beautiful light often falls on it. This, in his imagination, is why it matters so much. His worst fear is that Karen will leave, one day, and go back to a place where she once found lapis lazuli in the water.

Sailing yachts and kitchen appliances: he dreams of them often now. The thing which is nimble and defies the water; the thing which, superseded, might float for a while and then sinks.

Karen gets used to this dream of his. When he wakes and reaches for her hand, she just strokes it gently and says: 'That old dream, Tom. It's so rotten to you. I wish it would go.'

One morning, she says: 'I told Rachel about the Scanda-house. I explained there is nothing we can do. Just make it watertight and wait. She understands.'

And they're being so good about it now, his fair women. Hardly any tears from Karen after that first time; no sulking from Rachel. They've understood what's happened and that's that. In the mornings, when he leaves, there they are, chatting softly together, as if the future were going to arrive today. They eat their muesli. They raise their faces to his for a goodbye kiss, exactly as they always and always did.

He's the one who cries. Nobody sees him do it, not even Jason. He tries not to see himself do it. He dives down to the sea floor and switches off his lamp, so that darkness round him is as absolute as the darkness of the grave, and lets his tears fall. His sobs, through his breathing apparatus, sound unearthly.

He does little searching for human objects any more. He prefers lying in the dark. He's tired of the stories men tell. The only thing he's started to long for is to go beyond the coastal shelf, to go to the true deep, where all the variety of the ocean lives. He's begun to believe – at least with half his mind – that only if he is brave enough, insane enough, to go down into this vast darkness will he find the solution to the problem of the house.

One evening, Tom comes home and hears Karen talking on the telephone to her mother, Eva. He can understand quite a bit of Danish. Karen is telling Eva that she's waiting for her life to change. She says: 'I'm not living my life any more, Mama. I'm waiting to start it again, when I've got my studio.'

He sits down dumbly and listens to this conversation. He knows that Eva has offered to lend them money, but that the money offered is nowhere near enough and, even if it were, it couldn't be accepted because it couldn't be repaid. Eva is a kind woman and she has passed this quality of kindness onto Karen.

At supper, addressing both Karen and Rachel, Tom says: 'I want to talk about our situation. I promised you I'd find a way out of it. And I still mean to. I don't want you to think I've just given up.'

'No, Tom,' says Karen, 'you're not a person who gives up.'

'It's not your fault anyway,' says Rachel.

Tom pushes away his half-finished meal and lights a cigarette. He doesn't often smoke and the cigarette tastes old. 'I thought,' he says, 'I would have a word with the insurance company.'

Karen says: 'I don't think the insurers can do anything, Tom.'

'Well,' says Tom, 'they will have some idea about the future – about when the value gap might start to close.'

Rachel is looking at Tom's face intently, as though it were a map of the world. 'Do you think it will ever?' she asks.

'Yes,' says Tom. 'Yes'.

He sees the summer pass. The insurers say that they really do not know when the value gap may start to close and they dare not guess. The temperature of the sea rises and then starts to fall again. Tom promises himself that, before the winter comes, he will do the thing he has planned.

It requires the hiring of a boat. He chooses a Saturday morning in September when the air is bright. As he manoeuvres the boat out of the harbour, he looks back and sees, half hidden by trees, his new house, waiting.

He is four or five miles out when he throws the anchor. He can see the grey smudge of a ferry going towards Harwich and wonders whether, for some of the Dutch passengers coming over from the Hook of Holland, this may be their first sighting of England. When Karen first saw England, she and her friend Else said together: 'It looks a bit like home.'

He checks his equipment carefully. He knows certain important things are being done incorrectly: he should have a reserve valve on his cylinder; he should not be diving alone.

He lets himself tip backwards into the water and goes down slowly, barely moving his flippers, his lamp directed onto the depth gauge at his wrist. He has no idea how far he has to dive before he starts to see it, the life of the true deep. For the first hundred feet of his fall, there seems to be nothing but himself and the drifting bladderwrack and the bubbling of his own breathing.

But then they start to swim into his light: shoals of silver herring; the brown swirl of an eel; a kite-shaped ray with its dancing tail; the blue bodybags of squid; the fingers of cuttlefish; the first red fronds of deepwater seaweed.

For a while, he hangs still, poised where he is, turning and turning his head so that his lamp beam makes an arc and every arc reveals a new picture. He opens his arms to everything he sees, like he used to open his arms to Rachel when she was a small child. With every suck of compressed air that he takes, his feeling of elation increases.

He goes lower, lower. He's no longer looking at his depth gauge. And then, just ahead of him, he sees a dark mass and feels his body pressed by an underwater current. The mass moves by him and on, and thousands of brownfish rush from its path and Tom knows that something vast is down there with him and he chooses to believe that he's found a whale.

He turns and starts to follow it. He scans it with his lamp, but he can see nothing, only the small fish darting from its path. He wants to touch it, to hold onto it, to become its passenger. He wants it to lead him down. *Only by going deeper and further can anything be solved.*

Tom doesn't know whether he can keep pace. He has to swim as fast as he can, taking in a lot of air, but he does keep pace until he feels the mass suddenly drop away beneath him. It drops and he's stranded there alone, at some mid-point, foolishly kicking his flippered feet. Then he makes the steepest dive he's ever made in his life. Briefly, he thinks of Jason's face wearing a look of terror, then of Jane Fonda wearing a striped leotard and hanging from a wallbar by her feet, and then of nothing, nothing but the beauty of the dive. It doesn't matter whether the thing that leads him down is a whale or not. It's a whale in his mind, just as the Scoutmaster and the thurifer were real people in his mind. It is something alive which, in its every moment of existence, can express its own individual purpose. He has only to follow it and he will attain perfect clarity of thought. The deeper he goes, the more euphoric he feels.

And then, without warning he's in darkness. He remembers it from his sea-bed crying, this darkness-of-the-grave, and with a heavy arm reaches up to switch on his lamp. But no light appears. The battery of his lamp is used up.

In a mere few seconds he feels a drunken sickness come on and now he can't say if this darkness is the real, external darkness of the deep sea or only a darkness of his mind. Far, far away, weak and soft, he hears Karen's voice say: 'Oh! This darkness of us northerners, this blackness of ours . . .'

Sick as he feels, he knows that he must take control. Karen must be his light now, Karen and Rachel, there on the dry cliff, in a dry wind, with the sun on their hair.

He starts to swim up. But he's lost all sense of time. For how long has he been following the imaginary whale? And how deep is he? Without a light to shine on his depth gauge, he has no means of knowing.

So one question only remains, the question of equity: is the sum of water above him greater than the corresponding sum of compressed air left in the cylinder, or is the sum of the air greater than the sum of the water? He says it like a mantra, over and over, to calm him, to keep his sickness in check: *Which is greater? Which is greater?*

Somewhere far above him his bossy angels wait in the bright September sun and all he can keep trying to do is swim upwards to meet them.

\* \* \* \* \*

**Susan Hill**: Aldeburgh, with its echoes of Crabbe and more recently its music festival, has acted as a magnet to writers over the years. Brought up on the east coast, Susan Hill was drawn to the Suffolk resort by Britten's *Sea Interludes* and each winter throughout the 1970s she rented a cottage on the sea front. These were productive years for Hill. The clear, vibrant air seemed charged with an intensity and the stories began to flow as she tramped for miles along the shore. The result is a series of moving tales set on this bleak stretch of coast, notably her novella *The Albatross* and several short stories including *The Custodian* in the collection *A Bit Of Singing And Dancing* (1973).

# The Custodian
## SUSAN HILL

At five minutes to three he climbed up the ladder into the loft. He went cautiously, he was always cautious now, moving his limb warily, and never going out in bad weather without enough warm clothes. For the truth was that he had not expected to survive this winter, he was old, he had been ill for one week, and then the fear had come over him again, that he was going to die. He did not care for his own part, but what would become of the boy? It was only the boy he worried about now, only he who mattered. Therefore, he was careful with himself, for he had lived out this bad winter, it was March, he could look forward to the spring and summer, could cease to worry for a little longer. All the same he had to be careful not to have accidents, though he was steady enough on his feet. He was seventy-one. He knew how easy it would be, for example, to miss his footing on the narrow ladder, to break a limb and lie there, while all the time the child waited, panic welling up inside him, left last at the school. And when the fear of his own dying did not grip him, he was haunted by ideas of some long illness, or incapacitation, and if he had to be taken into hospital, what would happen to the child, then? *What would happen?*

But now it was almost three o'clock, almost time for him to leave the house, his favourite part of the day, now he climbed on hands and knees into the dim, cool loft and felt about among the apples, holding this one and that one up to the beam of light coming through the slats of the roof, wanting the fruit he finally chose to be perfect, ripe and smooth.

The loft smelled sweetly of the apples and pears laid up there since the previous autumn. Above his head, he heard the scrabbling noises of the birds, house martins nesting in the eaves, his heart lurched with joy at the fresh realization that it was almost April, almost spring.

He went carefully down the ladder, holding the chosen apple. It took him twenty minutes to walk to the school but he liked to arrive early, to have the pleasure of watching and waiting, outside the gates.

65

The sky was brittle blue and the sun shone, but it was very cold, the air still smelled of winter. Until a fortnight ago there had been snow, he and the boy had trudged back and forwards every morning and afternoon over the frost-hard paths which led across the marshes, and the stream running alongside of them had been iced over, the reeds were stiff and white as blades.

It had thawed very gradually. Today, the air smelled thin and sharp in his nostrils. Nothing moved. As he climbed the grass bank onto the higher path, he looked across the great stretch of river, and it gleamed like a flat metal plate under the winter sun, still as the sky. Everything was pale, white and silver, a gull came over slowly and its belly and the undersides of its wings were pebbly grey. There were no sounds here except the sudden chatter of dunlin swooping and dropping quickly down, and the tread of his own feet on the path, the brush of his legs against grass clumps.

He had not expected to live this winter.

In his hand, he felt the apple, hard and soothing to the touch, for the boy must have fruit, fruit every day, he saw to that, as well as milk and eggs which they fetched from Maldrun at the farm, a mile away. His limbs should grow, he should be perfect.

Maldrun's cattle were out on their green island in the middle of the marshes, surrounded by the moat of steely water, he led them across a narrow path like a causeway, from the farm. They were like toy animals, or those in a picture seen from this distance away, they stood motionless, cut-out shapes of black and white. Every so often, the boy was still afraid of going past the island of cows, he gripped the old man's hand and a tight expression came over his face.

'They can't get at you, don't you see? They don't cross water, not cows. They're not bothered about you.'

'I know.'

And he did know – and was still afraid. Though there had been days, recently, when he would go right up to the edge of the strip of water, and stare across at the animals, he would even accompany Maldrun to the half-door of the milking parlour, and climb up and look over, would smell the thick, sour, cow-smell, and hear the splash of dung on to the stone floor. Then, he was not afraid. The cows had great, bony haunches and vacant eyes.

'Touch one,' Maldrun had said. The boy had gone inside and put out a hand, though standing well back, stretched and touched the rough pelt, and the cow had twitched, feeling the lightness of his hand as if it were an irritation, the prick of a fly. He was afraid, but getting less so, of the cows.

So many things were changing, he was growing, he was seven years old.

Occasionally, the old man woke in the night and sweated with fear that he might die before the boy was grown, and he prayed, then, to live ten more years, just ten, until the boy could look after himself. And some days it seemed possible, seemed, indeed, most likely, some days he felt very young, felt no age at all, his arms were strong and he could chop wood and lift buckets, he was light-headed with the sense of his own youth. He was no age. He was seventy-two. A tall bony man with thick white hair, and without any spread of spare flesh. When he bathed, he looked down and saw every rib, every joint of his own thin body, he bent an arm and watched the flicker of muscle beneath the skin.

As the path curved round, the sun caught the surface of the water on his right, so that it shimmered and dazzled his eyes for a moment, and then he heard the familiar, faint, high moan of the wind, as it blew off the estuary a mile or more away. The reeds rustled dryly together like sticks. He put up the collar of his coat. But he was happy, his own happiness sang inside his head, that he was here, walking along this path with the apple inside his hand inside his pocket, that he would wait and watch and then, that he would walk back this same way with the boy, that none of those things he dreaded would come about.

Looking back, he could still make out the shapes of the cows, and looking down, to where the water lay between the reed-banks, he saw a swan, its neck arched and its head below the surface of the dark, glistening stream, and it too was entirely still. He stopped for a moment, watching it, and hearing the thin sound of the wind and then, turning, saw the whole, pale stretch of marsh and water and sky, saw for miles, back to where the trees began, behind which was the cottage and then far ahead, to where the sand stretched out like a tongue into the mouth of the estuary.

He was amazed, that he could be alive and moving, small as an insect across this great, bright, cold space, amazed that he should count for as much as Maldrun's cows and the unmoving swan.

The wind was suddenly cold on his face. It was a quarter past three. He left the path, went towards the gate, and began to cross the rough, ploughed field which led to the lane, and then, on another mile to the village, the school.

Occasionally, he came here not only in the morning, and back again in the afternoon, but at other times when he was overcome with sudden anxiety and a desire to see the boy, to reassure himself that he was still there, was alive. Then, he put down whatever he might be doing and came, almost running, stumbled and caught his breath, until he reached the railings and the closed, black gate. If he waited there long enough, if it was dinner or break time, he saw them all come streaming and tumbling out of the green painted doors, and he watched desperately until he saw him, and he could loosen the grip of his hands on the railings, the thumping of his heart eased, inside his chest. Always, then, the boy would come straight down to him, running over the asphalt, and laughed and called and pressed himself up against the railings on the other side.

'Hello.'

'All right are you?'

'What have you brought me? Have you got something?'

Though he knew there would be nothing, did not expect it, knew that there was only ever the fruit at home-time, apple, pear or sometimes, in the summer, cherries or a peach.

'I was just passing through the village.'

'Were you doing the shopping?'

'Yes. I only came up to see . . .'

'We've done reading. We had tapioca for pudding.'

'That's good for you. You should eat that. Always eat your dinner.'

'Is it home-time yet?'

'Not yet.'

'You will be here won't you? You won't forget to come back?'

'Have I ever?'

Then, he made himself straighten his coat, or shift the string shopping bag over from one hand to the other, he said, ' You go back now then, go on to the others, you play with them,' for he knew that this was right, he should not keep the child standing here, should not show him up in front of the rest. It was only for himself that he had come, he was eaten up with his own concern, and fear.

'You go back to your friends now.'

'You will be here? You will be here?'

'I'll be here.'

He turned away, they both turned, for they were separate, they should have their own ways, their own lives. He turned and walked off down the lane out of sight of the playground, not allowing himself to look back, perhaps he went and bought something from the shop, and he was calm again, no longer anxious, he walked back home slowly.

He did not mind all the walking, not even in the worst weather. He did not mind anything at all in this life he had chosen, and which was all-absorbing, the details of which were so important. He no longer thought anything of the past. Somewhere, he had read that an old man has only his memories, and he had wondered at that, for he had none, or rather, they did not concern him, they were like old letters which he had not troubled to keep. He had, simply, the present, the cottage, and the land around it, and the boy to look after. And he had to stay well, stay alive, he must not die yet. That was all.

But he did not often allow himself to go up to the school like that, at unnecessary times, he would force himself to stay and sweat out his anxiety and the need to reassure himself about the child, in some physical job, he would beat mats and plant vegetables in the garden, prune or pick from the fruit trees or walk over to see Maldrun at the farm, buy a chicken, and wait until the time came so slowly around to three o'clock, and he could go, with every reason, could allow himself the pleasure of arriving there a little early, and waiting beside the gates, which were now open, for the boy to come out.

'What have I got today?'

'You guess.'

'That's easy. Pear.'

'Wrong!' He opened his hand, revealing the apple.

'Well, I like apples best.'

'I know. I had a good look at those trees down the bottom this morning. There won't be so many this year. Mind, we've to wait for the blossom to be sure.'

'Last year there were hundreds of apples. *Thousands.*' He took the old man's hand as they reached the bottom of the lane. For some reason he always waited until just here, by the white-beam tree, before doing so.

'There were *millions* of apples!'

'Get on!'

'Well, a lot anyway.'

'That's why there won't be so many this year. You don't get two crops like that in a row.'

'Why?'

' Trees wear themselves out, fruiting like that. They've to rest.'

'Will we have a lot of pears instead then?'

'I daresay. What have you done at school?'

'Lots of things.'

'Have you done your reading? That's what's the important thing. To keep up with your reading.'

He had started the boy off himself, bought alphabet and word picture

69

books from the village, and, when they got beyond these, had made up his own, cut out pictures from magazines and written beside them in large clear letters on ruled sheets of paper. By the time the boy went to school, he had known more than any of the others, he was 'very forward', they had said, though looking him up an down at the same time for he was small for his age.

It worried him that the boy was still small, he watched the others closely as they came out of the gates and they were all taller, thicker in body and stronger of limb. His face was pale and curiously old looking beside theirs. He had always looked old.

The old man concerned himself even more, then, with the fresh eggs and cheese, milk and fruit, watched over the boy while he ate. But he did eat.

'We had meat and cabbage for dinner.'

'Did you finish it?'

'I had a second helping. Then we had cake for pudding. Cake and custard. I don't like that.'

'You didn't leave it?'

'Oh no. I just don't like it, that's all.'

Now, as they came on to the marshes, the water and sky were even paler and the reeds beside the stream were bleached, like old wood left out for years in the sun. The wind was stronger, whipping at their legs from behind.

'There's the swan.'

'They've a nest somewhere about.'

'Have you seen it?'

'They don't let you see it. They go away from it if anybody walks by.'

'I drew a picture of a swan.'

'Today?'

'No. Once. It wasn't very good.'

'If a thing's not good you should do it again.'

'Why should I?'

'You'll get better then.'

'I won't get better at drawing.' He spoke very deliberately, as he so often did, knowing himself, and firm about the truth of things, so that the old man was silent, respecting it.

'He's sharp,' Maldrun's wife said. 'He's a clever one.'

But the old man would not have him spoiled, or too lightly praised.

'He's plenty to learn. He's only a child yet.'

'All the same, he'll do, won't he? He's sharp.'

But perhaps it was only the words he used, only the serious expression on his face, which came of so much reading and all that time spent alone with the old man. And if he was, as they said, so sharp, so forward, perhaps it would do him no good?

He worried about that, wanting the boy to find his place easily in the world, he tried hard not to shield him from things, made him go to the farm to see Maldrun, and over Harper's fen by himself, to play with the gamekeeper's boys, told him always to mix with the others in the school playground, to do what they did. Because he was most afraid, at times, of their very contentment together, of the self-contained life they led, for in truth they needed no one, each of them would be entirely happy never to go far beyond this house: they spoke of all things, or of nothing, the boy read and made careful lists of the names of birds and moths, and built elaborate structures, houses and castles and palaces out of old matchboxes, he helped with the garden, had his own corner down beside the shed in which he grew what he chose. It had been like this from the beginning, from the day the old man had brought him here at nine months' old and set him down on the floor and taught him to crawl, they had fallen naturally into their life together. Nobody else had wanted him. Nobody else would have taken such care.

Once, people had been suspicious, they had spoken to each other in the village, had disapproved.

'He needs a woman there. It's not right. He needs someone who knows,' Maldrun's wife had said. But now, even she had accepted that it was not true, so that, before strangers, she would have defended them more fiercely than anyone.

'He's a fine boy, that. He's all right. You look at him, look. Well, you can't tell what works out for the best. You can never tell.'

By the time they came across the track which led between the gorse bushes and down through the fir trees, it was as cold as it had been on any night in January, they brought in more wood for the fire and had toast and the last of the damson jam and mugs of hot milk.

'It's like winter. Only not so dark. I like it in winter.'

But it was the middle of March now, in the marshes the herons and redshanks were nesting, and the larks spiralled up, singing through the silence. It was almost spring.

So, they went on as they had always done, until the second of April. Then, the day after their walk out to Derenow, the day after they saw the kingfisher, it happened.

From the early morning, he had felt uneasy, though there was no reason he could give for his fear, it simply lay, hard and cold as a stone in his belly, and he was restless about the house from the time he got up.

71

The weather had changed. It was warm and clammy, with low, dun-coloured clouds and, over the marshes, a thin mist. He felt the need to get out, to walk and walk, the cottage was dark and oddly quiet. When he went down between the fruit trees to the bottom of the garden the first of the buds were breaking into green but the grass was soaked with dew like a sweat, the heavy air smelled faintly rotten and sweet.

They set off in the early morning. The boy did not question, he was always happy to go anywhere at all but when he was asked to choose their route, he set off at once, a few paces ahead, on the path which forked away east, in the opposite direction from the village and leading, over almost three miles of empty marsh, towards the sea. They followed the bank of the river, and the water was sluggish, with fronds of dark green weed lying below the surface. The boy bent, and put his hand cautiously down, breaking the skin of the water, but when his fingers came up against the soft, fringed edges of the plants he pulled back.

'Slimey.'

'Yes. It's out of the current here. There's no freshness.'

'Will there be fish?'

'Maybe there will. Not so many.'

'I don't like it.' Though for some minutes he continued to peer between the reeds at the pebbles which were just visible on the bed of the stream. 'He asks questions,' they said. 'He takes an interest. It's his mind, isn't it – bright – you can see, alert, that's what. He's forever wanting to know.' Though there were times when he said nothing at all, his small, old-young face was crumpled in thought, there were times when he looked and listened with care and asked nothing.

'You could die here. You could drown in the water and never, never be found.'

'That's not a thing to think about. What do you worry over that for?'

'But you could, you could.'

They were walking in single file, the boy in front. From all the secret nests down in the reed beds, the birds made their own noises, chirring and whispering, or sending out sudden cries of warning and alarm. The high, sad call of a curlew came again and again, and then ceased abruptly. The boy whistled in imitation.

'Will it know it's me? Will it answer?'

He whistled again. They waited. Nothing. His face was shadowed with disappointment.

'You can't fool them, not birds.'

'You can make a blackbird answer you. You can easily.'

'Not the same.'

'Why isn't it?'

'Blackbirds are tame, blackbirds are garden birds.'

'Wouldn't a curlew come to the garden?'

'No.'

'Why wouldn't it?'

'It likes to be away from things. They keep to their own places.'

As they went on, the air around them seemed to close in further, it seemed harder to breathe, and they could not see clearly ahead to where the marshes and mist merged into the sky. Here and there, the stream led off into small, muddy pools and hollows, and the water in them was reddened by the rust seeping from some old can or metal crate thrown there and left for years, the stains which spread out looked like old blood. Gnats hovered in clusters over the water.

'Will we go onto the beach?'

'We could.'

'We might find something on the beach.'

Often, they searched among the pebbles for pieces of amber or jet, for old buckles and buttons and sea-smooth coins washed up by the tides, the boy had a collection of them in a cardboard box in his room.

They walked on, and then, out of the thick silence which was all around them came the creaking of wings, nearer and nearer and sounding like two thin boards of wood beaten slowly together. A swan, huge as an eagle, came over their heads, flying low, so that the boy looked up for a second in terror at the size and closeness of it, caught his breath. He said urgently, 'Swans go for people, swans can break your arm if they hit you, if they beat you with their wings. Can't they?'

'But they don't take any notice, so come on, you leave them be.'

'Oh, they might.' He watched the great, grey-white shape go awkwardly away from them, in the direction of the sea.

A hundred yards further on at the junction of two paths across the marsh, there was the ruin of a water mill, blackened after a fire years before, and half broken down, a sail torn off. Inside, under an arched doorway, it was dark and damp, the walls were coated with yellowish moss and water lay, brackish, in the mud hollows of the floor.

At high summer, on hot, shimmering blue days they had come across here on the way to the beach with a string bag full of food for their lunch, and then the water mill had seemed like a sanctuary, cool and silent, the boy had gone inside and stood there, had called softly and listened to the echo of his own voice as it rang lightly round and round the walls.

Now, he stopped dead in the path, some distance away.

'I don't want to go.'

'We're walking to the beach.'

'I don't want to go past that.'

'The mill?'

'There are rats.'

'No.'

'And flying things. Things that are black and hang upside down.'

'Bats? What's to be afraid of in bats? You've seen them, you've been in Maldrun's barn. They don't hurt.'

'I want to go back.'

'You don't have to go into the mill, who said you did? We're going on to where the sea is.'

*'I want to go back now.'*

He was not often frightened. But, standing there in the middle of the hushed stretch of fenland, the old man felt again disturbed himself, the fear that something would happen, here, where nothing moved and the birds lay hidden, only crying out their weird cries, where things lay under the unmoving water and the press of the air made him sweat down his back. Something would happen to them, something . . .

What could happen?

Then, not far ahead, they both saw him at the same moment, a man with a gun under his arm, tall and black and menacing as a crow against the dull horizon, and as they saw him, they also saw two mallard ducks rise in sudden panic from their nest in the reeds, and they heard the shots, three shots that cracked out and echoed for miles around, the air went on reverberating with the waves of terrible sound.

The ducks fell at once, hit in mid-flight so that they swerved, turned over, and plummeted down. The man with the shotgun started quickly forward and the grasses and reeds bent and stirred as a dog ran, burrowing, to retrieve. 'I want to go back, *I want to go back.*'

Without a word, the old man took his hand, and they turned, walked quickly back the way they had come, as though afraid that they too, would be followed and struck down, not caring that they were out of breath and sticky with sweat, but only wanting to get away, to reach the shelter of the lane and the trees, to make for home.

Nothing was ever said about it, or about the feeling they had both had walking across the marshes, the boy did not mention the man with the gun or the ducks which had been alive and in flight, then so suddenly dead. All that evening, the old man watched him, as he stuck pictures in a book, and tore up dock leaves to feed the rabbit, watched for signs of left-over fear. But he was only, perhaps, quieter than usual, his face more closed up, he was concerned with his own thoughts.

In the night, he woke, and got up, went to the boy and looked down through the darkness, for fear that he might have had bad dreams and woken, but there was only the sound of his breathing, he lay quite still, very long and straight in the bed.

He imagined the future, and his mind was filled with images of all the possible horrors to come, the things which could cause the boy shock and pain and misery, and from which he would not be able to save him, as he had been powerless today to protect him from the sight of the killing of two ducks. He was in despair. Only the next morning, he was eased, as it came back to him again, the knowledge that he had, after all, lived out the winter and ahead of them lay only light and warmth and greenness.

Nevertheless, he half-expected that something would still happen to them, to break into their peace. For more than a week, nothing did, his fears were quieted, and then the spring broke, the apple and pear blossom weighed down the branches in great, creamy clots, the grass in the orchard grew up as high as the boy's knees, and across the marshes the sun shone and shone, the water of the river was turquoise, and in the streams, as clear as glass, the wind blew warm and smelled faintly of salt and earth. Walking to and from the school every day, they saw more woodlarks than they had ever seen, quivering on the air high above their heads, and near the gorse bushes, the boy found a nest of leverets. In the apple loft, the house martins hatched out and along the lanes, dandelions and buttercups shone golden out of the grass.

It was on the Friday that Maldrun gave the boy one of the farm kittens, and he carried it home close to his body beneath his coat. It was black and white like Maldrun's cows. And it was the day after that, the end of the first week of spring, that Blaydon came, Gilbert Blaydon, the boy's father.

He was sitting outside the door watching a buzzard hover above the fir copse when he heard the footsteps. He thought it was Maldrun bringing over the eggs, or a chicken – Maldrun generally came one evening in the week, after the boy had gone to bed, they drank a glass of beer and talked for half an hour. He was an easy man, undemonstrative. They still called one another, formally, 'Mr Bowry,' 'Mr Maldrun.'

The buzzard roved backwards and forwards over its chosen patch of air, searching.

When the old man looked down again, he was there, standing in the path. He was carrying a canvas kitbag.

He knew, then, why he had been feeling uneasy, he had expected this, or something like it, to happen, though he had put the fears to the back of his mind with the coming of sunshine and the leaf-breaking. He felt no hostility as he looked at Blaydon, only extreme weariness, almost as though he were ill.

There was no question of who it was, yet above all he ought to have expected a feeling of complete disbelief, for if anyone had asked, he would have said that he would certainly never see the boy's father again. But now he was here, it did not seem surprising, it seemed, indeed, somehow inevitable. Things had to alter, things could never go on. Happiness did not go on.

'Will you be stopping?'

Blaydon walked slowly forward, hesitated, and then set the kitbag down at his feet. He looked much older.

'I don't know if it'd be convenient.'

'There's a room. There's always a room.'

The old man's head buzzed suddenly in confusion, he thought he should offer a drink or a chair, should see to a bed, should ask questions to which he did not want to know the answers, should say something about the boy. *The boy.*

'You've come to take him . . .'

Blaydon sat down on the other chair, beside the outdoors table. The boy looked like him, there was the same narrowness of forehead and chin, the same high-bridged nose. Only the mouth was different, though that might simply be because the boy's was still small and unformed.

'You've come to take him.'

'Where to?' He looked up. 'Where would I have to take him to?'

But we don't want you here, the old man thought, we don't want anyone: and he felt the intrusion of this younger man, with the broad hands and long legs sprawled under the table, like a violent disturbance of the careful pattern of their lives, he was alien. *We don't want you.*

But what right had he to say that? He did not say it. He was standing up helplessly, not knowing what should come next, he felt the bewilderment as some kind of irritation inside his own head.

He felt old.

In the end, he managed to say, 'You'll not have eaten?'

Blaydon stared at him. 'Don't you want to know where I've come from?'

'No.'

'No.'

'I've made a stew. You'll be better for a plate of food.'

'Where is he?'

'Asleep in bed, where else would he be? I look after him, I know what I'm about. It's half-past eight, gone, isn't it? What would he be doing but asleep in his bed, at half-past eight?'

He heard his own voice rising and quickening, as he defended himself, defended both of them, he could prove it to this father or to anyone at all, how he'd looked after the boy. He would have said, what about you? Where have you been? What did you do for him? But he was too afraid, for he knew nothing about what rights Blaydon might have – even though he had never been near, never bothered.

'You could have been dead.'

'Did you think?'

'What was I to think? I knew nothing. Heard nothing.'

'No.'

Out of the corner of his eye, the old man saw the buzzard drop down suddenly, straight as a stone, on to some creature in the undergrowth of the copse. The sky was mulberry coloured and the honeysuckle smelled ingratiatingly sweet.

'I wasn't dead.'

The old man realized that Blaydon looked both tired and rather dirty, his nails were broken, he needed a shave and the wool at the neck of his blue sweater was unravelling. What was he to say to the boy then, when he had brought him up to be so clean and tidy and careful, had taken his clothes to be mended by a woman in the village, had always cut and washed his hair himself? What was he to tell him about this man?

'There's hot water. I'll get you linen, make you a bed. You'd best go up first, before I put out the stew. Have a wash.'

He went into the kitchen, took a mug and a bottle of beer and poured it out, and was calmed a little by the need to organize himself, by the simple physical activity.

When he took the beer out, Blaydon was still leaning back on the old chair. There were dark stains below his eyes.

'You'd best take it up with you.' The old man held out the beer.

It was almost dark now. After a long time, Blaydon reached out, took the mug and drank, emptying it in four or five long swallows, and then, as though all his muscles were stiff, rose slowly, took up the kitbag, went towards the house.

When the old man had set the table and dished out the food, he was trembling. He tried to turn his mind away from the one thought. That

Blaydon had come to take the boy away.

He called and when there was no reply, went up the stairs. Blaydon was stretched out on his belly on top of the unmade bed, heavy and motionless in sleep.

While he slept, the old man worried about the morning. It was Saturday, there would not be the diversion of going to school, the boy must wake and come downstairs and confront Blaydon.

What he had originally said, was, your mother died, your father went away. And that was the truth. But he doubted if the boy so much as remembered; he had asked a question only once, and that more than two years ago.

They were content together, needing no one.

He sat on the straight-back chair in the darkness, surrounded by hidden greenery and the fumes of honeysuckle, and tried to imagine what he might say.

'This is your father. Other boys have fathers. This is your father who came back, who will stay with us here. For some time, or perhaps not for more than a few days. His name is Gilbert Blaydon.

Will you call him 'father' ?, will you . . .

'This is . . .'

His mind broke down before the sheer cliff confronting it and he simply sat on, hands uselessly in front of him on the outdoors table, he thought of nothing, and on white plates in the kitchen the stew cooled and congealed and the new kitten from Maldrun's farm slept, coiled on an old green jumper. The cat, the boy, the boy's father, all slept. From the copse, the throaty call of the night-jars.


'You'll be ready for breakfast. You didn't eat the meal last night.'

'I slept.'

'You'll be hungry.' He had his back to Blaydon. He was busy with the frying pan and plates over the stove. What had made him tired enough to sleep like that, from early evening until now, fully clothed on top of the bed! But he didn't want to know, would not ask questions.

The back door was open on to the path that led down between vegetable beds and the bean canes and currant bushes, towards the thicket. Blaydon went to the doorway.

'Two eggs, will you have?'

'If . . .'

'There's plenty.' He wanted to divert him, talk to him, he had to pave the way. The boy was there, somewhere at the bottom of the garden.

'We'd a hard winter.'

'Oh, yes?'

'Knee deep, all January, all February, we'd to dig ourselves out of the door. And then it froze – the fens froze right over, ice as thick as your fist. I've never known like it.'

But now it was spring, now outside there was the bright, glorious green of new grass, new leaves, now the sun shone.

He began to set out knives and forks on the kitchen table. It would have to come, he would have to call the boy in, to bring them together. What would he say? His heart squeezed and then pumped hard, suddenly, in the thin bone-cage of his chest.

Blaydon's clothes were creased and crumpled. And they were not clean. Had he washed himself? The old man tried to get a glimpse of his hands.

'I thought I'd get a job,' Blaydon said.

The old man watched him.

'I thought I'd look for work.'

'Here?'

'Around here. Is there work?'

'Maybe. I've not had reason to find out. Maybe.'

'If I'm staying on, I'll need to work.'

'Yes.'

'It'd be a help, I daresay?'

'You've a right to do as you think fit. You make up your own mind.'

'I'll pay my way.'

'You've no need to worry about the boy, if it's that. He's all right, he's provided for. You've no need to find money for him.'

'All the same . . .'

After a minute, Blaydon walked over and sat down at the table.

The old man thought, he is young, young and strong and fit, he has come her to stay, he has every right, he's the father. He is . . .

But he did not want Blaydon in their lives, did not want the hands resting on the kitchen table, and the big feet beneath it.

He said, 'You could try at the farm. At Maldrun's. They've maybe got work there. You could try.'

'Maldrun's farm?'

'It'd be ordinary work. Labouring work.'

'I'm not choosy.'

The old man put out eggs and fried bread and bacon onto the plates, poured tea, filled the sugar basin. And then he had no more left to do, he had to call the boy.

But nothing happened as he had feared it, after all.

He came in. 'Wash your hands.' But he was already half way to the sink, he had been brought up so carefully, the order was not an order but a formula between them, regular, and of comfort.

'Wash your hands.'

'I've come to stay.' Blaydon said at once, 'for a bit. I got here last night.'

The boy hesitated in the middle of the kitchen, looked from one to the other of them, trying to assess this sudden change in the order of things.

'For a week or two,' the old man said. 'Eat your food.'

The boy got on to his chair. 'What's your name?'

'Gilbert Blaydon.'

'What have I to call you?'

'Either.'

'Gilbert, then.'

'What you like.'

After that, they got on with eating; the old man chewed his bread very slowly, filled, for the moment, with relief.

Maldrun took him on at the farm as a general labourer and then their lives formed a new pattern, with the full upsurge of spring. Blaydon got up, and ate his breakfast with them and then left, there was a quarter of an hour which the old man had alone with the boy before setting off across the marsh path to school, and in the afternoon, an even longer time. Blaydon did not return, sometimes, until after six.

At the weekend, he went off somewhere alone, but occasionally, he took the boy for walks; they saw the heron's nest, and then the cygnets, and once, a peregrine, flying over the estuary. The two of them were at ease together.

Alone, the old man tried to imagine what they might be saying to each other, he walked distractedly about the house, and almost wept, with anxiety and dread. They came down the path, and the boy was sitting up on Blaydon's shoulders, laughing and laughing.

'You've told him.'

Blaydon turned, surprised, and then sent the boy away. 'I've said nothing.'

The old man believed him. But there was still a fear for the future, the end of things.

The days lengthened. Easter went by, and the school holidays, during which the old man was happiest, because he had so much time with the boy to himself, and then it was May, in the early mornings there was a fine mist above the blossom trees.

'He's a good worker,' Maldrun said, coming over one evening with the eggs and finding the old man alone. 'I'm glad to have him.'

'Yes.'

'He takes a bit off your shoulders, I daresay.'

'He pays his way.'

'No. Work, I meant. Work and worries. All that.'

What did Malrun know? But he only looked back at the old man, his face open and friendly, drank his bottled beer.

He thought about it, and realized that it was true. He had grown used to having Blaydon about, to carry the heavy things and lock up at night, to clear out the fruit loft and lop off the overhanging branches and brambles at the entrance to the thicket. He had slipped into their life, and established himself. When he thought of the future without Blaydon, it was to worry. For the summer was always short and then came the run down through autumn into winter again. Into snow and ice and cold, and the north-east wind scything across the marshes. He dreaded all that, now that he was old. Last winter, he had been ill once, and for only a short time. This winter he was a year older, anything might happen. He thought of the mornings when he would have to take the boy to school before it was even light, thought of the frailty of his own flesh, the brittleness of his bones, he looked in the mirror at his own weak and rheumy eyes.

He had begun to count on Blaydon's being here to ease things, to help with the coal and wood and the breaking of ice on pails, to be in some way an insurance against his own possible illness, possible death.

Though now, it was still only the beginning of summer, now, he watched Blaydon build a rabbit hutch for the boy, hammering nails and sawing wood, uncoiling wire skilfully. He heard them laugh suddenly together. This was what he needed, after all, not a woman about the place, but a man, the strength and ease of a man who was not old, did not fear, did not say 'Wash your hands', 'Drink up all your milk', 'Take care.'

The kitten grew, and spun about in quick, mad circles in the sun.

'He's a good worker.' Maldrun said.

After a while, the old man took to dozing in his chair outside, after supper, while Blaydon washed up, emptied the bins and then took out the shears, to clip the hedge or the grass borders, when the boy had gone to bed.

But everything that had to do with the boy, the business of rising and eating, going to school and returning, the routine of clothes and food and drink and bed, all that was still supervised by the old man. Blaydon did not interfere, scarcely seemed to notice what was done. His own part in the boy's life was quite different.

In June and early July, it was hotter than the old man could ever remember. The gnats droned in soft, grey clouds under the trees, and over the water of the marshes. The sun shone hard and bright and still the light played tricks so that the estuary seemed now very near, now very far away. Maldrun's cows tossed their heads, against the flies which gathered stickily in the runnels below their great eyes.

He began to rely more and more upon Blaydon as the summer reached its height, left more jobs for him to do, because he was willing and strong, and because the old man succumbed easily to the temptation to rest himself in the sun. He still did most of the cooking but he would let Blaydon go down to the shops and the boy often went with him. He was growing, his limbs were filling out and his skin was berry-brown. He lost the last of the pink-and-whiteness of babyhood. He had accepted Blaydon's presence without question and was entirely used to him, though he did not show any less affection for the old man, who continued to take care of him day by day. But he became less nervous and hesitant, more self-assured, he spoke of things in a casual, confident voice, learned much from his talks with Blaydon. He still did not know that this was his father. The old man thought there was no reason to tell him – not yet, not yet, they could go on as they were for the time being, just as they were.

He was comforted by the warmth of the sun on his face, by the scent of the roses and the tobacco plants in the evening, the sight of the scarlet bean-flowers clambering higher and higher up their frame.

He had decided right at the beginning that he himself would ask no questions of Blaydon, would wait until he should be told. But he was not told. Blaydon's life might have begun only on the day he arrived here. The old man wondered if he had been in prison, or else abroad, working on a ship, though he had no evidence for either. In the evenings they drank beer together and occasionally played a game of cards, though more often, Blaydon worked at something in the garden and the old man simply sat, watching him, hearing the last cries of the birds from the marshes.

With the money Blaydon brought in, they bought new clothes for the boy, and better cuts of meat, and then, one afternoon, a television set arrived with two men in a green van to erect the aerial.

'For the winter,' Blaydon said. 'Maybe you won't bother with it now. But it's company in the winter.'

'I've never felt the lack.'

'All the same.'

'I don't need entertainment. We make our own. Always have made our own.'

'You'll be glad of it once you've got the taste. I told you – it's for the winter.'

But the old man watched it sometimes very late in the evenings of August and discovered things of interest to him, new horizons were opened, new worlds.

'I'd not have known that,' he said. 'I've never travelled. Look at what I'd never have known.'

Blaydon nodded, He himself seemed little interested in the television set. He was mending the front fence, staking it all along with old wood given him by Maldrun at the farm. Now, the gate would fit closely and not swing and bang in the gales of winter.

It was on a Thursday night towards the end of August that Blaydon mentioned the visit to the seaside.

'He's never been,' he said, wiping the foam of beer from his top lip. ' He told me. I asked him. He's never been to the sea.'

'I've done all I can. There's never been the money. We've managed as best we could.'

'You're not being blamed.'

'I'd have taken him, I'd have seen to it in time. Sooner or later.'

'Yes.'

'Yes.'

'Well – I could take him.'

'To the sea?'

'To the coast, yes.'

'For a day? It's far enough.'

'A couple of days, I thought. For a weekend.'

The old man was silent. But it was true. The boy had never been anywhere and perhaps he suffered because of it, perhaps at school the others talked of where they had gone, what they had seen, shaming him; if that was so, he should be taken, should go everywhere, he must not miss anything, must not be left out.

'Just a couple of days. We'd leave first thing Saturday morning and come back Monday. I'd take a day off.'

He had been here three months now, and not missed a day off work.

'You do as you think best.'

'I'd not go without asking you.'

'It's only right. He's at the age for taking things in. He needs enjoyment.'

'Yes.'

'You go. It's only right.'

'I haven't told him, not yet.'

'You tell him.'

When he did, the boy's face opened out with pleasure, he licked his lips nervously over and over again in his excitement, already counting until it should be time to go. The old man went upstairs and sorted out clothes for him, washed them carefully and hung them on the line, he began himself to anticipate it all. This was right. The boy should go.

But he dreaded it. They had not been separated before. He could not imagine how it would be, to sleep alone in the cottage, and then he began to imagine all the possible accidents. Blaydon had not asked him if he wanted to go with them. But he did not. He felt suddenly too tired to leave the house, too tired for any journeys or strangers, he wanted to sit on his chair in the sun and count the time until they should be back.

He had got used to the idea of Blaydon's continuing presence here, he no longer lived in dread of the coming winter. It seemed a long time since the days when he had been alone with the boy.

They set off very early on the Saturday morning, before the sun had broken through the thick mist that hung low over the marshes. Every sound was clear and separate as it came through the air, he heard their footsteps, the brush of their legs against the grasses long after they were out of sight. The boy had his own bag, bought new in the village, a canvas bag strapped across his shoulders. He had stood up very straight, eyes glistening, already his mind was filled with imaginary pictures of what he would see, what they would do.

The old man went back into the kitchen and put the kettle on again, refilled the teapot for himself and planned what he was going to do. He would work, he would clean out all the bedrooms of the house and sort the boy's clothes for any that needed mending; he would polish the knives and forks and wash the curtains and walk down to the village for groceries, he would bake a cake and pies, prepare a stew, ready for their return.

So that, on the first day, the Saturday, he scarcely had time to think of them, to notice their absence and in the evening, his legs and back ached, he sat for only a short time outside, after his meal, drunk with tiredness, and slept later than usual on the Sunday morning.

It was then that he felt the silence and emptiness of the house. He walked about it uselessly, he woke up the kitten and teased it with a feather so that it would play with him, distract his attention from his own solitude. When it slept again, he went out, and walked for miles across the still, hot marshes. The water between the reed beds was very low and even dried up altogether in places, revealing the dark, greenish-brown slime below. The faint, dry whistling sound that usually came through the rushes was absent. He felt parched as the countryside after this long, long summer, the sweat ran down his bent back.

He had walked in order to tire himself out again but this night he slept badly and woke out of clinging nightmares with a thudding heart, tossed from side to side, uncomfortable among the bedclothes. But tomorrow he could begin to count the strokes of the clock until their return.

He got up feeling as if he had never slept, his eyes were pouched and blurred. But he began the baking, the careful preparations to welcome them home. He scarcely stopped for food himself all day, though his head and his back ached, he moved stiffly about the kitchen.

When they had not returned by midnight on the Monday, he did not go down to the village, or across to Maldrun's farm to telephone the police and the hospitals. He did nothing. He knew.

But he sat up in the chair outside the back door all night with the silence pressing in on his ears. Once or twice his head nodded down on to his chest, he almost slept, but then jerked awake again, shifted a little, and sat on in the darkness.

He thought, they have not taken everything, some clothes are left, clothes and toys and books, they must mean to come back. But he knew that they did not. Other toys, other clothes, could be bought anywhere.

A week passed and the summer slid imperceptibly into autumn, like smooth cards shuffled together in a pack, the trees faded to yellow and crinkled at the edges.

He did not leave the house, and he ate almost nothing, only filled and refilled the teapot, and drank.

He did not blame Gilbert Blaydon, he blamed himself for having thought to keep the boy, having planned out their whole future. When the father had turned up, he should have known what he wanted at once, should have said, 'Take him away, take him now,' to save them this furtiveness, this deception. At night, though, he worried most about the effect it would have on the boy, who had been brought up so scrupulously, to be tidy and clean, to eat up his food, to learn. He wished there was an address to which he could write a list of details about the boy's everyday life, the routine he was used to following.

He waited for a letter. None came. The pear trees sagged under their weight of ripe, dark fruit and after a time it fell with soft thuds into the long grass. He did not gather it up and take it to store in the loft, he left it there for the sweet pulp to be burrowed by hornets and grub. But sometimes he took a pear and ate it himself, for he had always disapproved of waste.

He kept the boy's room exactly as it should be. His clothes were laid out neatly in the drawers, his books lined on the single shelf, in case he should return. But he could not bother with the rest of the house, dirt began to linger in corners. Fluff accumulated greyly beneath beds. The damp patch on the bathroom wall was grown over with moss like a fungus when the first rain came in October.

Maldrun had twice been across from the farm and received no answer to his questions. In the village, the women talked. October went out in fog and drizzle, and the next time Maldrun came the old man did not open the door. Maldrun waited, peering through the windows between cupped hands, and in the end left the eggs on the back step.

The old man got up later and later each day, and went to bed earlier, to sleep between the frowsty, unwashed sheets. For a short while he turned on the television set in the evenings and sat staring at whatever was offered to him, but in the end he did not bother, only stayed in the kitchen while it grew dark around him. Outside, the last of the fruit fell onto the sodden garden and lay there untouched. Winter came.

In the small town flat, Blaydon set out plates, cut bread and opened tins, filled the saucepan with milk.

'Wash your hands,' he said. But the boy was already there, moving his hands over and over the pink soap, obediently, wondering what was for tea.

\* \* \* \* \*

**Pat Barker's** reputation as an important new novelist was already established in the 1980s with the publication of her first four novels, but it was the appearance of her highly acclaimed *Regeneration* trilogy in the eary '90s that brought her work to the attention of a much wider reading public. The first world war trilogy comprises *Regeneration, The Eye in the Door* and *The Ghost Road*, winner of the 1995 Booker Prize. *The Storm* is the memorable episode from *Regeneration* in which the psychologist Rivers decides to take a break from his work in the rehabilitation unit at Craiglockhart to visit an ex-patient, David Burns, on the Suffolk coast.

# The Storm
## PAT BARKER

Aldeburgh was the end of the line, but the train, as if reluctant to accept this, produced, as Rivers stepped down on to the platform, an amazing burst of steam. He stood, looking up and down, as the train's hissing subsided into grunts, and the steam cleared. Burns had promised to meet him, but his memory wasn't good, and, faced with the empty platform, Rivers was glad he had the address. But then, just as Rivers was resigning himself to finding the house on his own, Burns appeared, a tall, emaciated figure wearing a coat of stiff herringbone tweed that reached almost to the ground. He'd obviously been running, and was out of breath. 'Hello,' he said. Rivers tried to judge whether Burns looked better or worse. It was hard to tell. His face in the light of the naphtha flares was as expressionless as beaten bronze.

'How are you?' they asked simultaneously, and then laughed.

Rivers decided he should be the one to answer. 'A lot better, thanks.'

'Good,' Burns said. 'It's walking distance,' he added across his shoulder, already striding off. 'We don't need a taxi.'

They came out of the station and began walking downhill, through the quiet cold fringes of the town, past the church, through streets of huddled houses, and out on to the front.

The sea was calm, almost inaudible, a toothless mouth mumbling pebbles in the darkness. Instead of walking along the path, Burns struck out across the shingle and Rivers followed, to where the tide had laid bare a thin strip of sand. The crunch and slither of shingle under their feet blotted out all other sounds. Rivers turned, and saw the bones of Burns's face gleaming in the moonlight. He wondered what he made of the tangles of barbed wire that ran along the beach, with only two narrow channels left for fishing boats and for the lifeboat to come and go. But Burns seemed not to see the wire.

They stood together at the water's edge, two black shadows on the pale shingle, and small waves creamed over at their feet. Then the moon came out from behind a bank of dark cloud, and the fishermen's huts, the boats lined up in two short rows behind the wire, and the heaped nets, cast shadows behind them almost as sharply edged as day.

They returned to the path and began walking along the terrace of houses, which here and there had gaps. Many of the houses were shuttered and had sandbags piled against the front doors. 'The sea's been known to pay visits,' Burns said, following the direction of Rivers's gaze. 'I was here once when it flooded.' Evidently sandbags brought back no other memories.

'This is it,' he said a few minutes later, stopping in front of a tall but extremely narrow house. At this end of the foreshore the sea was much closer, turning and turning in the darkness. Rivers looked out and caught a glint of white. 'What's along there?'

'The marshes. More shingle. I'll show you tomorrow.'

They groped their way into the hall, closing the door carefully behind them before Burns switched on the light. His face, deeply shadowed from the unshaded bulb, peered anxiously at Rivers. 'I expect you'd like to go upstairs,' he said. 'I *think* I've given you a towel . . .' He looked like a child trying to remember what it was that grown-ups said to newly arrived guests. He also looked, for the first time, deranged.

Rivers followed him up the narrow stairs and into a small bedroom. Burns pointed out the bathroom and then went downstairs. Rivers put his bag down, bounced on the bed to test the mattress, and looked round. The walls were covered with paper of an indeterminate and confusing pattern, the background colour faded to the yellow of an old bruise. Everything smelled of the sea, as if the furniture had soaked it in. It reminded him of childhood holidays in Brighton. He splashed his face in the bowl, then, turning off the light, opened the shutters. His room overlooked the sea. The wind was rising, and with each gust the coils of wire twitched as if they were alive.

No sign of Burns's parents. Rivers had mistakenly assumed he was being invited to meet them, since a large part of Burns's letter had dealt with their anxieties about his future. But apparently not. This was probably their room. The house was so narrow there couldn't be more than one, or at the most, two small rooms on each floor.

The evening passed pleasantly enough. No mention of Burns's illness, no mention of the war. These were evidently taboo topics, but they talked about a great range of other things. Whatever else the war had done to Burns, it had certainly deepened his love for his native county. Suffolk flowers, birds, churches, he was knowledgeable about them all. More recently, he'd become interested in the preservation of country crafts. 'Old Clegg', who was apparently something of a local character, had promised to teach him flint-knapping, and he seemed to be looking forward to that. Even before the war he'd been very much a countryman in his interests, rather like Siegfried in a way, though without Siegfried's passion for hunting.

When the conversation turned to other matters, Burns was very much the bright sixth former, idealistic, intolerant, naive, inclined to offer sweeping generalizations as fact, attractive in the freshness of his vision as such boys often are. Rivers thought how misleading it was to say that the war had 'matured' these young men. It wasn't true of his patients, and it certainly wasn't true of Burns, in whom a prematurely aged man and a fossilized schoolboy seemed to exist side by side. It did give him a curiously ageless quality, but 'maturity' was hardly the word. Still, he was better than he'd been at Craiglockhart, so perhaps his conviction that if he could only get back to Suffolk and forget the war he would be all right had been proved correct. But then why am I here? Rivers thought. Despite Burns's reluctance to mention his illness, Rivers didn't believe he'd been invited to Suffolk to talk about church architecture. But it would be quite wrong to force the pace. Whatever was bothering him, he would raise the matter in his own time.

Rivers woke the following morning to find the beach shrouded in mist. He leant on the window sill, and watched the fishing boats return. The pebbles on the beach were wet, though not from rain or tide. The mist clung to them like sweat, and the air tasted of iron. Everything was so quiet. When a gull flew in from the sea and passed immediately overhead, he heard the creak of its wings.

Burns was already up, in the kitchen by the sound of things, but not, Rivers thought, preparing breakfast. Nothing in the way of dinner or supper had appeared the night before, and Rivers had hesitated, on his first evening, to go into the kitchen and forage for food, though he suspected that might be the only way of getting any.

He washed, dressed, shaved, and went downstairs. By this time the mist on the beach had begun to thin, but it was cold for the time of year, and the sight of a fire in the first floor living room was welcome. He went down a further flight of stairs into the kitchen and found Burns at the kitchen table with a pot of tea.

'There's some cereal,' he said, pointing.

He sounded shy again, though last night he'd begun to talk quite freely by the end of the evening, just as Rivers, caught between the roar of the fire and the roar of the sea, had started nodding off to sleep. 'I'm sorry I had to go to bed so early,' Rivers said, reaching for the cereal packet.

' 'S all right.' Visibly, he remembered what it was he was supposed to ask next. 'Did you have a good night?'

'Fine.' Rivers bit the reciprocal question back. He'd heard part of Burns's night. Obviously, however hard Burns tried to thrust memories of the war behind him, the nightmare followed.

The doorbell rang, and Burns got up to answer it. 'This is Mrs Burril's day for sorting me out,' he said.

Mrs Burril was a remarkably silent person, but she managed, without words, to make it clear their presence was superfluous.

Burns said, 'I thought we might go for a walk.'

The mist had thinned but not cleared. It moved in slow, cold currents over the marshes, where drainage ditches and sump holes reflected a steely light at the sky. Reeds whispered, with a noise like the palms of hands being rubbed together. It was difficult to breathe, difficult even to move, and they spoke in low voices when they spoke at all.

They walked along a narrow raised path that divided the marshes from the river. Small yachts rode at anchor, the breeze just strong enough to make their rigging rattle, not a loud sound, but persistent and rather disturbing, like an irregular heart beat. Nothing else here could disturb. The estuary lay flat and peaceful under a shrunken, silver sun, and nothing moved, except the reeds, until a flight of ducks whistled past.

Rivers had begun to realize how remarkable the area was. A strip of land, at times no more than a hundred yards wide, divided the estuary from the North Sea. Walking out along this strip, away from the town, into the bleached shingle distances, you became aware of two separate sounds: the roar and suck of waves on shingle, and the lulling sound of the river among its reeds. If you moved to the left, the crunch and chop of boots on shingle cut out the gentler river sounds. If to the right, the tapping of rigging and the lapping of water dominated, though you could still hear that the sea was there,

They turned and looked back at the huddled town. 'You know, I love this place,' Burns said. 'I wouldn't like you to think I'd left London just because of the raids. Actually it wasn't the raids, it was the regular meal-times, You know, everybody sitting down to eat. Waiting for food to be put in front of them, And father going on about the war. He's a great believer in the war, my father.'

'Will they be coming to Suffolk at all?'

'No, I shouldn't think so. They're both very busy in London.' They turned and walked on. 'It's best we don't see too much of each other at the moment. I am not a sight for sore eyes.'

A squat, circular building had begun to loom up out of the mist. It looked rather like a Martello tower, Rivers thought, but he hadn't known they'd been built as far north as this.

'This is the most northerly,' Burns said, slithering down the slope on to the beach. Rivers followed him across the shingle and down into the dank high moat that surrounded the tower. In its shadow, all water sounds, whether hissing waves or lapping water, abruptly ceased. Ferns grew from the high walls of the moat; and the tower, where the look-out turret had crumbled away, was thronged with bindweed, but the overall impression was of a dead place.

The sea must flood the moat at high tide, for all kinds of debris had been washed up and left. Driftwood, the torn-off wing of a gull, bits of blue and green glass. A child would have loved it, picking over these pieces.

'We used to play here,' Burns said. 'Daring each other, you know. Who could go all the way up?'

There was a door, but it had planks nailed across it. Rivers peered through a crack and saw stone steps going down.

'Strictly forbidden. They were always afraid we'd get trapped in the cellars.'

'I suppose they flood, don't they? At high tide?'

'Yes. There's all kinds of stories told about it. People chained up and left to drown. I think we rather liked that. We used to sit down there and pretend we could see ghosts.'

'It feels like a place where people have died. I mean, violent deaths.'

'You feel that, do you? Yes. I expect that's why we liked it. Bloodthirsty little horrors, boys.'

Rivers wasn't sorry when they climbed the bank of shingle and stood on the beach in the strengthening sunlight again.

'Do you feel up to a longish walk?' Burns asked.

'Yes.'

'All right. We can follow that path.'

They walked four or five miles inland, and came out into a wood where great golden tongues of fungus lapped the trees, and a mulch of dead leaves squelched underfoot. Rather to Rivers's surprise they stopped at a pub on the way back, though no food was available. Burns could drink apparently, and did, becoming in the process quite flushed and talkative, though nothing was said about his illness.

They arrived back in the late afternoon with every bone and muscle aching. Mrs Burril had obviously built up the fire before she left, and it was rescuable, just about. Rivers knelt in front of it, sticking strips of cereal packet through the bars, and blowing when he got a flame. 'Have you any newspapers?'

'No,' Burns said.

No, Rivers thought, silly question. Once the fire was burning well, Rivers went out and bought cakes and biscuits for tea, which he served in front of the fire, tucking in himself and not looking to see whether Burns ate or not. He ate, sitting on the hearth rug, his wind-reddened arms clasped about his knees, and the firelight playing on his face.

After the plates were cleared away, Rivers asked if he might work for a couple of hours. He was writing a paper on the Repression of War Experience which he was due to give to the British Medical Association in December, and he knew, once he got back to Craiglockhart, there would be very little time. He worked at the table in the window, with his back to the room. He began by reading through what he'd written so far on the evil effects that followed from patients trying to suppress their memories of war experience, and was about to start writing when it occurred to him he was in the same room as a man who was doing just that.

Why do I go along with it? he thought. One answer, the easy answer, was that he was no longer Burns's doctor. It was up to Burns now how he chose to manage his illness. But then he'd gone along with the suppression in Craiglockhart too. Whenever he'd tried to apply to Burns the same methods of treatment he used with everybody else, and used, for the most part, success-fully, his nerve had failed him. He'd told himself this was because of the peculiar nature of Burns's experience, the utter lack of any redeeming feature the mind could grasp and hold on to while it steadied itself to face the full horror. But was Burns's experience really worse than that of others? Worse than Jenkins's, crawling between the dismembered pieces of his friend's body to collect personal belongings to send back to the family? Worse than Prior's? *What shall I do with this gob-stopper?*

Corpses were everywhere in the trenches. Used to strengthen parapets, to prop up sagging doorways, to fill in gaps in the duckboards, Many of his patients treading on a dead body had been startled by the release of gas. Surely what had happened to Burns was merely an unusually disgusting version of a common experience. And I've let him, Rivers thought - no, that was unfair, that was *completely* unfair - I've let *myself* turn it into . . . some kind of myth. And that was unforgivable. He wasn't dealing with Jonah in the belly of the whale, still less with Christ in the belly of the earth, he was dealing with David Burns, who'd got his head stuck in the belly of a dead German soldier, and somehow had to be helped to live with the memory.

He turned and looked at Burns, who was still sitting on the hearth rug, though now he'd found himself a book and was reading, his tongue protruding slightly between his teeth. As he felt Rivers's gaze, he looked up and smiled. Twenty-two. He should be worrying about the Tripos and screwing up his courage to ask a girl to the May ball. And yet even now Rivers was nervous of raising the subject of his illness. Burns's instinc-tive reaction had been to get back to this house, to forget. And there had been some improvement under this regime, by day at least, though evidently not by night. If he wants to talk, he'll talk, Rivers thought, and turned back to his paper.

That evening, rather to Rivers's surprise, they went to the pub. He was surprised because he'd been assuming Burns was isolated here, but apparently all the locals knew him. They'd watched him growing up, summer by summer. The family had been staying here when war broke out. Burns had joined up along with most of the local lads, They all remembered him in his uniform, in the first days and weeks of the war, and perhaps that mattered a great deal. In London, Burns said, on his first trip out in civilian clothes, he'd been handed two white feathers.

Here, as soon as they pushed the bar door open, he was hailed by several people, and by one man in particular: 'Old Clegg'. Clegg had rheumy blue eyes, whose overflow had dried to a scurfy crust at his temples; three brown but very strong teeth; unidentifiable stains on his abdomen, and other stains, only too identifiable, further down. His conversation was so encrusted with salty Suffolk sayings that Rivers suspected him of deliberate self-parody. That, or leg-pulling. Once he'd discovered Rivers was interested in folklore, he was well away. Rivers spent a thoroughly enjoyable evening being initiated into the folklore of rural Suffolk. By closing time, he was convinced Clegg was possibly the most unreliable informant he'd ever had. For sheer imaginative flights of fancy none of the Melanesians came anywhere near him. 'That man is a complete fraud,' he said as they left the pub.

But Burns disagreed. 'He's not a fraud, he's a rogue. Anyway as long as he teaches me flint-knapping, I don't care.'

Next morning the weather had changed. At dawn there was a strip of clear blue on the horizon, fading to yellow, but the sky darkened rapidly, until, by mid morning, the clouds humped, liver-coloured, and the sea was dark as iron. The wind had risen during the night, sweeping away the last remnants of mist. At first it came in little gusts, lifting the thin carpet in the hall, swirling dust in corners, then in blasts that made waves on the surface of the estuary, rocking the yachts until the rattle of their rigging became a frenzy, while on the beach great waves swelled like the muscles of an enormous animal, rising to crests that hung and seethed along their full length, before toppling over in thunder and bursts of spray.

Rivers worked on his paper all morning, looking up now and then to find the window mizzled with rain. Burns slept late, having had another bad and very noisy night. He appeared just before noon, pink eyed and twitching, and announced he was going to the White Horse to see Clegg and arrange a definite time for his flint-knapping session. Clegg was proving rather difficult to pin down.

'Git him up agin' a gorse bush, bor,' Rivers said, in a passable imitation of Clegg's voice. 'He ont back away then.'

'That's girls in kissing season, Rivers.'

'Is it? Well, I shouldn't go kissing Clegg. I doubt if flint-knapping's worth it.'

He was immersed in his paper again before Burns left the house.

He came back an hour later, looking rather pleased with himself. 'Thursday.'

'Good.'

'I thought we might go for a walk.'

Rivers looked at the rain-spattered glass.

'It's died down a bit,' Burns said, not altogether convincingly.

'All right, I could do with a break.'

The sea was racing in fast. The fishermen's huts were empty, the boats hauled up high above the last stretch of shingle, with the fishing nets in dark heaps behind them. Either they'd not been out today or they'd turned back early, for Rivers had seen none of them come in. Even the seabirds seemed to be grounded, huddled in the lee of the boats, watching the town with unblinking amber eyes.

Faced with this sea, the land seemed fragile. Was fragile. To the north, cliffs were scoured away, to the south, notice boards were buried up to their necks in shingle. And the little Moot Hall that had once stood at the centre of the town was now on the edge of the sea.

They walked as far as Thorpeness, then turned back, not talking much, since the wind snatched the breath from their mouths. The sea had covered the thin strip of sand, so they had to walk along the steep shelf of shingle, a lopsided business that set the back as well as the legs aching.

It took them two hours, there and back, and Rivers was looking forward to the fire and - if he could contrive it - toasted tea cakes for tea. Breakfast, lunch and dinner, he could do without, but afternoon tea *mattered*. His boot squelched on something soft. Looking down, he saw the place was littered with cods' heads, thirty or more, with blood-stained gills and staring eyes. It gave him no more than a slight *frisson*. Obviously the fishermen gutted their catch and threw the offal away. But Burns had stopped dead in his tracks and was staring at the heads, with his mouth working. As Rivers watched, he jerked his head back, the same movement that had been so common when he first arrived at Craiglockhart.

'It's all right,' he said, when Rivers went back for him. But it was obviously very far from all right.

They got back to the house. Rivers made tea, though Burns didn't manage to eat anything.

After tea they went out and piled sandbags against the doors, struggling with the heavy bags through driving rain and then struggling again to close the storm shutters. The air was full of spray and blown spume.

'We should've done that earlier,' Burns said, wiping the rain from his face and blinking in the firelight. He was very concerned to pretend everything was normal. He sat on the hearth rug, in his favourite position, while the wind buffeted and slogged the house, and talked about his drink with Clegg and various items of local gossip. But he jumped from topic to topic, assuming the connections would be obvious when very often they were not. His mood, once he'd got over the shock of seeing the cods' heads, seemed to be almost elated. He said more than once that he loved storms, and he seemed, at times, to be listening to something other than the roar of wind and sea.

Closing his eyes, Rivers could imagine the town entirely given over to the storm, bobbing on the tide of darkness like a blown eggshell, without substance or power to protect. Burns's conversation became more and more disconnected, the jerking of his head more pronounced. Piling up sandbags, followed by the nearest thing to a bombardment nature could contrive, was not what Rivers would have prescribed. He was prepared to sit up with Burns, if he wanted to stay up, but Burns started talking about bed rather earlier than usual. Probably he took bromides. Rivers would have liked to advise him to stop, since they certainly wouldn't help the nightmares, but he was determined to let Burns be the first to raise the subject of his illness.

The evening ended with nothing to the point having been said. Rivers went to bed and undressed in the darkness, listening to the wind howl, and imagined Burns in the room above, also listening. He read for a while, thinking he might be too tense to go to sleep, but the fresh air and the struggle with the wind along the beach to Thorpeness had tired him out. His eyelids started to droop and he switched off the light. The whole house creaked and groaned, riding the storm like a ship, but he enjoyed that. He'd always found it possible to sleep deeply on board ship, though on land sleep often eluded him.

He was woken by what he immediately took to be the explosion of a bomb. Less than a minute later, while he was still groping for the light switch, he heard a second boom and this time managed to identify it as the sound of a maroon. The lifeboat, no doubt. He was getting our of bed to go to the window when he remembered that he probably ought not to open the shutters, for he could hear from the whistling of wind and lashing of rain that the storm had by no means blown itself out. His heart was pounding, unreasonably, since there was nothing to be afraid of. He supposed it was having come straight from London with its incessant talk of air raids that had made him identify the sound so positively as a bomb.

He lay back and a moment or two later heard footsteps padding past the door of his room. Obviously Burns too had been woken up. Probably he was going downstairs to make himself a cup of tea, perhaps even to sit up the rest of the night.

The more Rivers thought about Burns sitting alone in the kitchen, the more he thought he ought to get up. The sounds of the storm had now been joined by running footsteps. He wouldn't find it easy to sleep again anyway.

The kitchen was empty, and didn't seem to have been disturbed since last night. He told himself that he'd been mistaken, and Burns was still in bed. By now rather anxious, perhaps unreasonably so, he went upstairs and peered into Burns's room. The bedclothes had been pushed back, and the bed was empty.

He had no idea what he should do. For all he knew midnight walks - or rather three am walks - were a habit of Burns's when the nights were particularly bad. Surely he wouldn't go out in this. Rivers heard shouts, followed by more running footsteps. Obviously other people were out in it. Quickly, he returned to his own room, pulled on socks, boots and coat, and went out into the storm.

A small group of figures had gathered round the lifeboat, three of them holding storm lanterns. The overlapping circles of light shone on yellow oilskins glistening with wet, as the men struggled to clear the shingle from the planks that were used to launch the boat. Silver rain slanted down into the lighted area, while beyond, pale banks of shingle faded into the darkness.

A knot of bystanders had gathered by the hut, separate from the labouring figures around the boat. Convinced that Burns must be among them, Rivers ran across to join them, but when he looked from face to face Burns was not there. A woman he thought to be familiar, but couldn't immediately identify, pointed to the marshes south of the town.

As he turned and began walking quickly towards the marshes, he was dimly aware of the boat hitting the sea, and of the waves surging up around her. He left the shelter of the last houses, and the wind, roaring across the marshes, almost knocked him off his feet. He dropped down from the path and walked along beside the river where he was slightly sheltered, though the wind still howled and the yacht rigging thrummed, a sound like no other he had heard. He could see fairly clearly most of the time. Once, the moon freed itself from the tatters of black cloud, and then his own shadow and the shadow of the tower were thrown across the gleaming mud.

Looking at the tower, Rivers thought again how squat and unimpressive it was, and yet how menacing. A resemblance that had merely nagged at him before returned to his mind with greater force. This waste of mud, these sump holes reflecting a dim light at the sky, even that tower. It was like France. Like the battlefields. A resemblance greater by night than by day, perhaps, because here, by day, you could see things grow, and there nothing grew.

- *They were always afraid we'd get trapped in the cellars.*
- *I suppose they flood, don't they? At high tide?*

Rivers climbed on to the path, trying to work out where the tide was and whether it was rising or falling, but he could hear only the crash of breaking waves and feel the drizzle of blown spume on his face. In spite of his mud-clogged boots and aching thighs, he started to run, As he neared the tower, a stronger blast of wind sent him staggering off the path. He was slithering and floundering through mud, calling Burns's name, though the sound was snatched from his mouth and carried off into the whistling darkness.

He slid down on to the beach. An outgoing wave sucked shingle after it, but the entrance to the moat was clear. He hesitated, peering into the darkness, afraid that an unusually powerful wave might trap him in there. He called 'David', but he knew he couldn't be heard and would have to go down, into the black darkness, if he were ever to find him.

He groped his way into the moat, steadying himself against the wall. It was so wet, so cold, so evil-smelling, that he thought perhaps the tide had already reached its height and was now falling. At first he could see nothing, but then the moon came out from behind a bank of cloud, and he saw Burns huddled against the moat wall. Rivers called 'David' and realized he was shouting when there was no need. Even the howl of the storm sounded subdued in the shelter of the moat. He touched Burns's arm. He neither moved nor blinked. He was staring up at the tower, which gleamed white, like the bones of a skull.

'Come on, David.'

His body felt like a stone. Rivers got hold of him and held him, coaxing, rocking. He looked up at the tower that loomed squat and menacing above them, and thought, *Nothing justifies this. Nothing nothing nothing.* Burns's body remained rigid in his arms. Rivers was aware that if it came to a fight he might not win. Burns was terribly emaciated, but he was also thirty years younger. His surrender, when it came, was almost shocking. Suddenly his body had the rag-doll floppiness of the newborn. He collapsed against Rivers and started to shake, and from there it was possible to half lead, half push him out of the moat and up on to the relative safety of the path.

At the kitchen table, wrapped in a blanket, Burns said, 'I couldn't seem to get out of the dream. I woke up, I *knew* I was awake, I could move and yet . . . it was still there. My face was dripping. I could taste it.' He tried to laugh. 'And then the bloody maroon went off.'

There were no electric lights. The power lines must be down. They were talking by the light of an oil lamp that smoked and smelled, and left wisps of black smoke like question marks on the air.

'I think we can do without this now,' Rivers said, walking across to the window and pulling the curtains back. He opened the windows and shutters. The storm had almost blown itself out. A weak light seeped into the room, falling on Burns's red eyes and exhausted face.

'Why don't you go to bed? I'll bring you a hot-water bottle if you've got such a thing.'

Rivers saw him settled into bed. Then he went out to the butchers in the High Street, which he'd already noticed was surprisingly well stocked, bought bacon, sausages, kidneys, eggs, took them home and fried them. As he was spooning hot fat over the eggs, he remembered his reaction when he was looking up at the tower. *Nothing can justify this*, he'd thought. *Nothing nothing nothing*. He was rather glad not to be faced with the task of explaining that statement to Siegfried.

He sat down at the table and began to eat. He was still chasing the last dribble of egg yolk with a triangle of toast when Mrs Burril came in. She looked at the plates. 'Cracked, did you?' Two unpacked bags later she added, 'Thought you might.'

'Is the boat back?'

'Not yet. I keep busy.'

Rivers went upstairs to check on Burns and found him still asleep. The room was full of books, stacked up on tables and chairs, spilling over on to the floor. Church architecture, country crafts, ornithology, botany and - a slight surprise - theology. He wondered whether this was an expression of faith, or a quest for faith, or simply an obsession with the absence of God.

One of the reasons the books had to be stacked on tables and chairs was that the bookcase was already full of other books: boys' annuals, the adventure stories of Henty, Scouting for Boys. Games too: Ludo and Snakes and Ladders, a bat for beach cricket, collections of pebbles and shells, a strip of bladderwrack. All these things must have been brought here, or collected here, summer by summer, and then outgrown, but never thrown away, so that the room had become a sort of palimpsest of the young life it contained. He looked at Burns's sleeping face, and then tiptoed downstairs.

The lifeboat came back later that morning. Rivers looked out of the living room window and saw it beached at the water's edge, in that narrow space between the coils of tangled and rusting wire. He went out to watch.

The men were laying down the flat wooden skids over which the boat would be winched slowly back into place. A small group of villagers, mainly relatives of the crew, had gathered and were talking in low voices. The sea was choppy, but with none of the menace of the previous night. A light drizzle had begun to fall, matting the surface hairs on the men's jerseys and woollen caps.

When he got back, he found Burns stirring, though not yet up.

'Are they back?' he asked.

'Yes, they're hauling her up now.'

Burns got out of bed and came across to the window. The drizzle had become a downpour. The lifeboat, now halfway up the beach, was obscured by sheets of smoking rain.

'Be a load off Mrs Burril's mind. She's got two sons in the crew.

'Yes. She said.'

'You mean she spoke?'

'We had quite a chat. I didn't know the lifeboat was such a family matter.'

'Oh, yes. You see it on the memorial in the church. Not a good idea, really. From the woman's point of view.' A long pause. Then Burns added, 'You get the same thing in a battalion. Brothers joining up together.'

Rivers went very still. This was the first time Burns had volunteered any information at all about France. Even in Craiglockhart, where he couldn't altogether avoid talking about it, the bare facts of his war service had had to be prised out of him.

'You know, you'll be writing letters and suddenly you realize you've written the same name twice.'

Rivers said carefully, 'That must be one of the worst jobs.'

'You get used to it. I did it for eighty per cent of the company once.

A long silence. Rivers was beginning to think he'd dried up, but then he said, 'That was the day before the Somme. They got out there, and there was this bloody great dyke in the way. You couldn't see it from the trench because there were bramble bushes round it. And it wasn't on the map. Everybody bunched up, trying to get across it. German machine-gunners had a field day. And the few who did manage to get across were cut to pieces on the wire. General came round the following day. He said, "My God, did we really order men to attack across that?" Apparently we were intended to be a diversion from the main action. Further south.'

Slowly, Burns began to talk. He'd been promoted captain at the age of twenty-one, and this promotion coincided with the run-up to the Somme campaign. In addition to all the other strains, he'd been aware of a widespread, though unvoiced, opinion in the company that he was too young for the command, though in length of service he had been senior.

The story was one Rivers was well used to hearing: healthy fear had given way to indifference, and this in turn had given way to a constant, overwhelming fear, and the increasing realization that breakdown was imminent. 'I used to go out on patrol every night,' Burns said. 'You tell yourself you're *setting a good example*, or some such rubbish, but actually it's nothing of the kind. You can't let yourself know you want to be wounded, because officers aren't supposed to think like that. And, you see, next to a battle, a patrol is the best chance of getting a good wound. In the trenches, it's shrapnel or head injuries. On patrol, if you're lucky, it's a nice neat little hole in the arm or leg. I've seen men cry with a wound like that.' He laughed. 'Cry for joy. Anyway, it wasn't my luck. Bullets went round me, I swear they did.' A pause. 'It was going to happen anyway, wasn't it?'

'The breakdown? Oh yes. You mustn't attribute breaking down to that one incident.

'I went on for three days afterwards.'

'Yes, I know.'

They talked for over an hour. Near the end, after they'd been sitting in silence for a while, Burns said quietly, 'Do you know what Christ died of?' Rivers looked surprised, but answered readily enough. 'Suffocation. Ultimately the position makes it impossible to go on inflating the lungs. A terrible death.'

'That's what I find so horrifying. Somebody had to *imagine* that death. I mean, just in order to invent it as a method of execution. You know that thing in the Bible? "The imagination of man's heart is evil from his youth"? I used to wonder why pick on that? Why his *imagination*? But it's absolutely right.'

Rivers, going downstairs to make the tea, thought that a curious thing had happened during that conversation. For the first time, Burns had been able to put the decomposing corpse into some kind of perspective. True, he hadn't managed to talk about it, but at least it hadn't prevented him, as it so often had in the past, from talking about other, more bearable aspects of his war experience. Yet, at the same time, Rivers's own sense of the horror of the event seemed actually to have increased. It *was* different in kind from other such experiences, he thought, if only because of the complete disintegration of personality it had produced. He was very fond

101

of Burns, but he could discern in him no trace of the qualities he must have possessed in order to be given that exceptionally early command. Not that one could despair of recovery. Rivers knew only too well how often the early stages of change or cure may mimic deterioration. Cut a chrysalis open, and you will find a rotting caterpillar. What you will never find is that mythical creature, half caterpillar, half butterfly, a fit emblem of the human soul, for those whose cast of mind leads them to seek such emblems. No, the process of transformation consists almost entirely of decay. Burns was young, after all. If today really marked a change, a willingness to face his experiences in France, then his condition might improve. In a few years' time it might even be possible to think of him resuming his education, perhaps pursuing that unexpected interest in theology. Though it was difficult to see him as an undergraduate. He had missed his chance of being ordinary.

\* \* \* \* \*

**M R James:** This son of a Suffolk clergyman established a brilliant reputation as a medievalist at King's Cambridge. He eventually became University Chancellor but is best remembered for the ghost stories he wrote to amuse fellow students. *Oh Whistle And I'll Come To You My Lad* first appeared in *Ghost Stories of an Antiquary* (1904). With its golf course, a martello tower and the village of Aldsey (Bawdsey) on the far side of the estuary, the Suffolk coastal resort of Burnstow is a thinly disguised version of Felixstowe.

# 'Oh Whistle And I'll Come To You My Lad'
## M R JAMES

'I suppose you will be getting away pretty soon, now Full term is over, Professor,' said a person not in the story to the Professor of Ontography, soon after they had sat down next to each other at a feast in the hospitable hall of St. James's College.

The Professor was young, neat and precise in speech.

'Yes,' he said; 'my friends have been making me take up golf this term, and I mean to go to the East Coast – in point of fact to Burnstow – (I dare say you know if) for a week or ten days, to improve my game. I hope to get off to-morrow.'

'Oh, Parkins,' said his neighbour on the other side, 'if you are going to Burnstow, I wish you would look at the site of the Templar's preceptory, and let me know if you think it would be any good to have a dig there in the summer.'

It was, as you might suppose, a person of antiquarian pursuits who said this, but, since he merely appears in this prologue, there is no need to give his entitlements.

'Certainly,' said Parkins, the Professor: 'if you will describe to me whereabouts the site is, I will do my best to give you an idea of the lie of the land when I get back; or I could write to you about it, if you would tell me where you are likely to be.'

'Don't trouble to do that, thanks. It's only that I'm thinking of taking my family in that direction in the Long, and it occurred to me that, as very few of the English preceptories have ever been properly planned, I might have an opportunity of doing something useful on off-days.'

The Professor rather sniffed at the idea that planning out a preceptory could be described as useful. His neighbour continued:

'The site – I doubt if there is anything showing above ground – must be down quite close to the beach now. The sea has encroached tremendously, as you know, all along that bit of coast. I should think, from the map, that it must be about three-quarters of a mile from the Globe Inn, at the north end of the town. Where are you going to stay?'

'Well, *at* the Globe Inn, as a matter of fact,' said Parkins; 'I have engaged a room there. I couldn't get in anywhere else; most of the lodging-houses are shut up in winter, it seems; and, as it is, they tell me that the only room of any size I can have is really a double-bedded one, and that they haven't a corner in which to store the other bed, and so on. But I must have a fairly large room, for I am taking some books down, and mean to do a bit of work; and though I don't quite fancy having an empty bed – not to speak of two – in what I may call for the time being my study, I suppose I can manage to rough it for the short time I shall be there.'

'Do you call having an extra bed in your room roughing it, Parkins?' said a bluff person opposite. 'Look here, I shall come down and occupy it for a bit; it'll be company for you.'

The Professor quivered, but managed to laugh in a courteous manner.

'By all means, Rogers; there's nothing I should like better. But I'm afraid you would find it rather dull; you don't play golf, do you?'

'No, thank Heaven!' said rude Mr Rogers.

'Well, you see, when I'm not writing I shall most likely be out on the links, and that, as I say, would be rather dull for you, I'm afraid.'

'Oh, I don't know! There's certain to be somebody I know in the place; but, of course, if you don't want me, speak the word, Parkins; I shan't be offended. Truth, as you always tell us, is never offensive.'

Parkins was, indeed, scrupulously polite and strictly truthful. It is to be feared that Mr Rogers sometimes practised upon his knowledge of these characteristics. In Parkins's breast there was a conflict now raging, which for a moment or two did not allow him to answer. That interval being over, he said:

'Well, if you want the exact truth, Rogers, I was considering whether the room I speak of would really be large enough to accommodate us both comfortably; and also whether (mind, I shouldn't have said this if you hadn't pressed me) you would not constitute something in the nature of a hindrance to my work.'

Rogers laughed loudly.

'Well done, Parkins!' he said. 'It's all right. I promise not to interrupt your work; don't you disturb yourself about that. No, I won't come if you don't want me; but I thought I should do so nicely to keep the ghosts off.'

Here he might have been seen to wink and to nudge his next neighbour. Parkins might also have been seen to become pink. 'I beg pardon, Parkins,' Rogers continued; 'I oughtn't to have said that. I forgot you didn't like levity on these topics.'

'Well,' Parkins said, 'as you have mentioned the matter, I freely own that I do *not* like careless talk about what you call ghosts. A man in my position,' he went on, raising his voice a little, 'cannot, I find, be too careful about appearing to sanction the current beliefs on such subjects. As you know, Rogers, or as you ought to know; for I think I have never concealed my views —'

'No, you certainly have not, old man,' put in Rogers *sotto voce*.

' — I hold that any semblance, any appearance of concession to the view that such things might exist is equivalent to a renunciation of all that I hold most sacred. But I'm afraid I have not succeeded in securing your attention.'

'Your *undivided* attention, was what Dr Blimber actually *said*,' Rogers interrupted, with every appearance of an earnest desire for accuracy. 'But I beg your pardon, Parkins: I'm stopping you.'

'No, not at all,' said Parkins. 'I don't remember Blimber; perhaps he was before my time. But I needn't go on. I'm sure you know what I mean.'

'Yes, yes,' said Rogers, rather hastily — 'just so. We'll go into it fully at Burnstow, or somewhere.'

In repeating the above dialogue I have tried to give the impression which it made on me, that Parkins was something of an old woman — rather hen-like, perhaps, in his little way; totally destitute, alas! of the sense of humour, but at the same time dauntless and sincere in his convictions, and a man deserving of the greatest respect. Whether or not the reader has gathered so much, that was the character which Parkins had.

On the following day Parkins did, as he had hoped, succeed in getting away from his college, and in arriving at Burnstow. He was made welcome at the Globe Inn, was safely installed in the large double-bedded room of which we have heard, and was able before retiring to rest to arrange his materials for work in apple-pie order upon a commodious table which occupied the outer end of the room, and was surrounded on three sides by windows looking out seaward; that is to say, the central window looked straight out to sea, and those on the left and right commanded prospects along the shore to the north and south respectively. On the south you saw the village of Burnstow. On the north no houses were to be seen, but only the beach and the low cliff backing it. Immediately in front was a strip – not considerable – of rough grass, dotted with old anchors, capstans, and so forth; then a broad path; then the beach. Whatever may have been the original distance between the Globe Inn and the sea, not more than sixty yards now separated them.

The rest of the population of the inn was, of course, a golfing one, and included few elements that call for a special description. The most conspicuous figure was, perhaps, that of an *ancien militaire*, secretary of a London club, and possessed of a voice of incredible strength, and of views of a pronouncedly Protestant type. These were apt to find utterance after his attendance upon the ministrations of the Vicar, an estimable man with inclinations towards a picturesque ritual, which he gallantly kept down as far as he could out of deference to East Anglian tradition.

Professor Parkins, one of whose principal characteristics was pluck, spent the greater part of the day following his arrival at Burnstow in what he had called improving his game, in company with this Colonel Wilson: and during the afternoon – whether the process of improvement were to blame or not, I am not sure – the Colonel's demeanour assumed a colouring so lurid that even Parkins jibbed at the thought of walking home with him from the links. He determined, after a short and furtive look at that bristling moustache and those incarnadined features, that it would be wiser to allow the influences of tea and tobacco to do what they could with the Colonel before the dinner-hour should render a meeting inevitable.

'I might walk home to-night along the beach,' he reflected – 'yes, and take a look – there will be light enough for that – at the ruins of which Disney was talking. I don't exactly know where they are, by the way; but I expect I can hardly help stumbling on them.'

This he accomplished, I may say, in the most literal sense, for in picking his way from the links to the shingle beach his foot caught, partly in a gorse-root and partly in a biggish stone, and over he went. When he got up and surveyed his surroundings, he found himself in a patch of somewhat broken ground covered with small depressions and mounds. These latter, when he came to examine them, proved to be simply masses of flints embedded in mortar and grown over with turf. He must, he quite rightly concluded, be on the site of the preceptory he had promised to look at. It seemed not unlikely to reward the spade of the explorer;

enough of the foundations was probably left at no great depth to throw a good deal of light on the general plan. He remembered vaguely that the Templars, to whom this site had belonged, were in the habit of building round churches, and he thought a particular series of the humps or mounds near him did appear to be arranged in something of a circular form. Few people can resist the temptation to try a little amateur research in a department quite outside their own, if only for the satisfaction of showing how successful they would have been had they only taken it up seriously. Our Professor, however, if he felt something of this mean desire, was also truly anxious to oblige Mr Disney. So he paced with care the circular area he had noticed, and wrote down its rough dimensions in his pocket-book. Then he proceeded to examine an oblong eminence which lay east of the centre of the circle, and seemed to his thinking likely to be the base of a platform or altar. At one end of it, the northern, a patch of the turf was gone – removed by some boy or other creature *ferae naturae*. It might, he thought, be as well to probe the soil here for evidences of masonry, and he took out his knife and began scraping away the earth. And now followed another little discovery: a portion of soil fell inward as he scraped, and disclosed a small cavity. He lighted one match after another to help him to see of what nature the hole was, but the wind was too strong for them all. By tapping and scratching the sides with his knife, however, he was able to make out that it must be an artificial hole in masonry. It was rectangular, and the sides, top, and bottom, if not actually plastered, were smooth and regular. Of course it was empty. No! As he withdrew the knife he heard a metallic clink, and when he introduced his hand it met with a cylindrical object lying on the floor of the hole. Naturally enough, he picked it up, and when he brought it into the light, now fast fading, he could see that it, too, was of man's making – a metal tube about four inches long, and evidently of some considerable age.

By the time Parkins had made sure that there was nothing else in this odd receptacle, it was too late and too dark for him to think of undertaking any further search. What he had done had proved so unexpectedly interesting that he determined to sacrifice a little more of the daylight on the morrow to archaeology. The object which he now had safe in his  pocket was bound to be of some slight value at least, he felt sure.

Bleak and solemn was the view on which he took a last look before starting homeward. A faint yellow light in the west showed the links, on which a few figures moving towards the club-house were still visible, the squat Martello tower, the lights of Aldsey village, the pale ribbon of sands intersected at intervals by black wooden groynes, the dim and murmuring sea. The wind was bitter from the north, but was at his back when he set out for the Globe. He quickly rattled and clashed through the shingle and gained the sand, upon which, but for the groynes which had to be got over every few yards, the going was both good and quiet. One last look behind, to measure the distance he had made since leaving the ruined Templars' church, showed him a prospect of company on his walk, in the shape of a rather indistinct personage, who seemed to be making great efforts to catch up with him, but made little, if any, progress. I mean that there was an appearance of running about his movements, but that the distance between him and Parkins did not seem materially to lessen. So, at least, Parkins thought, and decided that he almost certainly did not know him, and that it would be absurd to wait until he came up. For all that, company, he began to think, would really be very welcome on that lonely shore, if only you could choose your companion. In his unenlightened days he had read of meetings in such places which even now would hardly bear thinking of. He went on thinking of them, however, until he reached home, and particularly of one which catches most people's fancy at some time of their childhood. 'Now I say in my dream that Christian had gone but a very little way when he saw a foul fiend coming over the field to meet him.' 'What should I do now,' he thought, 'if I looked back and caught sight of a black figure sharply defined against the yellow sky, and saw that it had horns and wings? I wonder whether I should stand or run for it. Luckily, the gentleman behind is not of that kind, and he seems to be about as far off now as when I saw him first. Well, at this rate he won't get his dinner as soon as I shall; and, dear me! it's within a quarter of an hour of the time now. I must run!'

Parkins had, in fact, very little time for dressing. When he met the Colonel at dinner, Peace – or as much of her as that gentleman could manage – reigned once more in the military bosom; nor was she put to flight in the hours of bridge that followed dinner, for Parkins was a more than respectable player. When, therefore, he retired towards twelve o'clock, he felt that he had spent his evening in quite a satisfactory way, and that, even for so long as a fortnight or three weeks, life at the Globe would be supportable under similar conditions – 'especially,' thought he, 'if I go on improving my game.'

As he went along the passages he met the boots of the Globe, who stopped and said:

'Beg your pardon, sir, but as I was a-brushing your coat just now there was somethink fell out of the pocket. I put it on your chest of drawers, sir, in your room, sir – a piece of pipe or somethink of that, sir. Thank you, sir. You'll find it on your chest of drawers, sir – yes, sir. Good night, sir.'

The speech served to remind Parkins of his little discovery of that afternoon. It was with some considerable curiosity that he turned it over by the light of his candles. It was of bronze, he now saw, and was shaped very much after the manner of the modern dog-whistle; in fact it was – yes, certainly it was – actually no more nor less than a whistle. He put it to his lips, but it was quite full of a fine, caked-up sand or earth, which would not yield to knocking, but must be loosened with a knife. Tidy as ever in his habits, Parkins cleared out the earth on to a piece of paper, and took the latter to the window to empty it out. The night was clear and bright, as he saw when he had opened the casement, and he stopped for an instant to look at the sea and note a belated wanderer stationed on the shore in front of the inn. Then he shut the window, a little surprised at the late hours people kept at Burnstow, and took his whistle to the light again. Why, surely there were marks on it, and not merely marks, but letters! A very little rubbing rendered the deeply-cut inscription quite legible, but the Professor had to confess, after some earnest thought, that the meaning of it was as obscure to him as the writing on the wall to Belshazzar. There were legends both on the front and on the back of the whistle. The one read thus:

FLA

FUR        BIS

FLE

The other:

QUIS EST ISTE QUI VENIT

'I ought to be able to make it out,' he thought; 'but I suppose I am a little rusty in my Latin. When I come to think of it, I don't believe I even know the word for a whistle. The long one does seem simple enough. It ought to mean, "Who is this who is coming?" Well, the best way to find out is evidently to whistle for him.'

He blew tentatively and stopped suddenly, startled and yet pleased at the note he had elicited. It had a quality of infinite distance in it, and, soft as it was, he somehow felt it must be audible for miles round. It was a sound, too, that seemed to have the power (which many scents possess) of forming pictures in the brain. He saw quite clearly for a moment a vision of a wide, dark expanse at night, with a fresh wind blowing, and in the midst a lonely figure – how employed, he could not tell. Perhaps he would have seen more had not the picture been broken by the sudden surge of a gust of wind against his casement, so sudden that it made him look up, just in time to see the white glint of a sea-bird's wing somewhere outside the dark panes.

The sound of the whistle had so fascinated him that he could not help trying it once more, this time more boldly. The note was little, if at all, louder than before, and repetition broke the illusion – no picture followed, as he had half hoped it might. 'But what is this? Goodness! what force the wind can get up in a few minutes! What a tremendous gust! There! I knew that window-fastening was no use! Ah! I though so – both candles out. It's enough to tear the room to pieces.'

The first thing was to get the window shut. While you might count twenty Parkins was struggling with the small casement, and felt almost as if he were pushing back a sturdy burglar, so strong was the pressure. It slackened all at once, and the window banged to and latched itself. Now to relight the candles and see what damage, if any, had been done. No, nothing seemed amiss; no glass even was broken in the casement. But the noise had evidently roused at least one member of the household: the Colonel was to be heard stumping in his stockinged feet on the floor above, and growling.

Quickly as it had risen, the wind did not fall at once. On it went, moaning and rushing past the house, at times rising to a cry so desolate that, as Parkins disinterestedly said, it might have made fanciful people feel quite uncomfortable; even the unimaginative, he thought after a quarter of an hour, might be happier without it.

Whether it was the wind, or the excitement of golf, or of the researches in the preceptory that kept Parkins awake, he was not sure. Awake he remained, in any case, long enough to fancy (as I am afraid I often do myself under such conditions) that he was the victim of all manner of fatal disorders: he would lie counting the beats of his heart, convinced that it was going to stop work every moment, and would entertain grave suspicions of his lungs, brain, liver, etc. – suspicions which he was sure would be dispelled by the return of daylight, but which until then refused to be put aside. He found a little vicarious comfort in the idea that someone else was in the same boat. A near neighbour (in the darkness it was not easy to tell his direction) was tossing and rustling in his bed, too.

The next stage was that Parkins shut his eyes and determined to give sleep every chance. Here again over-excitement asserted itself in another form – that of making pictures. *Experto crede*, pictures do come to the closed eyes of one trying to sleep, and are often so little to his taste that he must open his eyes and disperse them.

Parkins's experience on this occasion was a very distressing one. He found that the picture which presented itself to him was continuous. When he opened his eyes, of course, it went; but when he shut them once more it framed itself afresh, and acted itself out again, neither quicker nor slower than before. What he saw was this:

A long stretch of shore – shingle edged by sand, and intersected at short intervals with black groynes running down to the water – a scene, in fact, so like that of his afternoon's walk that, in the absence of any landmark, it could not be distinguished therefrom. The light was obscure, conveying an impression of gathering storm, late winter evening, and slight cold rain. On this bleak stage at first no actor was visible. Then, in the distance, a bobbing black object appeared; a moment more, and it was a man running, jumping, clambering over the groynes, and every few seconds looking eagerly back. The nearer he came the more obvious it was that he was not only anxious, but even terribly frightened, though his face was not to be distinguished. He was, moreover, almost at the end of his strength. On he came; each successive obstacle seemed to cause him more difficulty than the last. 'Will he get over this next one?' thought Parkins; 'it seems a little higher than the others.' Yes; half climbing, half throwing himself, he did get over, and fell all in a heap on the other side (the side nearest to the spectator). There, as if really unable to get up again, he remained crouching under the groyne, looking up in an attitude of painful anxiety.

So far no cause whatever for the fear of the runner had been shown; but now there began to be seen, far up the shore, a little flicker of something light-coloured moving to and fro with great swiftness and irregularity. Rapidly growing larger, it, too, declared itself as a figure in pale, fluttering draperies, ill-defined. There was something about its motion which made Parkins very unwilling to see it at close quarters. It would stop, raise arms, bow itself toward the sand, then run stooping across the beach to the water-edge and back again; and then, rising upright, once more continue its course forward at a speed that was startling and terrifying. The moment came when the pursuer was hovering about from left to right only a few yards beyond the groyne where the runner lay in hiding. After two or three ineffectual castings hither and thither it came to a stop, stood upright, with arms raised high, and then darted straight forward towards the groyne.

It was at this point that Parkins always failed in his resolution to keep his eyes shut. With many misgivings as to incipient failure of eyesight, over-worked brain, excessive smoking, and so on, he finally resigned himself to light his candle, get out a book, and pass the night waking, rather than be tormented by this persistent panorama, which he saw clearly enough could only be a morbid reflection of his walk and his thoughts on that very day.

The scraping of match on box and the glare of light must have startled some creatures of the night – rats or what not – which he heard scurry across the floor from the side of his bed with much rustling. Dear, dear! the match is out! Fool that it is! But the second one burnt better, and a candle and book were duly procured, over which Parkins pored till sleep of a wholesome kind came upon him, and that in no long space. For about the first time in his orderly and prudent life he forgot to blow out the candle, and when he was called next morning at eight there was still a flicker in the socket and a sad mess of guttered grease on the top of the little table.

After breakfast he was in his room, putting the finishing touches to his golfing costume – fortune had again allotted the Colonel to him for a partner – when one of the maids came in.

'Oh, if you please,' she said, 'would you like any extra blankets on your bed, sir?'

'Ah! thank you,' said Parkins. 'Yes, I think I should like one. It seems likely to turn rather colder.'

In a very short time the maid was back with the blanket.

'Which bed should I put it on, sir?' she asked.

'What? Why, that one – the one I slept in last night,' he said, pointing to it.

'Oh yes! I beg your pardon, sir, but you seemed to have tried both of 'em; leastways, we had to make 'em both up this morning.'

'Really? How very absurd!' said Parkins. 'I certainly never touched the other, except to lay some things on it. Did it actually seem to have been slept in?'

'Oh yes, sir!' said the maid. 'Why, all the things was crumpled and throwed about all ways, if you'll excuse me, sir – quite as if anyone 'adn't passed but a very poor night, sir.'

'Dear me,' said Parkins. 'Well, I may have disordered it more than I thought when I unpacked my things. I'm very sorry to have given you the extra trouble, I'm sure. I expect a friend of mine soon, by the way – a gentleman from Cambridge – to come and occupy it for a night or two. That will be all right, I suppose, won't it?'

'Oh yes, to be sure, sir. Thank you, sir. It's no trouble, I'm sure,' said the maid, and departed to giggle with her colleagues.

Parkins set forth, with a stern determination to improve his game.

I am glad to be able to report that he succeeded so far in this enterprise that the Colonel, who had been rather repining at the prospect of a second day's play in his company, became quite chatty as the morning advanced; and his voice boomed out over the flats, as certain also of our own minor poets have said, 'like some great bourdon in a minster tower.'

'Extraordinary wind, that, we had last night,' he said. 'In my old home we should have said someone had been whistling for it.'

'Should you, indeed!' said Parkins. 'Is there a superstition of that kind still current in your part of the country?'

'I don't know about superstition,' said the Colonel. 'They believe in it all over Denmark and Norway, as well as on the Yorkshire coast; and my experience is, mind you, that there's generally something at the bottom of what these country-folk hold to, and have held to for generations. But it's your drive' (or whatever it might have been: the golfing reader will have to imagine appropriate digressions at the proper intervals).

When conversation was resumed, Parkins said, with a slight hesitancy 'Apropos of what you were saying just now, Colonel, I think I ought to tell you that my own views on such subjects are very strong. I am, in fact, a convinced disbeliever in what is called the "supernatural." '

'What!' said the Colonel, 'do you mean to tell me you don't believe in second-sight, or ghosts, or anything of that kind?'

'In nothing whatever of that kind,' returned Parkins firmly.

'Well,' said the Colonel, 'but it appears to me at that rate, sir, that you must be little better than a Sadducee.'

Parkins was on the point of answering that, in his opinion, the Sadducees were the most sensible persons he had ever read of in the Old Testament; but, feeling some doubt as to whether much mention of them

113

was to be found in that work, he preferred to laugh the accusation off.

'Perhaps I am,' he said; 'but - Here, give me my cleek, boy! – Excuse me one moment, Colonel.' A short interval. 'Now, as to whistling for the wind, let me give you my theory about it. The laws which govern winds are really not at all perfectly known – to fisher-folk and such, of course, not known at all. A man or woman of eccentric habits, perhaps, or a stranger, is seen repeatedly on the beach at some unusual hour, and is heard whistling. Soon afterwards a violent wind rises; a man who could read the sky perfectly or who possessed a barometer could have foretold that it would. The simple people of a fishing-village have no barometers, and only a few rough rules for prophesying weather. What more natural than that the eccentric personage I postulated should be regarded as having raised the wind, or that he or she should clutch eagerly at the reputation of being able to do so? Now, take last night's wind: as it happens, I myself was whistling. I blew a whistle twice, and the wind seemed to come absolutely in answer to my call. If anyone had seen me –'

The audience had been a little restive under this harangue, and Parkins had, I fear, fallen somewhat into the tone of a lecturer; but at the last sentence the Colonel stopped.

'Whistling, were you?' he said. 'And what sort of whistle did you use? Play this stroke first.' Interval.

'About that whistle you were asking, Colonel. It's rather a curious one. I have it in my – No; I see I've left it in my room. As a matter of fact, I found it yesterday.'

And then Parkins narrated the manner of his discovery of the whistle, upon hearing which the Colonel grunted, and opined that, in Parkins's place, he should himself be careful about using a thing that had belonged to a set of Papists, of whom, speaking generally, it might be affirmed that you never knew what they might not have been up to. From this topic he diverged to the enormities of the Vicar, who had given notice on the previous Sunday that Friday would be the Feast of St. Thomas the Apostle, and that there would be service at eleven o'clock in the church. This and other similar proceedings constituted in the Colonel's view a strong presumption that the Vicar was a concealed Papist, if not a Jesuit; and Parkins, who could not very readily follow the Colonel in this region, did not disagree with him. In fact, they got on so well together in the morning that there was no talk on either side of their separating after lunch.

Both continued to play well during the afternoon, or, at least, well enough to make them forget everything else until the light began to fail them. Not until then did Parkins remember that he had meant to do some more investigating at the preceptory; but it was of no great importance, he reflected. One day was as good as another; he might as well go home with the Colonel.

As they turned the corner of the house, the Colonel was almost knocked down by a boy who rushed into him at the very top of his speed, and then, instead of running away, remained hanging on to him and panting. The first words of the warrior were naturally those of reproof and objurgation, but he very quickly discerned that the boy was almost speechless with fright. Inquiries were useless at first. When the boy got his breath he began to howl, and still clung to the Colonel's legs. He was at last detached, but continued to howl.

'What in the world *is* the matter with you? What have you been up to? What have you seen?' said the two men.

'Ow, I seen it wive at me out of the winder,' wailed the boy, 'and I don't like it.'

'What window?' said the irritated Colonel. 'Come pull yourself together, my boy.'

'The front winder it was, at the 'otel,' said the boy.

At this point Parkins was in favour of sending the boy home, but the Colonel refused; he wanted to get to the bottom of it, he said; it was most dangerous to give a boy such a fright as this one had had, and if it turned out that people had been playing jokes, they should suffer for it in some way. And by a series of questions he made out this story: The boy had been playing about on the grass in front of the Globe with some others; then they had gone home to their teas, and he was just going, when he happened to look up at the front winder and see it a-wiving at him. *It* seemed to be a figure of some sort, in white as far as he knew – couldn't see its face; but it wived at him, and it warn't a right thing – not to say not a right person. Was there a light in the room? No, he didn't think to look if there was a light. Which was the window? Was it the top one or the second one? The seckind one it was – the big winder what got two little uns at the sides.

'Very well, my boy,' said the Colonel, after a few more questions. 'You run away home now. I expect it was some person trying to give you a start. Another time, like a brave English boy, you just throw a stone – well, no, not that exactly, but you go and speak to the waiter, or to Mr Simpson, the landlord, and – yes – and say that I advised you to do so.'

The boy's face expressed some of the doubt he felt as to the likelihood of Mr Simpson's lending a favourable ear to his complaint, but the Colonel did not appear to perceive this, and went on:

'And here's a sixpence – no, I see it's a shilling – and you be off home, and don't think any more about it.'

The youth hurried off with agitated thanks, and the Colonel and Parkins went round to the front of the Globe and reconnoitred. There was only one window answering to the description they had been hearing.

'Well, that's curious,' said Parkins; 'it's evidently my window the lad was talking about. Will you come up for a moment, Colonel Wilson? We ought to be able to see if anyone has been taking liberties in my room.'

They were soon in the passage, and Parkins made as if to open the door. Then he stopped and felt in his pockets.

'This is more serious that I thought,' was his next remark. 'I remember now that before I started this morning I locked the door. It is locked now, and, what is more, here is the key.' And he held it up. 'Now,' he went on, 'if the servants are in the habit of going into one's room during the day when one is away, I can only say that – well, that I don't approve of it at all.' Conscious of a somewhat weak climax, he busied himself in opening the door (which was indeed locked) and in lighting candles.

'No,' he said, 'nothing seems disturbed.'

'Except your bed,' put in the Colonel.

'Excuse me, that isn't my bed,' said Parkins. 'I don't use that one. But it does look as if someone had been playing tricks with it.'

It certainly did: the clothes were bundled up and twisted together in a most tortuous confusion. Parkins pondered.

'That must be it,' he said at last: 'I disordered the clothes last night in unpacking, and they haven't made it since. Perhaps they came in to make it, and that boy saw them through the window; and then they were called away and locked the door after them. Yes, I think that must be it.'

'Well, ring and ask,' said the Colonel, and this appealed to Parkins as practical.

The maid appeared, and, to make a long story short, deposed that she had made the bed in the morning when the gentleman was in the room, and hadn't been there since. No, she hadn't no other key. Mr. Simpson he kep' the keys; he'd be able to tell the gentleman if anyone had been up.

This was a puzzle. Investigation showed that nothing of value had been taken, and Parkins remembered the disposition of the small objects on tables and so forth well enough to be pretty sure that no pranks had been played with them. Mr and Mrs Simpson furthermore agreed that neither of them had given the duplicate key of the room to any person whatever during the day. Nor could Parkins, fair-minded man as he was, detect anything in the demeanour of master, mistress, or maid that indicated guilt. He was much more inclined to think that the boy had been imposing on the Colonel.

The latter was unwontedly silent and pensive at dinner and throughout the evening. When he bade good night to Parkins, he murmured in a gruff undertone:

'You know where I am if you want me during the night.'

'Why, yes thank you, Colonel Wilson, I think I do; but there isn't much prospect of my disturbing you, I hope. By the way,' he added, 'did I show you that old whistle I spoke of? I think not. Well, here it is.'

The Colonel turned it over gingerly in the light of the candle.

'Can you make anything of the inscription?' asked Parkins, as he took it back.

'No, not in this light. What do you mean to do with it?'

'Oh, well, when I get back to Cambridge I shall submit it to some of the archaeologists there, and see what they think of it; and very likely, if they consider it worth having, I may present it to one of the museums.'

'M!' said the Colonel. 'Well, you may be right. All I know is that, if it were mine, I should chuck it straight into the sea. It's no use talking, I'm well aware, but I expect that with you it's a case of live and learn. I hope so, I'm sure, and I wish you a good night.'

He turned away, leaving Parkins in act to speak at the bottom of the stair, and soon each was in his own bedroom.

By some unfortunate accident, there were neither blinds nor curtains to the windows of the Professor's room. The previous night he had thought little of this, but to-night there seemed every prospect of a bright moon rising to shine directly on his bed, and probably wake him later on. When he noticed this he was a good deal annoyed, but, with an ingenuity which I can only envy, he succeeded in rigging up, with the help of a railway-rug, some safety-pins, and a stick and umbrella, a screen which, if it only held together, would completely keep the moonlight off his bed. And shortly afterwards he was comfortably in that bed. When he had read a somewhat solid work long enough to produce a decided wish for sleep, he cast a drowsy glance round the room, blew out the candle, and fell back upon the pillow.

He must have slept soundly for an hour or more, when a sudden clatter shook him up in a most unwelcome manner. In a moment he realized what had happened: his carefully-constructed screen had given way, and a very bright frosty moon was shining directly on his face. This was highly annoying. Could he possibly get up and reconstruct the screen? or could he manage to sleep if he did not?

For some minutes he lay and pondered over the possibilities; then he turned over sharply, and with all his eyes open lay breathlessly listening. There had been a movement, he was sure, in the empty bed on the opposite side of the room. To-morrow he would have it moved, for there must be rats or something playing about in it. It was quiet now. No! the commotion began again. There was a rustling and shaking: surely more than any rat could cause.

I can figure to myself something of the Professor's bewilderment and horror, for I have in a dream thirty years back seen the same thing happen; but the reader will hardly, perhaps, imagine how dreadful it was to him to see a figure suddenly sit up in what he had known was an empty bed. He was out of his own bed in one bound, and made a dash towards the window, where lay his only weapon, the stick with which he had propped his screen. This was, as it turned out, the worst thing he could have done, because the personage in the empty bed, with a sudden smooth motion, slipped from the bed and took up a position, with outspread arms between the two beds, and in front of the door. Parkins watched it in a horrid perplexity. Somehow, the idea of getting past it and escaping through the door was intolerable to him; he could not have borne – he didn't know why – to touch it; and as for its touching him, he would sooner dash himself through the window than have that happen. It stood for the moment in a band of dark shadow, and he had not seen what its face was like. Now it began to move, in a stooping posture, and all at once the spectator realized, with some horror and some relief, that it must be blind, for it seemed to feel about it with its muffled arms in a groping and random fashion. Turning half away from him, it became suddenly conscious of the bed he had just left, and darted towards it, and bent over and felt the pillows in a way which made Parkins shudder as he had never in his life thought it possible. In a very few moments it seemed to know that the bed was empty, and then, moving forward into the area of light and facing the window, it showed for the first time what manner of thing it was.

Parkins, who very much dislikes being questioned about it, did once describe something of it in my hearing, and I gathered that what he chiefly remembers about it is a horrible, an intensely horrible, face *of crumpled linen*. What expression he read upon it he could not or would not tell, but that the fear of it went nigh to maddening him is certain.

But he was not at leisure to watch it for long. With formidable quickness it moved into the middle of the room, and, as it groped and waved, one corner of its draperies swept across Parkins' face. He could not – though he knew how perilous a sound was – he could not keep back a cry of disgust, and this gave the searcher an instant clue. It leapt towards him upon the instant, and the next moment he was half-way through the window backwards, uttering cry upon cry at the utmost pitch of his voice, and the linen face was thrust close into his own. At this, almost the last possible second, deliverance came, as you will have guessed: the Colonel burst the door open, and was just in time to see the dreadful group at the window. When he reached the figures only one was left. Parkins sank forward into the room in a faint, and before him on the floor lay a tumbled heap of bed-clothes.

Colonel Wilson asked no question, but busied himself in keeping everyone else out of the room and in getting Parkins back to his bed; and himself, wrapped in a rug, occupied the other bed for the rest of the night. Early on the next day Rogers arrived, more welcome than he would have been a day before, and the three of them held a very long consultation in the Professor's room. At the end of it the Colonel left the hotel door carrying a small object between his finger and thumb, which he cast as far into the sea as a very brawny arm could send it. Later on the smoke of a burning ascended from the back premises of the Globe.

Exactly what explanation was patched up for the staff and visitors at the hotel I must confess I do not recollect. The Professor was somehow cleared of the ready suspicion of delirium tremens, and the hotel of the reputation of a troubled house.

There is not much question as to what would have happened to Parkins if the Colonel had not intervened when he did. He would either have fallen out of the window or else lost his wits. But it is not so evident what more the creature that came in answer to the whistle could have done than frighten. There seemed to be absolutely nothing material about it save the bed-clothes of which it had made itself a body. The Colonel, who remembered a not very dissimilar occurrence in India, was of opinion that if Parkins had closed with it it could really have done very little, and that its one power was that of frightening. The whole thing, he said, served to confirm his opinion of the Church of Rome.

There is really nothing more to tell, but, as you may imagine, the Professor's views on certain points are less clear cut than they used to be. His nerves, too, have suffered: he cannot even now see a surplice hanging on a door quite unmoved, and the spectacle of a scarecrow in a field late on a winter afternoon has cost him more than one sleepless night.

\* \* \* \* \*

**Raffaella Barker** is the daughter of the novelist Elspeth Barker and the poet George Barker and her first novel *Come And Tell Me Some Lies* (1994) is based on her own childhood in north Norfolk. She still lives in the county with her family and the Norfolk countryside has provided the setting for subsequent novels including *The Hook* (1996), *Hens Dancing* (1998) and most recently *Summertime* (2002). *Sea Lavender*, set on the coast at Staitheley (Blakeney) is taken from *Phosphorescence* her story for teenagers published earlier this year (2003).

# Sea Lavender
## RAFFAELLA BARKER

My grandfather Jack's funeral is on his birthday. It is the worst and the best day it could be held on. On the Norfolk train with Mum, I look out as we pass familiar landmarks. It is a cruelly beautiful day, a day meant for being outside. The estuary with the tide out, somewhere near the beginning of our journey, has the criss cross tracks of sand pipers and flat footprints of shoveller ducks in the mud. I look at it but instead I see the marshes, a low tide and me and Jack crouched in ankle deep water, catching flat fish in our hands. I was six the first time I caught one, and Dad has the photograph of both of us, wet and laughing, holding out our fish, Jack standing behind me in his shirtsleeves, his eyes the colour of the summer sky behind him.

'How can he not be here now?' I speak my thoughts, and am surprised to hear my voice in the quiet early morning train carriage. Mum squeezes my hand, and I need more memories to push back the tide of loss which creeps up on me as we come nearer to Staitheley.

'Do you remember when Jack gave you Cactus?' Mum is smiling, she knows this memory well too. I was eight, carrying my school bag, back off the bus from school. Jack and Grandma had come to tea. Mum used to wear an apron a lot then and she was always baking things. I think it was jam tarts that time, but it could have been my favourite chocolate buns. She came to the door, wiping her floury hands on her blue striped apron.

'Jack and Grandma are in the garden,' she said. 'They've got someone with them.' I can see them still in my mind, framed by the door, in two chairs under the apple tree and Jack standing up when he saw me, leading me to the hammock and there was Cactus asleep with a bow round his neck.

'A grown up girl like you needs a puppy,' Jack said, and he handed me a collar and lead. 'Look after him and he will look after you.' It was such a treat, and it wasn't even my birthday. Jack just loved surprises.

121

In Dad's car on the way from the station, I find I am locked still in my memories. I don't want to talk. Mum and Dad are in the front with me and Cactus sitting behind them and it's just like it used to be except that everything is different. I hug Cactus, his warm round body is comforting and solid. I wish I could take him back to London with me.

'Where's Grandma?'

I can see a sliver of Dad's face, his pale eyes like Jack's in the rear view mirror. 'At home. We're going there now to pick her up so we can all go to church together.'

It must be the light, or just the way I'm feeling, but Grandma's front garden with rocketing lupins and roses cascading, and the blue front door in the middle of honeysuckle, is the saddest thing I have ever seen.

'I can't get out of the car, Mum,' I whisper, hugging Cactus. 'I'm afraid.' Dad goes in, and the sight of Grandma, with her best lipstick on, and holding Tike in the doorway makes me feel better. I follow Mum to the house, and stand with my eyes on the floor until Grandma hugs me.

'Oh Lola, I am so pleased to see you,' she says into my hair and I hug her back as tightly as I possibly can. She releases me, and I struggle to make myself speak:

'I wish I had come before, Grandma, last weekend I mean. 'There. I've said it. She knows now. Grandma squeezes my hand, and smiles, 'I know. Of course you do. And Jack knew too.'

I have never been to church without both Jack and Grandma. Often when I was small they would take me to the Sunday service and back to lunch with them afterwards, and all of us with Mum and Dad too attended every Easter and Christmas service.

We sit in the same pew as usual, but Jack is small in his coffin in front of us. Grandma is small too, and Dad and my Uncle John on either side of her are huge like rocks around her. There are too many people, all looking at me with kind sad eyes. I know so many faces, it is bewildering to try and look at them, acknowledge them and still keep myself from crying. I glance at Mum, she has her head down, and I copy her.

Afterwards, in the churchyard I see Josh and his parents, and Josh knods as I pass with Grandma towards the gate. Grandma doesn't even look at Josh's Mum and Dad, although their faces are next to us, full of sympathy and sadness. Jack is going to be buried on The Point next to Uncle James. We have to go in boats out there. I am worried about Grandma. She is weary and cold today, I don't think she much wants to get in a boat, but she does it, her hair ruffling in the breeze, and she sits down holding my hand tight.

'Everyone is welcome back at the village hall for tea' shouts Dad, to the people still spilling out on to the quay from the churchyard. We head out to sea with Reverend Horace and the undertakers who are all really fisherman friends of our family, wearing hired suits and sad faces. Our family is diminished. There aren't enough with just Grandma and her two big sons, Mum and me and Great Aunt Phyllis, Jack's sister whom we only ever saw at Christmas when she slept through everything except the Queen's Speech on telly. Phyllis has to bring her dog, a fat short-legged labrador called Jean. Jean barks hoarsely all the time we are in the boats, but Phyllis does not utter a single word. No one does actually. The motor chugs to life, bringing the smell of two stroke petrol. The familiarity of the sound and scent ease my sadness as we make our way across the creek to The Point. The burial is surreal, I almost feel as if I am watching it from above. The things that should be very difficult, like getting the coffin off the boat, are easy, maybe because Billy and the other fishermen help Dad and John do that. Reverend Horace holds his prayer book and leads us to the burial site. The walk, which is the bit that should be easy, is so sad it is almost impossible to do. Every step I know Grandma is thinking of Uncle James as well as Jack, and I cannot stop crying; my tears are hot channels in my skin now, and even the sea breeze doesn't dry them.

Mum puts her arm around me, 'Darling Lola, I shouldn't have let you come,' she murmurs, wiping my face with her handkerchief. Her scent on it cuts through the soft summer marsh smell of salt water, outboard engine oil and succulent samphire. I push her away, 'No, Mum, I'm all right. I'm glad I'm here. I belong.' I am so surprised by what I have just said that I stop crying. Mum and I look at one another in silence. *'May the Lord bless and keep the soul of our brother Jack.'*

Reverend Horace used to fish with Jack for sea bass and sea trout every summer. Late at night they would head out along the sandy beach of The Point, one in the water, waist deep in huge waders, the other walking on the beach, a long net dragging the shallow seabed between them. In the holidays, on Saturday nights, I was allowed to go too, and I walked behind the net with a box for the catch. Sometimes Dad came instead of Reverend Horace, and he walked deeper in the sea in his wet suit with Jack rowing a bit futher out in the darkness. The beach at night is one of my favourite places. Jack taught me to love it when I was first allowed out at night aged about seven. And what I still love is the glittering, mysterious night sea, and in it, just out of sight, dolphins and fish and unimaginable creatures., They are there, but we cannot see them as it is as if they inhabit a parallel world to ours as we walk on the moonlit sand.

It is mid afternoon when Grandma steps towards the grave and throws a tiny posy of lilac and sea lavender in. I stand by her side, hoding hands with her, until she raises her eyes to look out to sea and I know she has said goodbye. Across the channel, a red smear catches my eye.

'They've lit the boat,' says Dad. And I can make out the dark carcass of the burning boat cloaked in flames over on the mainland. We chug back across the water, Grandma sitting bolt upright, her eyes never leaviing the burning boat, and Dad guides us through the inlets to a mooring where we can see it without being noticed too much by the crowd around it. The afternoon light melts, changes shape and reforms in the heat of the flames and the black clad mourners look like burnt scraps tossed onto the marshes by the wind as they walk back to the village hall for tea.

Mum finds me playing with little Sadie in the car park.

'I'm going now,' she says, 'Will you come with me?'

I nod, although the idea of anywhere existing now except here on the marshes is impossible to imagine. But being here without Jack is worse. Billy Lawson, one of the fisherman undertakers drives us to the station. As we climb up from the sea and over into the next valley, my phone trills, as if woken from a magic sleep. I have six messages from Harry, three from Jessie and a couple from Pansy and Freda. I have never had this many messages before. I have never had any from Harry, and now I don't want them. I read the first one. It is some rubbish about how to get a new ring tone that sounds like a loo flushing. At the end Harry has added. 'Heh Heh Atta Girl, Flash in the Pan - Yeah.'

Honestly, what is the point? Does he know where I have been or what I am doing? He is an idiot. 1 delete everything else without reading it. The phone trills again and I look at the screen. It is from Josh and Sadie at the Staitheley village hall.

*'You look so sad. What can we do to help? Your loving friends Josh and Sadie Christie.'*

I turn to press my forehead against the car window so Mun doesn't see my face. I wish I had come here last weekend to see Jack. And even more I wish Mum and Dad were still together and we all lived at home in Staitheley with Cactus. It is the thought of Cactus that finally makes me howl, hugged by Mum in the back of Billy Lawson's car.

\* \* \* \* \*

*Landlines*

**Edward Storey** was born near Peterborough in 1930. Several generations of his family have lived and worked in the fens and for over thirty years Storey has been a solitary chronicler of this unique landscape in over twenty volumes of essays, poetry, autobiography and short stories. He is vice president of the John Clare Society and wrote *A Right To Song* in 1982, a long awaited biography of the poet. Having lived in East Anglia most of his life, Storey and his wife recently moved to the Welsh border where distance from his homeland has brought the flat landscape into sharper focus. *Funeral In The Fens* is one of the 'Tales from East Anglia' broadcast in 2001 on BBC Radio 3.

# Funeral In The Fens

## EDWARD STOREY

It was when Stephen received a telephone call from Geof's third wife, Maggie, to say that he had died that morning of a heart attack, that he knew he would have to forget about his last trip home and go to his friend's funeral. He'd always had a soft spot for Geof, not only because he was such a fine musician but because he'd always been a good, reliable companion – a constant joker, fond of a few pints, and a game of cricket. It was his passion for that innocent sport, as much as his dance-band engagements, that led to the break-up of his first marriage. His second marriage failed, ironically, when his new wife fell in love with the team's wicket-keeper and, a year later, ran off with him to Devon. Geof vowed he would not marry again and for four years went back to his old temptations. But the two pints now became five and his flirtations with other women lacked discretion.

Then along came Maggie, the thirty-five-year old daughter of a local farmer, who took Geof in hand, put him in charge of the sales office on the farm, and eventually married him. When Maggie's father died she inherited the farms and a large Victorian house, two miles east of Denham, surrounded by a thousand acres of rich black soil. The nearest other farm was no more than a white speck on the horizon. They were linked with the world only by the long rows of pylons, the long man-made drains that kept the Fens fertile and dry, and the telephone.

And so Maggie was ringing Stephen. 'I'd be ever so grateful if you would come,' she said. 'You can stay with us. We've plenty of room. Our son, Jeremy and his partner, Kate, will be here. They're coming up from London. And maybe Geof's brother, Jack, will be staying, though he's in a poor state these days.'

Stephen paused to think for a moment and then asked Maggie to remind him of Geof's age. 'Sixty-one,' she said. 'You should know that.

Which makes you fifty-eight. Right?'

Her frankness almost hurt. 'Frightening, isn't it,' he said quietly. 'Two more years and I'll be able to retire. Then what will I do with myself?'

'Better not look too far ahead,' Maggie replied. 'Life can be very unpredictable.'

The moment those words sped irretrievably down the line Maggie knew she had said the wrong thing. 'Sorry, Steve, that was rather tactless of me.'

There was a slight pause before she added, 'I hope that won't put you off coming to the funeral.'

Stephen waited for a moment before saying 'What time is it?'

'Two o'clock, St Mary's Church. But come to the house first. I'm sure there'll be several people who'd like to see you again. By the way, no flowers by request. Donations to the British Heart Foundation, should you feel like it.'

It was a beautiful September day as Stephen drove down to Cambridgeshire. The harvest had been gathered in early that summer and most of the fields already ploughed for re-sowing. It wasn't so much the unfolding space that he first noticed but the smell. That rich soil had a smell like no other. His grandfather used to say it still smelt of Anglo-Saxon England, of primeval forests buried under thousands of years of decaying foliage and then floods. There was something about it that called you back.

He had not been back to his home town of Denham in the Fens for fifteen years and could hardly blame any of his old acquaintances if they didn't recognise him. He had not only put on weight but also grown a beard. He thought that he'd severed his connections with the place when he accepted an appointment as a music-teacher in Cumbria ten years ago.

Having grown up in the Fens he'd not found it easy to live among mountains. The awesome grandeur that inspired others only left him with a depressing claustrophobia that made him restless. Although he was grateful to have been given a job at a crucial time of his life, he still longed for more elbow room and a greater sense of freedom. At the same time he knew that he could not go back to live in the Fens. As an ambitious young man he'd found them culturally stultifying. His dream then was to become a member of a major symphony orchestra and, when his playing days were over, to take up conducting, for which he believed he had a natural talent.

Stephen's family had a long tradition in brass bands. His father, grandfather and four uncles were all bandsmen and, as a boy, he was taught to the play the cornet. By the age of nine he was already a popular soloist, appearing as a guest-artist throughout East Anglia. Then, as a teenager, he was taken to a live orchestral concert in London and fell in love with classical music. He immediately switched from cornet to trumpet, won a scholarship to music college, and later passed an audition for the Bournemouth Symphony Orchestra.

Tragically for him, it was a shorter career than he'd expected and he still harboured a deep resentment over the reason why his dreams were so completely turned upside-down, if not ruined. A car accident, which had left him with a broken jaw and no front teeth, meant his playing days were already over. If only he had not agreed to rush home to Denham that weekend for his cousin Julia's wedding, that accident would not have happened. His reluctance to go back to the Fens because of that incident alienated him from the place and it's people.

When he was invited to go out to New Zealand as the professional coach of one of the country's top brass bands, he eagerly accepted. It was to be a five-year contract to begin with but there was every possibility that it would be extended for at least another three years and, if successful, he might even decide to settle there. It may have looked as if his life had come full circle but at least he would be conducting and working in a land of opportunity.

Although they were to be some of the happiest years of his adult life, they too came to an end sooner than expected. The New Zealand Government, whilst grateful for his contribution to the country's cultural life, especially with the young, now believed that they had enough home-grown talent who deserved a chance to carry on the good work.

So Stephen returned to England, to become again a music-teacher, this time in a large comprehensive school in Yorkshire, a county that had always produced some of the finest brass bands in the world. Within eighteen months he had formed his own Yorkshire Youth Concert Band, which soon began to win area and national contests.

The only Denham friend that he'd kept in touch with during all these years was Geof Tyler, who was three years older and, as a young trombonist, had been as popular as Stephen – more so in some ways because he had joined a well-known dance band and became an idol with the girls.

The other difference was that Stephen had never married, whereas Geof had been married three times. He used to tease Stephen for remaining single and putting his career first. 'You have to think about what will happen to you when your playing days are over,' he said, 'and the adoring crowds have all gone home. There's a lot to be said for coming home to the same bed every night.'

Stephen drove slowly into the town of Denham, looking for changes more than familiar landmarks. The house where he was born had gone, so too had the corner shop. A small estate of modern bungalows stood where the cricket field used to be, and what had been his and Geof's favourite pub, was now a Chinese takeaway.

He turned down into Blackmoor Fen and along Vermuyden's Drain to Maggie's farm. Several members of the family and friends were already there and Jeremy was going round with a tray of sherry. Stephen declined but introduced himself and asked for Maggie. Jeremy nodded towards the foot of the stairs.

She was still very attractive, even in her elegant black dress and large hat. The moment she saw Stephen she stepped quickly into the room to welcome him. 'Steve! How lovely to see you. Thank you for coming. Have a good journey?'

'Not bad, considering it's Friday. I must say, Maggie, you're looking absolutely fantastic – if that's not a tactless thing to say on such a day.'

'That's more than I can say about you, old bean. You've put on a lot of weight since we last met, and forgotten to shave . . . And you haven't even got a drink.'

'I declined. Not keen on sherry.'

'Would you like me to get you a scotch?'

Before he could answer, Jeremy announced that the funeral cars had arrived. Geof and Maggie had never been church-goers but, like most country people, they believed that things should be done properly. The church was full, nearly everyone wore black, the service was traditional, the burial in Denham cemetery conducted with old-fashioned solemnity and, because the request for no flowers had been respected, there was no vying between relatives and friends over the most expensive wreaths.

Back at the house there was the customary spread of cold meats, pies, salads, sandwiches and cakes, and a chance for everyone to talk about the old times, including their favourite anecdotes about Geof. For those who did not want a cup of tea there was beer, or spirits. Knowing that it was going to be a long evening, Stephen decided to stay with tea, for the time being.

At six o'clock Jeremy and Kate announced that they had to leave because they had an important meeting in London in the morning. As Maggie did not look surprised, Stephen assumed that she had already been told that they would not be staying over-night. Geof's brother Jack, who'd not been well enough to attend the funeral, was not there either

Soon others began to leave, offering well-intended but inadequate phrases such as 'You know where we are, Maggie . . .' and 'You must come and have dinner with us before the winter sets in.'

By seven o'clock there were only Maggie's brother Clive and his wife Marjory left. The house suddenly felt very quiet and empty. Clive tried to keep the conversation going by saying, 'Has Maggie had chance to tell you, Steve, that the Isle of Ely Youth Band is looking for a new conductor? Not a full-time job, I'm afraid, but I thought it might interest you.'

'But I don't retire for another two years, Clive, and by then I shall be too old.'

'You don't have to wait until you retire,' said Marjory. 'They need someone now. Besides, it's time you came back to your roots.

Stephen was amused at the suggestion. 'But what would I do for a living?'

'You could always help me,' Maggie said. 'Now that Geof's gone I shall need help in the office. You do know how to use a computer, don't you?'

'Just what have you three been cooking up between you? You know I couldn't come back here.'

'Tell me why not,' said Marjory. 'The place needs someone like you. You've the flair and the experience to make things happen.'

'Besides,' Clive added, 'I'm on the Board of Governors and could put in a good word for you. You could almost name your own terms. But we would like to make an appointment before Christmas because of the Band's commitments.'

'That's out of the question,' Stephen said. 'I'd have to give two term's notice, even if I was tempted to consider it. In any case, I'm looking forward to my retirement.'

'Well, the job's there if you want it,' said Clive as he and Marjory prepared to leave. 'Why don't you sleep on it?'

Sitting alone with Maggie in that large house, surrounded by so much space, darkness and silence, Stephen felt uneasy. Looking at Maggie he couldn't help thinking that Geof had been third time lucky. She was attractive, capable and practical, and had clearly given Geof the kind of love he'd always needed.

She refilled their glasses then asked, 'You don't have to rush off at crack of dawn, do you?'

'No, but I ought to be away by ten-thirty, I think. Why?'

'I was rather hoping that we could have gone to the cemetery together. This afternoon seemed so unreal. I still can't believe it's happened.'

Stephen readily agreed. 'I was planning to visit my parents' grave before leaving Denham, anyway.'

He did not sleep well that night. His head was too full of doubts, memories, the events of the day, and Maggie. He had believed her when she said earlier that she was going to find it hard to live without Geof, but he also knew she was a survivor and would get on with her life. At the same time, running two farms would not be easy. He felt terribly sorry for her. He also began to feel sorry for himself. Being reminded of his childhood, the house where he grew up, his parents and disappointments, made him feel as if he'd been to his own funeral that day. But no one can go back, whatever the loss. The past is always dead. He was a very different person from the young man who'd left Denham all those years ago. It was now a town full of ghosts, and he was one of them.

The following morning was no better. He and Maggie drove to the cemetery in separate cars so that he could leave immediately afterwards. When their visits to the graves were over they stood outside the gates, wondering what to say to each other.

Eventually Maggie asked, 'Do you think you'll ever come back, Steve?'

'What, to live? I doubt it. Whether I'll come back to visit the place again who knows.'

He walked Maggie to her car, opened the door and kissed her goodbye. 'I'll phone you next week.' She could keep back her tears no longer. With a brief wave and an attempted smile, she drove off.

Stephen felt rooted to the spot and waited until her car was out of sight. Then he left, leaving the town and the smell of the Fens behind him. What does call a man back to a place? The land? Or something else? By the time he'd reached the A1 he was trying to think about his concert that evening. 'We can only belong to where we are going,' he said, 'not to where we have been.'

But he wasn't convinced.

\* \* \* \* \*

**Jon McGregor** was born in Bermuda and brought up in Norfolk before going to university. *What The Sky Sees*, published in Granta 2002, is set in the fens but owes much to the author's cycle rides through Breckland and the Norfolk countryside as a teenager. McGregor's novel, *If Nobody Speaks of Remarkable Things* (2002), was published by Bloomsbury and he is currently working on a second novel.

# What The Sky Sees

## JON McGREGOR

In the summer the sky is most times blue. A blue so pure and bright that it hurts to look into it. A blue so deep that if you tip your head back and lose the land from the edges of your vision then you become dizzy and have to hold something to steady yourself, for fear of slipping and falling in. The light which pours from out of this blueness sears everything it reaches, grants beauty where there was none. Anonymous fields of wheat become crowds of ears of grain, stagnant canals and drains become millions of glittering waterdrops, tarmac roads become shattered diamonds placed gently into soft black felt. In the summer, the sky is blue and lifted high, transforming the landscape and the actions of the people who live in it, a shimmering blue silence from which there is no hiding place save beneath the surface of the land.

In the autumn the sky is most times white, a ragged dirty white, and you wonder how this could be the same sky but it is. As the earth turns thick and hard beneath it, the sky seems to be struggling to remain unbroken. Cutting winds come from beyond the horizon, slicing across the land, ripping the sheeted clouds which protect the sky. Slashes of light emerge through these tears, running across the fields like searchlights before vanishing over the horizon and leaving the land as sullen as before. The colours of the earth change, and both landscape and lives turn faces away from the sky in preparation for the cold to come. Fields and ditches prepare coats of fallen leaves for themselves, rivers swell. People who grew up in other places claim they can smell the changing of the seasons, but that means nothing here. All we can smell is the richness of the earth. We know the seasons are changing only by the shape and the colour of the sky, stretched over us from horizon to horizon, the length and breadth of a day.

*Landlines*

In the winter the sky is most times grey. A dark and bruising grey. The days shorten, the distance between the horizons shrivels, and what little light seeps down is thick and lifeless. There is no danger of falling into the sky at these times, our bodies and our lives anchored to the ground by the weight of the colour of the light. The earth hides secrets at these times, and the land is silent, save for the shriek of winds which the old people will tell you come all the way from Siberia. Sometimes the drains and the canals will freeze, and be covered in snow, and sometimes these snows will come fast in the night and block the roads so that the landscape is nothing but whiteness, all lines and textures concealed. At times it seems as though the land is giving back light to the sky, begging it to lessen the weight of its greyness and trying to hold off the load.

In the spring the sky is all of these colours, and more. Spring comes gradually here, clusters of bright flowers breaking through the surface of the soil and buds of palest green squeezing out of dry branches while the sky fades to light grey, then white, and finally a faint blue. The air cleanses itself then, with a warm wind from the south and sudden bursts of fresh sparkling rain. The sky lifts away from the ground, the horizons drawing apart to stretch it taut and let space and light flood back into our lives. This is the time when change is a daily force, woodlands smeared green overnight, fields purpled with lavender behind your back. This is the time when the floods come, and the ditches and the barriers have to be built a little deeper and a little higher, and the crops have to be replanted. But still, with all this life bursting up towards the sky, still the earth holds secrets. And still the sky watches.

People who grow up in other places talk about the hills having eyes, but that means nothing here. The land is level here and all we have watching over us is the sky, the ever-present, the always watching. People who grow up having hills to climb and valleys to shelter in think of the sky as neutral, as an emptiness sometimes covered over by clouds, but here the sky is all, arching over our lives.

I was seventeen the first time I kissed a girl. She had long dark hair and she took my face in her hands and pushed her mouth on to mine. She seemed to know what she was doing; I certainly didn't. She drew away just as I was beginning to understand what it was that I had been missing, and told me that she would like to see me again in the evening. That we should go somewhere, do something. She vanished inside her house, leaving me to walk away with the taste of her on my wind-cracked lips.

The bus from March, where she lived then, to my father's house in Upwell, where he still lives today, passes down through Wimblington and then swings around to follow the B1098 parallel to Sixteen Foot Drain. It was a journey I made every day, from the school where I was studying for A levels, to my father's house where I helped on the farm in the evenings. The road beside the Sixteen Foot is perfectly straight and lifted above the level of the fields, and looking out of the window on that newly kissed afternoon I felt like we were passing through the sky.

By the time the day had faded to black my father was asleep and ready for another early morning of work. With the taste of her on my lips and the spark she had put in my belly still dancing there, I slipped the car keys from the hook on the wall and took his car. I had driven before, pulling trailers of straw and silage along farm tracks, but I had no licence to be on the road and I knew my father would never give me permission. But she had said she wanted to see me, to go somewhere and do something, and I wasn't about to stay at home with those words in my head and wipe the salt taste of her away. Perhaps, now, I would. But I was seventeen then and things were different.

The drive to her house was easy enough, uneventful. The roads were empty and straight, and the sky was letting in enough moonlight to steer by. But the drive to her house was filled with my questions and her voice and my mouth and her hands and her face and her hair all at once in my head, one after the other, all at once. What had she meant when she said we should go somewhere? And why, when I'd been circling her for months, had she waited until now to show her interest? I didn't understand, but I had her taste and I wanted more.

I soon discovered that she didn't want to go somewhere at all, just to sit beside me in the car and drive through the flatness of the landscape, looking down across the fields from the raised-up road. We drove through Westry, over Twenty Foot Drain, past Whittlesey (and as we passed through Pondersbridge she put her hand on my thigh and kissed my ear). We crossed the Forty Foot Bridge, drove through Ticks and West Moor, the windows open to the damp rich smell of a summer night in the fens (and beside West Moor I put my hand into the length of her hair). We crossed Old Bedford and New Bedford rivers, drove through Ten Mile Bank, Salters Lode and Outwell (and on the edge of Friday Bridge she asked me to stop the car and we kissed for a very long time).

135

*Landlines*

When we finally stopped we looked out across the fields and talked, about the things people talk about when they suddenly come together in that way. Home, and family, and dreams, and awkward silences. Then she turned to me and lifted my thin woollen jumper over my head, the wool snagging against my tingling skin and giving me tiny electric shocks. Starting from a point beneath my belly button she traced a line with her finger, around the edge of my ribcage and over my nipple, down under my chest cavity and up over my other nipple, around the other edge of my ribcage and back down to my belly button - a glorious heart shape burned on to my body by her fingernail. Sometimes, now, I redraw that shape myself, hoping to regain that moment. Sometimes, now, I think of her hair and wonder why I can no longer remember the way it smelled that night.

I remember the way she watched me as I undid the buttons of her shirt and looked at her breasts. I couldn't bring myself to touch them, not then, not so soon, and eventually she took my fingers and placed them there herself. I drew tiny heart shapes around the dark patches around her nipples, and then pulled her close to kiss her again, electrified by her skin on my skin. I can remember the touch of her whisper on my face as we told each other things we had never spoken before and asked for extravagant promises we believed we could keep. And I can remember the way she looked in the rear-view mirror of my father's car when I drove away from her house, knowing that life would be different now and terrified that it would be taken away from me. But I can't remember the way her hair smelled that night, it no longer smells that way.

This place that I have grown up in is a landscape of straight lines, a field of vision dominated by the parallel and the perpendicular. The straightest line of all is the hard blur of the horizon, a single unbending line which encircles the day. When I was a child I used to spin round with my eyes on the horizon, trying to spot the places where the line curved or turned or bent; but I never could, and the mystery of the encircling straight line stayed with me, troubled me, comforted me.

All other lines find their way to the horizon line, sooner or later. The high lines, the connecting lines: the railway tracks, telegraph wires, canals and drains and rivers, all banked and lifted up above the level of the fields and houses. Years ago, playing in the field while my father worked, I looked up to see a line of boats processing grandly through the sky. I think they must have been barges navigating the Sixteen Foot to Lynn, but at the time all I knew was these boats way above my head.

The other lines are the boundary lines, the low lines. There are no hedges between fields here, only ditches. Ditches mark boundaries, and suck the water off the fields, serve as the barriers which stop the sea coming back to reclaim what it rightfully owns; and you can never go far before you find somebody re-cutting the ditches of their land, making them a little deeper, a little wider, one eye on the sky, always wondering when the rains will come and swell the rivers by those few inches too far.

Floods. Sometimes the lines of this place are obliterated, and all that is left is flatness from horizon to horizon. This obliteration is always an act of nature, weather come from the sky to erase the man-made geometry and restore a resemblance to the sunken sea this place once was. Sometimes it will be rain, swelling the rivers until they break out of the embankments and sandbags and rush over the fields, ignoring the prayers of the farmers and settling across hundreds of acres for weeks at a time so that the sky can be seen from below as well as above, clouds and seabirds gliding across the land. Sometimes it will be snow, covering everything, blocking drains and roads, muffling sound as well as vision until mothers forbid children to leave their houses for fear of them losing their way.

I don't remember my mother telling me not to go out, but I suppose I would have been too young.

Sometimes it will be fog which obliterates our geometry, hiding even the horizon, veiling the sky. Sometimes the fog will come in with the floods, and our world will be utterly alien, unmappable, precarious.

The same floods that obliterate also bring life to the land, make our soil the richest in the country. At ploughing time the smell of the earth's nutrients seems to hang in the air, a smell like apple bruises and horse chestnut shells, a smell of pure energy. Sometimes, as a child, I would put my ear to the clodded ground and believe I could hear the richness of the soil, a richness my father claimed would grow five-pound notes if you planted a shilling. I suppose it must have been a similar sound to that which children hear when they listen to shells and hear the sea, but I didn't know that at the time. I had never been to the ocean. The sea regularly came to us, after all, since we lived on land which belonged to the sea.

Flatness, straight lines, a man-made geometry; this is the landscape I grew up in, a landscape encircled by the unbroken straight line of the horizon.

And this is the journey that I never forget. It's a journey I make often, driving into town, but it's this journey I never forget, the night I returned to my father's house from hers, the night when I knew that things were going to be different.

I drove with my hand on my chest, feeling the burn of her finger there still, and I drove along the straight road with the moonlight shining off the Sixteen Foot. She had told me many things I thought I'd never hear, talking about us and we and our as if something had already been decided. Driving along that road I realized that something already had, that I would not after all be able to endure a life of solitude as my father had learned to do. I considered it to be an awakening, a welcoming to adulthood, and it felt right that it should take place out on the road with the sky taking up most of my field of vision and the land flat and dark on all sides.

It was sudden, it was so sudden.

First I was driving along the empty road thinking about her, and then there was a man in the road looking over his shoulder at me and I was driving into him. I don't know where he came from, I don't know why I didn't see him sooner. He was not there and then he was there and I didn't have time to do anything. I didn't have time to flinch, or to throw my hands up to my face, or to shout. I didn't even have time to take my fingers from inside my jumper, and as the car hit him I was flung forwards and crushed my hand against the steering wheel. As the car hit him his arms lifted up to the sky and his back arched over the bonnet and his legs slid under one of the wheels and his whole body was dragged down to the road and out of sight.

His arms lifted up to the sky, his arching back.

The sound his body made when my father's car struck him, it was too loud, too firm, it sounded as though I had driven into a fence rather than a man, it was a thump, it was a smack. And the sound he made, a sound which is always in the back of my throat now, a muffled split-second of a scream.

His arms lifted up to the sky, even his fingers pointing upwards, as if there was something he could reach up there to pull himself clear. His back arching over the bonnet of my father's car before being dragged down. The last I saw before my head hit my chest. The jolt and the lurch as he was lost beneath the wheels. His lifted arms, the sound he made, the lurch of the car, my hand crushed between my chest and the steering wheel.

138

Then stillness and quiet and me turning the engine off and my heart rattling inside me.

He lay on his back with his legs underneath him, looking up at the night. His legs were so far underneath him that I supposed they were most probably broken. I stood by the car looking at him for a long time before I moved towards him. He made no sound, there was no sound anywhere, the night was quiet and the moon bright and the air still and there was a man lying dead in the road a few yards from me. It didn't feel real, and there are times, now, when I wonder whether it really did happen at all; but then I remember the way his neck felt when I touched my fingers against the vein there. Not cold, but not warm either, not warm enough, the temperature of a stillborn calf. There was no pulse to feel, the man's eyes were seeing nothing. I looked at him some more, at his broken body on the tarmac, his eyes, his open mouth.

He was wearing a white shirt, and a red V-necked jumper, and a frayed tweed jacket. His arms were up beside his head, and his fists were tightly clenched. A broken half bottle of whisky was hanging from the pocket of his jacket. There didn't seem to be any blood anywhere; there were dirty black bruises on his face, but no blood. His clothes were ripped across the chest, but there was no blood. I didn't understand how a man could be dragged under the wheels of a car and not bleed. I didn't understand how he could not bleed and die so quickly.

The whites of his eyes looked yellow under the moonlight.

I didn't understand who he was, why he had been on the road in the middle of the night, how I had not seen him, why he was dead. I didn't know what to do. I knelt beside him, looking out across the fields, up at the sky, at my father's car, at my shaking hands, up to the sky.

The words we've been given by our ancestors to name these places have no poetry. There's no elegance or grandeur in our geographical vocabulary. Our waterways are called drains; not rivers or streams or becks or burns, but drains. And even then they are marked not by old legends but by civil engineering. The Thirty Foot Drain. The Sixteen Foot Drain. The closest our ancestors could bring themselves to come to grandeur was in the naming of the Hundred Foot Drain. Our farms are not named for fancy, but anonymity. Lower Field Farm. Middle Field Farm. Sixteen Foot Farm. Names that give no clue to map readers, outsiders. Names that will never find their way on to tourist maps or guidebooks. People don't come here because they've been drawn by the romantic sound of the place; people don't come here much at all, and so the landscape remains mostly empty and retains its beauty. The poetry of this place is not in the names but in the shapes, the flatness, the bigness, the completeness of the landscape. Only what is beneath the surface of the earth is hidden, everything else between you and the horizon is visible.

The poetry is in the hidden also. In the unseen movements taking place beneath the surface. The cycles of growth and decay which take place in these fields, the nitrates and minerals and salts which come from the sea and crackle life into the roots of the crops. It's the quietness of these hidden processes which so enthrals me, the stateliness of such magical things. This is not poetry which can be named, or fitted on to a picture postcard, this is non-poetry. A secret kept from all except those who have stood and watched the changing of the fields, the colours of the sky, the patterns of the land.

The girl I'd made my journey to that night taught me the words I now use about this place that I love. I think that is why I felt so strongly about her; that, and the promise she held in her fingertips. She talked about the land and the sky in a way that made what I'd always felt make sense. She told me that on a clear day the horizon is about ten miles away and that since the average adult can walk twice that in a day then our landscape is the size of the time from dawn until dusk. She said that ours is the only place so unceasingly flat for this to hold true and that this was a gift. She told me that the flood times are echoes of a past when our land was under salt water and that they're a reminder that we only remain here by the grace of the sea and the sky. She said we should always remember this.

She told me, and I can't remember her exact words because I had her breast pressing against my mouth at the time, but she told me that our sky was so much greater than in other places that it was our reference point in ways that other people could never understand. They say the hills have eyes she said, but we have no hills here and she smiled and I understood.

She said lots of things like this, and I was instantly in love with her language, with the connection she felt with this place, with the way she touched my skin. She made me love this place, and she made me realize why I loved this place, and she made me realize why people from other places do not.

People don't often come here to visit, because they don't understand all this; outsiders don't make their homes here by choice. And people who do stray into these flatlands often get lost, floundering along the roads and tracks from one side of the day to the other without ever reaching the place they're looking for.

(He was an outsider, the man I met that night. I can remember looking at him, into his face, thinking I don't know you, I don't know who you are, I've not seen your face before, you're not from this place, you don't belong here. And that almost took the edge off it, made what I'd done seem a little less terrible. I don't know this man I kept thinking, I don't owe him anything. If he hadn't been dead I think I would have been demanding an apology from him for spoiling my evening. What had he been doing, walking down this road, my road, half-drunk, not looking where he was going? Why should I feel bad for his stupidity? I remember I got it into my head that he was probably from Nazeby, and I remembered my father saying that nothing of worth could ever come out of Nazeby. And so although I felt bad that I had killed a man, and although it is something which keeps me awake in the dark hours, I didn't feel bad that it was this man. And I had my reasons for not doing the right thing that night, on that journey, for doing what I did.)

I had my reasons. Although I've often regretted it, and although I've often thought perhaps my reasons were not enough, I know I would do the same again. I was young then, and scared, and the sky hung so high over me that I couldn't look up until it was done. If I'd been older when I made that journey then perhaps I would have been stronger, perhaps my thoughts would have been clearer. But I was seventeen, and I had never knelt beside a dead man before. So I drove away. I stood up, and turned away from the man, and walked back to my father's car, and drove away. I didn't look in the rear-view mirror, and I didn't turn around when I slowed for the junction. I suppose it was at that stage that I began to realize what had happened, what I had done. I had driven my father's car into a man, and then over him, and now he was dead. I felt a sort of sickness in me, a watery dread, starting somewhere down in my guts and rising to the back of my throat. My hands were locked on the wheel, I couldn't blink.

I knew before I reached my father's house that I would have to return to the man. The man, the body, the victim, the corpse, the man; whichever word I used made me flinch. But I knew I had to return, that I couldn't leave him laid out on the road like that with his legs neatly folded under his back. I knew that when he was found then somehow I would be found too, and the girl who'd drawn upon my bare chest would not even look me in the eye, and I knew that I couldn't let that happen.

So I fetched a spade from a shed at my father's farm and drove back to where I had hit the man. It sounds so terrible now, so mercenary, cowardly. Absurd. But it's what I did, and I had my reasons. I took the spade, and I walked down the embankment to the field below the road and I took off my thin jumper and began to dig.

I was used to digging. I knew how to strike an angle, break and shift, break and shift, pile the soil neatly so it can be replaced. The field had only recently been harvested, and the stubble was still in the ground. I laid sections of topsoil to one side. I was thinking clearly, working quickly but properly, ignoring the purpose of the hole I was digging. Once, when I was knee-deep in the ground, I looked up the bank and realized what I was doing. But I couldn't see the man, so I managed to swallow the sickness and dig some more. And all this time, the sound of metal on soil, the sky over me.

I dug a hole in the earth until I was in it up to my waist, breaking and shifting, breaking and shifting, metal on soil and soil on metal. My shoes and my trousers became heavy and dark with it, my face and my arms and my chest creased with sweat and dirt. And all the while the sickness rising in my throat, the dead man on the road, the sound of metal on soil, the sky above me.

It was deep enough, it was done. So long as it was further into the ground than the blades of ploughs could reach then it was deep enough, most probably. I walked up the embankment to the road, wanting to hurry and get it done, but holding back from what I had to do. He was still there, he would always be still there, me stood over him under the sky, him lying still on the road, broken.

To touch him.

I would have to touch him. I would have to pick him up and carry him down the embankment and into the hole I had made in the ground. I could hardly bring myself to look at him, and I would have to touch him. Put him in the hole in the ground, the hole I had made, the death I had made in the hole I had made in the earth. I bent down to take his arms. I could smell whisky on his face. I stopped, unwilling to touch him, unwilling to follow my reasons. They were good reasons, but perhaps they were not enough. But then I remembered her skin on my skin and her eyes and I knew I could do anything not to lose that and gripped his elbows and lifted them up to my waist. I backed away towards the embankment and his legs unfolded from beneath him, his head rolling down into his armpit, his half bottle of whisky falling from his pocket and breaking on the road. I didn't stop, I kept dragging him away, away from the road, down the bank, into the field.

I laid him down, this man, beside the hole in the earth which I had made for him, and I rolled him over into it. He fell face down, and I felt bad about that, about his face in the mud.

I returned to the place on the road and picked up the pieces of glass, caught in the moonlight, and threw them down on to his back and then I took the spade and began to pile the earth on to him. This man.

I threw soil upon him until he was gone, until the soil pressed so hard on him that he was no longer a man or a body or a victim or an anything. Just an absence, hidden under the ground. It was only then that I looked up at the sky, dark and silent over me, the moon now hidden by a cloud. I clenched my eyes shut and bit my lip until it bled. And when I returned to my father's house, I showered for hours, long after the hot water tank had emptied and I was left standing beneath a trickle of icy water.

When the dawn comes, when the first light slides in from the east, the sky is the colour of marbles. Thinnest grey, glass, frozen. Behind you, everything is dark still, silhouettes and shadows clinging to the last of the night-time, but as you look to the eastern edge of the horizon there is light.

The sky first, unveiling its shape for the day, cloud formations, texture; then giving that first thin light down to the lines of the land. And if you have the time to stand and watch, you can trace the movement of the light into the morning, the lines of fields and roads creeping towards you and then away to the west until the whole geometry of the day is revealed and the water in the drains begins to steam and shine. And gradually, you will notice the workers arriving, stepping from minibuses and spreading out in long lines across the fields, shadows, crouching, shuffling along the crop lines.

When the mid-morning comes, the sky is the colour of flowering linseed, a pale-blue hint of the full colour to come. Sometimes there will be clouds, joining together to form arches from horizon to horizon, stretching, tearing, scattering patterns across the fields.

Sometimes these clouds bring rain, puddles falling from the air and sinking into the earth, and the sky will darken for a moment. But then the rain will pass and the sky will be brighter. Cleaner. And now the workers are more visible, returning to their trays and boxes after the rain, lifting food from the ground, sorting, trimming, laying down and moving along the line. Occasionally one will stand, stretching an aching back, arching his spine and lifting cramped arms to the sky before returning to the soil.

When lunch time comes, when there is a moment of stillness and silence, the sky is the colour of the summer noon. This blue has no comparison, it is just the pure deep blue of the summer noon in this place. There are no clouds, there is no movement, and you hold your breath and turn around and follow the circle of the unbending horizon line. The workers eat their lunch in silence, gathered beside the road, looking out across the fields the way fishermen watch the sea. The workers spend their days lifting food from the soil; celery, spring onions, leeks, lettuces, fragile growth which would be ruined by machinery. But at noon they pause, and the sky stares down at the earth as if challenging it to reveal its secrets, and gravity seems to be reversed for a moment.

When the late afternoon comes, when the light is only beginning to fade from the day, the sky is the colour of a freshly forming bruise. The workers are slowing their pace, pausing more frequently to savour the warmth of the soil in their hands, aware now of the slight chill in the air, waiting for the word that the day is over. It was at a moment like this, sitting here as a child and watching the work of harvest, that an old farmer once told me the story about the whale. His father had discovered it, while leading the horses in ploughing; a whale's skeleton, with the jawbone intact and the entire ribcage in place. It was in such good condition, because of the peat in the soil, that they used it in place of timber when they built Upwell's church—the jaws for the door frame and the ribs for the beams in the roof. I'm not sure now if the story was true, but at the time the ghost of that great lost whale haunted my sleep, and kept me away from the church.

When the evening comes, before the embers of the closing of the day, the sky is the colour of my father's eyes. A darkening, muddied blue, hiding shadows and gradually turning away. Awake still, alive, just, but going. Going gently. The workers have left the field and collected their pay, measured by the weight of the food they have gathered, and the marks of their footprints are fading, dusted over with soil blown by a wind from the sea.

I married the first girl I kissed. Some people said that was the wrong thing to do, that I should have gone with other girls, that everyone falls in love with the first girl but that doesn't mean you should marry her. But they were wrong. Some people said they were jealous of us, of our romance, of our reckless commitment, but they were wrong as well. I was in love with her, and I think I still am, but I have never been convinced that she was The One or anything as dramatic as that. I was simply terrified that she would leave and I would never find another girl to draw shapes on my chest and kiss me in the dark hours. So I married her, and ever since I've been terrified that she would find out what I did that night, on my journey back from her house. Why I flinch at the sound of metal on soil, why I drive so slowly at night. She still doesn't know.

We married before we got the chance to go to university. I had to take over my father's farm, and it seemed to make sense for her to move in and help me, to become farmers and turn the soil of the fields where we grew up. My father could no longer work because he had a heart attack that summer. I heard the dogs barking at the tractor in the yard and went outside to see him clutching his chest and turning blue, so I dragged him from the cab into the mud and began to hammer on his chest. I was determined that he wouldn't be lost to the land as well, and I beat his heart with my fists and forced air into his lungs until the blue faded from his skin.

When I remember it now, it's always from a height, me kneeling over my father in the mud of the yard, as if I can see it the way the sky saw it, the dogs circling and barking and me shouting at my father until he could hear me again.

Now my father, the giant man who could pull down trees with his bare hands, the magician who could breathe life into a handful of seeds, now he sits in an armchair clutching a hot-water bottle and watching the sky change colour outside. He refuses to watch television, choosing instead to listen to the radio while he keeps his vigil on the land and sky. Sometimes when I take him his evening meal he will tell me something he's heard on the radio, a concert recording, a weather forecast, a news report, and I'm scared that one day he'll hear my secret coming from the radio.

But he never has done, yet. Often I just sit with him and listen to his short creaking breaths, thankful that he is not yet ready to lay beneath the ground.

My wife doesn't sit with us at these times. She reads, or does the accounts, waiting for me to reassure myself that my father is still well. We do most things together, planting the crops, harvesting, ploughing the soil, and when there is no work to be done we walk the paths beside the drains and talk and look at the sky fading. The evening is when the fields beside the drain smell richest, the warmth of the day evaporating from the soil into the air and bringing with it the smell of the fertility which produces such rich harvests year after year. We walk, and we look at our fields, and we watch the sky, and we hold each other.

We never had children, and although this is sad for us both it has meant that we have spent our evenings growing closer, talking our way into each other or resting in silences. We've moved together the way rail tracks move together as they approach the horizon, and I'm very glad I took my father's car that night and let her draw upon my body.

And yet.

And yet that same night, that same journey I made which took me to her is the same journey which keeps us from ever being one, for we are not so close at all; the secret I hid in the ground is as much between us as if he were lying in our bed.

Sometimes I've tried to tell her, convinced myself that she would understand, that she could forgive me. I imagine myself saying that I have to tell her something very important, that she might be shocked or upset but that she should try and understand. And I imagine her stopping what she is doing and turning to me, joining her small hands in the hollow of my back and saying I can tell her anything. In my head I'm then able to say that a long time ago I drove into a man and killed him and that because I was scared and because I didn't know what to do I dug a hole and buried him. And in my head she kisses my tears away. And in my head she throws cups and saucers at my feet and tells me to leave. I'm ashamed that I don't know her well enough to know how she would react; but I don't and so I've always stopped on the edge of speaking. I know what a danger my secret is and I think it is safer where it remains, buried.

One time I saw a man metal-detecting in the field where my secret is buried. I was driving past and I saw his car parked up on the verge and a faint line of footprints leading out across the soil. The light was clear and strong behind him and he was no more than a silhouette, his shadow rippled across the plough furrows. I sat in my car watching him, the sweeps of his scanner like a pendulum, moving towards the place. Twice

I saw him stoop to the ground and dig with a small shovel. Twice I saw him stand and kick the earth back into place and continue his steady sweeping. I wanted to go and tell him to stop, but I couldn't think of a good way of doing so, it wasn't my land, I had no right. He would surely have asked permission, and anyway he was doing no damage so soon after ploughing. He was moving towards the near edge of the field. He must have walked out to the middle and begun there. I don't know what he thought he'd find in these fields, there's no history here, not the sort which gets into museums anyway. There have never been dramatic finds of Saxon villages here, no burial mounds or hidden treasures. The only artefacts our ploughs have ever dragged up are rusted iron anchors from when this flatness was the sea.

The effects of ploughing on the soil can be unpredictable. There are the intended effects, the ripping up of hardened ground, the replenishing of nutrients, the breaking of the soil to strengthen it like scar tissue, always in perfect lines. We pride ourselves on the absolute straightness of our plough lines, fixing our eyes with perfect concentration upon distant points for as long as the blade is in the earth. But you can never tell what happens to the earth beneath these lines. Those rusted anchors sometimes found, they've been sunk in this soil ever since it was drained, and sometimes the turning of the earth will bring them closer to the surface and sometimes it will send them further down.

And so it is with my secret, buried down there at the edge of the field. When I dream of him, it's with a sound of the plough metal on soil, the roar of stones and earth as he either tumbles further down or is thrust to the surface. Sometimes I dream that he's been dragged away from the edge of the field, or turned upright with his arms stretched out towards the sky. When I picture him being found it's always his hands, open-palmed, that break the flat surface of the land. And whenever I see him in those dark hours, his face is hidden, covered with mud, only the tufts of a still growing beard sticking through the mask.

I was thinking all this when I watched the man swinging his metal detector back and forth that day. And I was thinking all this when I watched him stop, close to the edge of the field, and dig. I felt that this was the moment I'd been fearing, storing up my dreams until now. I hadn't expected it to happen this way, I'd imagined it differently. Him being dragged into the air by the blades of a plough, scooped into the sky by a ditch-digger, a sudden brutal discovery, not a man with a metal detector easing clods of soil away from his face and hands.

I've long been scared watching ploughing, not just in this field but in all the fields around here. You can see from miles away when a farmer is ploughing, because the gulls rise up in a dense white cloud behind the blades, picking out the worms and insects thrown up by the turning earth, and you can follow them as they rise and fall back and forth across the field. Always in a perfectly straight line. Once I had to help the farmer plough this field, dragging the blades across the spot where my secret is hidden, and I was so scared that I thought I might follow my father and have to have my chest beaten in the mud and be left to sit indoors. But nothing was revealed that time.

And this day, as I sat watching the man slowly digging, I realized that I wasn't scared. My father would disown me, but the truth would be spoken and there would be nothing hidden, everything would be above the surface beneath the sky.

I got out of my car to stand beneath the sky, lifting my arms and staring into the brightest part of it. It felt like an epiphany. The man in the field looked up at me, and I looked down at him, ready for what he was about to say, ready to make my confession at last. But he just looked at me, packed his tools into a bag, and began hurrying back to his car, stumbling slightly across the furrows. I walked over to him as he was putting his equipment into the boot of his car, and he looked at me nervously. Perhaps he hadn't asked permission from the farmer after all. Did you find anything I asked him, and he said no nothing and got straight into his car and drove away.

I stayed for a while, leaning against my car and looking out across the field, looking at the small pile of earth the man had dug out of the ground. I'd been surprised by my reaction, and I was almost disappointed now. I wondered if that meant the time was right to tell my wife, to sit her down and tell the truth, to hear her reaction and accept her reaction.

I wanted to do this, but I couldn't.

And now here I am again, driving down the road which flanks that field for the millionth time. And this time is no less anxious than the rest, my hands locked on the wheel, my eyes not blinking.

Except the field's not there today. The floods have come again, and this road is like a causeway across the sea. The water reaches as far as the horizon, interrupted only by the fixed points of telegraph poles like the masts of sunken boats. The horizon is close today, a vague boundary somewhere between here and the water and the sky, confused by the thick fog which hangs over the flooded fields.

The road is busy today, cars ahead of and behind me, piercing red lights suspended in a long line through the fog. People are driving very slowly, and I wonder if there are roadworks.

And then it happens, and my secret is revealed.

I'm driving, and I'm looking as always at the place where it happened. And I see bright lights and men in white overalls standing knee-deep in the water. The lights cut through the fog and I see police officers standing on the embankment and a small white tent on the verge. There are two police vans in the road, and it's these that have caused the traffic to slow; a policeman is waving cars past a few at a time, and everyone is looking down to the water where the men in white overalls are doing something with poles and tape. I can hardly breathe, there's a rushing sound in my ears.

The policeman waves at me to stop, and I think I recognize him. He walks over to my window and asks me to wind it down. He tells me we were at school together and I smile and say oh yes and there's a moment of silence. A funny do this isn't it he says then and I say oh yes and I know he's waiting for me to ask him what has happened but I say nothing. There's a generator somewhere, I can hear its muffled rattle.

Yes he says, they found a body, well a kind of body, in the water down there, floating, face down. They think it's been buried down there near twenty years he says, they think the flood water must have disturbed the soil and brought it out. Not much left of it now though he says. I don't think they'll find out who it is, and he straightens up and looks at the traffic. Best let you go on he says. How's the wife, how's your father he asks and I say fine they're both fine thanks I'll be seeing you I say and I press my foot gently down on the accelerator and drive slowly into the fog.

Behind me in my mirror I see him standing looking at the traffic, a line of white lights leading towards him. I see the police vehicles, I see the tent, I see the men wading in the water, and then they've faded into the fog and I am almost home.

And what will happen when I reach home? Everything has changed, but nothing has changed. My wife will still meet me in the hallway with a kiss and touch my thinning hair. I'll still take a meal to my father, and although he might tell me the news of the discovery it will be with a tone no different to what he normally uses. We'll still sit in silence and listen to his creaking breaths, the dogs will still bark when the daylight fades. My secret has been revealed, but it has not been revealed at all. Even if they find out who he was, they have no reason to connect him to me. And he was no one from here anyway, no one from here has gone missing for a long, long time.

So I am safe as I always was, my wife will still want to touch me, I will still wake in the morning and have fields to look out over.

But I'm not safe at all. Each year of holding this secret has eaten away at me, as each flood has carried layers of soil away from the grave I made. And the truth is now barely hidden at all, straining to break out of the thinness of me which holds it in. My wife has come to know something is wrong, and how very wrong it is, and she thinks less of me for it, I know. When she kisses me now she is always first to pull away. When she touches me she is searching, looking for the way in. And her knowledge of my hiding has made her bitter, I know, I can smell it in her hair at night, a worn out smell, a growing old smell.

I drive into the yard and the dogs come barking out to meet me. I sit in my car for a moment, fearful of what I know I must do, too weak to open the door of the car. The lights of my house are clear and warm, spilling into the foggy night. I feel tired, I feel so tired, I want to lie down and sleep and wake when all this has passed. The strength and the relief I felt that day I saw the man metal-detecting, that day I thought my secret would be unearthed to the sky, those feelings have evaporated now, and now all I feel is weak and old. I get out of the car and walk to the house, pushing the dogs away, and meet my wife in the hallway. I look at her, I say nothing. I serve the meal she has prepared for my father and take it through to him. They found a body in a field down the road he says. I know I heard I reply. I can't think it was anyone from round here he says. No I say, I shouldn't think so. He eats his food in small mouthfuls and asks if I'm okay and I look out of the window and say yes thanks I'm fine.

In the spring, when the dark fields turn a pale green, it's possible to watch the new shoots swing from east to west through the day. Later, as the crops become taller and thicker, this movement will become imperceptible; but while the shoots are still small you can watch them following the brightest part of the day. I think this is part of why I feel so old now, why my skin feels thin and grey, because I've forgotten to turn through the day, have stooped, wilted.

I'm not a religious man, but I know about sin. I know what it means to carry that load inside you, shielding it from the light of day, straining to hide it behind ever thinning defences. And I know now that eventually the defences must give way, the load break free, the earth give up its secrets to the sky. And I know that time has come. In the dark hours of last night, while my wife slept beside me, I made a discovery. The load inside me, the sin which has been growing with each moment of deceit, is not what I thought it was at all. It's not that I killed the man, nor even that I dug a hole and buried him face down and told nobody. My sin is in the reasons I had for digging that hole. Fear. Cowardice. But more than these the thinking of him as an outsider, as someone who didn't belong and so didn't matter. This is the weight I've been carrying, and I've not even known until now. Can a man be guilty of something he doesn't even realize he's done? Does a seed planted by mistake still grow?

The mists of yesterday have disappeared now, the sky is reflected clearly in the flooded fields. The day is so open and clear that the great ship of Ely Cathedral is just visible across the water, and I wonder whether that might be a place I could go to put down what I've been carrying and can carry no more. But it's like I said, I'm not a religious man.

The air has a chill to it, a dampness; the air tastes salty like I remember her lips tasted that first night. She is walking beside me now, we are walking the road beside what should be the Sixteen Foot Drain, keeping an eye on the flood levels. The dogs are running ahead, their barking crisp, their claws clicking on the tarmac.

I think of my father, watching this sky through the window, listening to the radio, tasting the burn from his weakened heart. I remember how he used to love walking these roads, when he had time, how he would hoist me up on to his shoulders so I could see further across the land than him. Can you see anything he'd say, what's there, what's there? And I'd make things up, dragons, castles, so as not to disappoint him or let him know that it was really more of the same, that our landscape just kept going.

It was only later I realized that that was what was magical about it, when the girl who is now my wife told me.

I think of my mother, of the story our family has which is never told, of where she might be now.

And I think of the man with his face turned to me and his arms reaching up into the sky, and I wonder who he was. Whether anyone still wonders where he might be now, whether he's been one of the missing persons cases they sometimes show after the local news.

I feel a warmth on my back, and I turn my face to the brightest part of the sky. I stop walking, and she stops and looks at me. I look out across the flooded fields towards the hard blur of the horizon, I look at her. I tell her there is something I have to tell her, that she might be upset or angry but that I have to tell her. She moves closer to me, she joins her small hands in the hollow of my back, she asks me to tell her what it is. And I tell her, in a strong clear voice, that the same night I kissed her in my father's car I drove into a man and killed him and buried him in a hole in these fields. I tell her this, and I tell her my reasons for doing this, and I tell her I am sorry but that I know sorry may not be enough. I speak these words and then I am silent and she looks at me.

And in that flat landscape, under the arch of the pure blue sky, I wait for her to speak.

\* \* \* \* \*

**Sylvia Townsend Warner's** first novel *Lolly Willowes* (1926) about a spinster's escape into witchcraft established her as a distinctive new voice, but throughout a long and distinguished career she only returned to the supernatural near the end of her life with the collection *Kingdoms Of Elfin* (1977) from which *Elphenor And Weasel* is taken. This, like most of her short stories, first appeared in *The New Yorker*.

# Elphenor and Weasel
## SYLVIA TOWNSEND WARNER

The ship had sailed barely three leagues from Ijmuiden when the wind backed into the east and rose to gale force. If the captain had been an older man he would have returned to port. But he had a mistress in Lowestoft and was impatient to get to her; the following wind, the waves thwacking the stern of the boat as though it were the rump of a donkey and tearing on ahead, abetted his desires. By nightfall, the ship was wallowing broken-backed at the mercy of the storm. Her decks were awash and cluttered with shifting debris. As she lurched lower, Elphenor thrust the confidential letter inside his shirt, the wallet of mortal money deeper in his pocket, and gave his mind to keeping his wings undamaged by blows from ripped sails and the clutches of his fellow-passengers. Judging his moment, he took off just before the ship went down, and was alone with the wind.

His wings were insignificant: he flew by the force of the gale. If for a moment it slackened he dropped within earshot of the hissing waves, then was scooped up and hurled onward. In one of these descents he felt the letter, heavy with seals, fall out of his breast. It would be forever private now, and the world of Elfin unchanged by its contents. On a later descent, the wallet followed it. His clothes were torn to shreds, he was benumbed with cold, he was wet to the skin. If the wind had let him down he would have drowned willingly, folded his useless wings and heard the waves hiss over his head. The force of the gale enclosed him, he could hardly draw breath. There was no effort of flight; the effort lay in being powerlessly and violently and almost senselessly conveyed – a fragment of existence in the drive of the storm. Once or twice he was asleep till a slackening of the wind jolted him awake with the salt smell of the sea beneath him. Wakened more forcibly, he saw a vague glimmer on the face of the water and supposed it might be the light of dawn; but he could not turn his head. He saw the staggering flight of a gull, and thought there must be land not far off.

The growing light showed a tumult of breakers ahead, close on each other's heels, devouring each other's bulk. They roared, and a pebble beach screamed back at them, but the wind carried him over, and on over a dusky flat landscape that might be anywhere. So far, he had not been afraid. But when a billow of darkness reared up in front of him, and the noise of tossing trees swooped on his hearing, he was suddenly in panic, and clung to a bough like a drowning man. He had landed in a thick grove of ilex trees, planted as a windbreak. He squirmed into the shelter of their midst, and heard the wind go on without him.

Somehow, he must have fallen out of the tree without noticing. When he woke, a man with mustachios was looking down on him.

'I know what you are. You're a fairy. There were fairies all round my father's place in Suffolk. Thieving pests, they were, bad as gypsies. But I half liked them. They were company for me, being an only child. How did you get here?'

Elphenor realised that he was still wearing the visibility he had put on during the voyage as a measure against being jostled. It was too late to discard it – though the shift between visible and invisible is a press-button affair. He repressed his indignation at being classed with gypsies and explained how the ship from Ijmuiden had sunk and the wind carried him on.

'From Ijmuiden, you say? What happened to the rest of them?'

'They were drowned.'

'Drowned? And my new assistant was on that ship! It's one calamity after another. Sim's hanged, and Jacob Kats gets drowned. Seems as though my stars meant me to have you.'

It seemed as though Elphenor's stars were of the same mind. To tease public opinion he had studied English as his second language; he was penniless, purposeless, breakfastless, and the wind had blown his shoes off. 'If I could get you out of any difficulties – ' he said.

'But I can't take you to Walsham Borealis looking like that. We'll go to old Bella, and she'll fit you out.'

Dressed in secondhand clothes too large for him and filled with pork pie, Elphenor entered Walsham Borealis riding pillion behind Master Elisha Blackbone. By then he knew he was to be assistant to a quack in several arts, including medicine, necromancy, divination, and procuring.

Hitherto, Elphenor, nephew to the Master of Ceremonies at the Elfin

Court of Zuy, had spent his days in making himself polite and, as far as in his tailor lay, ornamental. Now he had to make himself useful. After the cautious pleasures of Zuy everything in this new life, from observing the planets to analyzing specimens of urine, entertained him. It was all so agreeably terminal: one finished on thing and went on to another. When Master Blackbone's clients overlapped, Elphenor placated those kept waiting by building card houses, playing the mandora, and sympathetic conversation – in which he learned a great deal that was valuable to Master Blackbone in casting horoscopes.

For his part, Master Blackbone was delighted with an assistant who was so quick to learn, so free from prejudice, and, above all, a fairy. To employ a fairy was a step up in the world. In London practice every reputable necromancer kept a spiritual appurtenance – fairy, familiar, talking toad, airy consultant. When he had accumulated the money, he would set up in London, where there is always room for another marvel. For the present, he did not mention his assistant's origin, merely stating that he was the seventh son of a seventh son, on whom any gratuities would be well bestowed. Elphenor was on the footing of an apprentice; his keep and training were sufficient wages. A less generous master would have demanded the gratuities, but Master Blackbone had his eye on a golden future, and did not care to imperil it by more than a modest scriptural tithe.

With a fairy as an assistant, he branched out into larger developments of necromancy and took to raising the Devil as a favour. The midnight hour was essential and holy ground desirable – especially disused holy ground: ruined churches, disinhabited religious foundations. The necromancer and the favoured clients would ride under cover of night to Bromholm or St Benet's in the marshes. Elphenor, flying invisibly and dressed for the part, accompanied them. At the Word of Power he became visible, pranced, menaced, and lashed his tail till the necromancer ordered him back to the pit. This was for moonlight nights. When there was no moon, he hovered invisibly, whispering blasphemies and guilty secrets. His blasphemies lacked unction; being a fairy he did not believe in God. But the guilty secrets curdled many a good man's blood. A conscience-stricken clothier from a neighbouring parish spread such scandals about the iniquities done in Walsham Borealis that Master Blackbone thought it wisest to make off before he and Elphenor were thrown into jail.

They packed his equipment – alembics, chart of the heavens, book of spells, skull, etc. – and were off before the first calm light of an April morning. As they travelled southward Elphenor counted windmills and church towers and found windmills slightly predominating. Church towers were more profitable, observed Master Blackbone. Millers were rogues and cheats, but wherever there was a church you could be sure of fools; if Elphenor were not a fairy and ignorant of Holy Writ he would know that fools are the portion appointed for the wise. But for the present they would lie a little low, shun the Devil, and keep to love philtres and salves for the itch, for which there is always a demand in spring. He talked on about the herbs they would need, and the henbane that grew around Needham in Suffolk, where he was born and played with fairies, and whither they were bound. 'What were they like?' Elphenor asked. He did not suppose Master Blackbone's fairies were anything resplendent. Master Blackbone replied that they came out of a hill and were green. Searching his memory, he added that they smelled like elderflowers. At Zuy, elderflowers were used to flavour gooseberry jam – an inelegant conserve.

At Zuy, by now, the gardeners would be bringing the tubs of myrtle out of the conservatories, his uncle would be conducting ladies along the sanded walks to admire the hyacinths, and he would be forgotten; for in good society failures are smoothly forgotten, and as nothing had resulted from the confidential letter it would be assumed he had failed to deliver it. He would never be able to go back. He did not want to. There was better entertainment in the mortal world. Mortals packed more variety into their brief lives – perhaps because they knew them to be brief. There was always something going on and being taken seriously: love, hate, ambition, plotting, fear, and all the rest of it. He had more power as a quack's assistant than ever he would have attained to in Zuy. To have a great deal of power and no concern was the life for him.

Hog's grease was a regrettable interpolation in his career. Master Blackbone based his salves and ointments on hog's grease, which he bought in a crude state from pork butchers. It was Elphenor's task to clarify it before it was tinctured with juices expressed from herbs. Wash as he might, his hands remained greasy and the smell of grease hung in his nostrils. Even the rankest-smelling herbs were a welcome change, and a bundle of water peppermint threw him into a rapture. As Master Blackbone disliked stooping, most of the gathering fell to him.

It is a fallacy that henbane must be gathered at midnight. Sunlight raises its virtues (notably efficacious against toothache, insomnia, and lice), and to be at its best it should be gathered in the afternoon of a hot day. Elphenor was gathering it in a sloping meadow that faced south. He was working invisibly – Master Blackbone did not wish every Tom, Dick, and Harry to know what went into his preparations. Consequently, a lamb at play collided with him and knocked the basket out of his hand. As it stood astonished at this sudden shower of henbane, Elphenor seized it by the ear and cuffed it. Hearing her lamb bleat so piteously, its mother came charging to the rescue. She also collided with Elphenor and, being heavy with her winter fleece, sent him sprawling. He was still flat on his back when a girl appeared from nowhere, stooped over him, and slapped his face, hard and accurately. To assert his manly dignity he pulled her down on top of him – and saw that she was green.

She was a very pretty shade of green – a pure delicate tint, such as might have been cast on a white eggshell by the sun shining through the young foliage of a beech tree. Her hair, brows, and lashes were a darker shade; her lashes lay on her green cheek like a miniature fern frond. Her teeth were perfectly white. Her skin was so nearly transparent that the blue veins on her wrists and breasts showed through like some exquisitely marbled cheese.

As they lay in an interval of repose, she stroked the bruise beginning to show on his cheek with triumphant moans of compassion. Love did not heighten or diminish her colour. She remained precisely the same shade of green. The smell, of course, was that smell of elderflowers. It was strange to think that exactly like this she may have been one of the fairies who played with Elisha Blackbone in his bragged-of boyhood, fifty years back. He pushed the speculation away, and began kissing her behind the ear, and behind the other ear, to make sure which was the more sensitive. But from that hour love struck root in him.

Eventually he asked her name. She told him it was Weasel. 'I shall call you Mustela,' he said, complying with the lover's imperative to rename the loved one; but in the main he called her Weasel. They sat up, and saw that time had gone on as usual, dusk had fallen and the henbane begun to wilt.

When they parted, the sheep were circling gravely to the top of the hill, the small grassy hill of her tribe. He flew leisurely back, swinging the unfilled basket. The meagre show of henbane would be a pretext for going off on the morrow to a place where it grew more abundantly; he would have found such a place, but by then it was growing too dark for picking, and looking one way while flying another he had bruised his cheek against a low-growing bough. At Zuy this artless tale would not have supported a moment's scrutiny; but it would pass with a mortal, though

157

it might be wise to substantiate it with a request for the woundwort salve. For a mortal, Master Blackbone was capable of unexpected intuitions.

The intuitions had not extended to the reverence for age and learning which induced Elphenor to sleep on a pallet to the windward. Toward morning, he dreamed that he was at the foot of the ilex; but it was Weasel who was looking down at him, and if he did not move she would slap his face. He moved, and woke. Weasel lay asleep beside him. But at the same time they were under the ilex, for the waves crashed on the screaming pebble beach and were Master Blackbone's snores.

At Zuy the English Elfindom was spoken of with admiring reprehension: its magnificence, wastefulness, and misrule, its bravado and eccentricity. The eccentricity of being green and living under a hill was not included. A hill, yes. Antiquarians talked of hill dwellings, and found evidence of them in potsherds and beads. But never, at any time, green. The beauties of Zuy, all of them white as bolsters, would have swooned at the hypothesis. Repudiating the memory of past bolsters, he looked at Weasel, curled against him like a caterpillar in a rose leaf, green as spring, fresh as spring, and completely contemporary.

She stirred, opened her eyes, and laughed.

'Shush!'

Though invisible, she might not be inaudible, and her voice was ringing and assertive as a wren's. She had come so trustingly it would be the act of an ingrate to send her away. Not being an ingrate he went with her, leaving Master Blackbone to make what he would of an early-rising assistant. They breakfasted on wild strawberries and a hunk of bread he had had the presence of mind to take from the bread crock. It was enough for Weasel, and when they came to a brook she twitched up a handful of minnows and ate them raw. Love is a hungry emotion, and by midday he wished he had not been so conventional about the minnows. As a tactful approach, he began questioning her about life in the hill, its amenities, its daily routine. She suddenly became evasive: he would not like it; it was dull, old-fashioned, unsociable.

'All the same, I should like to visit it. I have never been inside a hill.'

'No! You can't come. It's impossible. They'd set on you, you'd be driven out. *You're not green*'.

Etiquette.

'Don't you understand?'

'I was wondering what they would do to you if they found out where you woke this morning.'

158

'Oh, that! They'd have to put up with it. Green folk don't draw green blood. But they'd tear you in pieces.'

'It's the same where I come from. If I took you to Zuy, they might be rather politer, but they'd never forgive you for being green. But I won't take you, Weasel. We'll stay in Suffolk. And if it rains and rains – '

'I don't mind rain – '

'We'll find a warm, dry badger sett.'

They escaped into childishness and were happy again, with a sharpened happiness because for a moment they had so nearly touched despair.

As summer became midsummer, and the elder blossom out-lasted the wild roses and faded in its turn till the only true elderflower scent came from her, and the next full moon had a broader face and shone on cocks of hay in silvery fields, they settled into an unhurried love and strolled from day to day as through a familiar landscape. By now they were seldom hungry, for there was a large crop of mushrooms, and Elphenor put more system into his attendances on Master Blackbone, breakfasting soundly and visibly while conveying mouthfuls to the invisible Weasel (it was for the breakfasts that they slept there). Being young and perfectly happy and pledged to love each other till the remote end of their days, they naturally talked of death and discussed how to contrive that neither should survive the other. Elphenor favoured being struck by lightning as they lay in each other's arms, but Weasel was terrified by thunder – she winced and covered her ears at the slightest distant rumble – and though he talked soothingly of the electric fluid and told her of recent experiments with amber and a couple of silk stockings, one black, one white, she refused to die by lightning stroke.

And Master Blackbone, scarcely able to believe his ears, madly casting horoscopes and invoking the goddess Fortuna, increasingly tolerant of Elphenor's inattention, patiently compounding his salves unassisted, smiling on the disappearances from his larder, was day after day, night after night, more sure of his surmise – till convinced of his amazing good fortune he fell into the melancholy of not knowing what best to do about it, whether to grasp fame single-handed or call in the help of an expert and self-effacingly retire on the profits. He wrote a letter to an old friend. Elphenor was not entrusted with this letter, but he knew it had been written and was directed to London. Weasel was sure Master Blackbone was up to no good – she had detested him at first sight. They decided to keep a watch on him. But their watch was desultory, and the stranger was already sitting in Master Blackbone's lodging and conversing with him when they flew in and perched on a beam.

The stranger was a stout man with a careworn expression. Master Blackbone was talking in his best procuring voice.

'It's a Golconda, an absolute Golconda! A pair of them, young, in perfect condition. Any manager would snap at them. But I have kept it dark till now. I wanted you to have the first option.'

'Thanks, I'm sure,' said the stranger. ' But it's taking a considerable chance.'

'Oh no, it isn't. People would flock to see them. You could double the charges – in fact you should, for it's something unique – and there wouldn't be an empty seat in the house. Besides, it's a scientific rarity. You'd have all the illuminati. Nobs from the colleges. Ladies of fashion. Royal patronage.'

The stranger said he didn't like buying pigs in pokes.

'But I give you my word. A brace of fairies – lovely, young, amorous fairies. Your fortune would be made.'

'How much do you want?'

'Two-thirds of the takings. You can't say that's exorbitant. Not two-thirds of the profits, mind. Two-thirds of the takings and a written agreement.'

The stranger repeated that he didn't like buying pigs in pokes, the more so when he had no warrant the pigs were within.

'Wait till tonight! They come every night and cuddle on that pallet there. They trust me like a father. Wait till they're asleep and throw a net over them, and they're yours.'

'But when I've got them to London, suppose they are awkward, and won't perform? People aren't going to pay for what they can't see. How can I be sure they'll be visible?'

Master Blackbone said there were ways and means, as with performing animals.

'Come, Weasel. We'll be off.'

The voice was right overhead, loud and clear. Some cobwebs drifted down.

Elphenor and Weasel were too pleased with themselves to think beyond the moment. They had turned habitually toward their usual haunts and were dabbling their feet in the brook before it occurred to Elphenor that they had no reason to stay in the neighbourhood and good reason to go elsewhere. Weasel's relations would murder him because he was not green, Master Blackbone designed to sell them because they were fairies. Master Blackbone might have further designs: he was a necromancer, though a poor one; it would be prudent to get beyond his magic circle. Elphenor had congratulated himself on leaving prudence behind at Zuy. Now it reasserted itself and had its charm. Prudence had no charm whatever for Weasel; it was only by representing the move as reckless that he persuaded her to make it.

With the world before them, he flew up for a survey and caught sight of the sea, looking as if ships would not melt in its mouth – which rather weakened the effect of his previous narrative of the journey from IJmuiden to the ilexes. Following the coastline they came to Great Yarmouth, where they spent several weeks. It was ideal for their vagrant purposes, full of vigorous, cheerful people, with food to be had for the taking – hot pies and winkles in the market place, herring on the quayside where the fishing boats unloaded. The air was rough and cold, and he stole a pair of shipboy's trousers and a knitted muffler for Weasel from a marine store near the Custom House. He was sorry to leave this kind place. But Weasel showed such a strong inclination to go to sea, and found it so amusing to flaunt her trousers on the quayside and startle her admirers with her green face, that she was becoming notorious, and he was afraid Master Blackbone might hear of her. From Yarmouth they flew inland, steering their course by church towers. Where there is a church tower you can be sure of fools, Master Blackbone had said. True enough; but Elphenor tired of thieving – though it called for more skill in villages – and he thought he would try turning an honest penny, for a change. By now he was so coarsened and brown-handed that he could pass as a labouring man. In one place he sacked potatoes, in another baled reeds for thatching. At a village called Scottow, where the sexton had rheumatism, he dug a grave. Honest-pennying was no pleasure to Weasel, who had to hang about invisibly, passing the time with shrivelled blackberries. In these rustic places which had never seen a circus or an Indian peddler, her lovely green face would have brought stones rattling on their heels.

Winter came late that year and stealthily, but the nights were cold. Nights were never cold in Suffolk, she said. He knew this was due to the steady temperature under the hill, but hoping all the same she might be right he turned southward. He had earned more than enough to pay for a night at an inn. At Bury St Edmunds he bought her a cloak with a deep hood, and telling her to pull the hood well forward and keep close to his heels he went at dusk to a respectable inn and hired the best bedroom they had. All went well, except that they seemed to look at him doubtfully.

In his anxiety to control the situation he had reverted to his upper-class manner, which his clothes did not match with. The four-poster bed was so comfortable that he hired the room for a second night, telling the chambermaid his wife had a headache and must not be disturbed. It was certainly an elopement, she reported; even before she had left the room, the little gentleman had parted the bed curtains and climbed in beside the lady. After the second night there was no more money.

They left on foot, and continued to walk, for there was a shifting, drizzling fog which made it difficult to keep each other in sight if they flew. Once again they stole a dinner, but it was so inadequate that Elphenor decided to try begging. He was rehearsing a beggar's whine when they saw a ruddy glow through the fog and heard a hammer ring on an anvil. Weasel as usual clapped her hands to her ears; but when they came to a wayside forge the warmth persuaded her to follow Elphenor, who went in shivering ostentatiously and asked if he and his wife could stand near the blaze: they would not get in the way, they would not stay long. The blacksmith was shaping horseshoes. He nodded, and went on with his work. Elphenor was preparing another whine when the blacksmith remarked it was no day to be out, and encouraged Weasel, who stood in the doorway, to come nearer the fire.

'Poor soul, she could do with a little kindness,' said Elphenor. 'And we haven't met with much of it today. We passed an inn, farther back' – it was there they had stolen the heel of a Suffolk cheese – 'but they said they had no room for us.'

Weasel interrupted. 'What's that black thing ahead, that keeps on showing and going?'

The blacksmith pulled his forelock. 'Madam. That's the church.'

They thanked him and went away, Elphenor thinking he must learn to beg more feelingly. The blacksmith stood looking after them. At this very time of year, too. He wished he had not let slip the opportunity of a Hail Mary not likely to come his way again.

The brief December day was closing when they came to the church. The south porch, large as a room, was sheltered from the wind, and they sat there, huddled in Weasel's cloak. 'We can't sleep here,' Elphenor said. For all that, he got up and tried the church door. It was locked. He immediately determined to get in by a window. They flew round the church, fingering the cold panes of glass, and had almost completed their round and seen the great bulk of the tower threatening down on them, when Weasel heard a clatter overhead. It came from one of the clerestory windows, where a missing pane had been replaced by a shutter. They wrenched the shutter open, and flew in, and circled downward through darkness, and stood on a flagstone pavement. Outlined against a window was a tall structure with a peak. Fingering it, they found it was wood, carved, and swelling out of a stem like a goblet. A railed flight of steps half encircled the stem. They mounted the steps and found themselves in the goblet. It was like an octagonal cupboard, minus a top but carpeted. By curling round each other, there would be room to lie down. The smell of wood gave them a sense of security, and they spent the night in the pulpit.

He woke to the sound of Weasel laughing. Daylight was streaming in, and Weasel was flitting about the roof, laughing at the wooden figures that supported the crossbeams – carved imitations of fairies, twelve foot high, with outstretched turkey wings and gaunt faces, each uglier than the last. 'So that's what they think we're like,' she said. 'And look at her! She pointed to the fairy above the pulpit, struggling with a trumpet.

Exploring at floor level, Elphenor read the Ten Commandments, and found half a bottle of wine and some lozenges. It would pass for a breakfast; later, he would stroll into the village and see what could be got from there. While he was being raised as the Devil at Walsham Borealis, he had learned some facts about the Church of England, one of them that the reigning monarch, symbolically represented as a lion and a unicorn, is worshipped noisily on one day of the week and that for the rest of the week churches are unmolested. There was much to be said for spending the winter here. The building was windproof and weatherproof. Weasel was delighted with it, and, for himself, he found its loftiness and spaciousness congenial, as though he were back in Zuy – a Zuy improved by a total removal of its inhabitants. He had opened a little door and discovered a winding stone stairway behind it when his confidence in Church of England weekdays was shaken by the entrance of two women with brooms and buckets. He beckoned to Weasel, snatched her cloak from the pulpit, and preceded her up the winding stairs, holding the bottle and the lozenges. The steps were worn; there was a dead crow on one of them. They groped their way up into darkness, then into light; a window showed a landing and a door open on a small room where some ropes dangled from the ceiling. Weasel seized a rope and gave it a tug, and would have tugged at it more energetically if Elphenor had not intervened, promising that when the women had gone away she could tug to her heart's content. Looking out of the cobwebbed window, he saw the churchyard far below and realized they must be a long way up the tower.

163

But the steps wound on into another darkness and a dimmer lightness, and to another landing and another door open on another room. This room had louvred windows high up in the wall, and most of its floor space was taken up by a frame supporting eight bells, four of them upside down with their clappers lolling in their iron mouths. This was the bell chamber, he explained. The ropes went from the bells into the room below, which was the ringing chamber. There was a similar tower near Zuy; mortals thought highly of it, and his tutor had taken him to see it.

Weasel began to stroke one of the bells. As though she were caressing some savage sleeping animal, it presently responded with a noise between a soft growl and a purr. Elphenor stroked another. It answered at a different pitch, deeper and harsher, as though it were a more savage animal. But they were hungry. The bells could wait. The light from the louvred windows flickered between bright and sombre as the wind tossed the clouds. It was blowing up for a storm.

They would be out of the wind tonight and for many nights to come. January is a dying season, there would be graves to dig, and with luck and management, thought Elphenor, he might earn a livelihood and be a friend to sextons here and around. Weasel would spare crumbs from the bread he earned, scatter them for birds, catch the birds, pluck and eat them: she still preferred raw food, with the life still lively in it. On Sundays, she said, they would get their week's provisions; with everybody making a noise in church, stealing would be child's play. The pulpit would be the better for a pillow, and she could soon collect enough feathers for a pillow, for a feather mattress even: one can always twitch a pillowcase from the washing line. The wine had gone to their heads; they outbid each other with grand plans of how they would live in the church, and laughed them down, and imagined more. They would polish the wooden fairies' noses till they shone like drunkards' noses; they would grow water-cresses in the font; Elphenor would tell the complete story of his life before they met. Let him begin now! Was he born with a hook nose and red hair? He began, obediently and prosily. Weasel clamped her eyes open, and suppressed yawns. He lost the thread of his narrative. Drowsy with wine, they fell asleep.

He woke to two appalling sounds. Weasel screaming with terror, a clash of metal. The bell ringers had come to practise their Christmas peal, and prefaced it by sounding all the bells at once. The echo was heavy on the air as they began to ring a set of changes, first the scale descending evenly to the whack of the tenor bell, then in patterned steps to the same battleaxe blow. The pattern altered; the tenor bell sounded midway, jolting an arbitrary finality into the regular measure of eight. With each change of position the tenor bell accumulated a more threatening insistency, and the other bells shifted round it like a baaing flock of sheep.

Weasel cowered in Elphenor's arms. She had no strength left to scream with; she could only tremble before the impact of the next flailing blow. He felt his senses coming adrift. The booming echo was a darkness on his sight through which he saw the bells in their frame heaving and evading, evading and heaving, under a dark sky. The implacable assault of the changing changes pursued him as the waves had pursued the boat from Ijmuiden. But here there was no escape, for it was he who wallowed broken-backed at the mercy of the storm. Weasel lay in his arms like something at a distance. He felt his protectiveness, his compassion, ebbing away; he watched her with a bloodless, skeleton love. She still trembled, but in a disjointed way, as though she were falling to pieces.

He saw the lovely green fade out of her face. 'My darling,' he said, 'death by lightning would have been easier.' He could not hear himself speak.

The frost lasted on into mid-March. No one went to the bell chamber till the carpenter came to mend the louvers in April. The two bodies, one bowed over the other, had fallen into decay. No one could account for them, or for the curious weightless fragments of a substance rather like sheet gelatine which the wind had scattered over the floor. They were buried in the same grave. Because of their small stature and light bones they were entered in the Register of Burials as *Two Stranger Children*.

\* \* \* \* \*

**Julia Bell** was an editor and tutor based at the University of East Anglia where she co-edited the literary magazine *Pretext* and the *Creative Writing Coursebook*. She has also co-edited *England Calling* (2001), a collection of short stories for the 21st century from which *Gap Kids* is taken. Bell's first novel *Massive* (2002) is followed by *Out There* to be published in 2004.

# Gap Kids
## JULIA BELL

They've opened another Starbucks on London Street. Haven't even put the signs up yet and there's people milling around on the cobbles, drinking lattes and cappuccinos from great white beakers that look like they were made for babies. A blur of khaki and trainers, skateboards and mobile phones. Something in me resists as I pass them, makes me want to go to the markets instead, where the coffee tastes of chicory and there's always a layer of scum on the top of the water.

I go in anyway, but I feel a bit guilty ordering a three-quid mochaccino, as if I'm doing something bad for my morals. Residual shame from the time Psycho Sue caught me in McDonald's sinking my teeth into a Big Mac. 'Oh Janis, lass, whorraya doing in hia?' There was nothing I could do to deny it. The evidence was in my hand, half chewed. 'Ya'r a Fair Weather Wendy ya are, Janis,' she said, dumping a load of Womyn's Collective 'Meat is McMurder' flyers on my table. How could I tell her about the cravings then? *I want more*, I wanted to scream at her. More than thirty quid a week and smoking Cheap Cil's slate and living in a house that has gone past being cared about, with the dole on my back every five minutes. *More*. The talk about communities and alternatives: it wasn't a political point, it was pointless.

There's a queue at the end where you're supposed to collect your drinks. The students they're employing haven't quite got used to the idea of slick service and the old ladies are confused by the system of paying and then waiting. They look anxiously at the red faces preparing their drinks as if they're being ripped off.

While I'm waiting a group of girls comes in, petite replicas of the glossy fashion pages: summer sportswear and string handbags, water bottles and books.

One of the girls waves at me. 'Hiya!'

166

For a minute I can't quite place her. A fellow student, I know, but name, year, subject evade me. I smile back and wave, then realise it was a mistake, she's coming over to talk to me.

'All right,' I say, 'how's things?'

'Great! Just taking it easy for a bit. Having a bit of time off, working out what to do next, you know?'

Yeah, I think, I know.

'Anyway, what d'you get?'

'Oh. A Desmond.'

'You what?'

'A Desmond. A two two. Desmond Tutu.'

She looks at me, not quite sure what to say. 'Oh, er, well done.'

'It's all right. I was pissed off about it last week, but - ' I shrug.

She smiles and nods encouragingly. Now I remember: Carolyn Giles, Women and Literature, last semester. She didn't see the point of feminism. Our generation are so *over* all that,' she whispered in my ear during one of the lectures. 'I mean I *like* wearing lipstick, y'know what I mean?'

'What about you?' I ask.

'A first,' she says, her grin widening. 'I got a first.'

'Well done.'

We smile at each other. I don't have anything to say to her.

'You still writing?'

'Oh. Yeah. Just bits and pieces.' *That's* why I came into town. To procrastinate. Anything's better than pottering around the fiat in this heat while the computer throbs away idly on the desk, like toothache. I promised myself that I'd finish my novel when I got my degree, but I've hardly written a word since the results.

'You going to watch the match?'

'The match?'

'England Germany.'

'Oh.' That match.

'We're having a party,' she says, 'a barbecue, tonight, to watch it. You want to come?'

'Sounds great,' I say, trying to be non-committal.

'Come on,' she says. She's being insistent, writing the address down on a Starbucks information leaflet. 'We've got Widescreen TV and cocktails.'

'All right then,' I say, more to get rid of her than because I mean it. If Fiona were here she'd be complaining. 'Football,' she always said, 'is a game men play with their balls, and since I have nothing to do with either

I don't see why I should care.' She was fond of lines like this - 'His mother should have thrown him away and kept the stork' or 'Men are like rollercoasters, stay on too long and you start to feel sick' - she had lots of them stuck in her memory like fridge magnets.

'You will come, won't you?'

'Thanks, Carolyn,' I say, this time remembering to smile. Her persistence is touching. She must think I'm worth it. 'I'll try and make it,' I say. 'Sounds fun.'

On the way back from the centre, weaving through the knot of medieval streets, the whole town seems to be melting. This heatwave is unexpected, no one's had a chance to acclimatise yet.

They've done up the Slug and Lettuce, the one by the cathedral. Looking through the window, it's like a Gap advert. Beanbags and trestle tables, fake tans and sports sandals. Gaggles of red, beery boys in England shirts clog up the pavement outside.

'Cheer up, love.' One of them is in my face, livid with drink.

'Fuck off,' I say, broadening my shoulders, making myself butch.

He shouts something back, but I'm across the road now, past the cathedral. I dig my hands into my faded 50Is and childishly comfort myself with the things I will buy when I sell my novel for millions of pounds. I try to smile.

I turn into Magdalen Street and the shops begin to get cheaper, scruffier. Someone shouts at me from across the road.

'Janis!' It's Kenny. Kenny lives in the bedsit underneath my flat, little more than a bathroom, a kitchen and a lounge-bedroom. 'Yar all right?' he roars, stepping out into the traffic to talk to me.

'Yes ta,' I say, reaching out a hand to steady him as he staggers on to the kerb.

'Yar going to watch the match?'

'Maybe,' I say.

'I'm going up the Ironmongers,' he says, 'but I'll be in the Tavern later.'

I like Kenny, he looks out for people. Trouble is, these days, he can't really see them too well. He used to work on the rigs out of Yarmouth, fucked his back in some accident, and now he's pissing away his compensation. Since the Tavern got Sky Sports we watch the football together, me nursing halves of lager to his halves of whisky. Man U, always Man U. Unlike the rest of the country, people round here like winners.

'Later, Kenny,' I tell him. 'I'll come and find you later.'

'Nice one, girl.'

He slaps me on the back and staggers forward. His eyes are swimming. I doubt if he'll last until the evening. Not in this heat.

He's been sick outside his fiat. Down the wall by the guttering. There's flecks of blood in it by the look of it.

Once I'm in, I want to go out again. The heat is oppressive, the damp smell that rises from Kenny's flat suffocating. Fiona would hate this; living so close to men. She always said she wanted to live like the Amazons. 'Women give you all the emotional support you need,' she said. 'Men don't know what the word means.'

I lie on the sofa and try to read but the words swim in front of my eyes. It's too hot to think. Every now and then the sound of roaring - *En-ger-land, En-ger-land, En-ger-land* - jerks me out of my dozing.

I suppose I will watch the match. Since I've been living here I've got into it again. I was born in 1966: 'Best year for football this country's ever seen,' according to Dad. Which meant that I had to like football whatever. Sacrilegious not to. We watched it together on the telly. He said he couldn't afford to take me to matches, though he would go occasion-ally with Uncle Ted, or Barry, his best mate, in his battered gold Capri. On my eighth birthday he bought me a Liverpool scarf.

There's a commotion of coughing and swearing outside. I get up and look out of the window. It's Kenny and some bloke from the pub. I've seen him before: greasy baseball cap, slimy bomber jacket with the padding escaping at the sleeves. I can't make out what Kenny's saying; all his words are tonally berserk, like someone's messing with the pitch control.

'Fach off. FACH off. Ahll be ahrit. Yaar NO yaAR no.'

Kenny's holding a T-shirt to his head. There are big oily patches of blood down the front of his shirt. He's swaying all over the shop. He should probably go up the hospital, but he won't. Last time he went in about his back they tried to dry him out and he nearly died.

Greasy Baseball Cap gets it together to open the door. There's a crash as it swings back on its hinges and more swearing and then someone sitting down, the creak of springs. Silence. The roar of traffic from the ring road. I wonder if there's anything I should do.

There's blood spots on the tarmac, a grisly trail leading from the car park round the back to the flats. I knock on the window.

'YAAARRR?'

'You all right, Kenny?'

Greasy Baseball Cap comes to the door without his bomber jacket, showing a ripped and greying T-shirt with IBIZA SUNSHINE in faded fluorescent letters on the front.

'Kenny's indisposed,' he says in a strangely composed voice, comedy posh.

'Is he all right?'

'I'm looking after him.'

His skin is plump, fleshy, made childish by glasses that are sub-NHS: blue plastic frames taped up on one side with Elastoplast. He's got the hiccups but he's trying to hide it.

'Er, OK. I'll leave you to it.'


Carolyn's written the address in curvy handwriting. *Pottergate*, a cobbled street still inside the city walls. It's early, probably too early to arrive, but I can't face going back inside the flat. Not with Greasy Baseball Cap downstairs.

I take the long way round, following the city walls, all the way down the river, past Cow Tower and up through Cathedral Close where they film costume dramas outside the Queen Anne houses. It's so picture-postcard it hurts.

When Fiona left for London she said she'd miss the scenery. 'Norwich is so pretty,' she always said.

Pretty vacant, more like.


A lad in a red Ronald McDonald wig opens the door. I recognise him vaguely, friend of one of the students, maybe even Carolyn's boyfriend. He looks surprised to see me. We stare at each other for just too long.

'Er. Come in, come in,' he says, finally.

He steps back and leads me through the house to the kitchen. It smells of paint; the hall is a new, soft orange, the floor shiny polished wood, the kitchen a pale toothpaste green. Carolyn is opening bags of nachos, cracking the lids on tubs of hummus.

'Oh, hi.' She looks a bit surprised. 'You're here.'

'I brought some booze.' I hold up a fourpack of Stella.

'Great!' We look at each other. She smiles uncertainly. I'm beginning to wish I hadn't come. 'Everyone else is out the back. What d'you think of the house? We did it ourselves.'

I don't know what to say. 'Gorgeous.'

'We bought it between us.'

'You *bought* it?' How horribly grown up.

'Well, Nikki's dad secured it, but we've got our names on the deeds. Kind of made sense really, house prices and all that. I'll show you round.'

The house is impeccable. Her bedroom is a dark blue with stars painted on the ceiling and material draped over the headboard. This obsession with home decorating has passed me by a bit - I blame *Blue Peter* myself, all those bloody washing-up bottles and rolls of sticky-back plastic.

'Couldn't live with this colour though,' I say, trying to sound authoritative rather than catty.

'Really?' she says, disappointed. 'D'you think? Maybe it is a bit strong.'

When I was her age I was at Greenham, shivering in Cheap Cil's bender, joining hands around the fence, talking revolution over a damp campfire, people throwing stones at us from passing cars. Psycho Sue earned her 'Psycho' label for battering a copper and getting six months for it. We thought we were saving the world. We thought we were all going to die in World War Three. Now, I wonder why we cared so much. No one else seems to any more. Everybody wants an ecstasy lifestyle - doesn't even matter if they don't take the drugs.

I look at Carolyn swinging her hips in her Joseph skirt. I bet she really regrets inviting me here. I crack a ringpull off a can of Stella with a defiant hiss. Well, I'm here now, might as well get drunk.

They've put the telly outside on the patio. Massive great box with a screen like a cinema. A dozen kids are sat out on the grass on rugs and cushions and beanbags. I recognise quite a few of them. One of them puts a joint behind his back.

'S'all right,' I say, 'I'm not anyone's mother.' I flop down on the grass next to the boy in the red Ronald McDonald wig. 'Hot enough for you?' I ask, smiling. He doesn't look away from the screen.

Up close I can see that the wig is making him overheat - his temples are beaded with sweat.

'Nuh, boiling,' he says, nodding his head.

They're still building up to it. Shots of the crowd, wigs, warpaint, Liverpool flags, BCFC, Man U, the Gunners, even some sad bastard in a Canaries shirt.

'What's the score going to be then?' I ask.

'Two nil,' he says, definitively, his eyes drifting from the screen to watch Carolyn as she comes outside with a tray of crisps. I watch his eyes dropping down her figure, lingering on her breasts. 'I put twenty quid on it.'

'Oh.' I shift myself about on the grass and take another swig of beer. A boy in a white England shirt puts burgers on the barbecue. They hiss and spit and catch fire. They've let the coals get too hot, but I won't interfere.

'Fuckin' hell, Simon, you trying to set fire to yourself?'

'Piss off, Dan.'

Carolyn comes over and sits next to me. 'Pringles?' she asks, offering me the bowl. I shake my head.

'No ta. They make me feel like I'm living in an advert.'

'Oh.' She looks crestfallen. I wish I wasn't in such a bitchy mood. 'Dan?'

He reaches across me to grab a handful. 'Thanks, babe,' he says, winking at her.

She giggles. 'You look a twat in that wig.'

'Love you too,' he says, crunching on a wedge of crisps. Smithereens of reconstituted potato cover his England top.

'Messy bastard. You need a bib.'

'Ah fuck off,' he says with his mouth full.

This abuse goes on for ages. I pretend not to notice, watch the screen, finish my beer, open another one. The air is thick with barbecue smoke, and in the distance is the noise of chanting from the pubs. Then a roar and the players are coming on to the pitch. Someone turns up the volume. With the super-surround sound, the cheering is deafening. I get expectant goosebumps. Nothing else is happening now. The streets will be as empty as they were for Diana's funeral.

'Ooh, it's David,' Carolyn says breathily.

'You like him?' I ask.

'Yeah, don't you?'

'He's a fucking shirtlifter,' Dan says, before I can reply. 'SHE-RA. SHE-RA.'

Carolyn giggles.

They play the German national anthem. Everyone hisses, as if at the baddie in a panto.

'Send 'em off,' Dan shouts. 'Twwoooniiil, you bastards.'

For the first five minutes everyone stares at the TV. All the players are nervous. They're over-kicking the ball, marking each other too hard, neither side can settle into a rhythm. Dan shouts 'Penalty!' or 'Free kick!' every time Germany touch the ball.

England get a free kick. Beckham takes it.

'Come on, lover,' Carolyn says as the camera closes in on him kicking the ball, shorts flapping around his thighs like sails. 'Do it for me, David.' The ball lands at the feet of the Germans.

'POOF,' Dan says, giving the finger to the TV.

After fifteen minutes it gets strangely boring. We're not playing as a team. Everyone running back to defend and nobody passing the ball around in midfield. Beckham is too much the star to be a team player. He's been strutting around, puffing out his cheeks, hands on hips, waiting for free kicks so he can do his balletic little superstar turns.

Carolyn stands up to fetch more drinks.

'Get us a beer, there's a love,' Dan says.

'She's not your love,' I say, almost by reflex.

Scholes kicks the ball at goal but it flies high above the crossbar.

'OH!' Dan sits up, thumps the grass. 'You what?' He half turns towards me.

'Never mind,' I say.

At half-time it's still nil-nil. I've had three cans and my head feels tight and fuzzy.

'We're playing like fucking *donkeys*,' Dan says, scuffing the grass with his trainers.

I lie back and look at the back of the house. Must be eighteenth century or very early nineteenth. Old, anyway. The brickwork looks like it's been recently repointed and the woodwork is shiny with new paint.

'You own this place then?' I ask, more for something to say than because I'm interested.

Dan laughs. '*Me?* He shakes his head. 'The girls got it sorted. I pay the rent. Couldn't afford a place like this on my wages.'

'Here you are, carnivore.' Carolyn stands over him, holding out a burger. Her wraparound skirt flaps open, giving him a flash of her knickers. He blinks. Tomato sauce drips in a thick splodge on to his jeans.

Second half and immediately Germany get a free kick.

'Fuck off, Krauts!' Dan shouts, flinching away from the screen as Ziege boots the free kick. It floats over the crossbar.

'We won the war, you wankers.'

'You didn't,' I say.

Dan turns to me.

'You didn't win the war.'

He narrows his eyes. 'You trying to be funny?'

*No, I'm trying to pick a fight*, I think. I take another swig of beer. 'You're all right,' I say. 'I'm pissed.'

I suppose I feel a bit guilty. There were loads of Germans at Greenham. Made some of us look almost right-wing. Selma and Hilde; they wouldn't buy food from shops because they said it propped up the system, so they ate what they could catch or steal from other people's vegetable plots until Hilde got pneumonia and they had to go back to Berlin. Selma complained that the English countryside hadn't proved at all nourishing or fruitful, 'not like in your poems'. But the truth was that they were scared in case radioactivity had leaked out and contaminated everything. They were living on acorns and blackberries in the end, gathered from fields miles away. I wonder what they're doing now, if they're watching this game.

England surge forward again. Michael Owen could score but - *argh* - the ball won't sit down for him. I find that I have been pulling up handfuls of grass.

'Come on, come *on*.'

It happens in slow motion. Or maybe it takes so long to sink in that by the time we've realised it's a goal they're already on the replay. Beckham kicks the ball perfectly, like it's on the end of a string attached to his boot. It bounces between two bewildered German defenders and on to the head of Alan Shearer. Bang. In the back of the net. The cheering could be heard in outer space. All over town you can hear it. No one louder than us.

'OH YEEESSS. FUCKING YEEEESSSS. SHE-RA, SHE-RA.'

Germany are retaliating almost immediately. There is a different kind of urgency now, the game picks up pace and momentum. We've got to hang on; they've got to score. Germany seem to have far too much possession but they keep missing their shots on goal. We're winning because of their mistakes.

Dan can hardly watch. He covers his eyes with his hands whenever Germany get a free kick.

'Come on, one more goal. One more. OH! Ince, you fucking *tosser*.'

Ten minutes to go, and it's like we've all crawled closer to the telly. I'm surprised how much I care. If England win, I think to myself, if England win I'll finish my book, get out of here. Make enough money to skip town, go travelling, maybe even go visit Selma and Hilde, or go to Spain for a bit, get a tan, maybe even get a girlfriend.

Eight minutes to go, and still nothing is safe. Barmby gives away a dangerous free kick. Oh Christ, we can't let them score, not so late in the day.

Dan is silent, holding his breath.

'We're going to win,' says Carolyn cheerfully. 'I'll go and get the champagne.'

'Shh,' Dan says. 'Don't say that, it's bad luck.'

Countdown time - oh no, three minutes of time added on. Too much, too much, anything can happen in three minutes. I watched Man U beating Bayern Munich in the Tavern with Kenny. Two goals in two minutes.

Then the whistle. At last, we won. Dan's eyes are wet round the edges. 'Fucking hell,' he says. Then he stands up and lets out a big roar and starts jumping around with the rest of us. We're all kissing and shouting.

Dan picks up Carolyn and spins her round. He loses his balance and they fall backwards into the bushes.

'Aaww, Dan.' Carolyn gets up. 'For fuck's sake, I've got mud on my skirt.'

Dan looks at me and shrugs, then grins some more. 'SHE-RA, SHE-RA.'

I go inside to get more beer. My legs are spongy, drunken. I try not to trip over the TV wires on my way.

I fix my hair in the mirror of their cork-tiled bathroom. They've even got an old cast-iron bath, like the one in the Flake advert. I nick some expensive hair gel from the shelf above the sink. A pro-vitamin *system* for extra gloss, it says on the bottle. When I've flattened my hair into a black cap, I trace the lines under my eyes with my fingertips. I think of Carolyn and her friends with their smooth skin, and I can't stop the sinking feeling that I didn't make the best of my looks when I had them.

Carolyn's in the kitchen, rubbing at her skirt with a cloth.

'It's great we won,' she says, 'but Dan's really doing my head in.' Her cheeks are flushed, her hair is ruffled, she looks drunk. 'He would have been unbearable if we'd lost. I know you're not supposed to say this but I only ever watch football if England are playing. I can't stand it otherwise and Dan's gone mental over this tournament. He's been watching all the matches, even the ones with Eastern European teams in. I mean, who wants to watch Yugoslavia? Tell you the truth, he's pissing us off a bit.' She lowers her voice. 'Me and Nikki used to go out with him. Not together mind, but you know - ' She shrugs and giggles. 'It was all right when we were students but now - I mean, he hasn't got a degree or anything and we only agreed to let him rent a room off us as a kind of short-term thing. You know? He's kind of getting in the way.'

'You've got a twig in your hair,' I say, picking it out for her.

Outside, Dan's having a heated debate about Alan Shearer with Simon, who's still trying to cook things on the barbecue.

175

'I tell ya, he's a fucking donkey. Worst England captain ever. You watch what happens to the team when he retires.'

'Ah, Dan man, how can you say that? He scored the fucking goal. Against *Germany*. Come on.'

'Here you go,' I say, dropping the fourpack on the grass. 'Beer.'

Dan looks up at me and smiles. 'Cheers, darling.'

*I'm not your darling*, I think, but then wonder why I'm arguing with him. I smile back. 'Shame about your bet.'

'I know, twenty quid down the Swanee. That was next week's drink money, that was.'

'You still working at the Norwich Union then?' Simon asks, sparking the tip of a joint.

'Nah, I jacked it in last month. Trying to get a bit of DJ-ing, you know.' He sighs. 'But I was thinking I might go to Essex for a bit, back to my mum's.' He looks at Carolyn, who's coming out with a big portable stereo. 'Nothing to keep me here really.'

Carolyn puts on some dance music. The kind of drubbing bass and hissing treble that they tried to ban, once upon a long time ago when young people en masse were still dangerous.

She starts to dance; swaying in her stack heels, moving her arms.

'C'mon everybody,' she says, looking at me. 'We won.'

\* \* \* \* \*

**Mary Mann** achieved considerable success as the writer of romantic fiction but her many novels have long been out of print. During her years at Shropham in south Norfolk Mann was confronted by widespread deprivation. Conditions that brutalised the rural workforce inspired the remarkable collection of stories published in 1903 as *The Fields Of Dulditch*, tales of human endurance in a world of cruelty and superstition that stand alongside those of Thomas Hardy. *The Lost Housen* originally appeared in this collection.

# The Lost Housen
## MARY MANN

On the high road, a couple of miles from the village of Dulditch, but yet within the boundary of that parish, in the midst of a plot of garden ground all waste and uncultivated, the ruins of the two cottages stand which were known to the countryside by the above designation. The position of the 'Lost Housen' is very lonely and remote from any dwelling. They are divided by the acre and a half of ground in which they stand from the wood which runs at the back and on one side of them; on the other side is an osier-bed, and beyond that the river; in front runs the road, from which a straggling, untrimmed hedge all but hides them.

Some forty years ago on the same site stood the turnpike lodge, and the place is still believed to be haunted by the ghost of the gate-keeper, brutally murdered in his bed by a tramp in the midst of the silence and darkness of a winter night. His body, dragged round the osier-bed, was found next morning in the river, too shallow even at that time of year to conceal the ugly crime.

For years after the last toll had been paid on the Runwich Road, the gate removed, and the lodge fallen to decay, the site remained unoccupied, owing to the loneliness of the situation, to the dampness of the surroundings, to the spirit of the murdered lodge-keeper hovering where the vapours lingered among the shivering osiers or rising mist-like from the river.

It was not until old Ambrose Crouch, the Dulditch blacksmith, died, leaving his few pounds of savings between his two sons, that the building of the two hideous cottages, which at present occupy the position of the old toll-house was begun.

The tale goes that the blacksmith, having enjoyed several years of married life without issue, and being anxious for a couple of strong sons to help him in his trade and to save the wages of journeymen, made a bargain with the Almighty (whose name was familiar in his mouth more in cursing than in prayer) that if He would give him a pair of male children, Ambrose for his part would see to it that they bore respectively the longest and the shortest names in the Bible. When, within the year, Mrs. Crouch presented her husband with twin boys, those poor unconscious infants were accordingly burdened with the names of Og and Maher-shalal-hash-baz to carry through life.

Thus cruelly handicapped from the beginning, the race of life run by the two sons, for whom old Ambrose, after his ignorant and superstitious fashion, had prayed, was far from being a creditable one. Only Og, after all, helped his father to beat the sparks from the glowing iron in the forge, to shoe the cart-horses, lifting huge, unflinching hoofs for the operation, standing patient on the little green before the blacksmith's door. For anger in the Crouch family was apt to wax as hot and as dangerous as the great bars the men handled so unconcernedly amid the leaping flames, and words of rage and cursing sounded often above the ringing blows of the hammer on the anvil; and Maher – it was by this comparatively insignificant appellation that the owner of the formidable baptismal title was know in Dulditch – who was of a quiet and timid disposition, slipped away from the paternal roof one evening and did not return.

He only went as far as the next village, where he addressed himself to the profession of bricklaying, the noise and the heat of the blacksmith's work being repugnant to him; but it was very seldom afterwards that his father set eyes on the still, white face, the strange-looking blue eyes, the sleek, black hair of his truant son.

In those days the rural population was more averse even than at present from movement. Among the more old-fashioned of them one hears continually still of sons who for twenty years have not seen mothers living a few parishes distant; of sisters within walking distance who never meet. A man who lives within a hundred yards of the workhouse was overtaken the other day by the doctor of that institution, who, knowing the pedestrian, pulled up to ask him why, on a working day, he was attired in his Sunday suit, and whither he was bound with such a determined gait.

'I'm a goin' to see faather,' the man said. 'Tis a matter o' twenty year come th' thutty-fust o' next month sin' I sot eyes on th' old chap last. He be a getting' along i' yares now; and me and my missus ha' set a wonderin' how 'e fare. So I ha' tuk a holiday and rid myself up, and I be a goin' to make my moind aisy by a glint on 'm at last.'

The doctor, having sympathised with the somewhat tardy filial anxiety, offered a seat in his gig to help the pilgrim on his road, an honour the pilgrim, however, declined; and, with evident surprise that the whereabouts of 'faather' was not universally known, pointed across the way to the big white poor-house, intimating that unlovely edifice as his destination.

He had lived within a stone's-throw of the miserable old pauper father for a score of years without feeling the impulse to cross the road to see him.

So Ambrose Crouch had only the one son and the wife to curse at, to batter with hard words and cruel blows. The mother was a woman slow of tongue, with eyes like Maher's, dull and blue as his, and with the same still gaze. How she aroused her husband's fury is not known; it is said that she never attempted retaliation. As for Og, he also seemed to be cowed by the fierce old man, and took his brother's portion of oaths and stripes as well as those due to himself with apparent resignation.

But the day came when the weakness of old age and illness robbed the tyrant of his power, and then did Og and his mother show of what material they were made.

'Th' po'r ol' chap were a bad ol' warmint, but he were th' best o' th' lot, arter all,' the neighbours said, and said truthfully. For his sins he suffered terribly now. There was never a blow that was not paid back to him with interest; he was starved; he was terrified; he was tortured. He escaped from his bed once at noonday, and, in his night-shirt, ran about the village imploring the neighbours to take care of him and protect him. Old Brose Crouch was more terrifying in his frantic dread and in that scant attire than ever he had been in the height of his splendid strength and his unrestrained passion, cursing and swearing and wielding his mighty hammer at the forge. The women hid away from him, doors were slammed in his face.

Finally he was captured by wife and son and taken back to his bed again. Og pushed him homeward in a wheelbarrow, abashed and beaten, the poor old bare legs dangling helpless. The woman stalked before, silent, her thin lips drawn inward, the great pale blue eyes gazing into vacuity, by no means discomposed at forming one in such a procession.

Life was strong in the miserable old man. Starvation, exposure, ill-treatment of all kinds failed to kill him. He was found lying insensible upon the snow in his front garden early one morning. His head was cut and bruised, his arm and leg were broken; yet even then he did not die at once, but lived long enough to swear before witnesses that he had fallen from his window in his sleep, and that his son, who had ever treated him with kindness and attention, had had no hand in the disaster.

But the nearest neighbours had heard a cry for mercy in the night; there were signs of a struggle in the bedroom. The village people, excited by the presence of the police among them and athirst for a tragedy, insisted that Og Crouch should at once be taken to Runwich Gaol and hanged there. To their intense disappointment the culprit got off with a six months' imprisonment for assault, the father protesting his son's innocence to the last, dying – fortunately for him – just before that son's release.

Those cottages the blacksmith and the bricklayer undertook to erect with some of their father's savings were long in the building. The men were suspicious of interference in the work, and from foundation stone to topmost bricks in the chimney did everything themselves. Consequently in architectural design, in beauty, and in finish the 'lost housen' left much to be desired. Before paint or paper or whitewash was put on the walls, the brothers, tired of the expense of lodgings, had moved into that cottage which they meant to occupy, and amid the squalid confusion of the miserable place had installed their mother to keep house.

Perhaps it was not to be expected that such a trio should live in peace. It was soon abundantly evident which one among them meant to be master. On the shoulders of Og, it seemed, his father's mantle had fallen. He swore at and beat his mother, cursed and fought his brother to his heart's content. The fear that Jemima Crouch had never shown of her husband she exhibited in a marked degree now of her son. She had seen him grow from childhood to middle age; she knew so much of him, she knew nothing that was not terrible. In her dread of Og Jemima drew near to the son who was so like herself in outward seeming – possessing the same tall, stooping figure, the same air of stillness and reserve upon the white, well-featured face, the same blue eyes, which never lit up, but gazed with their indescribable look into space.

If Maher sympathised with his mother's fears, or felt them on his own account, is not known. He was sparing of speech to an extraordinary degree, and his attitude was ever that of defence rather than defiance. He received what Og dealt out to him in food and fisticuffs, although his own share in the little patrimony had been equal with his brother's, and in spite of the fact that, physically, he was better made and far stronger, with long arms and enormously strong hands, which were quite equal to the task of retaliation.

Having once settled down in the miserable half-finished place, through whose single-brick walls the wet oozed and the wind blew, Og delayed to enter upon the finishing touches which should have made the home habitable. He guarded the remnant of the money carefully, carrying it on his own person night and day. They could live very well without paint on the 'win-skirtin'' and the 'windies,' he declared. What was the good of whitewash or wall-paper while the 'chimney' smoked, as he put it forcibly, 'like-hell'? Jemima, who had been used to a particularly neat and, for her class, even luxurious home in her husband's time, groaned with rheumatism and shivered with ague all the winter through. What Maher could do without outlay of capital for materials he did, but surreptitiously and in a half-hearted way. He cut wedges of wood to stop the rattling of the windows, and daubed a trowelful of mortar over the chinks in the chimney through which the smoke poured. But the effort needed to bring the outer door into closer connection with the doorstep was apparently too great for him, and in the work of cultivating the garden he never got further than spitting meditatively upon the soil over the spade upon which he leant.

Since the money had come into their possession the idea of adding to it by earning a day's wage had been abandoned by both the brothers. Og, who, as has been said, carried the purse, spent his days at the nearest public-house, where he drank himself into a savager, more brutal condition; while Maher sat silent with his silent mother, or roamed about the miserable place with his hands in his pockets, making a melancholy survey of its deficiencies.

Then Og fell ill, the cold and the damp telling first on him, apparently the strongest of the three. He began with bronchitis and went on to inflammation of the lungs and to 'ammonia'; and being a hard drinker upon whom the necessary stimulants took no effect, he lay very quickly at death's door.

On the fifth day, when the doctor came out of the bedroom, where a paraffin lamp, sending forth a most abominable stench, burnt day and night in a feeble struggle against the damp and chill of the place, he stopped to speak to Maher, sitting idle and alone in the living-room, his hands in his trousers pockets, his long legs, reaching nearly to the opposite wall, stretched before him, his blue eyes fixed vacantly.

'This brother of yours is in a very critical state, my man,' the doctor said, pausing in the act of screwing his clinical thermometer into its case. 'His temperature is a hundred and seven this morning. If that temperature be maintained till evening he will die.'

Maher's eyes wandered slowly to the doctor's face and fixed themselves there for a long minute before he spoke.

'And if 't don't?' he asked at length.

'If the temperature declines, and the little strength the man at present has is maintained, there is a chance for him – he may recover. The next few hours will decide. I am sorry to tell you that in my opinion he is far more likely to die – and that quickly – than to live.'

The young man said nothing. His eyes continued to be fixed on the doctor's face. There was something disagreeably fascinating in that long silent stare. What an odd-looking figure the man was, with his white complexion and in his white workman's dress! There was no play of expression in the face; the features were as emotionless and as still as those of a dead man.

'That old woman always gives me the creeps,' the doctor said to himself with irritation, thinking of Jemima Crouch, sitting silent, gaunt, and upright by the bedside; 'her son is as bad.'

'I ha' heared the folk let on,' said Maher, speaking slowly, with his hushed and far-off voice, 'as how when a man lay at th' p'int o' death – his breath, which in an or'nary way he live by, a lavin' on 'm – I ha' heared say at them times the breath 'f a livin' human critter brathed into 's nost'ils and down 's tr'ut – ef so be as sech can be found as 'll go t'rough with' 'casion – 'ull bring that feller-suff'rer back from 's mortial plight.'

Maher's rare speech was slow and difficult, and by the time he had reached the end of it the doctor had put away his thermometer, had buttoned his great-coat, had settled his hat on his head.

'And what,' he asked as he drew on his driving gloves, 'what do you suppose your patient would be doing while you were whistling into his nostrils and blowing down his windpipe?'

'What?' Maher asked, having paused to watch the other button his gloves and turn to depart.

The doctor turned round upon him, the outer door in hand.

'Why, he'd be kicking the bucket, my good fellow,' the cheerful doctor said with a laugh. 'By the time you'd cured your man he'd be as dead as Moses.'

Then he went, and Maher sat for long hours over the smoky fire, and

182

gazed at the opposite wall.

At night Mrs Crouch always gave up her post in the sick-room to Maher, she repairing to her own bed for a few hours' rest. The mother and son stood for a few minutes over the fire before going their several ways.

'How du 'e fare?' Maher asked.

'Better,' she answered. 'To my thinkin' he ain't i' th' chechyud yit. He be a goin' to live.'

Maher's jaw fell open, his dull, mournful eyes widened; he said nothing, but gazed stupidly upon his mother. She, for her part, gave her report with nothing of that trembling joy with which a mother might be expected to welcome her son back from the grave.

'He be asleep,' she said, 'and his breathin's reg'lar. The pantin' and the ruttlin' on his chist 's left 'm. So 've the burnin' faver left 'im. He's all of a sweat.'

She sat down, with a groan for her aching bones, in the chair Maher had vacated, and her strange eyes fixed themselves miserably upon the hot wood-ashes in the grate. Og objected to the expenditure for coal, and they burnt what bits of wood they found about the place.

'Tis all to begin over agin,' she said, whispering the words to the fire, leaning forward over her folded arms. 'He's managing' (manageable) 'in 's ways now, t'rough his wakeness, but give 'm 's strength, and we've a worse devil among us agin than iver's father were – a cru'ler, selfiger, dartier-mouthed devil.'

'Th' doctor let on as he were a goin',' Maher reminded her slowly.

'Ah!' she said. A quavering, long-drawn 'Ah!' that expressed a great deal – her contempt of the doctor's opinion, her better knowledge of her son's condition among other things.

'We shall ha' to give 'm back the money agin,' Maher said reflectively.

She only nodded at the fire, rocking herself to and fro over her folded arms.

Maher contemplated her in one of his long silences.

'We han't done it yit,' he said at length with more than usual emphasis. 'Maybe we shorn't ha' to du 'it arter all.'

With that he turned away from his mother, and walked with something of decision in his shambling step into the adjoining room to take up his watch over the invalid.

Before the doctor started on his rounds on the following morning he received a message to the effect that his presence was not needed at the

'Lost Housen,' Og Crouch having died in the night. The man of medicine had left direction with Mrs Crouch that, in this too probable termination of the case, word should be sent him, as the cottage was out of his way; and he now signed the death certificate with a light heart and an easy conscience. He had a patient to see at a distance of fifteen miles in the opposite direction, and the weather was particularly bad that morning, so that the good man was glad to shorten his rounds.

'That shambling half idiot, his brother, didn't try his famous recipe for putting breath into his respiratory organs, I suppose?' he inquired jocosely of the messenger, the Dulditch carpenter, who had already measured the big blacksmith for his coffin, and who had volunteered to let the doctor know of the death. The man did not understand the allusion, and had it explained to him amid much chuckling on the doctor's part.

By night all Dulditch knew the story – how Maher Crouch had tried to save his brother's life by breathing down the dying man's throat.

The experiment had been tried before in the memory of one or two of the villagers, not with success in any case, it seemed.

Gentleman George Ganders was full of information on the point for the benefit of the neighbours who passed his gate, his housekeeper Queenie Mask's mother's uncle having been operated on in like fashion when at his last extremity. Gentleman George related the occurrence with bated breath, for a 'cur'ous thing had happened on the 'casion, as Queenie, who was a "quite" body and didn't want no pace o' work made, had let on – a won'erful cur'ous thing.' The dying uncle, Jabez by name, so it was told in the family, had rejected the breath so liberally offered in his hour of need, and had breathed his own 'sperrit' down Uncle Thomas's t'rut, the consequence being that Uncle Thomas had never been 'hisself agin' in any sense of the word, Jabez's 'sperrit,' after a sharp contest with the former inhabitant of the body, having at length 'hulled out th' sperrit' of Thomas. So that the living man grew, even in outward form, the 'moral' of the dead brother; and when asked, in the doubt of his identity naturally engendered in the family's mind, which of the two he was, had always unhesitatingly responded 'Jabez.'

'Th' wumman Queenie don't want no hape o' talk made on 't, as that happ'd har own fam'ly; but that were the long and th' short on 't as she gi'en th' account to me. An' I take it 'tis a wonnerful p'or look on for Maher, according',' Mr Ganders said.

After such a precedent it is not very surprising that in Dulditch great interest was felt in the case of Maher Crouch, and a curiosity doomed to remain unsatisfied. Those who caught a sight of the man reported him as looking whiter than ever, which was not satisfactory to the prevalent expectation, for Og had inherited the ruddy complexion of his father. But all admitted that he had a 'wonnerful cur'ous look' about the eyes. Asked to describe the look, they said it was 'kind o' wild like.' Now as Og had been always spoken of as a 'wild chap' since his father's death, it was decided that 'Og's sperrit was looking out of Maher's eyes,' and the rustic mind was gratified.

Those who had seen Maher had penetrated to that miserable living-room where he and his mother sat silent over the fire at the mercy of the volumes of smoke that poured down the chimney; of the wind that blew in by cranny and crevice and whirled about them; of the rain that flowed under the door, and ran down the inside of the window, and trickled from the walls. For, in the light of day Maher Crouch never again stirred abroad. When the shades of night came on, his long figure, white and ghost-like in his bricklayer's jacket, might be seen sometimes, creeping about among the mists that rose from the osier bed, wandering around the uncultivated space that was to have been the garden of the brothers' domain. At the sound of a passing foot-fall, at the approach of wheels, he would, even in the darkness, hurry away to hide; for the silent unsociable ways of the man had, since his brother's death, developed into a determined shunning of his kind.

What sort of life the mother and son led together was only a matter of conjecture in Dulditch. Mrs Crouch, who had been 'wonnerful shut-up and quite-like' always, and had made no friends among her neighbours, was shyer than ever of acquaintances, and had acquired since her son's death a nervous and suspicious manner, which those few people who succeeded in getting speech of her greatly resented. It is held to be mannerly in Dulditch for a woman to be as open-minded in her trouble as her joy. She should have no secret recesses in her mind – all the chambers should be thrown open, frankly and confidingly, to the friendly inquisition. There is nothing found so efficacious to ease the heartache as the popular expedient of having half a dozen women in to talk the matter over. One who refuses this form of consolation sows a grudge against her in the breast of her more generous-minded sister.

So it came to pass that in time the inhabitants of the 'Lost Housen' were regarded as an unneighbourly, ill-conditioned couple, and were left to their own silent and secret devices.

No one quite knew when Maher Crouch disappeared from the scene. It was rumoured that the mother was living alone long before it was definitely ascertained that her son had left her. And even when the fact became established, no one could make out to his satisfaction where or why the man was gone. That their life together had been most miserable all firmly believed; but there was division on the point of whether he or she had been the 'ill-condition'est.' Nothing more wretched than the white, scared face of the mother could have been imagined till the wild, ashen face of the son had been seen. A man that never smoked 'a pipe o'baccy,' leaning over his own or his neighbour's fence, nor took 'a mug o' ale, sociable-like,' in the 'White Hart' kitchen; a woman who had no answer to give when a neighbour 'passed the time o' day,' but who scuttled away from her kind as dumb and as wild as a frightened rabbit – who should say which was the least human of these?

So Maher at length crept away, leaving the mother, very old now, crippled with rheumatism and with a chronic asthma, quite alone. To all questions addressed to her she vouchsafed the briefest answer, or, when it pleased her, none at all. She did not know where he was gone, she did not know what he was doing, she did not know if he was ever coming back. As to whether she was sorry to be without him, whether she was afraid to live in such a solitary place alone, whether he had gone away in consequence of any unpleasantness, if he had left her enough money to live on, if he had treated her with kindness while with her – on these points when questioned she was absolutely silent.

It was impossible to get on with the woman, so 'onmannerly' was she; and the people, who through curiosity or kindness had valiantly made friendly advances, drew back and left her alone once more.

For years she lived so; alone with her memories of the past, with whatever secrets her life held. By the look of her face uncommonly ugly some of her reminiscences must have been.

As time went on her rheumatism grew worse, so that, by-and-by, she was quite disabled, and lay on her bed groaning and sometimes shrieking with pain. And in the daytime the little daughter of her nearest neighbour waited on her, 'riddin' up' her house, cooking her little food, rubbing her poor limbs with the horse-oils upon which the Dulditch people pin their faith for the 'rheumatics.' But when these duties were fulfilled (with that zeal and discretion to be expected of eleven years) the little maid would scamper off home. She was the eldest of nine, and her parents were among the poorest in the parish – glad enough of the 'shillin' a week and her wittles,' for which Dora, night and morning, walked the long distance between the 'Lost Housen' and her home. But for forty times that sum they would not force the child to sleep in the evil-looking place, falling quickly to decay and ruin through bad building and neglect, where the ghost of the murdered toll-gate keeper still stalked uneasily amid the river fog and the mists.

So that long before the shades of night fell upon the 'Lost Housen' Jemima Crouch was left alone.

For a year Dora walked to and from the cottages. Through evenings and mornings, making three hundred and sixty-five days, she trod the 'joyless fields' of winter, or waded through the same fields 'waist-deep in meadow sweet' in the lovelier half of the year. She made her short cut through the woods from 'faather's' to 'Miss Crouch's' when the bright leaves of the chestnut, the fierce, copper-hued leaves of the beech, the lemon-yellow leaves of the elm and the maple were falling softly about her ears with a sound as of pattering rain. She came through the woodland path in the early spring when those glorious-toned leaves lay a moist, smelling, rotting mass beneath her feet, and when the buds on the boughs overhead were aching to open:

> 'Ere a leaf was on a bush,
> In the time before the thrush
> Had thought about her nest.'

Through the rigours and delights of the year, then, little Dora ran the half-mile homeward, or walked to the scene of her day's labours with lagging feet. For she had a childish, exaggerated dread of the woman upon whom she waited, lying helpless on the bed, regarding the little maid with her wide, staring eyes, or shrieking horribly upon the stillness in her unbearable pain. There had been days in the early part of her service when the child, going her unwilling errand, had heard those shrieks in the distance and had cowered away in the wood, or hidden among the osiers for hours before she had found courage to go on. There had been foggy afternoons in winter when the mists floating up from the river in the form of a murdered toll-keeper's ghost has pursued the child to the very door of home. Awful experiences of unknown terrors, incommunicable sufferings burdening Dora's mind went to the earning of that shilling which was of so much value to the family comfort.

At last there came a day in winter when Dora, trembling, crying, distraught with fear, appeared in her home circle an hour before her appointed time. She had only an unintelligible tale to tell, and no one could satisfactorily determine why she was so frightened.

There had been a noise in the uninhabited one of the 'Lost Housen' of someone moving about there. In the broad light of day, and at first, the child had not been frightened, had even, it seems, offered to Mrs Crouch to discover who or what had taken up abode there, but had been forbidden to stir from the bedside. It was apparently the undisguised terror of Mrs Crouch herself which had communicated itself to her small attendant, increasing in the imaginative but ignorant mind of the latter to a perfect frenzy of fear of that hidden something moving about on the other side of the thin wall.

Something was there that breathed like the bull 'I' Rober'son's midder,' Dora said; that stumbled about the floor and fell against the wall like 'granfaather when 'e were in drink of a Sat'd'y night'; that was yet more awful a thousand times than the infuriated, bellowing bull or the intoxicated grandparent.

All through the long day the child had supported her terror of the hidden thing, cowering away from the dividing wall that at any moment might open to disclose a sight too awful for little girls to see and live. But when, as time went on, the pale woman on the bed, who had forgotten her pain in her fear, or who had managed to repress all the usual cries, intimated to Dora in a strained and agonised whisper that she dared not be left, that the child must promise for the love of God not to leave her as usual, but to stay at her side all night, for that she was afraid, horribly afraid; when she had clutched at the little hand and arm and had insisted, almost voiceless, but horribly, fearfully impressive, in the hoarse, painful whisper of extremist fear, that not for a moment must she be left alone with what was behind the wall; then the child with a wild cry had pulled herself from the woman's clutches, and, without waiting to look for hat or jacket, had flown from the house and torn homeward as if all the fiends of the bottomless pit had been behind her.

Dora was put to bed, her teeth chattering as with ague, and she screamed all night through at intervals, and muttered in her dreams; and in the morning, to her thankful relief, was found to be too feverish and headachy to start on her usual day's work.

It was Dora's mother, therefore, who on pushing open the door of the ill-fated house discovered the horrid sequel of the unknown terror of the day before.

Upon the bed, scratching and tearing at the air with distorted skeleton fingers, lay Mis' Crouch, the silence she had kept for so many years broken hideously at last by ceaseless babble of maniacal raving. Opposite her bed, hanging from a nail in the wall, was a thing terrible to look upon: the hidden horror of yesterday made visible for the destruction of the senses.

Dora's mother with one wild glance assured herself that what Mrs Crouch was addressing in hoarse confidential whisper, or in loud frenzied entreaty, was not, as she had at first thought, the last year's scarecrow out of the patch of wheat behind her own back door, cruelly maltreated, and hung up to frighten the sick woman. That it was indeed and in truth the dead body of Maher Crouch, who had hanged himself there before his mother's eyes. Then, having with desperate effort summoned strength of mind to slam the door upon the ugly sight, she ran as far as the 'White Hart (where brandy was at hand to recover her) and fainted on the doorstep.

The villagers, who came in a crowd to cut the suicide down, noticed that the rotten wall had given way in several places under the weight of Maher before he had at length found means of firmly fixing the nail upon which to strangle himself. Unpleasant to imagine the sight which must have taken place before the helpless mother's eyes! It was said in Dulditch, where people do not at all shrink from attributing crime or awarding judgment, that the woman's sin must indeed have been great, seeing that her punishment was so terrible.

It is not quite certain if it was from the desire to justify the Power which had so heavily smitten J'mima Crouch, or if it was from the revelations of her own disjointed but incessant ravings that the theory which now maintains about the family was formed. The basis in either case is unsound, for the self-accusations of a maniac cannot be accepted as evidence, and upon perfectly innocent people very heavy misfortunes daily fall.

However the truth may be, it is now held in Dulditch as a fact, undoubted and unalterable as the fact that the world was created in seven days and that Jonah existed for a period in the belly of a whale, that Jemima Crouch assisted her son Og in the attempt to slay his father, and afterwards urged on Maher to murder his brother, and was punished by having to witness the protracted death struggles of the latter, hanging himself with some difficulty before her eyes.

She is very old now, and passes her days in a ward of the pauper lunatic asylum, lying always helpless on her back. But from the way in which her eyes (full of the horror for which perhaps they had kept themselves vacant of expression so long) fix themselves on the white bare wall, and her twisted fingers scratch the air, it is evident she still sees the starting eyes, the protruded, horrid tongue, the blue, hideous face of the son always hanging himself before her.

The 'Lost Housen' are lost indeed now. It is little more than a heap of rubbish which marks the place where they stood.

\* \* \* \* \*

**Virginia Woolf** spent the summer of 1906 at Blo Norton Hall on the Norfolk - Suffolk border. She was then twenty four, and her first essays had just appeared in the *Guardian*. While there she managed to complete one of those 'beautiful brilliant' stories that had begun to take shape as she roamed the countryside. *The Journal Of Miss Joan Martyn* is set in the medieval hall and based in part on her reading of *The Paston Letters*. The story, one of her earliest attempts at fiction, was not published until 1979 in *Twentieth Century Fiction*. Had Woolf revised it she would have noticed the inconsistencies among the dates used.

# The Journal Of Mistress Joan Martyn
VIRGINIA WOOLF

My readers may know, perhaps, who I am. Therefore, although such a practice is unusual and unnatural – for we know how modest writers are – I will not hesitate to explain that I am Miss Rosamond Merridew, aged forty-five – my frankness is consistent! – and that I have won considerable fame among my profession for the researches I have made into the system of land tenure in mediaeval England. Berlin has heard my name; Frankfurt would give a soirée in my honour; and I am not absolutely unknown in one or two secluded rooms in Oxford and in Cambridge. Perhaps I shall put my case more cogently, human nature being what it is, if I state that I have exchanged a husband and a family and a house in which I may grow old, for certain fragments of yellow parchment; which only a few people can read and still fewer would care to read if they could. But as a mother, so I read sometimes not without curiosity, in the literature of my sex, cherishes most the ugliest and stupidest of her offspring, so a kind of maternal passion has sprung up in my breast for these shrivelled and colourless little gnomes; in real life I see them as cripples with fretful faces, but all the same, with the fire of genius in their eyes. I will not expound that sentence; it would be no more likely to succeed than if that same mother to whom I compare myself took pains to explain that her cripple was really a beautiful boy, more fair than his brothers.

At any rate, my investigations have made a travelling pedlar of me; save that it is my habit to buy and not to sell. I present myself at old farm houses, decayed halls, parsonages, church vestries always with the same demand. Have you any old papers to show me? As you may imagine the palmy days for this kind of sport are over; age has become the most merchantable of qualities; and the state moreover with its Commissions has put an end for the most part to the enterprise of individuals. Some official, I am often told, has promised to come down and inspect their documents; and the favour of the 'State' which such a promise carries with it, robs my poor private voice of all persuasion.

Still it is not for me to complain, looking back as I can look back, upon some very fine prizes that will have been of real interest to the historian, and upon others that because they are so fitful and so minute in their illumination please me even better. A sudden light upon the legs of Dame Elizabeth Partridge sends its beams over the whole state of England, to the king upon his throne; she wanted stockings! and no other need impresses you in quite the same way with the reality of mediaeval bodies, and so, proceeding upward step by step, with the reality of mediaeval brains; and there you stand at the centre of all ages: middle beginning or end. And this brings me to a further confession of my virtues. My researches into the land tenure in the 13th, 14th and 15th centuries have been made doubly valuable, I am assured, by the remarkable gift I have of presenting them in relation to the life of the time. I have borne in mind that the intricacies of the land tenure were not always the most important facts in the lives of men and women and children; I have often made so bold as to hint that the subtleties which delight us so keenly were more a proof of our ancestors' negligence than a proof of their astonishing painstaking. For what sane man, I have had the audacity to remark, could have spent his time in complicating his laws for the benefit of half a dozen antiquaries who were to be born five centuries after he was in the grave?

We will not discuss this argument on whose behalf I have given and taken many shrewd blows; I introduce the question merely to explain why it is that I have made all these enquiries subsidiary to certain pictures of the family life which I have introduced into my text; as the flower of all these intricate roots; the flash of all this scraping of flint.

If you read my work called 'The Manor Rolls' you will be pleased or disgusted according to your temperament by certain digressions which you will find there.

I have not scrupled to devote several pages of large print to an attempt to show, vividly as in a picture, some scene from the life of the time; here I knock at the serf's door, and find him roasting rabbits he has poached; I show you the Lord of the Manor setting out on some journey, or calling his dogs to him for a walk in the fields, or sitting in the high backed chair inscribing laborious figures upon a glossy sheet of parchment. In another room I show you Dame Elinor, at work with her needle; and by her on a lower stool sits her daughter stitching too, but less assiduously. 'Child, thy husband will be here before thy house linen is ready,' reproves the mother.

Ah, but to read this at large you must study my book! The critics have always threatened me with two rods; first, they say, such digressions are all very well in a history of the time, but they have nothing to do with the system of mediaeval land tenure; secondly, they complain that I have no materials at my side to stiffen these words into any semblance of the truth. It is well known that the period I have chosen is more bare than any other of private records; unless you chose to draw all your inspiration from the *Paston Letters* you must be content to imagine merely, like any other story teller. And that, I am told, is a useful art in its place; but it should be allowed to claim no relationship with the sterner art of the Historian. But here, again, I verge upon that famous argument which I carried on once with so much zeal in the *Historian's Quarterly*. We must make way with our introduction, or some wilful reader may throw down the book and profess to have mastered its contents already: O the old story! Antiquaries' Quarrels! Let me draw a line here then so —— and put the whole of this question of right or wrong, truth and fiction behind me.

On a June morning two years ago, it chanced that I was driving along the Thetford road from Norwich to East Harling. I had been on some expedition, a wild goose chase it was, to recover some documents which I believed to lie buried in the ruins of Caistor Abbey. If we were to spend a tithe of the sums that we spend yearly upon excavating Greek cities in excavating our own ruins what a different tale the Historian would have to tell!

Such was the theme of my meditations; but nevertheless one eye, my archaeological eye, kept itself awake to the landscape through which we passed. And it was in obedience to a telegram from this that I leapt up in the carriage at a certain point and directed the driver to turn sharply to the left. We passed down a regular avenue of ancient elm trees; but the bait which drew me was a little square picture, framed delicately between green boughs at the far end, in which an ancient doorway was drawn distinctly in lines of carved white stone.

As we approached, the doorway proved to be encircled by long low walls of buff coloured plaster; and on top of them, at no great distance was the roof of ruddy tiles, and finally I beheld in front of me the whole of the dignified little house, built like the letter E with the middle notch smoothed out of it.

Here was one of those humble little old Halls, then, which survive almost untouched, and practically unknown for centuries and centuries, because they are too insignificant to be pulled down or rebuilt; and their owners are too poor to be ambitious. And the descendants of the builder go on living here, with that curious unconsciousness that the house is in any way remarkable which serves to make them as much a part of it as the tall chimney which has grown black with generations of kitchen smoke. Of course a larger house might be preferable, and I doubt not that they would hesitate to sell this old one, if a good offer were to be made for it. But that is the natural, and unselfconscious spirit which proves somehow how genuine the whole thing is. You can not be sentimental about a house that you have lived in for five hundred years. This is the kind of place, I thought, as I stood with my hand on the bell, where the owners are likely to possess exquisite manuscripts, and sell them easily to the first rag man who comes along, as they would sell their pig wash, or the timber from the park. My point of view is that of a morbid eccentric, after all, and these are the people of truly healthy nature. Can't they write? they will tell me; and what is the worth of old letters? I always burn mine – or use them to tie over jam pots.

A maid came, at last, staring meditatively at me, as though she ought to have remembered my face and my business. 'Who lives here?' I asked her. 'Mr Martyn,' she gaped, as if I had asked the name of the reigning King of England. 'Is there a Mrs Martyn, and is she at home, and might I see her?' The girl waved me to follow, and led me in silence to a person who could, presumably, undertake the responsibility of answering my strange questions.

I was shown across a large hall, panelled with oak, to a smaller room in which a rosy woman of my own age was using a machine upon a pair of trousers. She looked like a housekeeper; but she was, the maid whispered, Mrs Martyn.

She rose with a gesture that indicated that she was not precisely a lady to receive morning calls, but was nevertheless the person of authority, the mistress of the house, who had a right to know my business in coming there.

There are certain rules in the game of the antiquary, of which the first and simplest is that you must not state your object at the first encounter. 'I was passing by your door; and I took the liberty – I must tell you I am a great lover of the picturesque, to call, on the chance that I might be allowed to look over the house. It seems to me a particularly fine specimen.'

'Do you want to rent it, may I ask,' said Mrs Martyn, who spoke with a pleasant tinge of dialect.

'Do you let rooms then?' I questioned.

'O no,' rejoined Mrs Martyn decisively: 'We never let rooms; I thought perhaps you wished to rent the whole house.'

'It's a little big for me; but still, I have friends.'

'As well, then,' broke in Mrs Martyn, cheerfully, setting aside the notion of profit, and looking merely to do a charitable act; 'I'm sure I should be very pleased to show you over the house – I don't know much about old things myself; and I never heard as the place was particular in any way. Still it's a pleasant kind of place – if you come from London.' She looked curiously at my dress and figure, which I confess felt more than usually bent beneath her fresh, and somewhat compassionate gaze; and I gave her the information she wanted. Indeed as we strolled through the long passages, pleasantly striped with bars of oak across the whitewash, and looked into spotless little rooms with square green windows opening on the garden, and where I saw furniture that was spare but decent, we exchanged a considerable number of questions and answers. Her husband was a farmer on rather a large scale; but land had sunk terribly in value; and they were forced to live in the Hall now, which would not let; although it was far too large for them, and the rats were a nuisance. The Hall had been in her husband's family for many a year, she remarked with some slight pride; she did not know how long, but people said the Martyns had once been great people in the neighbourhood. She drew my attention to the 'y' in their name. Still she spoke with the chastened and clear sighted pride of one who knows by hard personal experience how little nobility of birth avails, against certain material drawbacks, the poverty of the land, for instance, the holes in the roof, and the rapacity of rats.

Now although the place was scrupulously clean and well kept, there was a certain bareness in all the rooms, a prominence of huge oak tables, and an absence of other decorations than bright pewter cups and china plates which looked ominous to my inquisitive gaze. It seemed as though a great deal must have been sold, of those small portable things that make a room look furnished. But my hostess' dignity forbade me to suggest that her house had ever been other than it was at present. And yet I could not help fancying a kind of wistfulness in the way she showed me into rooms that were almost empty, compared the present poverty to days of greater affluence, and had it on the tip of her tongue to tell me that 'Things had once been better.' She seemed half apologetic, too, as she led me through a succession of bedrooms, and one or two rooms that might have served for sitting rooms if people had had leisure to sit there, as though she wished to show me that she was quite aware of the discrepancy between such a house and her own sturdy figure. All this being as it was, I did not like to ask the question that interested me most – whether they had any books? and I was beginning to feel that I had kept the good woman from her sewing machine long enough, when she suddenly looked out of the window, hearing a whistle below, and shouted something about coming in to dinner. Then she turned to me with some shyness, but an expression of hospitality, and begged me to 'Sit down to dinner' with them. 'John, my husband, knows a sight more than I do of these old things of his, and I know he's glad enough of some one to talk to. It's in his blood I tell him,' she laughed, and I saw no good reason why I should not accept the invitation. Now John did not fall so easily beneath any recognised heading as his wife did. He was a man of middle age and middle size, dark of hair and complexion, with a pallor of skin that did not seem natural to a farmer; and a drooping moustache which he smoothed slowly with one well-shaped hand as he spoke. His eye was hazel and bright, but I fancied a hint of suspicion when its glance rested upon me. He began to speak however, with even more of a Norfolk accent than his wife; and his voice, and dress asserted that he was, in truth, if not altogether in appearance, a solid Norfolk farmer.

He nodded merely when I told him that his wife had had the kindness to show me the house. And then, looking at her with a twinkle in his eye he remarked, 'If she had her way the old place would be left to the rats. The house is too big and there are too many ghosts. Eh Betty?' She merely smiled, as though her share of the argument had been done long ago.

I thought to please him by dwelling upon its beauties, and its age; but he seemed little interested by my praises, munched largely of cold beef, and added 'ayes' and 'noes' indifferently.

A picture painted perhaps in the time of Charles the First, which hung above his head, had so much the look of him had his collar and tweed been exchanged for a ruff and a silk doublet, that I made the obvious comparison.

'O aye,' he said, with no great show of interest, 'that's my grandfather; or my grandfather's grandfather. We deal in grandfathers here.'

'Was that the Martyn who fought at the Bogne,' asked Betty negligently while she pressed me to take another slice of beef.

'At the Bogne,' exclaimed her husband, with query and even irritation – 'Why my good woman, you're thinking of Uncle Jasper. This fellow was in his grave long before the Bogne. His name's Willoughby,' he went on

196

speaking to me, as though he wished me to understand the matter thoroughly; because a blunder about such a simple fact was unpardonable, even though the fact itself might not be of great interest.

'Willoughby Martyn: born 1625 died 1685: he fought at Marston Moor as Captain of a troop of Norfolk men. We were always royalists. He was exiled in the Protectorate, went to Amsterdam; bought a bay horse off the Duke of Newcastle there; we have the breed still; he came back here at the Restoration, married Sally Hampton – of the Manor, but they died out last generation, and had six children, four sons and two daughters. He bought the Lower Meadow you know Betty,' he jerked at his wife, to goad her unaccountably sluggish memory.

'I call him to mind well enough now,' she answered placidly.

'He lived here all the last part of his life; died of small pox, or what they called small pox then; and his daughter Joan caught it from him. They're buried in the same grave in the church yonder.' He pointed his thumb, and went on with his dinner. All this was volunteered as shortly and even curtly as though he were performing some necessary task, which from long familiarity had become quite uninteresting to him; though for some reason he had still to repeat it.

I could not help showing my interest in the story, although I was conscious that my questions did not entertain my host.

'You seem to have a queer liking for these old fathers of mine,' he commented, at last, with an odd little scowl of humorous irritation. 'You must show her the pictures after dinner, John,' put in his wife; 'and all the old things.'

'I should be immensely interested,' I said, 'but I must not take up your time.'

'O John knows a quantity about them; he's wonderful learned about pictures.'

'Any fool knows his own ancestors, Betty;' growled her husband; 'still, if you wish to see what we have, Madam, I shall be proud to show you.' The courtesy of the phrase, and the air with which he held the door open for me, made me remember the 'y' in his name.

He showed me round the Hall, pointing with a riding crop to one dark canvas after another; and rapping out two or three unhesitating words of description at each; they were hung apparently in chronological order, and it was clear in spite of the dirt and the dark that the later portraits were feeble examples of the art, and represented less distinguished looking heads. Military coats became less and less frequent, and in the

18th century the male Martyns were represented in snuff coloured garments of a homely cut, and were briefly described as 'Farmers' or 'him who sold the Fen Farm' by their descendant. Their wives and daughters at length dropped out altogether, as though in time a portrait had come to be looked upon more as the necessary appendage of the head of the house, rather than as the right which beauty by itself could claim.

Still, I could trace no sign in the man's voice that he was following the decline of his family with his riding crop, for there was neither pride nor regret in his tone; indeed it kept its level note, as of one who tells a tale so well known that the words have been rubbed smooth of meaning.

'There's the last of them – my father,' he said at length, when he had slowly traversed the four sides of the Hall; I looked upon a crude canvas, painted with a literal brush. Perhaps the unskilful hand had brought out the roughness of the features and the harshness of the complexion; had found it easier to paint the farmer than to produce the subtle balance which, one might gather, blent in the father as in the son. The artist had stuffed his sitter into a black coat, and wound a stiff white tie round his neck; the poor gentleman had never felt at ease in them, yet.

'And now, Mr Martyn,' I felt bound to say, 'I can only thank you, and your wife for . . .'

'Stop a moment,' he interrupted, 'we're not done yet. There are the books.'

His voice had a half comic doggedness about it; like one who is determined, in spite of his own indifference to the undertaking, to make a thorough job of it.

He opened a door and bade me enter a small room, or rather office; for the table heaped with papers, and the walls lined with ledgers, suggested the room where business is transacted by the master of an estate. There were pads and brushes for ornament; and there were mostly dead animals, raising lifeless paws, and grinning with plaster tongues, from various brackets and cases.

'These go back beyond the pictures;' he said, as he stooped and lifted a great parcel of yellow papers with an effort. They were not bound, or kept together in any way, save by a thick cord of green silk, with bars at either end; such as you use to transfix bundles of greasy documents – butcher's bills and the year's receipts. 'That's the first lot,' he said ruffling the leaves with his fingers, like a pack of cards; 'that's No.1: 1480 to 1500.' I gasped, as anyone may judge: but the temperate voice of Martyn reminded me that enthusiasm was out of place, here; indeed enthusiasm began to look like a very cheap article when contrasted with the genuine thing.

'Ah indeed; that's very interesting; may I look? was all I said, though my undisciplined hand shook a little when the bundle was carelessly dropped into it. Mr Martyn indeed offered to fetch a duster before desecrating my white skin; but I assured him it was of no consequence, too eagerly perhaps, because I had feared that there might be some more substantial reason why I should not hold these precious papers.

While he bent down before a book case, I hastily looked at the first inscription on the parchment. 'The Journal of Mistress Joan Martyn,' I spelt out, 'kept by her at Martyn's Hall, in the county of Norfolk the year of our Lord 1480.'

'My grandmother Joan's diary,' interrupted Martyn, turning round with his arm full of books. 'Queer old lady she must have been. I could never keep a diary myself. Never kept one beyond the 10th of February, though I tried often. But here you see,' he leant over me, turning the pages, and pointing with his finger, 'here is January, February, March, April – and so on – a whole twelve months.'

'Have you read it then?' I asked, expecting, nay, hoping that he would say no.

'O yes, I've read it;' he remarked casually, as though that were but a simple undertaking. 'It took me some time to get used to the writing and the old girl's spelling is odd. But there are some queer things in it. I learnt a deal about the land from her, one way and another.' He tapped it meditatively.

'Do you know her history too?' I asked.

'Joan Martyn,' he began in the voice of a showman, 'was born 1495. She was the daughter of Giles Martyn. She was his only daughter. He had three sons though; we always have sons. She wrote this diary when she was twenty-five. She lived here all her life – never married. Indeed she died at the age of thirty. I daresay you might see her tomb down there with the rest of them.

'Now this,' he said touching a thick book bound in parchment, 'is more interesting to my mind. This is the household book of Jasper for the year 1583. See how the old gentleman kept his accounts; what they eat and drank; how much meat and bread and wine cost; how many servants he kept – his horses, carriages, beds, furniture, everything. There's method for you. I have a set of ten of them.' He spoke of them with greater pride than I had heard him speak of any of his possessions yet.

'This one too makes good reading of a winter's night,' he went on, 'This is the Stud Book of Willoughby; you remember Willoughby.'

199

'The one who bought the horse of the Duke, and died of smallpox,' I repeated glibly.

'That's so,' he nodded. 'Now this is really fine stuff, this one.' He went on, like a connoisseur, talking of some favourite brand of port. 'I wouldn't sell this for £20. Here are the names, the pedigrees, the lives, values, descendants; all written out like a bible.' He rolled some of the strange old names of these dead horses upon his tongue, as though he relished the sound like wine. 'Ask my wife if I can't tell 'em all without the book,' he laughed, shutting it carefully and placing it on the shelf.

'These are the Estate books; they go down to this year; there's the last of 'em. Here's our family history.' He unrolled a long strip of parchment, upon which an elaborate genealogical tree had been inscribed, with many faded flourishes and extravagances of some medieval pen. The boughs spread so widely by degrees, that they were lopped unmercifully by the limits of the sheet – a husband depending, for instance, with a family of ten children and no wife. Fresh ink at the base of all recorded the names of Jasper Martyn, my host, and his wife Elizabeth Clay: they had three sons. His finger travelled sagaciously down the tree, as though it were so well used to this occupation that it could almost be trusted to perform it by itself. Martyn's voice murmured on as though it repeated a list of Saints or Virtues in some monotonous prayer.

'Yes,' he concluded, rolling up the sheet and laying it by, 'I think I like those two best. I could say them through with my eyes shut. Horses or Grandfathers!'

'Do you study here a great deal then?' I asked, somewhat puzzled by this strange man.

'I've no time for study,' he returned, rather roughly, as though the farmer cropped up in him at my question. 'I like to read something easy in the winter nights; and in the morning too, if I wake early. I keep them by my bed sometimes. I say them to send myself to sleep. It's easy to know the names of one's own family. They come natural. But I was never any good at book learning, more's the pity.'

Asking my permission, he lit a pipe and began puffing forth great curls of smoke, as he ranged the volumes in order before him. But I kept No. One, the bundle of parchment sheets, in my hand, nor did he seem to miss it from the rest.

'You would be sorry to part with any of these, I daresay?' I hazarded, at last, covering my real eagerness with an attempt at a laugh.

'Part with them?' he returned, 'what should I part with them for?' The idea was evidently so remote that my question had not, as I feared, irritated his suspicions.

'No, no,' he went on, 'I find them too useful for that. Why, Madam, these old papers have stood out for my rights in a court of law before now; besides, a man likes to keep his family round him; I should feel – well kind of lonely if you take my meaning, without my Grandfathers and Grandmothers and Uncles and Aunts.' He spoke as though he confessed to a weakness.

'O,' I said, 'I quite understand – '

'I daresay you have the same feeling yourself Madam and down here, in a lonely place like this, company means more than you could well believe. I often think I shouldn't know how to pass the time, if it weren't for my relations.'

No words of mine, or attempt at a report of his words, can give the curious impression which he produced as he spoke, that all these 'relations', Grandfathers of the time of Elizabeth, nay Grandmothers of the time of Edward the Fourth, were just, so to speak, brooding round the corner; there was none of the pride of 'ancestry' in his voice but merely the personal affection of a son for his parents. All generations seemed bathed in his mind in the same clear and equable light: it was not precisely the light of the present day, but it certainly was not what we commonly call the light of the past. And it was not romantic, it was very sober, and very broad and the figures stood out in it, solid and capable, with a great resemblance, I suspect, to what they were in the flesh.

It really needed no stretch of the imagination to perceive that Jasper Martyn might come in from his farm and his fields, and sit down here alone to a comfortable gossip with his 'relations'; whenever he chose; and that their voices were very nearly as audible to him as those of the labourers in the field below, which came floating in, upon the level afternoon sunlight through the open window.

But my original intention of asking whether he would sell, almost made me blush when I remembered it now: so irrelevant and so impertinent. And also, strange though it may seem, I had lost for the time my proper antiquarian zeal; all my zest for old things, and the little distinguishing marks of age, left me, because they seemed the trivial and quite immaterial accidents of large substantial things. There was really no scope for antiquarian ingenuity in the case of Mr Martyn's ancestors, anymore than it needed an antiquary to expound the history of the man himself.

They are, he would have told me, all flesh and blood like I am; and the fact that they have been dead for four or five centuries makes no more difference to them, than the glass you place over a canvas changes the picture beneath it.

But on the other hand, if it seemed impertinent to buy, it seemed natural, if perhaps a little simpleminded, to borrow.

'Well, Mr Martyn,' I said at length, with less eagerness and less trepidation than I could have thought possible under the circumstances, 'I am thinking of staying for a week or so in this neighbourhood – at the Swan at Gartham indeed – I should be much obliged to you if you would lend me these papers to look through during my stay. This is my card. Mr Lathom, (the great landowner of the place) will tell you all about me.' Instinct told me that Mr Martyn was not the man to trust the benevolent impulses of his heart.

'O Madam, there's no need to bother about that,' he said carelessly, as though my request were not of sufficient importance to need his scrutiny. 'If these old papers please you, I'm sure you're welcome to 'em.' He seemed a little surprised, however, so that I added, 'I take a great interest in family histories, even when they're not my own.'

'It's amusing eno', I daresay, if you have the time,' he assented politely; but I think his opinion of my intelligence was lowered.

'Which would you like?' he asked, stretching his hand towards the Household Books of Jasper; and the Stud Book of Willoughby.

'Well, I think I'll begin with your grandmother Joan,' I said; 'I like beginning at the beginning.'

'O very well,' he smiled; 'though I don't think you'll find anything out of the way in her; she was very much the same as the rest of us – as far as I can see, not remarkable – '

But all the same, I walked off with Grandmother Joan beneath my arm; Betty insisted upon wrapping her in brown paper, to disguise the queer nature of the package, for I refused to let them send it over as they wished, by the boy who took the letters on his bicycle.

(1)

The state of the times, which my mother tells me, is less safe and less happy than when she was a girl, makes it necessary for us to keep much within our own lands. After dark indeed, and the sun sets terribly soon in January, we have to be safe behind the hall Gates; my mother goes out as soon as the dark makes her embroidery too dim to see, with the great keys on her arm. 'Is everybody within doors?' she cries, and swings the bells out upon the road, in case any of our men may still be working in the fields. Then she draws the Gates close, clamps them with the lock, and the whole world is barred away from us. I am very bold and impatient sometimes, when the moon rises, over a land gleaming with frost; and I think I feel the pressure of all this free and beautiful place – all England and the sea, and the land beyond – rolling like sea waves, against our iron gates, breaking, and withdrawing – and breaking again – all through the long black night. Once I leapt from my bed, and ran to my mother's room, crying, 'Let them in. Let them in! We are starving!' 'Are the soldiers there, child,' she cried: 'or is it your father's voice?' She ran to the window, and together we gazed out upon the silver fields, and all was peaceful. But I could not explain what it was that I heard; and she bade me sleep, and be thankful that there were stout gates between me and the world.

But on other nights, when the wind is wild and the moon is sunk beneath hurrying clouds, I am glad to draw close to the fire, and to think that all those bad men who prowl in the lanes, and lie hidden in the woods at this hour cannot break through our great Gates, try as they will. Last night was such a night; they come often in Winter when my father is away in London, my brothers are with the army, save my little brother Jeremy, and my mother has to manage the farm, and order the people, and see that all our rights are looked to. We may not burn the tapers after the church bell has struck 8 times, and so we sit round the logs, with the priest, John Sandys, and one or two of the servants who sleep with us in the Hall. Then my mother, who cannot be idle even by fire light, winds her wool for her knitting, sitting in the great chair which stands by the cheek of the hearth. When her wool gets tangled she strikes a great blow with the iron rod, and sends the flames and the sparks spurting in showers; she stoops her head into the tawny light, and you see what a noble woman she is; in spite of age – she is more than forty – and the hard lines which much thought and watching have cut in her brow. She wears a fine linen cap, close fitting to the shape of her head, and her eyes are deep and stern, and her cheek is coloured like a healthy winter apple. It is a great thing to be the daughter of such a woman, and to hope that one day the same power may be mine. She rules us all.

Sir John Sandys, the priest, is, for all his sacred office, the servant of my mother; and does her will simply and querulously, and is never so happy as when she asks him for advice, and takes her own. But she would scold me well if I ever whispered such a thing: for she is the faithful daughter of the Church, and reverences her priest. Again there are William and

Anne, the servants who sit with us, because they are so old that my mother wishes them to share our fire. But William is so ancient, so curved with planting and digging, so bruised and battered by the sun and the wind that one might as well ask the pollard willow in the fen to share one's fire, or join one's talk. Still, his memory goes back a great way, and if he could tell us, as he sometimes tries to begin, of the things he has seen in his day, it would be curious to hear. Old Anne was my mother's nurse; she was mine; and she still mends our clothes, and knows more about household things than any, save my mother. She will tell you, too, the history of each chair and table or piece of tapestry in the house; but most of all she likes to discuss with mother and Sir John the men whom it would be most suitable for me to marry.

As long as the light serves it is my duty to read aloud – because I am the only one who can read though my mother can write, and spell words beyond the fashion of her time, and my father has sent me a manuscript from London; called *The Palace of Glass* by Mr John Lydgate. It is a poem, written about Helen and the Siege of Troy.

Last night I read of Helen, and her beauty and her suitors, and the fair town of Troy and they listened silently; for though we none of us know where those places are, we see very well what they must have been like; and we can weep for the sufferings of the soldiers, and picture to ourselves the stately woman herself, who must have been, I think, something like my mother. My mother beats with her foot and sees the whole processions pass I know, from the way her eyes gleam, and her head tosses. 'It must have been in Cornwall,' said Sir John, 'where King Arthur lived with his knights. I remember stories I could tell you of all their doings, but my memory is dim.'

'Ah but there are fine stories of the Northmen, too,' broke in Anne; whose mother was from those parts; 'but I have sung them often to my Mister, and to you too Miss Joan.'

'Read on Joan, while there is light,' commanded my mother. Indeed, of all I think she listened closest, and was most vexed when the Curfew tolled from the Church nearby. Yet she called herself an old fool for listening to stories, when the accounts had still to be made up for my father in London.

When the light is out and I can no longer see to read, they begin talking of the state of the country; and telling dreadful stories of the plots and the bloody deeds that are going on all around us. But for all I can see, we are not worse now than we have always been; and we in Norfolk today are much the same as we were in the days of Helen, wherever she may have lived. Was not Jane Moryson carried off on the eve of her wedding only last year?

But anyhow, the story of Helen is old; my mother says it happened long before her day; and these robbings and burnings are going on now. So the talk makes me, and Jeremy too, tremble and think that every rattle of the big door, is the battering ram of some wandering highwayman.

It is far worse tho', when the time for bed comes, and the fire sinks, and we have to feel our way up the great stairs, and along the passages, where the windows shine grey, and so into our cold bed rooms. The window in my room is broken, and stuffed with straw, but gusts come in and lift the tapestry on the wall, till I think that horses and men in armour are charging down upon me. My prayer last night was, that the great gates may hold fast, and all robbers and murderers might pass us by.

(2)

The dawn, even when it is cold and melancholy, never fails to shoot through my limbs as with arrows of sparkling piercing ice. I pull aside the thick curtains, and search for the first glow in the sky which shows that life is breaking through. And with my cheek leant upon the window pane I like to fancy that I am pressing as closely as can be upon the massy wall of time, which is forever lifting and pulling and letting fresh spaces of life in upon us. May it be mine to taste the moment before it has spread itself over the rest of the world! Let me taste the newest and the freshest. From my window I look down upon the Church yard, where so many of my ancestors are buried, and in my prayer I pity those poor dead men who toss perpetually on the old recurring waters; for I see them, circling and eddying forever upon a pale tide. Let us, then, who have the gift of the present, use it and enjoy it: That I confess, is part of my morning prayer.

It rained steadily today, so that I had to spend the morning with my sewing. My mother was writing her letter to my father which John Ashe will take with him to London next week. My thoughts naturally dwelt upon this journey, and upon the great city which perhaps I may never see, though I am for ever dreaming of it. You start at dawn; for it is well to spend few nights on the road. John travels with three other men, bound to the same place; and I have often seen them set forth, and longed to ride with them. They gather in the courtyard, while the stars are still in the sky; and the people of the neighbourhood come out wrapped in cloaks and strange garments, and my mother carries out a tankard of strong Ale to each traveller; and gives it to him from her own hand. Their horses are laden with packs before and behind, but not so as to hinder them from starting out in a gallop if need be; and the men are well armed, and closely dressed in fur lined habits, for the winter days are short and cold, and maybe they will sleep beneath a hedge. It is a gallant sight in the dawn; for the horses champ and fret to be gone; the people cluster round. They wish their God speeds and their last messages to friends in London; and as the clock strikes four they wheel about, salute my mother and the rest, and turn sharply on their road. Many young men and women too, follow them some paces on the way till the mist comes between, for often men who set forth thus in the dawn, never ride home again.

I picture them riding all day along the white roads, and I see them dismount at the shrine of our Lady and do homage, pray to her for a safe journey. There is but one road, and it passes through vast lands, where no men live, but only those who have murdered or robbed; for they may not dwell with others in towns, but must pass their lives with the wild beasts, who murder also, and eat the clothes from your back. It is a fearful ride; but, truly, I think I should like to go that way once, and pass over the land, like a ship at sea.

At midday they reach an Inn – for there are Inns at all stages upon the journey to London, where a traveller may rest in safety. The landlord will tell you the state of the road, and he will ask you of your adventures, so that he may give warning to others who travel the same way. But you must press on, to reach your sleeping place before the dark lets loose all those fierce creatures who have lain hidden in the day. John has often told me how as the sun comes from the sky silence falls on the company, and each man has his gun swung beneath his hand, and even the horses prick their ears and need no urging. You reach the crest of the road, and look fearfully beneath you, lest something moves in the shade of the fir trees by the wayside. And then Robin, the cheerful Miller, shouts a snatch of a song, and they take heart, and step bravely down the hill, talking lest the deep breath of the wind, as of a woman who sighs deeply, may cast a panic into their hearts. Then some one rises in his stirrup and sees the spark of a lodging far off on the rim of the land. And if Our Lady is merciful to them they reach this in safety when we at home are on our knees in prayer for them.

(3)

My mother called me from my book this morning to talk with her in her room. I found her in the little chamber where my father is wont to sit, when he is at home, with the Manor Rolls and other legal papers before him. It is here that she sits when she has duty to do as the head of the household. I curtseyed deeply; thinking I had guessed already why she had sent for me.

She had a sheet spread before her, covered with close writing. She bade me read it; and then before I had taken the paper in my hand she cried, 'No – I will tell you myself.'

'Daughter,' she began, solemnly, 'it is high time that you were married. Indeed it is only the troubled state of the land' – she sighed – 'and our own perplexities, that have delayed the matter so long.'

'Do you think much of marriage?' she looked at me half smiling.

'I have no wish to leave you,' I said.

'Come, my child, you speak like a Babe,' she laughed, though I think she was well pleased at my affection.

'And besides, if you married as I would have you marry' – she tapped the paper – 'you would not go far from me. You might for instance rule over the land of Kirflings – your land would touch ours – You would be our good neighbour. The Lord of Kirflings is Sir Amyas Bigod, a man of ancient name.'

'I think it is a suitable match; such as a mother might wish for her daughter,' she mused, always with the sheet before her.

As I have only seen Sir Amyas once, when he came home with my father from the sessions at Norwich, and as on that occasion my only speech with him was to invite him gravely to drink the sack which I proffered, curtseying, I could not pretend to add anything to what my mother said. All I knew was that he had a fair, straight face; and if his hair was gray, it was not so gray as my father's, and his land bordered ours so that we might well live happily together.

'Marriage, you must know, my daughter,' went on my mother, 'is a great honour and a great burden. If you marry such a man as Sir Amyas you become not only the head of his household, and that is much, but the head of his race for ever and ever, and that is more. We will not talk of love – as that song writer of yours talks of love, as a passion and a fire and a madness.'

'O he is only a story teller, Mother,' I chimed in –

'And such things are not to be found in real life; at least I think not often.' My mother was used to consider gravely as she spoke.

'But that is beside the question. Here, my daughter,' and she spread the paper before her, 'is a writing from Sir Amyas, to your father; he asks for

207

your hand, and wishes to know whether there are other treaties for you and what dowry we will give with you. He tells us what he will provide on his part. Now I give you this paper to read by yourself; that you may consider whether this exchange seems to you a fair one.'

I knew already what lands and monies I had as my portion; and I knew that as the only daughter of my father my dowry was no mean one.

So that I might continue in this country which I love, and might live on close to my mother, I would take less than my right both of wealth and of land. But the gravity of the compact is such that I felt as though several years were added to my age, when my mother handed me the roll of paper. Since I was a child, I have always heard my parents talk of my marriage; and during the last two or three years there have been several contracts almost made I know, that came to nothing in the end. I lose my youth however, and it is high time a bargain were struck.

I thought, naturally, for a long time, until the dinner bell rung indeed at midday, of the general honour and burden, as my mother calls it, of marriage. No other event in the life of a woman can mean so great a change; for from flitting shadow like and unconsidered in her father's house, marriage suddenly forms her to a substantial body, with weight which people must see and make way for. That is of course, if her marriage is suitable. And so, every maiden waits this change with wonder and anxiety; for it will prove whether she is to be an honourable and authoritative woman for ever, like my mother; or it will show that she is of no weight or worth. Either in this world or in the next.

And if I marry well, the burden of a great name and of great lands will be on me; many servants will call me mistress; I shall be the mother of sons; in my husband's absence I shall rule his people, taking care for herds and crops and keeping watch on his enemies; within doors I shall store up fine linens and my chests shall be laden with spices and preserves; by the work of my needle all waste of time and use will be repaired and renewed so that at my death my daughter shall find her cupboards better lined with fine raiments than when I found them. And when I lie dead, the people from the countryside shall pass for three days before my body, praying and speaking good of me, and at the will of my children the priest shall say mass for my soul and candles shall burn in the church for ever and ever.

(4)

I was stopped in the midst of such reflections firstly by the dinner bell; and you must not be late, or you interfere with Sir John's grace and that means no pudding; and then, when I might have put myself more into the position of a married woman, Jeremy my brother insisted that we should go for a walk with Anthony, my father's chief steward – after my mother that is.

He is a cross man, but I like him because he is a faithful servant, and knows as much about land and sheep as any man in Norfolk. It was he also who broke Lancelot's head in last Michaelmas for using bad language to my mother. He is for ever tramping our fields, and knows them better and loves them more, so I tell him, than any human creature. He is wedded to this clump of earth, and sees in it a thousand beauties and gifts such as ordinary men see in their wives. And, as we have trotted by his side since we could walk alone, some of his affection has become ours too; Norfolk and the parish of Long Winton in Norfolk is to me what my own grandmother is; a tender parent, dear and familiar, and silent, to whom I shall return in time. O how blessed it would be never to marry, or grow old; but to spend one's life innocently and indifferently among the trees and rivers which alone can keep one cool and childlike in the midst of the troubles of the world! Marriage or any other great joy would confuse the clear vision which is still mine. And at the thought of losing that, I cried in my heart, 'No, I will never leave you – for a husband or a lover,' and straightway I started chasing rabbits across the heath with Jeremy and the dogs.

It was a cold afternoon, but a bright one; as though the sun were made of gleaming ice and not of fire; and its rays were long icicles that reached from sky to earth. They splintered on our cheeks, and went glancing across the fen. And the whole country seemed empty, save of a few swift rabbits, but very chaste and very glad in its solitude. We ran to keep warm, and chattered when the blood raced sparkling through our limbs. Anthony stalked straight on, as though his stride were the best thing in the world against the cold. Certainly when we came to a broken hedge, or a snare stretched for a rabbit, he took off his gloves and leant on his knee and took note of it as though it were a midsummer day. Once we came upon a strange man, slouching along the road, in rusty green, with the look of one who knows not which way to take. Anthony held my hand firmly; this was a Sanctuary man he said, prowling out of bounds in search of food. He had robbed or murdered, or perchance he was only a debtor. Jeremy swore he saw blood on his hands: but Jeremy is a boy, and would like to defend us all with his bow and arrows.

Anthony had some business at one of the cottages, and we came in with him out of the cold. But indeed, I could hardly stand the heat and the smell. Beatrice Somers, and her husband Peter live here, and they have children; but it was more like the burrow of some rabbit on the heath than the house of a man. Their roof was of brush, and straw, their floor was but the earth trodden bare of grass or flower; sticks burnt in the corner, and sent the smoke stinging into our eyes. There was but a rotten log on which a woman sat, nursing a baby. She looked at us, not with fright, but with distrust and dislike written clear in her eyes; and she clasped her child more closely. Anthony spoke to her as he would have spoken to some animal who had strong claws and a wicked eye: he stood over her, and his great boot seemed ready to crush her. But she did not move or speak; and I doubt whether she could have spoken, or whether snarling and howling was her only language.

Outside we met Peter coming home from the fen, and tho' he touched his forehead to us, he seemed to have no more human sense in him than his wife. He looked at us, and seemed fascinated by a coloured cloak which I wore; and then he stumbled into his burrow, to lie on the ground I suppose, rolled in dry bracken till morning. These are the people we must rule; and tread under foot, and scourge them to do the only work they are fitted to do; as they will tear us to pieces with their fangs. Thus Anthony spoke as he took us away, and then clenched his fists and and set his lips as though he were razing to the earth some such poor wretch already. Still the sight of that ugly face spoilt the rest of the walk; since it seemed that even my dear country bred pests like these. I saw such strange eyes staring at me from the furze bushes, and the tangles of the undergrowth.

It was like waking from a nightmare to enter our own clean hall, where the logs burnt tidily in the great chimney, and the oak shone bright; and my mother came down the staircase in her rich gown, with spotless linen on her head. But some of the lines on her face, and some of the sternness of her voice, had come there, I thought suddenly, because she always saw not far from her such sights as I had seen today.

## (5) - May

The spring which has now reached us means more than the mere birth of green growing things; for once again the current of life which circles round England is melted from its winter frost, and in our little island we feel the tide chafing at our shores. For the last week or two strange wayfarers have been seen on the roads, who may be either pilgrims or pedlars, or gentlemen travelling in parties to London or the North. And at this season the mind becomes eager and hopeful even though the body must stay motionless. For as the evenings lengthen and new light seems to well up from the West so one may fancy that a new whiter light of another kind is spreading over the land; and you may feel it hitting your eyelids as you walk or sit over your embroidery.

In the midst of such a stir and tumult, one bright May morning, we saw the figure of a man striding along the road, walking fast and waving his arms as though he conversed with the air. He had a great wallet at his back and we saw that he held a stout book of parchment in one hand at which he glanced occasionally: and all the while he shouted words in a kind of measure with his feet, and his voice rose up and down, in menace or in plaint till Jeremy and I shrank close against the hedge. But he saw us; and pulled off his cap and made a deep bow; to which I curtseyed as properly as I could.

'Madam,' he said, in a voice that rolled like summer thunder, 'may I ask if this is the road to Long Winton?'

'It is only a mile in front of you Sir,' I said, and Jeremy waved down the road with his stick.

'Then Sir,' he went on, shutting his book, and looking at once more sober and more conscious of the time and place, 'may I ask further where is the house I could sell my books most easily? I am come all the way from Cornwall, singing songs, and trying to sell the manuscripts I have with me. My wallet is still full. The times are not favourable to songs.'

Indeed the man, though ruddy of cheek, and lusty of frame, was as ill dressed as any hind; and his boots were so patched that walking must have been a penance. But he had a kind of gaiety and courtesy about him, as though the fine music of his own songs clung to him and set him above ordinary thoughts.

I pulled my brother's arm, and said, 'We belong to the Hall ourselves Sir, and we will gladly shew you the way. I should be very glad to see those books of yours.' His eye lost its merriment at once; and he asked me almost sternly, 'Can you read?'

'O Joan's always got her nose in a book,' called out Jeremy, starting to talk, and pulling me too.

'Tell us about your travels Sir. Have you been to London? What is your name?'

'I am called Richard Sir,' said the man smiling. 'Doubtless I have another name, but I never heard it. I come from Gwithian which is in

Cornwall; and I can sing you more Cornish songs, Madam, than any man in the Duchy.' He turned to me, and wound up with a flourish of one hand with the book in it. 'Here for instance – in this little volume, are all the stories of the Knights of the Round Table; written out by the hand of Master Anthony himself, and painted by the Monks of Cam Brea. I value this more than my wife or children; for I have none; it is meat and drink to me, because I am given supper and lodging for singing the tales in it; it is horse and staff to me, for it has lifted me over many miles of weary road; and it is the best of all companions on the way; for it has always something new to sing me; and it will be silent when I wish to sleep. There never was such a book!'

Such was the way he talked, as I have never heard any man talk. For in speaking he did not seem to speak his mind exactly, or to care whether we understood him. But words seemed dear to him whether he spoke them in jest or earnest. We reached our courtyard, and he straightened himself, flicked his boots with a handkerchief; and tried with many swift touches of his fingers to set his dress somewhat more in order than it was. Also he cleared his throat, as one preparing to sing. I ran to fetch my mother, who came slowly, and looked at him from an upper window before she would promise to hear him.

'His bag is stuffed with books, mother,' I urged; 'he has all the Tales of Arthur and the Round Table; I daresay he can tell us what became of Helen when her husband took her. O Mother, do let us hear him!'

She laughed at my impatience; but bade me call Sir John, for after all it was a fine morning.

When we came down the man Richard was walking up and down, discoursing to my brother of his travels; how he had knocked one man on the head, cried to the other, " 'Come on Rascal" and the whole lot had fled like,' here he saw my mother, and swept off his hat as was his way.

'My daughter tells me Sir that you come from foreign parts, and can sing. We are but country people; and therefore I fear very little acquainted with the tales of other parts. But we are ready to listen. Sing us something of your land; and then, if you will, you shall sit down to meat with us, and we will gladly hear news of the country.'

She sat down on a bench beneath the oak tree; and Sir John came puffing to stand by her side. She bade Jeremy open the Gates, and let any of our people in who cared to hear. They came in shyly and curiously, and stood gaping at Master Richard, who once again waved his cap at them.

He stood on a small mound of grass; and began in a high melodious voice, to tell the story of Sir Tristram and the Lady Iseult.

He dropped his gay manner, and looked past us all, with straight fixed eyes, as though he drew his words from some sight not far from him. And as the story grew passionate his voice rose, and his fists clenched, and he raised his foot and stretched forth his arms; and then, when the lovers part, he seemed to see the Lady sink away from him, and his eye sought farther and farther till the vision was faded away; and his arms were empty. And then he is wounded in Brittany; and he hears the Princess coming across the seas to him.

But I cannot tell how it seemed that the air was full of Knights and Ladies, who passed among us, hand in hand, murmuring, and seeing us not; and then the poplars and the beech trees sent grey figures, with silver gems, floating down the air; and the morning was full, suddenly, of whispers, and sighs, and lovers' laments.

But then the voice stopped; and all these figures withdrew, fading and trailing across the sky to the West where they live. And when I opened my eyes, the man, and the grey wall; the people by the Gate, slowly swam up, as from some depths, and settled on the surface, and stayed there clear and cold.

'Poor things!' spoke my mother.

Meanwhile Richard was like a man who lets something slip from his clasp; and beats thin air. He looked at us, and I had half a mind to stretch out a hand; and tell him he was safe. But then he recollected himself, and smiled as though he had reason to be pleased.

He saw the crowd at the Gate; and struck up a jolly tune, about a Nut Brown Maid and her lover, and they grinned and stamped with their feet. Then my mother bade us come in to dinner; and she sat Master Richard on her right side.

He eat like a man who has fed on hips and haws, and drunk water from the brook. And after the meat had been taken away, he solemnly swung round his wallet; and took from it various things; which he laid upon the table. There were clasps and brooches, and necklaces of beads: but there were also many sheets of parchment stitched together; though none of such a size as his book. And then seeing my desire he placed the precious volume in my hands and bade me look at its pictures. Indeed it was a beautiful work; for the capital letters framed bright blue skies, and golden robes; and in the midst of the writing there came broad spaces of colour, in which you might see princes and princesses walking in procession and towns with churches upon steep hills, and the sea breaking blue beneath them. They were like little mirrors, held up to those visions which I had seen passing in the air but here they were caught and stayed for ever.

'And have you ever seen such sights as these?' I asked him.

'They are to be seen by those who look,' he answered mysteriously. And he took his manuscript from me, and tied the covers safely across it. He placed it in his breast.

It was yellow and gnarled outside as the missal of any pious priest; but inside the brilliant knights and ladies moved undimmed, to unceasing melody of beautiful words. It was a fairy world that he shut inside his coat.

We offered him a night's lodging, nay more, if he would but stay and sing to us again. But he listened to our prayers no more than the owl in the ivy: saying merely, 'I must go on my way.' By dawn he was out of the house, and we felt as though some strange bird had rested on our roof for a moment, and flown on.

### (6) - Midsummer

There comes a week, or maybe it is only a day, when the year seems poised consciously on its topmost peak; it stays there motionless for a long or a short time, as though in majestic contemplation, and then slowly sinks like a monarch descending from his throne, and wraps itself round in darkness.

But figures are slippery things!

At this moment I have the feeling of one swung high into tranquil regions; upon the great back of the world. The peace of the nation, and the prosperity of our own small corner of it – for my father and brothers are at home – make a complete circle of satisfaction; you may pass from the smooth dome of sky, to our own roof without crossing any gulf.

Thus it seemed a most suitable time for our midsummer pilgrimage to the shrine of Our Lady at Walsingham; more especially as I have this year to give thanks for much, and to pray for more. My marriage with Sir Amyas is settled for the 20th day of December; and we are busy making ready. So yesterday I started at dawn, and travelled on foot in order to show that I approached the shrine with a humble spirit. And a good walk is surely the best preparation for prayers!

Start with your spirit fresh like a corn fed horse; let her rear and race, and bucket you hither and thither. Nothing will keep her to the road; and she will sport in dewy meadows, and crush a thousand delicate flowers beneath her feet.

But the day grows hot; and you may lead her, still with a springing step back to the straight way; and she will carry you lightly and swiftly, till the midday sun bids you rest. In sober truth, and without metaphor, the mind drives clearly through all the mazes of a stagnant spirit when a brisk pair of legs impels it; and the creature grows nimble, with its exercise. Thus I suppose I may have thought enough for a whole week lived indoors during those three hours that I spent striding along the road to Walsingham.

And my brain that was swift and merry at first, and leapt like a child at play, settled down in time to sober work upon the highway, though it was glad withal. For I thought of the serious things of life – such as age, and poverty and sickness and death, and considered that it would certainly be my lot to meet them; and I considered also those joys and sorrows that were for ever chasing themselves across my life. Small things would no longer please me or tease me as of old. But although this made me feel grave, I felt also that I had come to the time when such feelings are true; and further, as I walked, it seemed to me that one might enter within such feelings and study them, as, indeed, I had walked in a wide space within the covers of Master Richard's manuscript.

I saw them as solid globes of crystal; enclosing a round ball of coloured earth and air, in which tiny men and women laboured, as beneath the dome of the sky itself.

Walsingham, as all the world knows, is but a very small village on the top of a hill. But as you approach through a plain that is rich with green, you see this high ground rising above you for some time before you get there. The midday sun lit up all the soft greens and blues of the fen land; and made it seem as though one passed through a soft and luxurious land, glowing like a painted book; towards a stern summit, where the light struck upon something pointing upwards that was pale as a bone.

At last I reached the top of the hill, joining with a stream of other pilgrims, and we clasped hands, to show that we came humbly as human beings and trod the last steps of the road together, singing our Miserere.

There were men and women, and lame people and blind people; and some were in rags, and some had ridden on horseback; I confess that my eyes sought their faces curiously, and I thought desperately for a moment that it was terrible that flesh and fens should divide us. They would have strange, merry stories to tell.

But then the pale cross with the Image struck my eyes, and drew all my mind, in reverence towards it.

I will not pretend that I found that summons other than stern; for the sun and storm have made the figure harsh and white; but the endeavour to adore Her as others were doing round me filled my mind with an image that was so large and white that no other thought had room there. For one moment I submitted myself to her as I have never submitted to man or woman, and bruised my lips on the rough stone of her garment. White light and heat steamed on my bare head; and when the ecstasy passed, the country beneath flew out like a sudden banner unfurled.

## (7) - *Autumn*

The Autumn comes; and my marriage is not far off. Sir Amyas is a good gentleman, who treats me with great courtesy and hopes to make me happy. No poet could sing of our courtship; and, I must confess that since I have taken to reading of Princesses, I have sometimes grieved that my own lot was so little like theirs. But then they did not live in Norfolk at the time of the Civil Wars; and my mother tells me the truth is always finest.

To prepare me for my duties as a married woman, she has let me help her in the management of the house and lands; and I begin to understand how much of my time will be passed in thoughts which have nothing to do with men or with happiness. There are the sheep, the woods, the crops, the people, things all needing my care and judgement when my Lord is away as he will be so often; and if times are as troubled as they have been, I must also act as chief Lieutenant in the disposition of his forces against the enemy. And then there will be my proper work as a woman calling me within the house. Truly, as my mother says, there will be little time for Princes and Princesses! And she went on to expound to me what she calls her theory of ownership; how, in these times, one is as the Ruler of a small island set in the midst of turbulent waters; how one must plant it and cultivate it; and drive roads through it, and fence it securely from the tides; and one day perhaps the waters will abate and this plot of ground will be ready to make part of a new world. Such is her dream of what the future may bring to England; and it has been the hope of her life to order her own province in such a way that it may make one firm spot of ground to tread on at any rate. She bids me hope that I may live to see the whole of England thus solidly established; and if I do, I shall thank my mother, and other women like her.

But I confess that deeply though I honour my mother and respect her

216

words, I cannot accept their wisdom without a sigh. She seems to look forward to nothing better than an earth rising solid out of the mists that now enwreathe it; and the fairest prospect in her mind is, I believe, a broad road running through the land, on which she sees long strings of horsemen, riding at their ease, pilgrims stepping cheerily unarmed, and waggons that pass each other going laden to the coast and returning as heavily laden with goods taken from ships. Then she would dream of certain great houses, lying open to the sight, with their moats filled up and their towers pulled down; and the gate would open freely to any passer by; and there would be cheer for guest or serving man at the same table with the Lord. And you would ride through fields brimming with corn, and there would be flocks and herds in all the pasture lands and cottages of stone for the poor. As I write this down, I see that it is good; and we should do right to wish it.

But at the same time, when I imagine such a picture, painted before me, I cannot think it pleasant to look upon; and I fancy that I should find it hard to draw my breath upon those smooth bright ways.

Yet what it is that I want, I cannot tell, although I crave for it, and in some secret way, expect it. For often, and oftener as time goes by, I find myself suddenly halting in my walk, as though I were stopped by a strange new look upon the surface of the land which I know so well. It hints at something; but it is gone before I know what it means. It is as though a new smile crept out of a well known face; it half frightens you, and yet it beckons.

### *Last Pages*

My father came in yesterday when I was sitting before the desk at which I write these sheets. He is not a little proud of my skill in reading and writing; which indeed I have learnt mostly at his knee.

But confusion came over me when he asked me what I wrote; and stammering that it was a 'Diary' I covered the pages with my hands.

'Ah,' he cried, 'if my father had only kept a diary! But he, poor man, could not write his own name even. There's John and Pierce and Stephen all lying in the church yonder, and no word left to say whether they were good men or bad.' Thus he spoke till my cheeks were pale again.

'And so my grandson will say of me,' he went on. 'And if I could I should like to write a line about myself: to say "I am Giles Martyn; I am a middle sized man, dark skinned, hazel eyed, with hair on my lip; I can read and write, but none too easy. I ride to London on as good a bay mare as is to be found in the County." '

'Well what more should I say? And would they care to hear it? And who will *they* be?' he laughed; for it was his temper to end his speech with a laugh, even though he began it soberly.

'You would like to hear of your father,' I said; 'why wouldn't they care to hear of you?'

'My fathers were much the same as I am,' he said; 'they lived here, all of 'em; they ploughed the same land that I plough; they married women from the countryside. Why they might walk in the door this moment, and I should know 'em, and should think it nothing strange. But the future' – he spread out his hands – 'who can tell? We may be washed off the face of the earth, Joan.'

'Oh no,' I cried; 'I am certain we shall live here always.' This pleased my father secretly; for there is no man who cares more for his land and his name than he does; though he will always hold that had we been a prouder race, we should not have stayed so long in the same prosperity.

'Well then Joan, you must keep your writing.' he said; 'or rather, I must keep it for you. For you are going to leave us – not to go far though,' he added quickly; 'and names matter but little. Still, I should like to have some token of you when you are away; and our descendants shall have cause to respect one of us at least.' He looked with great admiration at the neat lines of my penmanship. 'Now my girl, come with me, to the Church, where I must see to the carving on my father's tomb.'

As I walked with him, I thought of his words and of the many sheets that lie written in my oaken chest. Winter had come round again since I made my first flourish so proudly. Thinking that there were few women in Norfolk who could do the like; and were it not that some such pride stayed with me I think that my writing would have ceased long before this. For, truly, there is nothing in the pale of my days that needs telling; and the record grows wearisome. And I thought as I went along in the sharp air of the winter morning, that if I ever write again it shall not be of Norfolk and myself, but of Knights and Ladies and of adventures in strange lands. The clouds even, which roll up from the west and advance across the sky take the likeness of Captains and of soldiery and I can scarcely cease from fashioning helmets and swords, as well as fair faces, and high headdresses from these waves of coloured mist.

But as my mother would say, the best stories are those that are told over the fire side; and I shall be well content if I may end my days as one of those old women who can keep a household still on a winter's evening, with her tales of the strange sights that she saw and the deeds that were done in her youth. I have always thought that such stories came partly out of the clouds, or why should they stir us more than any thing we can see for ourselves? It is certain that no written book can stand beside them.

Such a woman was Dame Elsbeth Aske, who, when she grew too old to knit or stitch and too stiff to leave her chair, sat with clasped hands by the fire all day long, and you had only to pull her sleeve and her eyes grew bright, and she would tell you stories of fights and kings, and great nobles, and stories of the poor people too, till the air seemed to move and murmur. She could sing ballads also; which she made as she sat there. And men and women, old and young, came long distances to hear her; for all that she could neither write nor read. And they thought that she could tell the future too.

Thus we came to the church where my fathers lie buried. The famous stone Carver, Ralph of Norwich, has lately wrought a tomb for my grandfather, and it lies almost finished now, above his body; and the candles were flaring upright in the dim church when we entered. We knelt and whispered prayers for his soul; and then my father withdrew in talk with Sir John; and left me to my favourite task of spelling out the names and gazing down at the features of my dead kinsmen and ancestors. As a child I know the stark white figures used to frighten me; especially when I could read that they bore my name; but now that I know that they never move from their backs, and keep their hands crossed always, I pity them; and would fain do some small act that would give them pleasure. It must be something secret, and unthought of – a kiss or a stroke, such as you give a living person.

\* \* \* \* \*

**Ruth Rendell** came to Suffolk in 1970 and several crime novels as well as a number of short stories, including *Weeds*, draw on her knowledge of East Anglia. Most of her time has been spent near the Essex border in the village of Polstead, notorious for the Victorian murder of Maria Marten in the Red Barn. *Weeds* first appeared in the collection *The Copper Peacock* (1991).

# Weeds

## RUTH RENDELL

'I am not at all sure', said Jeremy Flintwine, 'that I would know a weed from whatever the opposite of a weed is.'

The girl looked at him warily. 'A plant.'

'But surely weeds *are* plants.'

Emily Hithe was not prepared to enter into an argument. 'Let me try and explain the game to you again,' she said. 'You have to see if you can find a weed. In the herbaceous borders, in the rosebeds, anywhere. If you find one all you have to do is show it to my father and he will give you a pound for it. Do you understand now?'

'I though this was in aid of cancer research. There's not much money to be made that way.'

She smiled rather unpleasantly. 'You won't find any weeds.'

It cost two pounds each to visit the garden. Jeremy, a publisher who lived in Islington, had been brought by the Wragleys with whom he was staying. They had walked here from their house in the village, a very long walk for a Sunday afternoon in summer after a heavy lunch. Nothing had been said about fund-raising or playing games. Jeremy was already wondering how he was going to get back. He very much hoped to catch the twelve minutes past seven train from Diss to London.

The Wragleys and their daughter Penelope, aged eight, had disappeared down one of the paths that led through a shrubbery. People stood about on the lawn drinking tea and eating digestive biscuits which they had had to pay for. Jeremy always found country life amazing. The way everyone knew everyone else, for instance. The extreme eccentricity of almost everybody, so that you suspected people, wrongly, of putting it on. The clothes. Garments he had supposed obsolete, cotton frocks and sports jackets, were everywhere in evidence. He had thought himself suitably dressed but now he wondered. Jeans were not apparently correct wear except on the under-twelves and he was wearing jeans, an old, very clean, pair, selected after long deliberation, with an open-necked shirt and an elegantly shabby Italian silk cardigan. He was also wearing, in the top buttonhole of the cardigan, a scarlet poppy tugged up by its roots from the grass verge by Penelope Wragley.

The gift of this flower had been occasioned by one of George Wragley's literary anecdotes. George, who wrote biographies of poets, was not one of Jeremy's authors but his wife Louise, who produced best-sellers for children and adored her husband, was. Therefore, Jeremy found it expedient to listen more or less politely to George going on and on about Francis Thompson and the Meynells. It was during the two-mile-long trudge to the Hithe's garden that George related how one of the Meynell children, with appropriate symbolism, had presented the opium-addicted Thompson with a poppy in a Suffolk field, bidding him, 'Keep this for ever!' Penelope had promptly given Jeremy his buttonhole, which her parents thought a very sweet gesture, though he was neither a poet nor an opium addict.

They had arrived at the gates and paid their entry fee. A lot of people were on the terrace and the lawns. The neatness of the gardens was almost oppressive, some of the flowers looking as if they had been washed and ironed and others as if made of wax. The grass was the green of a billiard table and nearly as smooth. Jeremy asked an elderly woman, one of the tea drinkers, if Rodney Hithe did it all himself.

'He has a man, of course,' she said.

The coolness of her tone was not encouraging but Jeremy tried. 'It must be a lot of work.'

'Oh, old Rod's got that under control,' said the girl with her, a granddaughter perhaps. 'He knows how to crack the whip.'

This Jeremy found easy to believe. Rodney Hithe was a loud man. His voice was loud and he wore a jacket of loud blue and red checked tweed. Though seeming affable enough, calling the women 'darling' and the men 'old boy', Jeremy suspected he was the kind of person it would be troublesome to get on the wrong side of. His raucous voice could be heard from end to end of the garden, and his braying unamused laugh.

'I wouldn't want to find a weed,' said the grand-daughter, voicing Jeremy's own feelings. 'Not for a pound. Not at the risk of confronting Rod with it.'

Following the path the Wragleys had taken earlier, Jeremy saw people on their hands and knees, here lifting a blossoming frond, there an umbelliferous stalk, in the forlorn hope of finding treasure underneath. The Wragleys were nowhere to be seen. In a far corner of the garden, where geometric rosebeds were bounded on two sides by flint walls, stood a stone seat. Jeremy thought he would sit down on this seat and have a cigarette. Surely no one could object to his smoking in this remote and secluded spot. There was in any case no one to see him.

He was taking his lighter from his jeans pocket when he heard a sound from the other side of the wall. He listened. It came again, an indrawing of breath and a heavy sigh. Jeremy wondered afterwards why he had not immediately understood what kind of activity would prompt the utterance of these sighs and half-sobs, why he had at first supposed it was pain and not pleasure that gave rise to them. In any case, he was rather an inquisitive man. Not hesitating for long, he hoisted himself up so that he could look over the wall. His experience of the countryside had not prepared him for this. Behind the wall was a smallish enclosed area or farmyard, bounded by buildings of the sty and byre type. Within an aperture in one of these buildings, on a heap of hay, a naked girl could be seen lying in the arms of a man who was not himself naked but dressed in a shirt and a pair of trousers.

'Lying in the arms of' did not accurately express what the girl was doing but it was a euphemism Jeremy much preferred to 'sleeping with' or anything franker. He dropped down off the wall but not before he had noticed that the man was very deeply tanned and had a black beard and that the girl's resemblance to Emily Hithe made it likely this was her sister.

This was no place for a quiet smoke. He walked back through the shrubbery, lighting a cigarette as he went. Weed-hunting was still in progress under the bushes and among the alpines in the rock garden, this latter necessarily being carried out with extreme care, using the fingertips to avoid bruising a petal. He noticed none of the women wore high heels. Rodney Hithe was telling a woman who had brought a Pekinese that the dog must be carried. The Wragleys were on the lawn with a middle-aged couple who both wore straw hats and George Wragley was telling them an anecdote about an old lady who had sat next to P G Wodehouse at a dinner party and enthused about his work throughout the meal under the impression he was Edgar Wallace. There was some polite laughter. Jeremy asked Louise what time she thought of leaving.

'Don't you worry, we shan't be late. We'll get you to the station all right. There's always the last train, you know, the eight forty-four.' She went on confidingly, 'I wouldn't want to upset poor old Rod by leaving the minute

222

we arrive. Just between you and me, his marriage hasn't been all it should be of late and I'd hate to add to his troubles.'

This sample of Louise's arrogance rather took Jeremy's breath away. No doubt the woman meant that the presence of anyone as famous as herself in his garden conferred an honour on Rodney Hithe which was ample compensation for his disintegrating home life. He was reflecting on vanity and authors and self-delusion when the subject of Louise's remark came up to them and told Jeremy to put his cigarette out. He spoke in the tone of a prison officer addressing a habitual offender in the area of violent crime. Jeremy, who was not without spirit, decided not to let Hithe cow him.

'It's harmless enough out here surely.'

'I'd rather you smoked your filthy fags in my wife's drawing-room than in my garden.'

Grinding it into the lawn would be an obvious solecism. 'Here,' Jeremy said, 'you can put it out yourself,' and he did his best to meet Hithe's eyes with an equally steady stare. Louise gave a nervous giggle. Holding the cigarette end at arm's length, Hithe went off to find some more suitable extinguishing ground, disappeared in the direction of the house and came back with a gun.

Jeremy was terribly shocked. He was horrified. He retreated a step or two. Although he quickly understood that Hithe had not returned to wreak vengeance but only to show off his new twelve-bore to the man in the straw hat, he still felt shaken. The ceremony of breaking the gun he thought it was called was gone through. The straw-hatted man squinted down the barrel. Jeremy tried to remember if he had ever actually seen a real gun before. This was an aspect of country life he found he disliked rather more than all the other things.

Tea was still being served from a trestle table outside the French windows. He bought himself a cup of tea and several of the more nourishing biscuits. It seemed unlikely that any train passing through north Suffolk on Sunday evening would have a restaurant or even a buffet car. The time was coming up to six. It was at this point that he noticed the girl he had last seen lying in the arms of the bearded man. She was no longer naked but wearing a T-shirt and a pair of shorts. In spite of these clothes, or perhaps because of them, she looked rather older than when he had previously seen her. Jeremy heard her say to the woman holding the dog, 'He ought to be called a Beijingese, you know,' and give a peal of laughter.

He asked the dog's owner, a woman with a practical air, how far it

223

was to Diss.

'Not far,' she said. 'Two or three miles. Would you say two miles, Deborah, or nearer three?'

Deborah Hithe's opinion on this distance Jeremy was never to learn, for as she opened her mouth to speak, a bellow from Rodney silenced all conversation.

'You didn't find that in this garden.'

He stood in the middle of the lawn, the gun no longer in his hands but passed on for the scrutiny of a girl in riding breeches. Facing him was the young man with the tan and the beard, whom Jeremy knew beyond a doubt to be Deborah's lover. He held up, in teasing fashion for the provocation of Hithe, a small plant with a red flower. For a moment the only sound was Louise's giggle, a noise that prior to this weekend he would never have suspected her of so frequently making. A crowd had assembled quite suddenly, surely the whole population of the village, it seemed to Jeremy, which Louise had told him was something over three hundred.

The man with the beard said, 'Certainly I did. You want me to show you where?'

'He should never have pulled it out, of course,' Emily whispered. 'I'm afraid we forgot to put that in the rules, that you're not supposed to pull them out.'

'He's your sister's boy friend, isn't he?' Jeremy hazarded.

The look he received was one of indignant rage. 'My *sister*? I haven't got a sister.'

Deborah was watching the pair on the lawn. He saw a single tremor shake her. The man who had found the weed made a beckoning gesture to Hithe to follow him along the shrubbery path. George Wragley lifted his shoulders in an exaggerated shrug and began telling the girl in riding breeches a long pointless story about Virginia Woolf. Suddenly Jeremy noticed it had got much colder. It had been a cool, pale grey, still day, a usual English summer day, and now it was growing chilly. He did not know what made him remember the gun, notice its absence.

Penelope Wragley, having ingratiated herself with the woman dispensing tea, was eating up the last of the biscuits. She seemed the best person to ask who Deborah was, the least likely to take immediate inexplicable offence, though he had noticed her looking at him and particularly at his cardigan in a very affronted way. He decided to risk it.

Still staring, she said as if he ought to know, 'Deborah is Mrs Hithe, of course.'

The implications of this would have been enough to occupy Jeremy's thoughts for the duration of his stay in the garden and beyond, if there had not come at this moment a loud report. It was, in his ears, a shattering explosion and it came from the far side of the shrubbery. People began running in the direction of the noise before its reverberations had died away. The lawn emptied. Jeremy was aware that he had begun to shake. He said to the child, who took no notice, 'Don't go!' and then set off himself in pursuit of her.

The man with the beard lay on his back in the rose garden and there was blood on the grass. Deborah knelt beside him, making a loud keening wailing noise, and Hithe stood between two of the geometric rosebeds, holding the gun in his hands. The gun was not exactly smoking but there was a strong smell of gunpowder. A tremendous hubbub arose from the party of weed-hunters, the whole scene observed with a kind of gloating horrified fascination by Penelope Wragley, who had reverted to infantilism and watched with her thumb in her mouth. The weed was nowhere to be seen.

Someone said superfluously, or perhaps not superfluously, 'Of course it was a particularly tragic kind of accident.'

'In the circumstances.'

The whisper might have come from Louise. Jeremy decided not to stay to confirm this. There was nothing he could do. All he wanted was to get out of this dreadful place as quickly as possible and make his way to Diss and catch a train, any train, possibly the last train. The Wragleys could send his things on.

He retreated the way he had come, surprised to find himself tiptoeing which was surely unnecessary. Emily went past him, running towards the house and the phone. The Pekinese or Beijingese dog had set up a wild yapping. Jeremy walked quietly around the house, past the drawing-room windows, through the open gates and into the lane.

The sound of that shot still rang horribly in his ears, the sight of the red blood on the grass was still before his eyes. The unaccustomed walk might be therapeutic. It was a comfort, since a thin rain had begun to fall, to come upon a signpost which told him he was going in the right direction for Diss and it was only a mile and a half away. There was no doubt the country seemed to show people as well as nature in the raw. What a nightmare that whole afternoon had been, culminating in outrageous violence! How horrible, after all, the Wragleys and Penelope were and in a way he had never been suspected! Why were one's authors so awful?

225

Why did they have such appalling spouses and ill-behaved children? Penelope had stared at him when he asked her about Deborah Hithe as disgustedly as if, like that poor man, he had been covered in blood.

And then Jeremy put his hand to his cardigan and felt the front of it, patted it with both hands like a man feeling for his wallet, looked down, saw that the scarlet poppy she had given him was gone. Her indignation was explained. The poppy must have fallen out when he hoisted himself up and looked over the wall.

It was a moment or two before he understood the cause of his sudden fearful dismay.

* * * * *

**Ronald Blythe** was born in Suffolk and is best known for *Akenfield* (1969), his remarkable study of change in the English village. His output ranges through poetry, fiction and essays including *From The Headland* (1982) and the highly acclaimed *Word From Wormingford* (1997), the village in the Stour valley where he lives in an old farmhouse once home to the painter John Nash. Blythe has always been intrigued by the cultural life of the region and its provincial dramas are the subject of *Arnulf And Esther,* (p264) and *Master Of None* one of the series 'Tales from East Anglia' broadcast in 2001 on BBC Radio 3.

# Master Of None
## RONALD BLYTHE

Mr Hooper pushed his handcart through the dawn streets, the shaft high against his chest. It bore a coffin which slid around under the roped-down tarpaulin like a restless sleeper. Paper-boys were weaving their bikes from door to door. The hand-cart was rubber-shod and ran silently. No particular discretion was intended by its early delivery. It was simply that later tasks pressed and it made sense to take an empty coffin to where it had to be filled as the first job of a many-jobbed day. Mr Hooper spun his cart along with a kind of showy ease, a reminder of a youthful 'look, no hands!' He was a huge man with thrusting shoulders, massive hips and visible reserves of great strength, should it be needed. It was said of him that he could turn his hand to anything, that he could not be deflected, once started, that he would always have a go. No one remarked on his strange hands which were small for the rest of him, delicate, the colour of yellowing piano keys. Yet their ivory palms with their sooty lines were as tell-tale as an engraver's plate. Chimney-sweeping was but one of the numerous trades which brought him a bob or two but no standing. What was he? No one could rightly say. The town called him a character. Early risers acknowledged him from all directions. 'Mr Hooper . . . Mr Hooper . . .' His name ran around the cold streets.

This particular morning, however, Mr Hooper's dull resignation to the endless calls on his time gave the lie to what was happening in his head, which was in turmoil. For one thing he hadn't slept an hour all night – his wife could swear to it. She was known behind her back as the 'unofficial towncrier' and was as little and loud as her husband was big and speechless, which is sometimes the way in marriage. He had certainly not breathed a word to her as to what had been on his mind for the best part of a week. Round and round it went, this awful question of whether to apply or not to apply. Never once in his fifty-two years had he applied for anything, a job, a favour or help. People applied to *him*. Could he do this, would he do that? And by tomorrow if he didn't mind. The most admiring thing said of him was that he was 'allus on the goo', high praise in some quarters. He was not flattered. Jobs, jobs, jobs. Somewhere, rumbling round his workhorse carcass, were the seeds of rebellion, the fragile shoot of ambition, the growing lust for some specific identity and a hatred of being jack of all trades.

The coffin delivered and a score of other loads, the evening come, he went off to bellringing practise as usual, clumping his way up the tower stairs, his shoulders brushing the whitewash as usual. It was stuffy in the ringing chamber where a trapped wren beat its wings against a high window. The eight looped bell-ropes hung motionless. When Mr Hooper unlooped his the sally was still warm from where the afternoon sun had caught it through the lancet. Robin from the chemist's was caller and soon the bells were raised and off to Plain Bob Major. The soft sally fled and returned to Mr Hooper's delicate hands, one second free, the next held. This evening he rang woodenly and without his usual joy. As he lurched up and down he saw the Royal Arms board with its furious lions lashing their tails around the proud motto, and he remembered those same Arms above the advertisements in the newspaper which had caught his eye now almost a week ago.

He had been summoned to the Rectory to sweep the dining-room chimney, a useless business as Mr Hooper knew only too well, it being one of those chimneys that would never draw no matter what you did to it. Had he not knelt before it countless times, partly as supplicant, but mostly to thank it for providing him with a regular little income. Fire-lighters, matches and the Rector's densely-lettered newspaper lay on the fender.

'Draw, bugger you,' Mr Hooper intoned.

it was at this moment that his gaze encountered the Royal Arms and under them 'Crown Appointments'. He read on. A man of impeccable character between the ages of thirty and sixty was required for the Crown Appointment of Public Hangman. Only it wasn't quite put like this, more round the houses, as it were. Mr Hooper read and re-read it, faintly swaying on his knees. Three references were essential, as was respectability. Also a letter in the applicant's own hand. He was more awkward than usual when he came for the chimney money.

'Was there something more, Mr Hooper?'

'Yes, sir. I must have a character.'

'You hardly need me to give you that.'

'I *must* have it, sir.'

'Why, are you thinking of leaving us?'

In the silence that followed the Rector told himself it was no business of his, went to his study and did what he did dozens of times, writing on a piece of headed paper, 'To whom it may concern' . . . then laying on the 'character' thick. Servants, farmworkers, apprentices, girls applying for work at the silk factory, choirboys making their way in the world, each and all received the same glowing testimonial for whom it might concern. But old Hooper – what was he up to? Not for the first time the Rector felt a twinge of worry, rather than conscience, at his doling out characters flat. Later, he mentioned Mr Hooper's request to his wife who surprisingly said, 'I can't bear him.'

Mr Hooper needed to change out of his sweep suit if he was going to collect two more characters that day. Time was running out. There was a deadline. And so he astonished the unofficial towncrier by arriving home during work hours and demanding hot water for a good wash.

'I was having my after dinner lay-down,' his wife told the neighbours, 'so you can tell how early he was!'

Clean enough to call on a magistrate, Mr Hooper found Edward Drake, Esq. J.P. tying up strings of onions in his shed.

'Here, take a hold of this, Hooper,' he said, passing a ball of twine.

It took their combined strength to haul such an enormous string of onions to a rafter and let it sway and dangle there. Mr Drake turned out to be a far more inquisitive character-giver than the Rector, and blazed away as he did on the bench, demanding the full facts. Mr Hooper quavered before authority, shook inside and then, mesmerised by Mr Drake's glassy stare, dragged the cutting from *The Times* from his pocket. Mr Drake read it wonderingly.

'Why, you dark old horse, Hooper.'

He punched the Jack of all trades affectionately on the shoulder. Admiration made him red in the face.

'I'll support you all right! Right up to here, Hooper! By God, Hooper, you're the man for me!'

A strange excitement overcame Mr Drake. Was he not for ever telling young men who pinched cash or rode their bicycles without a light that hanging was too good for them? Had he not spent years collecting signatures to 'let justice take its course' when there was an outbreak of sentimentality at some death sentence? But never in his happiest dreams had he dared to think that he would have a hand in appointing the next

229

Public Hangman! He took Mr Hooper into the house and sat him down in the scullery and went off to compose a winning letter. It took him ages. Mr Hooper drank beer. How fat it was, Mr Drake's character. It bulged in its envelope and was sealed with wax, and was fit for the King to open it. It raved about Mr Hooper's peculiar qualification for the office, about his coolness, handiness and his patriotism, his nerveless ability to do what had to be done. The final sentence read, 'Frederick Hooper can be trusted by your Majesty's judiciary to take charge on the scaffold when the condemned would feel reassured and leave this world with his name on their lips'. Mr Hooper placed Mr Drake's letter with the Rector's and went off to old Miss Greenaway for a third. How easy it was to be someone. Why had he left it so long!

Miss Greenaway had been Mr Hooper's headmistress long, long ago. So long that it would be a miracle if she still recognised him. But when she answered his loud knock she said, 'Come in, Freddie. Wipe your feet and don't touch anything,' which is what she had said when he was twelve and running her errands and mending her hencoop, distempering her WC, and doing all those jobs which were to be his apprenticeship for what he was to become. This thought now struck home. She must be going on ninety, he reckoned. Her cottage reeked of Ronuk, roses and old lady. Group photos of her class stood on every table-top and he found himself scanning them for his own small face. There were cats on chairs. Tenderly dislodging one of them she ordered him to take its place.

'And keep those big feet in, Freddie. Now, what is it that I can do for you? Speak up.'

'Please, Miss Greenaway, can you give me a character?'

'I could, but I won't. What do you want a character for at your age?' So he was no longer twelve.

'I have to have something about me in writing.'

'Why?'

'It's about a jo – a vacancy I read about in the paper.'

'What paper?'

'The Suffolk Free Press,' he lied.

He saw that she had been reading a library book without glasses and was still scarily bright like she had been in school, although now bent over like a crochet hook. She looked down at him kindly.

'Freddie,' she said, 'you *have* a unique position in this town, one which I pride myself having found for you. That boy, I told myself, hasn't much of a head on him but he can turn his hand to anything. And haven't you proved me right? What would we do without you? Don't lean back on that chair – I won't tell you again. In any case, what point is your coming to me for what you call a 'character'. Your jobs apart, how am I to know what you have been getting up to all these years? How is your Mavis? Still gossiping, I expect. Why didn't you have any children? Don't answer this.'

There was a lengthy silence during which her presentation clock ticked away. She rose, called the cats and fed them in the kitchen. She then went to her bureau for a sheet of paper, slicing it in half – 'for the milkman' – and wrote in her fine girlish hand on the remaining piece, 'Freddie Hooper has been useful to me. I have watched him grow and become the man he is, useful to all. Catherine Greenaway (Miss) B.A.'

On the way home Mr Hooper purchased sixpenny-worth of stationery at the sweetshop and a stamp at the post office. For the next three days he wrote and re-wrote to the address in the advert, gnawing at his pen. It was almost a month later that the unofficial towncrier swooped upon the most amazing letter ever to have sped through the door of twelve, Ipswich Street. She carried it to where her husband was wringing the cockerel's neck at the top of the garden. He took it without explanation. When he ordered her to press his best suit, brush his bowler and buy him a tie, he knew that there was no further way of keeping her in the dark. So he told her.

It shook him, the effect it had on her. He thought he knew her through and through. Never could he have imagined the way she looked at him, the way she stepped back from him. He showed her first the Royal Arms on the newspaper cutting from the Rectory, and then those same glorious Arms on the letter from the Home Secretary, smiling as he drew her to his elevation. But she hung fire – was in fact ice. What was it that she was seeing in him?

'Mavis . . . '

The interview was for October 17th, her birthday as it happened. When he returned it was all over town – all over everywhere – had he but known it. But terrible disappointment was blotting out what he might have seen or heard in the normal way. All that he could do was to grasp the ordinariness of things, at routine, habit. He blundered out of his interview suit and into his workaday clothes, by which time it was bell practise. They rang Spliced Surprise Major with him as caller. Black sweat stained his armpits. Halfway through, Robin from the chemist's said something about having a headache and vanished. Then they all fled, leaving him standing. He looped the abandoned ropes and walked to the King's Arms, hearing its roar subside as he entered.

And thus it started, his new aloneness, the nosy questions. Such as, for example, would he still have to wear cotton gloves when he took the chalice even if he didn't get the job as Public Hangman? The intent was there, they said. It was why Mavis left him – the intent. Not all at once, but gradually, as the enormity of his intention sank in, he found himself existing in a familiar town that was without greeting. Women found him sensational and children horrible. Men found him interesting for the first time in his life, but reduced this to a nod. Most of the locals did not know what to think. He had overturned their limits. Once, when a youth was hanged at Norwich Gaol, Mr Hooper became the epicentre of a frisson so ghastly that he made a faint effort to move away. Years later he was still to be seen pushing his handcart through the streets, trilby well pulled down over his eyes, his boots splashing along. Once the thoughtful Rector preached on the Scapegoat, but to uncomprehending ears. Every now and then, the subject being so fascinating, Mr Hooper was asked to his face why he had done it. His replies were mumbled and unsatisfactory. They heard things such as 'the beauty of rope', 'being close to justice' and – fiercely, 'it wasn't the money'. This last they believed. Then what was it? Mr Hooper knew, but not how to put what he knew into words.

\* \* \* \* \*

**George Ewart Evans:** On arriving in the remote east Suffolk hamlet of Blaxhall just after the war Evans was unaware that his new friendship with elderly neighbours would change the course of his writing and lay the foundations of what has become known as Oral History. *Ask The Fellows Who Cut The Hay* (1956), a celebrated tribute to the people of Blaxhall, was followed by a series of remarkable books that explore the traditional rural culture of East Anglia. In 1973 Evans returned briefly to fiction with the publication of *Acky*, an affectionate collection of gently subversive stories about a wiley old horseman living on the edge of a broad heath in the village of Fenhall that catches perfectly the language and humour of Suffolk.

# The Shield
## GEORGE EWART EVANS

Until you had lived in the village of Fenhall for at least a couple of generations you were still a *furriner*; and as a foreigner you were expected to keep your place. A newcomer to Fenhall must always state his opinion in a very small voice indeed. In fact, it would be much better if he didn't state it at all. For although he couldn't help being seen about the village – after all a man has to live somewhere – the foreigner ought not to be as rash as to make himself heard. This, at least, is what Akerman Flatt thought of Mrs Horringer who'd shown a strong intention of settling in Peartree Cottage.

Now Mrs Horringer was a good woman with as much energy as a committee of public workers; and she hadn't been long in Fenhall before she was making herself felt. She got herself a place on the Parish Council, the Mothers' Union, the School Managers; and after she had been in the village for about four years she was elected President of the Women's Institute. As soon as she got to that position she began a drive to tidy up the village and to persuade it to enter the Best Kept Village Competition that was being organised in the county.

When Acky heard this he said: 'What's that owd man-woman a-doing on now? She's not been in the village five minutes afore she mun be gitting everybody organised – a-toeing the line like she's the schoolmistress and us togither is a lot o' kids. What's wrong with the place? Fenhall's one o' the best lil' owd villages in Suffolk. What she want cod-wallopin' about to tarn it upside down for to win some owd tin shield? Did you hear she got 'em to pull down thet owd barn just on the road at the corner o' Mr Tomlin's meadow? The owd place weren't much to look at; but it would have sarved right well for some'un to keep his pigs in!'

But Sarah was not altogether with him in this. As a member of the

233

Women's Institute her ears had been opened to the glories that would come to Fenhall if the village would only pull itself together and spruce itself up.

'It is,' Mrs Horringer had said, sounding a fighting note that had rarely been heard in the parish hall, 'One of the prettiest villages in the county. It only wants us to straighten its bonnet and trim the fravelings off its frock, if I may say so.'

So while Acky muttered and grumbled about the things they were doing to the village, Sarah sat at the other side of the hearth and lectured him:

'You're a-getting set in your ways, Acky Flatt. You're afraid of anything new. That's the trouble with you! You want us all in Fenhall to go no faster then an owd hodmedod. You want to keep up with the times like the President say; we want to put the village on the map.'

'Ha! Now you're talking, gel. You're a-talking some sense. I *am* right afeered of anything new when it's like thet President o' yourn. I'm so afeered I'd run a mile along the Ditton road if I see her a-coming. As for the village, it's a rare owd pity we didn't put a bar up on the gate afore this Mrs Horringer got here in the first place.'

But Acky used something else beside talk, as everyone knew when the tidying-up campaign began in earnest. For though his cottage was right on the edge of the heath, almost on the parish boundary, the enclosure at the side and the back of it – his *owd yard*, as Acky called it – was so much in need of tidying up it would almost be a waste of time for the village to enter the competition unless Acky did something about it. Not that he was a bad gardener: indeed, Akerman Flatt was one of the best gardeners in the parish. But he was also one of the best hoarders. He could not bear to part with anything that was likely to be of remote use to him about the house or his small piece of land: logs of wood, odd scraps of furniture, an old bicycle, a pair of cartwheels, the skeleton of an old cart, some old-fashioned forms turned out of the village school, an old washing machine he'd once picked up at a sale – so that the side of his yard was filled with what looked like the flotsam of a deserted village. Acky's yard was so spectacular that it had become famous in the neighbourhood.

Therefore Mrs Horringer could see it was no use her trying to put pressure on him to clear up his yard. She's been in the village long enough to know that. Her only hope was to get at him through his wife. For the next few weeks Sarah had more than her share of attention at Institute meetings; and she was soon won round to the organisers' way of thinking. And she promised to talk again to her husband. Sarah started her campaign; and at first Acky turned a broad back to it all; but after she had missed giving him a meal or two he saw he would have to put up at least a show of doing what she wanted him to. He said he'd tidy up his yard, pack most of the odds and ends away; and then set a row of early peas right across the garden to screen the patched-up shed from the roadway. He even helped to straighten up the old boundary stone – which was a few yards on the Ditton side of his cottage and had tilted over perilously. So far so good; Mrs Horringer was very pleased and congratulated Sarah at the next meeting of the Institute; and Sarah beamed like a midday sun. But Mrs Horringer added:

'There's still the matter of the bedsteads in the fence, Mrs Flatt. If you can get your husband to take those out and hide them somewhere, I do believe we have a good chance of winning this Shield.'

But Acky had already refused to do anything about the bedsteads, and Sarah had given up trying to persuade him. For he had told her in a voice she recognised as carrying the last words on the subject:

'Don't you ask me to rip those owd bedsteads out ma' fence, gel. I think a lot on 'em, and you know it! I wouldn't shift 'em for a bus-load o' Presidents. Whoi! There's half the history o' the Flatt family in them bedsteads. We can't use 'em lightly, gel. We got to treat 'em with some respect. There's the one with the painted picture on it: that's the one ma Uncle Ephraim laid on for five year with his artheritis, afore he went to a better place. Then there's the one with the brass knobs. That's ma grandfather's wedding bed; and the plain solid one – that's the one I was born on, gel; and if the owd slats hadn't kinda deciduated we'd be using on it now.'

The bedsteads, therefore, stayed in the fence; and the Women's Institute hoped that by the time of the judging of the competition there would be enough growth in the hedge to cover up at least some of its worst features. The hope was short-lived; for as time went on, it became clear that the brass and the curlecues on Acky's bedsteads were not going to be subdued even by the generous growth of a particularly lavish June – and June was the month of judging.

No one knew which day the judges would be coming out; and there were so many villages to be visited, no one could begin to guess. The Women's Institute organised their annual June outing to the seaside, as usual, without any misgivings. They would leave things as tidy as they could, and if the judges arrived on the day they were away it would make no difference.

But no one really believed the judges would come out on the 22nd June, the fine day the Institute chose for their outing. As soon as the two buses had left with the women, all marshalled by Mrs Horringer and her committee, Acky took his pipe and sat on the seat at the front of his cottage.

'It's suthen to have a bit o' peace,' he said to himself. 'No women a-puttering about the place. It will do some on 'em good to set up there on the beach and put up with a bit o' real competition from the seagulls.'

Yet by the time he had smoked a couple of pipes, had a look at his row of peas and got himself a bite to eat, Acky found the morning was tending to drag. So he decided to get out his bike and pedal over to Fordham. He wanted to see Fred Partridge about a young pig he had for sale; and maybe he'd call at the Ditton *Rose* on the way back for a pint and a bit of news.

The weather, after a chill start, got much warmer; and Acky, finding cycling thirsty work, changed his mind and went straight to the *Rose* for refreshment. The kitchen bar of the pub was half full of Ditton men who had called in for a drink, but chiefly to find out what was happening in the village that morning. Two strangers, they said, were walking about looking at Ditton as if they were figuring to buy it. Acky came in just as the landlord was clearing up the mystery:

'Don't you know! They're two o' the judges for the Best Trimmed Village Competition. They're coming back here for something to eat before they do the next village, Fenhall most likely.'

'Ooh, ah! I reckon you hit it Parcy. I been dinning my hid to recollect where I see that bloke in the overcoat afore.'

'What he want an owd duffel-coat on in this weather? It ain't cold.'

'Oh, that's to show he's a judge. Don't you understand? The other one has growed himself a beard for the same parpose.'

Acky stood listening quietly sipping his pint. But then they turned to him and began to chip him about his village entering for the Shield. He was a bit angry; all that was nothing to do with him. He'd heard enough about this Shield to last him a lifetime. And why did they want to bring it up on the one day there was a chance of a bit o' peace? Naturally, Acky didn't show he was annoyed: he just sat and looked as impassive as usual. But when Percy Pearce the landlord said to him with a sly wink at the others:

'I reckon, Acky, with that old yard and that fence o' yours, you're about the best support Ditton could have in this competition. You certainly put Fenhall right out o' the running.'

Acky now came a little way out of his shell:

'All right, Percy,' he said. 'You allus know which side o' the hedge the owd hin is a-going to lay the egg. But I tell you one thing: Ditton isn't going to win this Shield.' There was a silence after he'd said this, long enough for Acky to wonder what had made him open his mouth at all.

'Who is then?' the landlord asked.

'Whoi, Fenhall's going to win it!'

There was a loud cackle of laughter with everyone except Acky joining in. Acky took an old tin tobacco box out of his pocket, and when the laughter had died down he placed it on the counter with a bang:

'I'll take anybody for an even pound that Fenhall will win the competition!'

Four of the Ditton men came forward immediately and handed over their notes to the landlord, while Acky carefully counted four out of his tin box to cover them.

When Acky was back on the road a few minutes later he said to himself: 'Blast 'em all! What made me get mixed up in that? Now I got to do suthen right quick afore the judges have finished their dinner.' But a plan formed itself as he cycled quickly along the road back to Fenhall. As soon as he came to his cottage he propped his bike against the gate and hurried inside. A minute or two later he came out with a pick and a shovel. Acky worked hard for an hour, keeping a sharp eye on the road he had just travelled. Fortunately no traffic of any account passed, and no one saw what he was doing. But after he had finished his job he saw a car away in the distance approaching from the Ditton direction. He took his tools inside, and hid behind the thickest part of his fence. The car slowed up and the two judges got out.

'Ah, here's the boundary stone. Fine! Someone has even cleaned it up!'

'I wonder which village did that: Ditton or Fenhall?' asked the judge with the beard. 'But look at this fence! Atrocious! and the bedsteads! Some awkward customer won't cooperate, evidently. Too bad; but we'll have to put it down against them – and pretty heavily at that.'

As soon as the judges had gone, Acky went indoors, washed his hands and lay down on his bed to recover from his exertions.

That evening he happened to be crossing the Knoll up in the village just as the Institute coaches returned from the outing. As the women got out

Acky told them, as if he'd been one of the organisers:

'We been judged, ladies! We been judged; and I fare to think we ha'n't been found a-wanting.'

Of course the women were angry, remembering Acky's obstinacy; and Sarah showed him the length of her tongue as they walked across the heath to their cottage. But Acky said mildly: 'Don't jaw me, gel. Write it down on a postcard and I can read it in the marning.'

That night, however, he left his bed in the small hours while Sarah, who was still half asleep, grumbled about his taking up his old poaching ways again. He went downstairs and, taking his pick and shovel, quietly returned the boundary stone to its rightful place near his cottage, muttering to himself as he did so: 'It's better thar. I reckon I couldn't sleep in Ditton one night without getting a horrible nightmare!'

About a month later Fenhall heard the surprising but heartening news that they had won the Shield in the county Best Kept Village Competition. As soon as the news came through Acky received a visit from the President. She was loud in her thanks for the way he had cooperated, even though – as she said – she had no idea how he'd cleaned his place so quickly at the last moment. But after listening to her benevolently Acky told her, his head on one side and his words as smooth in his mouth as butter:

'You see ma'am, when I come to it I couldn't let the village down. I'm a kinda rough diamond as you moight say; and I got a soft heart – as my Sarah will tell you. And there's nawthen I wouldn't do for Fenhall. But if you'll excuse me now, ma'am, I now got to take a turn over to Ditton. They mun be some disappointed over thar; and I reckon it would be right neighbourly to consolate with them togither for an hour or two.'

\* \* \* \* \*

**Penelope Lively** is the author of many prize-winning novels and collections of short stories. She was shortlisted for the Booker Prize in 1977 for *The Road To Lichfield* and again in 1984 for *According To Mark* before winning it with *Moon Tiger* (1987). This widely acclaimed novel, like her autobiographical memoir *Oleander, Jacaranda*, draws on her childhood in Egypt during the war. Penelope Lively is also a popular children's author and has won both the Carnegie Medal and the Whitbread Award. Although transposed from Kent to Suffolk *A Clean Death,* is Liveley's most autobiographical piece of fiction. It appears in the omnibus edition of her short stories *Pack of Cards* (1986).

# A Clean Death
## PENELOPE LIVELY

The train windows were still painted midnight blue for the black-out. Here and there, people had scraped at the paint, making channels and circles of bare glass behind which fled the darkening landscape. They had left King's Cross at four, in twilight, would be home, Aunt Frances said, by seven at the latest. Do, she had announced at the ticket office, assembling her welter of Christmas shopping – parcels and boxes from Harrods, Fortnum's, Marshall and Snelgrove – do call me Frances, just, I don't really like aunt, and Clive would like to be Clive, I'm sure. And Carol, smiling sideways, not looking at her, had known she could not, would have to say 'you' now, for always, before ever picking her way round the problem. She huddled into her school coat, stiff with cold, her knees raw red between the top of her socks and hem of her skirt, and fingered again the ticket in her pocket, checked the brown suitcase in the rack, in which were her holiday clothes, her good tweed skirt and her two jerseys and the tartan wool dress bought today by Aunt Frances – Frances – with money sent by her father from India. The money had meant complicated arrangements of cheques and deposit accounts and Frances, irritated, queueing at the bank, glancing at her watch. Money from the bank in Calcutta, hot and crowded, rupees not pounds and shillings. Don't think of it, she told herself, the tears pressing again behind her eyelids, don't think of India. But it came, as it never ceased to do, clamorous with smells and sounds and what-used-to-be, and she sat, miserable with longing, watching the lights of Suffolk villages twinkle through the tattered black-out paint.

Frances in her corner, was wedged beside a young soldier with hair so short his head seemed almost shaven, and battledress that smelled of damp and sweat; she had flinched away from him, Carol could see, turning to the window, reading her London Library book. She looked up, caught Carol's eye, and said, 'Ipswich in another few minutes now – lovely thought!'

239

I've put you in the spare room, she had said earlier, not in with Marian, I thought you might rather be on your own, and Carol, who had feared to be classified with her cousins, as child, had been relieved. She did not know how to be with children, what to say, they made her feel awkward, inadequate. But I don't know how to be with grown-ups either, she thought, there is no one I talk to, I am quite by myself, it is as though I was some kind of thing there is only one of. At school she was not unpopular, but had no friends; she never walked with her arm round someone else's waist, or gathered over the tepid radiator in the form room, warming her hands and whispering. The other girls alarmed her; they were so worldly-wise; so cushioned by their confidence in how things were done, how to talk and act and respond. The school bewildered her, with the jungle of its customs and taboos. She remained uninitiated, an outsider, doing her best to use the right language, show the right interests, have the right emotions. She collected, as the others did, photographs of the royal family cut from newspapers; she stared at the battered fashion magazines passed from hand to hand, exhaustively discussed and analysed. At night, she lay silent in bed, hearing their whispers of cinemas and London musicals, and India created and re-created itself in the darkness, and she could hardly bear it. It set her apart from them, she knew; it was not quite the thing, to have been born in another country. It was not good to be different. She knew it, and felt inadequate; there was nothing she could do about it, nothing could make her one of them. Sometimes, not often, they asked her about India, but their curiosity was brief, it would evaporate within minutes. She would be talking – of the house, the garden, the heat, the people – and they would be gone, their attention switched, back with their own concerns. The other thing they never mentioned. The girl who had shown her round, her first day – one of the prefects – had said, 'Bad luck about your mother, Carol,' and she had known that it was unmentionable, death you did not talk about, like God, or love.

She had learned how she ought to be, what was expected, and was quietly pleased that she had learned so much. She made fewer mistakes now, was more acceptable. She was managing.

The train slid to a stop. Frances opened the door, and steam oozed up between carriage and platform, cold air gushing in, and country voices, voices all related to one another, Carol could hear. Accents. There was a girl at school who had an accent; that was not good either, she too was apart. Her parents did not pay, it was said, she had the Scholarship.

Listening, in streets, on buses, Carol felt dizzied, sometimes, by voices: different, the same, connected. Like the babel of tongues in an Indian bazaar. You have to know who you are, she thought, who other people are, or it is impossible, you do everything wrong. Often I do not know who I am.

They got out, festooned with parcels. If you could take the children's stocking presents, Frances said, and Nigel's train-set, I can manage the Fortnum's bag and the curtain stuff. And Clive will get the cases, no hope of a porter of course, not these days.

Clive had come up almost at once, out of the darkness, and Carol thought wildly: do I kiss him or not, I can't remember, is it all relations, or not men ones? But he solved the problem himself by holding out a hand, and they shook awkwardly, and yes, she said, I had a good term, and yes, it is lovely to think it's nearly Christmas.

In the car, bumping through the East Anglian night, Frances recounted the day. London was awful, she said, I can't tell you, the shops so crowded, such a struggle on the buses, but I got everything, nearly everything, there was a problem with John's school things, they hadn't the games socks in yet . . . She sounded tired but triumphant, like a huntsman at the end of the day, the job done. The road shone wet black in the car headlights and the fields that slid by were ribbed with snow; it was bitterly cold. A frost tonight, Clive said, Marian's cold seems a bit better – oh, and Mrs Binns left a pie in the oven for supper, she said give it another half hour or so, when you get back.

They were close, easy, in their concerns, the running of their lives. Once or twice, remembering, they passed questions to her, or comments, over the back of their seats. Is it this summer you do School Cert., Carol, or next? This village is called Kersey, the church is so pretty, you'll have to walk over one day and have a look.

They arrived, and the house seemed to burst, spilling out into the night like a ripe fruit; light, voices, the small shapes of children running and leaping beside the car. Dogs barking. Wireless music. The country night lay black and still and freezing all around, and here was this confident, unassailable place, waiting. The children bounced and shrieked. Did you find the balloons? they cried, and have you got my ribbon, and are there any sweets? Mummy! they shrieked, Mummy! And Frances was hugging and recounting and saying, oh, and here's Carol, say hello to Carol.

Hello, they said, and then their voices were back on that note of excitement and demand, and everyone was going into the house, shutting

241

out the darkness – the endless snowy fields, the black roads.

She woke early in the morning, perished with cold. She had got up in the night to put on her underclothes beneath her pyjamas, and then her jersey on top, and still had lain frozen in the bed, curled knees to chest, the rest of the bed an icy pond. She listened to the noises of the house expand around her: the children's scampering feet, their voices crooning to cats or dogs, the rattle of a boiler being filled, Frances and Clive talking in the bedroom. It was an old, wooden house; it rang and echoed. Presently she got up and went to the bathroom that Frances had said she should share with the children. It smelled of flannels and damp and toothpaste; there was a full pottie in the corner. She stripped to the waist, as you had to do at school, and washed under her arms, up her neck, over the growing breasts that she felt must be so obvious, that slopped and bounced under her jerseys.

She dressed and went downstairs. On the bottom step there was a dog, a great golden lion-headed thing, lying right across it. She stood there, not knowing what to do, and it did not move, but looked at her and away again. And then one of the children – Nigel, the youngest – came from some room and saw her and said, 'Are you frightened of her?' And before she could answer he had gone running into the kitchen and she could hear him shout, 'Daddy! She's frightened of Tosca – Carol's frightened of Tosca.'

She could hear them laughing. Frances said, 'I expect she's not used to dogs, darling.' She came out and tugged at the dog's collar, still laughing, saying what a stupid, soft old thing she was, wouldn't hurt a fly, you musn't mind her. And Carol could think of no reply: she was not afraid of dogs, liked them, but in India a dog may be rabid, you do not go near a strange dog, never. It was instinctive, now, the hesitation, a conditioned response, just as at night, always, she thought, for the rest of her life, she would feel unsafe without the shrouding security of a mosquito net.

Clive was in the kitchen, nursing a cat. He stroked and tickled it, talking baby-language to it so that Carol was both embarrassed and fascinated. There was something wrong, apparently, it was ill. 'Poor Mr Patch,' crooned Clive. 'Poor pussy. Poor patchums,' and the children gathered round soft with sympathy, offering it tit-bits. 'We are a terrible animal family, I'm afraid, Carol,' said Frances, frying bacon. 'Everybody is mad about animals. The children will show you the pony after breakfast.'

She trailed with the children, in a wind that cut through her mack, clutched her bare knees, was shown the garden and its secret places, the hens, the rabbit hutches, the pony, the orchard. And then they became involved in some game of their own and she came back into the house alone and stood at a loss in the kitchen, where Frances mixed things and talked to a woman washing up at the sink.

'This is Carol, Mrs Binns,' she said. 'My niece, you know.' And Carol felt herself appraised, not unkindly, not critically, just with the shrewdness of a person who liked to see what was what, how things were.

'You'll be much of an age with my Tom, I should imagine,' said Mrs Binns. 'Fourteen he was, in October. We'll have to get you together. He's at a loose end, in the holidays, Tom, there's no one much his age, not nearer than the village.'

At school there were girls who had, or who were rumoured to have, boyfriends. The reputation gave them an aura, of daring but also of distinction; they too were set apart, but in a desirable way. They had moved on a little, on and up. Carol knew no boys, had not, she thought, spoken to one since long ago, since nursery days on another continent. She stared at Mrs Binns in alarm.

'Mmmn,' said Frances. 'What a good idea,' and Carol, puzzled now, saw that for some reason it was not. But Mrs Binns, saying, 'Well, you must look in at the cottage, dear, your auntie'll tell you where it is,' had turned now to the table and taken up the pink and pimpled carcase of a chicken. 'I'll do this for you, Mrs Seaton, shall I?'

Frances looked at the chicken with distaste. 'Yes, please, if you would. A beastly job. I'd be sunk without you, I really would.'

Mrs Binns laughed. She stood at the sink, rummaging with deft, knowledgeable hands in the chicken's insides. 'It's a matter of what you're used to. I did my first bird when I was – oh, younger than Carol here.' Appalling things slid from within the chicken and lay on the draining-board. Frances, Carol saw, had turned firmly away, busy with her pie-dish. Carol said, 'In India you buy chickens live. They hang them up by their feet in the bazaar, in bunches.'

'How absolutely horrid!' Frances exclaimed; her voice was tense with emotion. Mrs Binns, halted in her work, looked up. Frances went on, vehemently, 'That is what is so awful about those places – they are so foul to animals. One really cannot stand it. I remember going to Morocco, before the war, and it simply spoiled the holiday, the way they treat the donkeys and things. You had to walk about trying not to notice – it was wretched, we were so glad to come home.'

Mrs Binns said in neutral tones, 'It's not nice to see, cruelty to animals.'

She swilled the chicken out under the tap and put it on a plate. 'His dad give Tom a gun for his birthday, for rabbiting, but he told him he's to use it properly, no maiming things, he's to see there's a clean death.'

Frances's face was set in disapproval. 'Mmmn, Isn't fourteen a bit young for a gun?'

Mrs Binns was packing the chicken with stuffing now. Crumbs of it fell from her fingers and lay on the table, smelling of herbs, of summer. 'Rabbits are terrible round us now – had all my cabbage. He's the makings of a good steady hand, Bob says – Tom has. Three he got, last week.'

'Mmmn,' said Frances again. She got up, putting away flour and fat. 'Could you do the bedrooms next Mrs Binns, and then I think the dining-room windows need a going over.'

At lunch, Frances and Clive talked of Mrs Binns. Clive said that she was a card, quite a character, and tales were recounted, remarks that Mrs Binns had made, her opinions, her responses. They were told with affection, with indulgence – much, Carol noted, as the children were spoken of in their absence. 'But,' said Frances. 'I cannot approve of that boy being given a gun. They *will* start them off slaughtering things so early, people like that, I hate it.'

Marian said in stricken tones, 'Does he kill rabbits, Tom? Oh, *poor* rabbits . . . Mummy, can't you tell him not to?'

'No, I can't, darling, it's not up to me. There, don't think about it – I don't expect he does it much. Finish up your sausage and then you can get down.'

One girl at school got letters from her boyfriend. It was known, and envied. She took them away and read them alone, in the cloakroom, and later could be seen, pink-faced and giggling, poring over selected passages with her best friend. Carol said, staring at the bowl of frost-nipped chrysanthemums in the middle of the table, 'Mrs Binns said I could go over to her cottage sometime.'

There was a silence. Clive picked up the cat and blew softly into its fur, murmuring to it. 'Poor Mr Patch,' he mumbled. 'How are your insides today? – how's your poor tummy?'

'Yes,' said Frances. 'Well, just as you like, Carol.' She began to clear the table. 'I think a walk this afternoon, to the village and back, I need some things from the post office, anyway.'

The landscape was black and white under huge white skies – black ploughlands striped with white runnels of snow, criss-crossed with the dark lines of hedges, trimmed with the stiff shapes of trees. They walked

244

along a road bordered by fawn-coloured rushes and grasses, each one starred and bearded with frost; icy wind poured through the skeletal hedges; there was a chain of crisp puddles along the uneven surface. The children skittered ahead, sliding on the ice, darting off into the fields on brief excursions. Clive and Frances walked arm in arm, Carol a few paces behind. Their talk and occasional laughter came back to her in irrelevant, incomprehensible snatches. I am so cold, she thought, colder than I have ever been, colder even than I am at school, will I ever be warm, how do people get warm, ever, in their lives? In India, in childhood, she had been too hot; always, one was sticky with sweat, looking for a place out of the sun. I cannot remember that now, she thought, I have no idea, really, how it was, it is like something in a book, something that happened to someone else. The gap had lengthened between her and the others; Frances, looking back over her shoulder, called, 'Not far now – we shall have to get you used to walking, Carol.'

At the house, in Frances's sitting room, on the desk, there was a photograph of her and her brother, Carol's father, in youth. Around seventeen or eighteen. It was a bad photograph, muzzy, and Carol had not at first recognised the faces. Then, her father's familiar features had somehow emerged, but displaced and distorted; the boy in the photograph was him, and yet not him. She thought of this, and of herself; her hands, thrust into the pockets of her school coat, were rigid with cold; it was three o'clock in the afternoon, there was no reason, it seemed to her, why this day should not go on for ever. She stumped behind Frances and Clive, through the sphere of that silent, suspended landscape; it is so lovely here in summer, Frances had said, quite perfect, you must come in August, in the holidays.

At nights, at school, the other girls planned and recalled; the long thin room in which she slept with eight others was filled with disembodied voices, whispering in the dark of holidays past and holidays to come, of what they had done and what they would do. The limbo of the term was put away; they roamed into other times, other places. And Carol lay silent; to roam, for her, had too many dangers. Recollection must be checked; that way lay disaster. And the other way? She had nothing there, either, to offer, no plans or expectations.

The children came running from a field, solemn-faced and important, with a dead bird they had found, a lapwing, bright-plumaged and uncorrupt, its eyes closed by filmy lids. Marian was on the brink of tears. Her father took the bird and they huddled round him, quiet and comforted, as he dug a grave, lined it with leaves, buried the body, marked the place with a ring of berries collected from the hedges. 'I don't expect it *felt* anything, Mummy, did it?' begged Marian. 'It didn't *hurt* it, did it?' And Frances said, 'No, darling, it would be just like going to sleep, it would hardly know anything about it.'

In the village, Frances bought things in the warm, cluttered post office that smelled of soap, matches and bacon; the children fingered and fidgeted, their voices shrill and confident. 'This is my niece Carol,' Frances explained, 'who is here for the Christmas holidays.' And the shop lady, petting the children, giving them each a toffee from a personal store behind the till, hesitated, the open tin in her hand, as also did Carol hesitate; we neither of us know, she thought in despair, what I am, if I am a child or not. The shop lady reached a decision, good or bad, and put the tin back on the shelf, unproffered.

On the way back, Marian pointed suddenly over the fields and said to Carol, 'That's Mrs Binns's cottage, down that track: they've got chickens and a dog called Toby.'

Carol stared over a grass field, patched with unmelted snow; smoke filtered from a chimney, barely darker than the sky; washing hung limp on a line in stiff geometric shapes of sheets, towels, shirts with outstretched arms.

On Christmas morning she lay in bed hearing the children open their stockings in their parents' room across the corridor; their high-pitched voices alternated with their parents' deeper ones like a series of musical responses, statement and commentary. She heard their feet pattering on the bare boards, the dogs barking in excitement; the animals too had Christmas presents – bones wrapped up in scarlet crêpe paper, beribboned rubber mice. The day proceeded through a series of ceremonies and rituals: after breakfast we have presents under the tree, before church we telephone grandmother, in the afternoon we walk to Clee Hill. Frances said, 'I forgot to tell you, Carol – tomorrow our old friends the Laidlaws are coming. Mark is fifteen so he will be someone for you, I thought – it is dull for you, being always with the younger ones.'

The children did not like her, she knew. At first they had been shy, the small boys arch, trying to appeal as they would appeal to a grown-up. But they saw her now for what she was, neither fish nor fowl, not exempt like them from adult obligations, but without adult privileges either. Sharp-eyed, they noted her position as a classless person, without position, and exploited their own the more; if she would not join in their games when they wanted her to they complained to Frances, and Carol felt her aunt's resentment, unstated but none the less evident. I have a hundred things to do, her silent back said, the least you could do is help to amuse them for a while. They danced round Carol, more agile in every way; they made her feel lumpish of mind and in body.

The prospect of Mark filled her with apprehension. He is at Marlborough, said Frances, he is awfully clever, he has such nice manners, we have always liked him so much.

They came, the Laidlaws; there were kisses and handshakes and the house was filled with talk, with people at ease with one another. Mark, Carol furtively noted, had longish hair that flopped over one eye and was dressed as a man – tweed jacket, grey flannels, grown-up tie. He sat next to Frances at lunch and talked with what Carol saw to be charming attention, listening when listening should be done, taking the initiative when that was appropriate. After lunch he played with the children – an absurd game of crawling on the floor, romping, and he was in no way diminished by it, it made him seem more grown-up, not less so. And Frances beamed upon him.

He had said to Carol, 'Where do you go to school?' She had replied to this. He had asked her how many School Cert. subjects she was doing and she replied to that too. And then there had been a silence, she had searched wildly for something to fill it, and seen that he wanted to get away from her, to get back to the others, that she did not interest him. 'It must have been awfully exciting, growing up in India,' he said. 'What was it like?' and India swirled in her head, a kaleidoscope of sights and sounds and responses, and there was nothing she could say. 'Yes,' she stammered. 'It was . . . I mean . . . Yes, I . . . ', and felt Frances's gaze upon her, observing, regretting. 'Have you ever seen Gandhi?' he asked, and she shook her head.

Later in the evening, Frances said, 'The Laidlaws are having a small party for Mark, at the New Year, but of course you will be gone by then, Carol – they were so sorry.'

It snowed in the night. She drew her curtains and saw the landscape powdered over, not deeply, but shrouded as it were, in a state of suspension once again, motionless. The children, outside, were rushing about trying to scoop up enough for snowballs or snowmen; they came in wet and querulous, their hands scarlet with cold. Their exhilaration disintegrated into tears and fretfulness; Frances was irritable. Later, she had letters to write, and the children wanted to go to the village, to buy sweets. Carol can take us, they cried, and Frances, relieved, said yes, of course, Carol can take you – wrap up well; don't let them run on the road, Carol.

They met him on the way back. She was walking behind the children, who were quiet now, amiable, tamed by chocolate. He came down the track from the cottage, the gun crooked over his arm, and they arrived together precisely at the gate. Marian said, 'Hello, Tom.'

He nodded, 'Hello.' And then he looked at Carol and smiled, and quite easily, without her eyes sliding away to left or right, without a problem, she smiled back. He said, 'Mum told me you were stopping with your auntie.'

The children wanted to see the gun. But their curiosity was tinged, even at this remove, with Frances's disapproval. In silence they watched him demonstrate its workings; his thin fingers clicked this and pressed that, ran over the sleek metal, caressed the polished butt. He was immensely proud of it; in his light voice, not yet broken, a boy's voice, but with its sudden odd lurches into manhood, he described the make and model. It was not a toy, it was real, serious, it marked him. It told him what he was. 'My dad gave it me for my birthday. My fourteenth. He reckoned you can learn to use a gun, then, when you're fourteen, it's time.'

The children were restive, moving away. Come on, they said, let's go, it's cold, let's go home.

Tom turned to Carol. 'I'll be going out tomorrow morning, shooting. Early, when it's getting light. Sevenish. You could come if you like.'

She said, 'Yes, please,' before she could stop to think. 'Right,' he said. 'Come by the cottage then, and we'll go.'

She walked back to the house amazed; things like this did not happen, it was astonishing, she could hardly believe it.

It was in the cold, wakeful reaches of the night that it struck her she should have told Frances, asked Frances. But now it was too late, Frances was asleep: at seven – before seven – she would not be about. And suppose she said no, or even just implied no? I have to go, Carol thought, I must go, it is the only thing that has ever happened to me.

She woke again long before dawn and lay looking at her watch every few minutes. When it said half past six she got up, making as little noise as possible, and dressed in all her warmest things. But she was warm already, for the first time in days, weeks, it seemed, and when she crept down the stairs, and opened the back door the air outside was tinged with mildness, she thought. The wind that met her face was not so keen, and the snow, in the drive, had melted. Only in the lee of the hedges it lay still in thickish drifts.

It was almost dark. The sky was streaked with light in the east; dark clouds lay like great fish along the horizon. She walked down the road and there was no one else in the world, except her; she was alone, and it was quite all right, she felt confident, at ease with things, she walked briskly with her hands in her pockets and there was beauty in the landscape that wheeled around her, she could see that. It was still and quiet, clenched in its winter state, but there was a flush of reddish brown on the plough, where the snow had melted, and the bare shapes of the trees on the skyline were of amazing delicacy, they held the suggestion of other times, the ripeness to come, summer.

She hesitated outside the cottage door; there was an easy murmuring of voices from inside, and the chink of crockery, and smells of toast and something frying. And then a man came out, at that moment, in old jacket and muffler, his trousers clipped ready for a bicycle – Tom's father; presumably – and told her to go in, Tom wouldn't be a moment.

Mrs Binns gave her a cup of tea, but she could not eat the food offered; she felt in her stomach all the instability of before a journey, before an event. But it was good, it was the best thing she had known, beyond things which must not be remembered, things from other times. Tom said little; he attended to the gun with oil and a rag and a stick, and when he had done he got up and said, 'We'll be off now, Mum,' and Carol rose too, in a state still of amazement. She felt quite comfortable, quite in place. I have a friend, she thought, and could hardly believe it.

He led her over the fields, up a shallow hillside. Out of the cottage, he became talkative. He told her about the ways of rabbits, and how you must go after them downwind, towards their burrows, towards the slope where he knew they would come out to graze around now. He had shot two, he said, the week before, and Carol said, no, three your mother said, and he corrected her, carefully – two it was, one I missed, I told Mum, she got it wrong. I'm not good with sighting, he said, seriously, not yet, and I've got a shake in my wrist, I'll have to work on that, and she nodded, intent, and stared at his wrists. They were bony wrists, white-knobbed, sticking out from the frayed sleeve of his too-short jersey. His hair was cut short, almost cropped, like the soldier in the London train. He spoke with the accent of the place, this place to which he belonged, where he had been born, where his parents had been born; sometimes she could not quite follow what he said. She thought confusedly of this, as they climbed the hill, the ground wet and springy under their feet; of her own speech, which was quite different, and of the place where she had been born, none of whose many tongues she spoke. Once, climbing a gate, he gave her the gun to hold for a moment; she felt the sting of the cold metal on her hands, and cradled it gingerly, with reverence.

They reached the side of the field where, he said, the rabbits would come. It ran downhill from a small copse, and she could see the brown markings of burrows at the top. He edged cautiously along the ditch until he came to a place in long grass where they could lie and wait. 'They might have heard us,' he said. 'We'll have to sit tight a bit, and they'll come out again.'

They lay flank to flank on the wet grass. She could feel its damp and cold creep through to her skin, and the faint warmth of his body beside hers. Their breath steamed. Occasionally they whispered a little; it was better, though, he said, to stay quiet. He seemed to expect nothing of her; if she had not complied, if she had infringed the rules in any way, he did not let her know. He let her hold the gun again, and she peered down the long barrel into the field and saw, suspended cinematically beyond it, the cropped turf with its dark enigmatic holes and scrapings of rich earth and pockets of snow. He said, 'They're a long time about it, usually they come out quicker than this, once you've sat quiet a bit,' and she could feel the tension in him; the rabbits mattered, they were the most important thing in his life just now. She said suddenly, amazed at her own temerity, 'What is it like, killing something, do you like it?' And turning to look at him, saw with shock that a slow tide of of colour had crept up his face.

'I don't like them dying,' he said, mumbling with his head to the ground, so that she could hardly hear. 'I hate that. The first time I came out with my dad, I felt sick, I didn't want to do it. I couldn't say, not to him. He gave me the gun, see, for my own. Now it's all right. They die quick, it's over just like that.' He looked at her, his face still red. 'It's not for the killing, it's not for that.'

She nodded. There wasn't anything to say. And then suddenly he touched her arm, pressed his fingers down on her coat, and she looked out towards the field and there was movement on the turf, something brown shifting against the green – two, three of them. One sat up, nosing the wind, and she saw its pricked ears, and, as it turned, the white scut.

He lifted the gun, aimed; she was clenched in excitement, breathless. And then he pressed the trigger, and the noise was startling, louder than ever she had imagined, but in the second before, in a fraction of a second,

250

something had happened out there and the rabbits had bolted, homed back on their burrows, gone. The field was empty.

She said, 'Oh . . .' He sat up, breaking the gun apart angrily, unloading. 'Won't they come out again?'

He shook his head. 'Not for hours, maybe. That's done it, that has. Something scared them.' His hands were shaking, she could see that, they had been shaking earlier too, when he lay still on the grass, aiming. Now he seemed almost relieved. 'Come on,' he said. 'Have to get back. Mum'll be wondering.'

They ran down the field; there was no longer any need to be quiet. At the gate he showed her how he could vault over it, and she, who was unathletic, who lumbered around hopelessly around the games pitch at school, found that she could do it also; there was no end, it seemed, to the surprises this day held. There are bits of me I know nothing about, she thought, I am not so clumsy after all, I can talk to people, I can feel part of something. The sky was crossed and recrossed by ragged flights of birds. 'What are they?' she asked. 'What kind of bird is that?' and he told her that those were rooks, and these on the plough, in the field, were lapwings, surprised at her ignorance but uncritical. 'Mum said you grew up somewhere else,' he said, 'somewhere foreign,' and she talked about India; she brought heat and dust and the sound of the place on to this wintry Suffolk field and it was painless, or almost so.

At the corner of the track to the cottage he asked her if she would like to come out again the next morning; she had half-expected this and yet not dared to hope. Such coincidence, in the normal way of things, of what you would like and what was available, did not happen. She said, 'Yes, please,' and thought it sounded childish, and blushed.

Back at the house, she was amazed to find it past breakfast-time, Frances clearing the table, the children staring as she came in at the kitchen door, Clive reading a letter. Frances sounded annoyed. '*There* you are, Carol, we were beginning to wonder, where have you been?'

She had prepared nothing, given no thought to this moment. She stood, silent with confusion, and then one of the children said, 'She's been shooting rabbits with Mrs Binns's Tom. We heard him ask her yesterday.'

Frances swept things off the table on to a tray. 'Oh, really. I can't imagine why you should want to, Carol, I must say.'

'Did he kill any rabbits?' said Marian.

Carol muttered, 'No.' She could feel her face scarlet; the day, and all that it held, died on Frances's kitchen floor; she felt dirty.

251

'Goody,' said Marian. 'Can I go out now?'

Clive had not spoken; he had put down his letter and was playing with the dog, gently pulling its ears, mumbling to it; Carol, catching his eye by accident, saw it go cold, excluding her. 'Well,' he said to the dog, 'walkies, is it? Walkies for a good girl?' The dog beamed and fawned and swished its feathered tail.

All that day was sourly flavoured with Frances's disapproval; nothing was said, but it hung in the air at lunchtime, in the afternoon, over tea. Mrs Binns did not come, for which Carol was grateful; there would have been references, Tom would have been mentioned, and that she could not endure.

In the afternoon there was a letter from her father, enclosed in one to Frances. She read it by the drawing-room fire, and it seemed to come not from another country but from another time; his familiar handwriting, speaking of the house, the garden, neighbours, referred to things that no longer were, they had perished long ago. 'Poor Tim,' said Frances, reading her own letter. 'He is so anxious to get home, pack things up out there. It must be trying for him, but it is not long now, he has booked his passage.' Carol read that the bulbuls had nested again in the bush outside the laundry, that the cannas were a lovely show this year, that the rains had come early; it was as though he were frozen in another age, her father, in an imagined world. She asked, in a sudden panic, 'Will he really be here this summer, here in England?' And Frances, preoccupied now with the demands of the children, of the hour, said that of course he would, he was bound to, the house was sold, the furniture to be packed and shipped. If you are writing to him, she went on, you had better put it in with mine, and save the stamp.

Lying awake, after everyone else had gone to bed, Carol knew that she would go with Tom in the morning. She had thought about it, on and off, all day; she felt grubby, condemned by Clive's cold eye, by the children's indignation. '*Poor* rabbits,' Marian said once. 'I think it's beastly. Horrid Tom,' and she had answered nothing, being without defence. Now, staring at the dim square of the window, she knew that she would go, had to go, whatever they thought, whatever happened. Guilt clutched her; she lay sleepless for most of the night.

He was waiting for her at the bottom of the track. 'Hello,' he said, 'I thought you weren't coming,' and his innocence compounded her guilt. She carried now the burden not only of what she was doing, but of the fact that he did not know what they were doing, did not know that what they did was wrong, despised by decent people.

They climbed the hill again. It was raining; the wind blew wet sheets into their faces and they walked with heads down, not talking much. At the gate Tom did not vault but climbed over; Carol noticed how thin his legs were, childishly thin, like his bony wrists. Walking behind him, she observed that his hair made a ducktail at the nape and that the cleft had the softness, the look of vulnerability that the back of a small boy's neck has. She saw, for a moment, the ghost of the child that he had recently been; Mark Laidlaw's stocky frame had suggested the man from whom he stood at one remove. She thought of her own body, which seemed always to scream out in conflict – the alien, uncontrollable breasts, the pudgy hands and face, the scar on her knee that remembered a fall when she was ten. Her body held her back; at the same time it dragged her inexorably onwards.

At the place where they had waited before, he gestured her down into the grass. They lay again side by side, staring through rain-studded greenery at the point in the field where something might happen. The time passed slowly; it stopped raining and a weak sun shone opalescent behind the clouds. Occasionally, they murmured to each other. 'Taking their time again,' he said. 'Hope I'll have better luck today.' And she nodded and murmured yes, hope so, and ssh! look, isn't that one? no, it's just a thistle, sorry. Something had lifted, things had eased once more, guilt had been put to flight; Frances, Clive and the children no longer hovered behind her shoulder. The crystal globes of water on the grass blades shivered with a thousand colours; the dried head of a summer flower held between delicate stalks a miniature of the landscape beyond – skyline trees, clouds; the sun on the back of her hand was a breath, a promise, of warmth.

And then, together, they saw it on the grass beside the burrow; a moment ago it had not been there and now suddenly there it was, quietly munching grass, bobbing away a yard or so, sitting up to sniff the wind.

He raised the gun, hesitated for what seemed far too long, fired.

The rabbit bucked into the air. Bucked, and at the same time screamed. The sound was hideous; it rang over the field, obscene in the quietness of the morning. She cried, 'You got it! You hit it!' and they jumped up together and ran across the grass.

And saw, together, at the same moment, that the rabbit was not dead. It lay threshing and writhing and as they came near it screamed again, humanly, like a hurt child, and they pulled up short and stood there in horror, a few yards off, staring. Blood welled from its ear; it writhed and twitched.

Tom was shaking. His voice was high-pitched, out of control, 'I got to do something. You got to kill them, when that happens, you got to finish them off.'

She said, 'Oh, I don't want to see!' and turned away, her hands over her eyes, but then turned back, moments later, and he was standing above the rabbit, white-faced, and the rabbit bleated again, and arched its back, and kicked. He said, 'I don't know what to do. I've seen my dad do it – you have to break their necks. I don't know how to do it.' He was distraught.

She covered her eyes again.

When she looked back he had the rabbit in his hands, and the rabbit was limp. Blood dripped from it. He put it on the ground and it lay still. He was shaking violently. He moved away a few paces and sat on the grass, turned from her, and she could see his whole body tremble. She felt sorry for him, and at the same time exasperated. She could not help him; they were quite separate now, it was as though they did not know each other; the whole fragile structure of confidence, the sense of being at ease with the world, had been destroyed with the rabbit. She saw Tom, wretched, and could think only: I am wretched, too, I hate myself, and what we have done, and what people must think of us for it.

He got up, without a word, and began to walk away down the field, and wordlessly she followed him. He carried the gun all anyhow, not with pride, cradled over his arm; it looked, now, disproportionately large, as though it had grown and he had shrunk.

At the road he turned to her. 'Don't say anything about what happened – not to my mum.'

She shook her head.

'Cheerio, then.'

'Goodbye.'

It was raining once more. She trudged towards the house; she was shrivelled with guilt. They did not know what had happened, could not know, but she felt that the very look of her announced the incident; she carried still, in her head, the rabbit's scream.

They were having breakfast. As she came into the kitchen silence fell and the children looked expectantly towards Frances.

Frances said, 'You'd better have something to eat, Carol'; her voice was not friendly. When Carol was sitting at the table, she went on, 'It would have been a good idea, you know, to mention that you were going out with Tom Binns again. Clive and I are responsible for you, while you are here.'

Carol stared at the table. 'I'm sorry,' she said.

Clive had not looked once at her. He kept his back half-turned. Now, he busied himself giving milk to the cat. He poured the creamy top from a bottle into a saucer and put it by the stove. 'There, Mr Patch,' he murmured. 'There. Come on then, puss.' The kitchen was filled with well-loved, well-tended animals.

'Did Tom kill a rabbit?' said Marian in her small, clear voice.

Scarlet-faced, Carol noted the bordered tablecloth: red flower, cluster of leaves, spray of berries, red flower again. 'Yes,' she muttered.

'Children,' said Frances. 'you can get down now and go up and do your teeth. Oh, and tidy your bedroom, please, Marian darling.'

They went. Clive said he thought he would just go now and do the hens and the pony before he went into Ipswich. He went.

Frances began to clear the table. The room was charged with feeling; once, she dropped a cup, and swore. Carol sat, the rabbit's scream still in her ears, behind and above the sounds of the children upstairs, of Frances running water at the sink, of the cat lapping milk.

Frances slapped plates on to the draining board and spoke again, her voice assured and tinged with indignation, 'What I cannot understand – what Clive and I cannot understand – is why you should *want* to. I daresay it has been a bit dull here for you given that the children are a good deal younger and I am frightfully busy what with little or no help these days, not like it was for people before the war, but we've tried to find things for you to do and had Mark Laidlaw over who I thought would be just right for you, so I simply cannot understand why . . .'

The room spun; Frances's voice roared. Carol wrung the tablecloth between her shaking fingers and burst out, 'He didn't mean to. Tom didn't mean to – he meant to do it like his father said, a clean death, not hurting it, and something went wrong, it wasn't. He felt awful about it. I don't think he'll go shooting again. *I* don't want to, not ever. I hated it. It was beastly, the rabbit being hurt like that.' She fought back tears.

Frances turned from the sink; she was staring now, in surprise, across the kitchen table. She said, 'What rabbit? What do you mean? I'm not talking about shooting rabbits, Carol, which is really neither here nor there, lots of people round here shoot rabbits and of course one wishes they wouldn't but there it is. I'm talking about why you should want to go off doing things with someone like Tom Binns, as though he were a friend or something, when surely you must realise that it really won't do. I don't know what Mrs Binns was thinking of, suggesting it, she is normally such a sensible woman.' She paused, and then went on, 'I know it has made things difficult for you, growing up out there in India, sometimes it is a bit confusing for you here, I daresay, but surely you must see that a boy like Tom Binns . . . well, it really doesn't do, you should know that, Carol.'

The rabbit's scream died away; in its place there came, all innocent and unaware, Tom's voice of yesterday, explaining the workings of the gun. She stared at her aunt in bewilderment and thought: I don't know what you are talking about, I knew I had done one thing and now you tell me I have done another. It came to her suddenly that there was no way, ever, that she could oblige everyone, could do both what was expected of her, and what her own discoveries of what she was would drive her to do; she would have to learn to endure the conflict, as her body endured the conflict of what she had been and what she was bound to be, like it or not.

\* \* \* \* \*

**Marilyn Tolhurst** was born in Ipswich and has spent most of her working life in East Anglia as a free-lance writer and editor. She is the author of many books, largely children's fiction and historical works for English Heritage. Her novel *The Stone Street* is set in Roman East Anglia. *Home Win* is one of a series of stories inspired by the region and its recent history.

# Home Win

## MARILYN TOLHURST

When asked, I always told people I came from East Anglia – an ancient kingdom a bit like Saxe-Coburg Gotha, with its own line of kings. Admittedly, the kings were called Wuffings, but bathos is a residential hazard, I find. I did not say I came from Suffolk; it sounded as if I was half-witted and chewed straw. Never, never did I own up to coming from Ipswich; I mean people have been known to laugh out loud, just at the name. I once heard someone on the radio say that certain place names were *intrinsically* funny, like Mablethorpe . . . like Wigan . . . like Ipswich.

My Dad, a foreigner, who got shunted into a siding there in 1945, and stayed, used to quote some wartime comic asking a railway porter: 'which switch is the right switch for Ipswich?' I have since wondered why it's funny, I mean Mablethorpe, yes, the place of the elderly aunt, Wigan, well, anything to do with wigs is funny, but Ipswich? Is it the witch bit, (old women on broomsticks) or the switch bit (electrical, bakelite probably) or just the combination of the ip and the switch (yippee, it's bakelite)?

I once discussed it with a friend from university who kept a straight face throughout and made comments about the conjunction of the 'ip' and the 'it' sounds, suggesting 'kip' and 'shit' (yeah, man, that's all they *do* in Ipswich). But when I told him I lived in Coprolite Street, he sank to the floor in a fit of snorting laughter. 'Coprolite,' he wheezed, when he could get the word out, 'that's dinosaur shit, isn't it?'

I knew that anyone with any gumption, any *ambition*, had to get away from a town like Ipswich. Cardinal Wolsey, the butcher's boy, came from Ipswich – as good a reason as any to build Hampton Court, I always thought. *I* left after grammar school, escaping to a London college, and after an initial phase of telling people that my father was a diplomat and I was brought up in Benghazi, I answered, when asked, that I came from East Anglia.

After college I worked in other places, Derby for instance, a name which is almost funny but not quite; Bristol, which was better, except for the rhyming slang, and then back in London again, which made me feel comfortably metropolitan and a long way from Coprolite Street. The boy was out of Ipswich, and, I felt confident, Ipswich was out of the boy. By then, I had made it a fair way up the corporate ladder and as a third tier manager I had a (smallish) house in Dulwich, a wife from the home counties and two kids at a smart school. It was time, of course, for fate to play its place-name joke. Head office was going to be relocated – to Ipswich. That was the reason I was standing on a platform at Ipswich Station, overnight bag in hand, depression creeping up on me like a sea mist. Tomorrow I was going to do a deal with the agents of a new office block.

I decided to walk to my hotel in town. I set off down Princes Street (which princes, I wondered, ever walked down here) and paused on the bridge over the River Gipping. *Gipping* for Christ's sake, where's the poetry, where's the Avon, in a name like that? It reminded me of the times I came home from college in the holidays and, looking down at the river, knew with gloomy certainty that I was home. Small town big time.

It is tidal, this stretch, where the Gipping runs into the Orwell estuary, and at low tide the mud banks used to be covered in swans. Despite that, the river always looked forlorn, like the town drain. It looked forlorn now, the banks concreted over, the swans gone. I put up my collar. It was November and getting murky, sodium lamps were coming on in the street giving the impression of a warehouse blaze in the distance. For a minute I lost my bearings, then, noticing Commercial Street, I turned into it out of curiosity to see if the tavern was still there.

I used to frequent the Commercial Tavern in my teenage years, usually in the company of Enterprising Bob who lived next door. It was a dingy pub then, a place for solitary drinkers who sloped in after work, dockers mostly, who would do you a deal on dodgy merchandise. The street was unrecognisable now, with a row of plastic-clad warehouses where the goods sidings used to be, and the timber yard replaced by a Macdonalds. The pub, however, clung to its ancestral spot, marooned in a sea of tarmac, looking meagre and self-conscious. It had been renamed the 'Tart and Vicar' or the 'Pig and Poker' or whatever bloody stupid name pubs have these days and it called itself a 'sports bar' with American pool and bar billiards. Only in Ipswich, I thought, would sports be so defined.

I went in for a pint, partly for old time's sake, and partly to kill time. I had a local paper I'd bought at the station and decided to comb the property section to see if I could possibly find somewhere to live. I'd just circled a Tudor farmhouse in the culture belt round Aldeburgh when someone approached my table.

'Well, you old *bugger*!'

I recognised the greeting even before I looked up.

'Hello Bob.'

To say that Bob Catchpole was my childhood friend is to misrepresent a complicated relationship. He was the alpha male in our little community of boys, and was by turns, hero, bully, rival. He wasn't daft, Bob; he was quite bright in a nousey Ipswich sort of way, but like the town, he was dull, sly, parochial and hopelessly unfashionable.

We shook hands, eyeing each other up, noting the relative state of our hairlines (his good, mine in retreat).

'Funeral?' he said, sitting down and nodding at my suit (charcoal grey, sombre tie).

'God no', I huffed. 'Just looking the old place up. Let me get you a pint.'

He winked. 'Got a complimentary one at the bar.'

He would have, I thought, as he strode off to get it. He was still wearing the same old donkey jacket but he had a jaunty, almost prosperous, look about him.

'How you doing then, Bob?'

'Oooh, tidy,' he said, sounding like his own dad. 'Can't complain.'

Last time I'd heard, Bob was selling packs of crinkle-cut chips to Post House hotels round the ring road.

'Still in the green grocery trade?' I enquired.

'Still got a hand in it,' he said. 'But Zintra runs that side of things now. I've moved into other areas.' He left a pause, expecting me to enquire about his business empire. I didn't oblige.

It was my mother who called him Enterprising Bob. My Dad, older and more cynical, used to call him 'that spiv'. He always had a scam going, even at school where he supplied doughnuts to the tuck shop from Yapp's bakery where he worked at weekends. I took a slug of my pint hoping the alcohol would inspire me to conversation. We tacked through ritual queries as to the health and welfare of wives and children. Then, on our second pint, we fell with more enthusiasm to football. This generated a little fug of warmth and fellow feeling. By our third pint we were swapping reminiscences about life in Coprolite Street.

It was a narrow street that sloped down to the docks, a stranded terrace of red brick houses crouching under the slab sides of warehouses and grain silos. Built, I suppose, for dock workers in the 19th century, it was named

259

after the flourishing trade in coprolite, identified then as fossilised dinosaur dung, and highly prized as a fertiliser. It turned out that the turd-shaped lumps dug up nearby, were naturally-occurring phosphates. Anyway, the stuff was ground up and shipped out from Ipswich.

My mother was born at number seventeen Coprolite Street and when she married, moved to number nineteen (the gypsy in her soul, she said). My grandparents lived at number twenty-seven, Bob and his family at number twenty-one (lucky for some, his dad inevitably said).

In a friendly haze of beer, Bob and I discussed our childhood exploits on The Barley, a strip of waste land behind the houses. In spite of its rural name it was a scrubby, cindery spot where boys mended their bikes and committed minor acts of arson, or later, had assignations with girls in the bomb shelter.

We were deep in conversation about the time we exploded a small cache of wartime ordinance when a tall woman with shoulder pads and clickety-click heels joined our table. She was wearing a lot of gold jewellery and looked like the manageress of a dress shop. In my beery state it took me a few seconds to recognise Bob's wife, Zintra. I stood up to do the metropolitan kiss-kiss thing when I remembered that this was Ipswich.

'Zintra!' I cried in alcoholic enthusiasm. 'You're looking great. Not a day older.'

'Older than what?' she said, sitting down.

This counted as a friendly Ipswich greeting and I went to get another round of drinks in. The last time I'd seen Bob and Zintra together was at their wedding, sometime in the seventies, Bob in pinstriped flares and a footballer's perm (his crinkle-cut, I called it) and Zintra in miles of satin and a hair-do you could break concrete on. The reception was held in a dismal church hall and her dad created a riot by getting rat-arsed and dancing on the tables. He was a Polish airman who had settled in Ipswich after the war. (It probably reminded him of Gadansk.) He kept the local green grocer's shop.

Weaving unsteadily back to our table, I tried my urban charm on Zintra.

'How's your old dad then? Still weighing spuds?'

'Dead,' she said. 'Two years ago.'

'Oh, I'm sorry to hear that. He was a good old boy.'

'He was eighty-five,' she said, as if the years conferred sainthood. I waited for Bob to say he'd had a good innings, and he obliged.

'So what's happened to the shop?'

'Rory, our eldest, took it over,' she said. 'He's got another shop out Foxhall way.'

'Quite a family business then. Are you still supplying the chips?'

From her pursed mouth I could tell this was the wrong question.

'We've moved on from that,' she said. 'We do all sorts of pre-packs now – julienne carrots, baby turnips, endive, that sort of thing. We supply hotels as far as Bury St Edmunds.'

'Well, well!' I cried. 'Vegetables never go out of fashion do they?'

'Did I tell you that Zintra's Dad bought The Barley?' said Bob. 'He used it as a market garden.'

I was genuinely surprised. The Barley was a casebook study in industrial blight. 'Christ, he must have got a good crop of nuts and bolts off that.'

Bob gave a loud guffaw. 'Coprolite, mate,' he said. 'Tons of the stuff. Spuds as big as yer head; marrows the size of bloody barrage balloons.'

We all laughed, even Zintra cracked her face a bit. I slapped Bob on the back. 'Talk about making the desert bloom.'

'Callum, our youngest, took it over when Dad died,' said Zintra, 'but he's got his own place at Bucklesham now. Five acres of glass. Organic.'

'So you're the green-grocery barons of Ipswich,' I said, raising my glass. 'I'll drink to that.'

'You gotta keep up,' said Bob complacently. 'Let me get you another pint.'

'Just a half,' I said, loosening my tie. 'I don't want to end up in the Gipping.'

'You been down the old street yet?' asked Zintra, with a knowing look.

'I haven't been down there since Mum died,' I said. 'I thought I'd take a look on my way up town.'

'We'll stroll over with you,' said Bob.

I felt a little light-headed when we finally got out of the pub, my good humour evaporating in the damp night air. We walked down to Stoke Bridge with Bob giving a running commentary on the townscape like a tour operator. There were clubs, a new cinema and a skateboard park by the river. My sense of dislocation was made worse by the drink. In the dark I could hear a faint tinkling sound.

'What's that noise?'

'Leisure craft in the marina,' said Bob. 'That's the spinnakers or whatever you call 'em.'

'Marina?' I peered into the dock. There was a flotilla of little boats bobbing in the water.

'The port's been moved down the river,' said Bob. 'The old dock basin's a marina now.'

I had a sudden feeling of outrage. This was *my* dock. This was where rust-bucket tankers tied up and shabby old blokes smoked Woodbines on the quay; it wasn't for fibre-glass gin palaces and prats in yachting caps.

*Landlines*

It was unnaturally quiet. Where were the Latvian sailors who used to be sick over our garden wall? Where were the blokes on bikes going to the night shift at Ransome's? Suspiciously, I walked along the colonnade under Read's warehouse. The smell of cattle feed had gone and there was no dusty trail of meal underfoot.

'Been a few changes lately,' said Bob, seeing my puzzled look.

We stopped in front of a warehouse that had been turned into a fish restaurant. My confusion deepened – fish and chips were what you ate in Ipswich, fried in lard. Zintra stopped to study the bill of fare and nodded approvingly. There was sea bass . . . monkfish . . . red snapper . . .

'We supply their fennel and herbs,' she said.

'What do they want with a fish restaurant here?' I cried.

'Same as they do anywhere else, I expect,' she answered smartly.

'But it's a dock!'

'Not any more,' said Bob. 'It's a waterfront amenity area.'

'Christ!'

Bob looked at me in grinning surprise. 'You hated it,' he said. 'Couldn't get away quick enough. Called it the arsehole of the Eastern Counties if I remember rightly.'

That had been some sort of joke about coprolite but I couldn't expect Bob to understand that. I struggled for words. 'Yes, but . . . but . . . it was *authentic*.'

They both laughed. 'If you mean it was dirty,' said Zintra, 'you'd be right.'

We walked on and I gave a sigh of relief when I saw that the old custom house was unchanged. But beyond it, looming upwards in the dark, was an unfamiliar outline. Where Coprolite Street should have opened on to the dockside, there was a block of flats in new red brick with tinted windows and jaunty little balconies. I gazed at it transfixed.

'Well?' Bob and Zintra were looking at me in triumphant expectancy.

'Where's the old street? Where's The Barley?'

'This is it,' said Bob, gesturing widely. 'Transformed!'

My sense of loss was so great, I could feel tears at the back of my eyes. Somewhere, dimly, I knew it was alcohol-induced nostalgia but I felt stricken with grief. Where was my childhood?

I half-heard Zintra telling me the details. 'Well, Dad bought The Barley, and then the houses one by one, till he'd got the whole row but the rents didn't amount to much so we got the tenants re-housed and knocked the old places down. They should have been condemned years ago.'

'Good parcel of land,' said Bob. 'Ripe for development. We had a bit of trouble getting the finance, mind. Had to fight off the big boys, but we made it in the end.'

'You built these?'

'Catchpole Quay,' said Bob, beaming with pride. 'Views down the river, jacuzzis, the lot.'

They were enjoying my open-mouthed amazement.

'We've got the penthouse flat, of course,' said Zintra. 'But we spend quite a bit of time in Florida these days.'

'Florida?' I said faintly.

'Time share,' said Bob. 'Wonderful golf.'

He was excited now and grabbing my arm, pointed across the dock.

'Remember the old maltings, down river? Big old place, empty for years?'

I nodded. As boys we had been responsible for smashing 90 per cent of the windows.

'It was very run-down,' said Bob. 'But with the profit I made on the flats, I bought the maltings and converted it to an office block. Lovely job. All cabled up for computers. Some London company's taking the lease; signing tomorrow.'

I nodded slowly, letting the information trickle through my nervous system till it hit full consciousness. Oh woe, cried something in my head; woe to the prodigal son who returns to a post-industrial commercial unit within easy reach of amenities.

'Well,' I said, trying to return his fat grin with a rictus of my own, and sifting my bankrupt brain for something to say. 'That's a turn-up for the books!'

They urged me in for a nightcap but I declined, saying I had to check into my hotel. We shook hands and they ambled off, but as I turned to go I was halted by a shout.

'By the way,' called Bob. 'I named the new offices Coprolite House, you know, for old time's sake.'

I waved. 'Very apt.'

The hangover had come on early. I leaned over the dock wall and looked down at the flotsam heaving gently on the tide. I felt slightly nauseous.

Welcome home, old son, I said to myself. Something tells me you're up shit street again.

* * * * *

263

# Arnulf and Esther

## RONALD BLYTHE

Returning from the shops, Frau Moser made her way to the town hall, there to take her ritual gaze at its statuary. Great men and women from the borough's history gesticulated with swords and crosses from a high Portland stone arcade; bishops, soldiers, a Romano-British princess, each figure fixed in a riot of carved foliage. There were *putti* and mottoes and all the orders of architecture twining about each other. Frau Moser loved this wildly civic building. It was the only thing in the otherwise intensely architecturally controlled little town which could remind her of Vienna. Which was odd because during all the years she and Arnulf had lived in that city they had never given its florid sculpture a second thought.

Thinking of Vienna – when did she not? – Frau Moser wondered for the thousandth time what it was which kept them from escaping until the eleventh hour? The Freuds and all their other friends had discreetly slipped abroad long since, quietly emptying the Berggasse. But she and Arnulf had waited until the waiting grew to be a grown-up version of the dangerous childhood game of last-across. Had they been brave or idiot? She tossed the question around in her head as she strode home, dodging phlegmatic women cowled in head-scarfs, groups of gunners from the barracks, sailors from the harbour and hordes of yelling boys and girls. It was Saturday morning. The Sabbath. These English, they were stolidly calm, just as the Germans were stolidly something else. How calm would they be when the latter arrived – as they must? What could stop them now that France had fallen? It was all a house of cards. Flattened; the Nazis would walk in. In which case, why had they – she and Arnulf – escaped? She could not be calm. Often she shook with terror. Certain 'incidents', as the newspapers called them, were starting to add up as they had done in Vienna less than a decade ago. Would they put off fleeing to America until the penultimate hour? What were they to do? Where were they to go, she and Arnulf? She

264

looked into the passing faces as if for answers. None was tremulous.

She could remember being quite amazingly calm in Vienna, even when she heard of the round-ups. Like the posturing town hall, she and Arnulf had let the strong and ornamental facade of their house on the Berggasse put on a brave front for them, and somehow it worked. Now and then from an upper window she had caught debating faces looking up. One grim day they discovered a well-drawn rat chalked on the fine front door, but there was never a brick through the glass, never entrance. It was uncanny. But she never shook and Arnulf most certainly did not. So why in England did she so shake into tears that passers-by would look away? And how, should they enquire, which they never did, could she explain? That she wept because they had escaped, yes, but into shabbiness. Shabbiness! They should think themselves lucky! Four young officers, swinging along in brand new uniforms, all shoulders-back and snowy grins, parted to let her through with elaborate good manners, and again she was back in the Berggasse house where thick curtains failed to block out bursts of marching feet. Once more she heard orders, laughter and a neighbour's cries. She and Arnulf had sat mute.

One day, just as they had finished breakfast, he had said, 'Listen to this,' and had read from an English poem:

> 'To throw away the key and walk away,
> Not abrupt exile, the neighbours asking why,
> But following a line with left and right,
> An altered gradient at another rate.'

She sat listening obediently, rather than attentively: he was working on his English.

'Well?'

Arnulf repeated the verse and would have done so yet again when the penny dropped.

'Oh, Arnulf – when?'

'Now. At once. Tomorrow.'

He then went to his consulting room as usual. Emerging after what seemed to her like a lifetime for dinner, he saw the modest case in which she had packed a few treasures, opened it and replaced them where they normally belonged.

'Not mother's silver clock!'

They ate their dinner in the family house in silence, hoping and praying that it would indeed be a Passover meal. Next day they left, Arnulf in his

265

open-necked Aertex shirt and herself in a Shantung dress and white cardigan – picnic garments. They did not, of course, throw away the key but placed it where anyone searching for them would expect to find it, in the Frau Doktor's handbag, along with just enough money for an excursion and her housekeeping cheque book. In every other respect they obeyed the English poem to the letter, walking away from the Berggasse to the Westbahn, and then along the everlasting Mariahilferstrasse to the railway station. This was uproarious with singing troops, banners, kit and girls. The small middle-aged woman smiled at them as she manoeuvred herself through their joyful confusion to the ticket office, whilst her tall thin husband hung on to the picnic basket. This contained, as well as cakes, sausages, coffee in a thermos flask and two novels, a Brownie camera and a towel, their passports and tickets to Berne. The tickets had arrived, miraculously, via New York, and the passports had but one more month's validity. Tickets, passports, Frau Moser had afterwards recalled, to seventeen Totman's Yard, their present 'temporary' yet inescapable address. It could have been Buchenwald, and she never forgot it. She asked God to make her thankful but for some reason He had not.

Totman's Yard was one of those packed Victorian courts reached by alleys which housed the labour force of dull towns. It was a tumble of blackened brick dwellings, shared lavatories and stand-pipes, and surprisingly private lives. A ghetto, thought Frau Moser the moment the Jewish Refugees' Association guided them into it.

'Not for long. Just for the time being. And such good sorts, such rough diamonds next door.'

Linen lines were hooked from a central mast to each cottage like a maypole. Dogs, cats and innumerable children perched on doorsteps. Seventeen contained four narrow rooms, a steep staircase, a porcelain sink, a copper, a gas-stove and, from behind, a view of a sluggish creek in which more boys and girls, and some gulls, shrieked. Across the Yard was a pub called The Volunteer, and a minute shop which sold sweets, paraffin, groceries, cigarettes, firewood and newspapers.

'Now, darling, remember what we agreed,' said Arnulf.

This was to make the best of things. Soon, any day now, he would be appointed chief consultant at one of the large mental institutions which were such a feature of this part of England. How could the untemperamental English go so mad? Psychoanalysis would let out their insanity. And he, Dr Arnulf Moser of the Berggasse, the student of

Sigmund Freud himself, would be offered the house which went with the appointment, a fine ugly red house with a huge garden in the grounds of the asylum. True, it would be a long way from Vienna, but it would also be far from Totman's Yard. Life, as he was beginning to see it, was a business of regulated escapes. One day, after the war, who knows, he might end where he began. Great cities, even when trammelled into slime and rubble by armies, like damaged woods greened again. His people would escape from their camps to cultivate them. History was, among many other things, a record of picking up the pieces.

Frau Moser's response to this cheeriness was a fleeting smile as her husband spoke, and a howl when he left her alone. He took evening walks by the harbour and she drew the black-out curtains and let herself go. She wept not for those losses which Arnulf never ceased to mourn – their paintings, books, jewels, clothes, the poor deserted cat Maxi – but for themselves in limbo. She was once weeping in what she knew to be a disgustingly uncontrolled way when accordion music broke in. Peeping through the net of an unlit bedroom, she saw a curious ballet-like scene. A young man was playing a glittering instrument, all filigree, pleats and mother-of-pearl, whilst women in pinafores and lads in braces waltzed. The scene was moonlit but aided by searchlights. For the first time Frau Moser wondered what would happen to such people when Hitler came. When Arnulf next left her alone her despair had vanished. She quite missed it, this long-permitted hollow into which she could void her unhappiness. The next-door woman noticed a difference in her.

'You're looking better, dear – more yourself.'

These crying fits over, Frau Moser took to observing her neighbours and accepting that they spied on her. The Yard was a bricked-in universe, mean yet vital, with its own pulse racing away day and night. Most of its inhabitants worked in the tent factory whose galvanised roof shone over it, although soon it would be camouflaged. Not that it mattered now, any more than the dragging of old farm vehicles across the country lanes to create barricades could matter. The Wehrmacht must flood through – what – who – could stop it? And immediately after that the processing camps would be set up, and through the mill she and Arnulf must go, whilst this working-class into whose crevice they had crept, pro tem, would be worked, worked, worked until they collapsed. Trained in such matters, she noted a lack of hysteria. Perhaps this foolish calm was epidemic, for Arnulf was behaving as though nothing worse than penury could happen, and spying out the land, as he called it. He made a list of all the hospitals, mental or otherwise, in the vicinity and chugged around in buses to see them. They were enormous, some an insane distance from their entrance gates and lost in foliage, all with chimney stacks which emitted a sickly plasma-like smoke which never quite got away, but hung around until the air absorbed it. Arnulf became his own inspectorate and jotted in his notebook, '500 beds (?), staff quarters, some kind of new recreational wing, therapy centre, close control; 1,000 beds (surely not, though probable), run-down; small, with patients in the garden; a workhouse,' and so on. The asylum at Hanger's Green could be progressive. Would Esther mind the Superintendent's Lodge? It was both heavy and poky. They could make a start here and then move on to London. One of these recces brought him to St Barbara's, a magnificent Victorian madhouse masquerading as an aristocratic country seat – coats of arms, heraldic flag and all. He looked up St Barbara in the public library; she was the patron saint of gunpowder. It was there that he wrote a brief letter requesting an interview, careful to add after his name just one of his many qualifications. Psychology was still a small world. One either knew everyone in it, or none.

This was the first of many such letters. Their courteously negative replies made Arnulf imperious, then touchy, then furious, then bewildered. These fellow professionals were masters of dismissal. One or two did welcome a chat over a cup of tea or glass of sherry 'when you are passing', but they knew how to show him out. What they could not say was that, for them, the glut of brilliantly qualified specialists from Germany and Austria was one of the problems of the war.

Thus two years passed. A Jewish Refugee Society paid the rent of ten shillings a week. Indeed, paid for everything. His inability to earn demoralised Arnulf. Nothing came in except the Society's monthly bare-bones cheque. Once, the Society forwarded a document on which he was to make a full inventory of all they had left behind – house, furniture, bank deposits, works of art, 'for future claims'. When he did so the figure became enormous. Who could take it seriously? Why oh why had they not sent money abroad – in 1935, say? People they knew had. Perhaps all those Streicher cartoons of the Jews as looters had had their effect. Why had they so carefully escaped – with nothing? Physician heal thyself, thought Arnulf, looking at the person he was then but finding no logic in what he did. Listing these lost possessions made Esther weep. During the two years she had managed to stow them away at the back of her mind, where they had started to become unmissed. Now here they were fully valuated and in full view – the watercolours, her mother's gilded bed, all the books and the beloved house itself with its stately run of steps up from the pavement and loud door-knocker.

'I know, I know, my darling.'

Arnulf cradled her head in his big hands.

'I have been trying to forget.'

'That is not a good thing to do. It is the Herr Doktor speaking.'

'You needn't worry; the town hall refuses to let me.'

'The *town hall*?'

'Yes, it reminds me of the Pestsaule.'

This was the famous Viennese plague pillar around which writhed carvings of everything from the Blessed Trinity down, and which was a kind of stone totem pole of the Christian imagination.

Arnulf said that he had scarcely glanced at the Pestsaule and had never noticed the town hall.

'Oh, come!'

His loftiness took her right back to their courting days when he was the highbrow student who affected never to have heard of some popular cult or other.

The inventory posted back to the Jewish Society, a line seemed to be drawn under the Berggasse, making it possible to take the narrowness of their present life more naturally, more for granted. The war went on and on, engulfingly so. It swallowed up the accordion player, who was never seen a gain. It left the Yard with old men and children, and young women running wild with Americans. They gave Esther the time of day, but nothing more. 'Mornin', Mrs Moser.' Arnulf they regarded suspiciously. At night they lay in bed listening to the crump and cough of anti-aircraft batteries, and staring up at the bumpy whitewashed ceiling, expecting it to fall. With little talk of Vienna and none of Jerusalem, they became like those animals which, during a hard winter, reduce all activity to the minimum. This inertia began to tell on Esther, this plus the Craven-A cigarettes which she endlessly smoked. For she acquired a sallow, pared-down look and an occasionally hectic eye. Arnulf began to look old.

This torpor evaporated quite suddenly. The woman who ran the Literary Institute called. There were several such clubs and societies in the town. They met in shabby none-too-warm rooms and fought each other for guest speakers. Some were political, others artistic. The Mosers had taken to sampling them, sitting at the back, often wanting to join in but aware of creating a tiny commotion when they did. Theirs was not so much an out of place accent as an out of place intelligence. They also sounded German. For the British this was a comical sound. Hitler, orating, brought the wrong kind of tears to their eyes. Thus, mouse-like at the rear of the monthly Literary Institute talks, it never crossed their minds that the chairman, this large woman with the 1920s shingle, knew exactly who Arnulf was. She advanced into the hallway with outstretched arms. She had never lost a speaker yet.

'Dr Moser! I have been meaning to call for ages. Mrs Moser!'

She had not; Ursula Bloom had let her down. Frantic, she had pawed through the membership file and there under 'interests' Dr Moser had written 'Goethe'. Would he, could he, speak on Goethe? The society had always *longed* to hear about Goethe.

Arnulf smiled. 'I will tell you about Hölderlin – how about that?

'Hölderlin . . .?'

'A great favourite of mine. I will talk about him. Translate some of him.'

At first Esther was delighted with this unexpected development, this coming back to life, but when Arnulf began to call his talk 'the Lecture', and had copies of his translations cyclostyled at the stationers so they could be handed out, and put all his honours and degrees on the poster, she became apprehensive. He was overreaching.

'Just talk, leibling, then read a few of the poems. That is all they expect.'

On the night, with the silver-black mop of hair greased to a shine and wearing a nice blue serge suit which cost fifteen shillings second-hand, and with his gold spectacles glittering, Arnulf was introduced as 'a most distinguished guest among us'. It was four years since he had last lectured. There was a full turn-out and he told the listening rows about the poet who had walked away, and about Hölderlin's madness which wasn't madness, and he should know, being a friend of Sigmund Freud. And he read from the *Diotime* verses so beautifully that Esther heard once more the dark boy sprawling on the Stadtpark grass, his head in her lap. He was right, she corrected herself, to turn this evening into a statement of who he was and what he was, and she felt proud of him.

Afterwards, there was the usual crowd around the tea-urn. A lot of elderly men and women who lived in Library books, youthful soldiers and sailors with Penguins jutting from their gasmask packs, grammar-schoolboys, aged clergymen, would-be writers, maidenly creatures with Proust in their handbags. And Mrs Seabrook. She was an occasional attendee but a notable one, with her piled yellow hair, fresh cotton dresses and diamond regimental brooch, her low rich voice and her breeding. For what else could one call it? Arnulf had seen her before, but she was seeing him for the first time. She was in her way a seer, shifting from vision to vision, discarding the last to take up the next. At the moment by the tea-urn her sights were not on Hölderlin but psychoanalysis. The medical qualifications after Arnulf's name on the programme, and his references to Freud and Jung, spread infinite prospects before her. As well as a seer, Pauline Seabrook was a disciple, a born follower to date of Mrs Baker Eddy, Krishnamurti, Major Douglas, Prunella Stack, Emile Coué ('Every day, in every way, I'm getting better and better') and Oswald Mosley. Her feeling for poetry was less peripatetic. She had listened with tears to Arnulf reading Holderlin. It was a virtue in her to give herself utterly to language. But when Hölderlin ended and reminiscences of Vienna began, Mrs Seabrook was once more on her way to a new master. (A new craze, her husband Colonel Seabrook called it.)

And so it was, a week later, and a heatwave at its height, that Arnulf once more caught a village bus from the town, one which bounced and rocked past St Barbara's Asylum into the deep and, for him, still unexplored countryside. This had little appeal for either him or Esther. They liked streets and parks. Beyond these they were both lost. Mrs Seabrook had sent him a pencilled map and the conductress assured him that he would be put down at the right spot. The summer hedges grew richer, denser, the tar bubbled under the tyres. There was a smell like hot sweet socks. Wearing the blue serge suit – it was a consultation – Arnulf felt faintly sick. The bus was like an oven. The conductress sang, 'I'll be seeing you'. So did the driver.

'In the ordinary way, dear Dr Moser, we would of course have fetched you, but the petrol ration, you know. However, there are compensations. You will adore the walk from the windmill where the bus will drop you. A fair old way, as they say in our part of the world, but a lovely, lovely way. I can't tell you how I envy those who walk that footpath for the first time! And then, at the end of it, a good English luncheon. I hope you have a good appetite to match.'

He refolded the letter. Before sending him these instructions she had encountered both Arnulf and Esther in the local Food office with the 'need to talk' written all over her. They scanned her face and in their emotional un-English way showed open solicitude. Esther laid a hand on Mrs Seabrook's brown arm.

'Oh, not me – my husband. But this is neither the place nor the time to bother you with my troubles. So unethical, please forgive me.'

271

Arnulf took the bull by the horns.

'You wish to consult me professionally?'

'My husband, the Colonel, should – must.'

'Do you understand what it would entail?'

Thinking he meant the fee, she said, 'Yes, yes, of course.'

Arnulf paused. She looked anxious. Then he agreed. A consultation. Esther drew back to study a poster about ration books. Mrs Seabrook was giving the address, ominously adding, 'And give yourself plenty of time.' Arnulf was contrasting the muted contralto of her voice with her fingers, which looked as if they did nothing but dig in the earth. She curled them up protectively when she noticed him staring. There was a wedding, an engagement and a signet ring, locked together on one finger.

On the way home Esther said, 'It is her who needs analysis.'

'Not, now, leibchen!'

The windmill stop proved to be ten miles from the town and the footpath to the farm a mile and a half of sagging, tangling undergrowth. No one had walked it for months. Bean scent made him sneeze. Arnulf was not made for this kind of opulence and plunged along like a swimmer in uncongenial waters, pressing his way through, looking ahead for land. The Seabrooks' farm came into view only when he was on top of it. There it lay, as it had done for centuries, in all its determined obscurity. He saw Mrs Seabrook waving and calling 'Cooeee . . .' He stumbled through the last of the corn and weeds to an untended lawn, sticky, spattered with pollen, clasping his cheap new briefcase and thunderingly angry. Put out. She stopped laughing and said, quietly in the low-register voice, 'Dear Dr Moser, you found us.'

She wore the blue cotton dress of the Hölderlin lecture but minus the regimental brooch. Her feet and legs were bare and scratched, her marvellous hair heaped high on a comb.

'What a scorcher! Real summer at last!'

She took him to a corner of the stackyard where a huge tablecloth was spread on the ground. Such piles of plates, cutlery, glasses – who else could be coming? Arnulf felt sweat trickling down his back and from under the tight trouser-band round his belly. He also felt disgusting. The tablecloth was spread in the full sun. Dogs had to be shooed away from it. There were far cries from a tennis court, maybe. Every now and then Spitfires and other planes took off from an airfield which could not be more than a few yards away, or so it felt. They made surprisingly little noise but cast black crosses on the burnt landscape. There was an uproar of larks. Mrs Seabrook took Arnulf's case and put it out of the sun, smoothing it as though it was of great value.

'First you deserve a drink. Second, we're going to have a lovely, lovely afternoon.'

She brought him beer in a tankard.

'Our own brew.'

No longer nauseous from the journey but foolishly uncomfortable in the suit, Arnulf's lips touched the chilly pewter with relief. He ached to sit but there were no chairs. Most of all he longed to be in a big cool room with shuttered windows, a room like his consulting room on the Berggasse, with its marble Persephone and glass-fronted bookcases and parquet floor. Its serenity surged through him. 'To throw away the key and walk away . . . '

'And what happened to the Mosers?' the prisoners at Auschwitz would ask in a whisper. '*They escaped.*'

A fragment of a psalm which had lodged, forgotten, amidst the lumber which he called the subconscious, rushed to the forefront of his mind, poignant, ravishing.

'Let the sighing of the prisoner come
before thee, according to the greatness
of thy power preserve those that are
appointed to die . . .'

'Make yourself comfortable, Dr Moser,' Mrs Seabrook was calling from the kitchen window. 'No standing on ceremony here!' She laughed, revealing well-shaped discoloured teeth. But when she saw him dabbing his forehead, she ran out to hurry him to a cloakroom. He washed and felt better. Now he must confront her with the purpose of his visit. The consultation. After they had eaten, naturally. When he mentioned it, he was surprised to see her momentarily put out. She brushed goosegrass from her skirt with slow considering movements to gain time.

'Now let me see . . . your bus goes at five. Hurrah! that means we have the whole afternoon. Goody, goody. And we'll certainly find a way to run you back to the windmill stop. We should be able to manage that! The war, what a damned nuisance!'

She carried food out, food such as Arnulf had not seen for years – fruit, salad, chicken, rice, home-made bread, masses of vegetables, all piled in old china and scrubbed wooden bowls. Seeing Arnulf's expression, she said, 'We're not going to let that Mr Schicklegruber get us down, are we!'

She rang a big brass handbell and instantly three children raced from the orchard, two boys and a girl. He guessed them to be somewhere between twelve and sixteen. They were naked.

'Put something on for lunch, darlings.'

They returned in khaki shorts.

'Edward, Eric, Pamela, say how do you do to Dr Moser.'

Their flawless naturist bodies spoke to him, not only of their mother's sun-worship phase, but of the singing phalanxes of Hitler Youth winding through the Austrian hills. Now that the layers of Mrs Seabrook's enthusiasms were coming into view, Arnulf's analyst's mind began to tick. But his haunches protested. He rolled from one to the other, sitting on the ground as long as he could. Then he stood – 'I'm afraid I'm not built for this!' Edward rushed to fetch a chair and returned with his father.

'My husband, Colonel Seabrook. Geoffrey, this is Dr Moser.'

Arnulf gripped the hand of a dying man of eighty or more, a man of great height and reduced flesh. He wore cricket whites and plimsolls. Where the shirt gaped, tufts of hair fluttered on the parchment skin like thistledown. A lifetime's engaging grin had set into its final rictus. All three children were strikingly like him and not at all like their mother. Each was his young self, Pamela too in a sense. He tucked into the food with appetite. It was 'Pass this and pass that' and, when the girl rose to wind her arms round his neck and rock him to and fro, 'Am I to suffer indigestion as well as – '

'Shush, Geoffrey.'

'It can hardly be a secret,' grinned the Colonel.

A month, thought Arnulf. A month, no more. So, married to someone very nearly twice her age, a progressive thinker – a charitable assessment – still very handsome, an artist, a sucker for false prophets, a good mother, a poor farmer, and currently, like half the females who sought 'help' on the Berggasse, entranced by Sigmund and his heirs. Arnulf recognised all the symptoms, and he remembered the old advice, which, boiled down, was, 'Get yourself a job'. However, there might well be a need for some medical help after the funeral. He found himself grieving for the lovely children who were about as deathless a group as could be imagined, and who were so untouched by corruption. Corruption, elegant in flannels, was holding out his glass for wine, more wine. Something else occurred to Arnulf. Had a new widow in her grief come to him in Vienna, would he not have listened? Of course he would. So why feel this guilt about accepting Mrs Seabrook as a patient? Hölderlin had brought her to him. Others would follow. He and Esther were at last taking the first steps away from the route which led to Totman's Yard. The war itself would end.

Luncheon over, he was shown the farmhouse. There were pots of wild flowers, oil lamps, billowing curtains, sleeping cats, fat chintzy chairs and scattered books. Mrs Seabrook was as good as her word. Guiding Arnulf to a nook with wing-chairs and port, she said, 'Now to business,' and disappeared. Her husband emerged from the shadows, held up the decanter and looked pleased.

'We are honoured. We don't get this every day.'

When Arnulf suggested that it might be rather chilly sitting inside after the garden – he meant for his host – Colonel Seabrook replied, 'Not nearly as cold as I am going to be before the summer is out.'

There was a vast silence. Arnulf became professional.

'What kind of treatment are you having?'

'Quinine and the Sacraments.'

Tennis shrieks and some lowing as milking time drew near. 'I am a very old-fashioned sort of chap, Dr – Moser, was it? – and he told Arnulf all about his cancer, which didn't hurt, or hurt much, and how, because there was so little of him left, there was little left to die. 'But my wife is taking it badly.'

'Forgive me, but I sense she is taking it very well. She is strong and she has the family.'

It was the hour for platitudes.

The Colonel was greatly amused. His jaw-crack of a smile widened wickedly.

'You don't know her – how could you? I will tell you something. It is my wife who is putting off my death, not me. That is why you are here, to make me put up a fight. She tells me you are a famous chap in your way, knew Freud and all that kind of thing. But dear, dear old chap, what *can* you do? I am eighty-seven. Married late, had the children at the last minute – good-looking bunch, don't you think? – and I am still being adored. My wife is a very enthusiastic girl – you'll find out. Enthusiastic about everything. Taking this up, that up. Never a dull moment. Never ill herself. Had those babies – well you can see there couldn't have been many complications. Runs this farm, even does some of the ploughing. I'm not much help these days. Very gone on me still. Lucky old Geoff, that's me. And very lucky at the end. You can't wait, you know. You will see when your time comes. She'll have this place, my reduced pension, and the children. There's nothing in the bank. What else can I tell you?'

Mrs Seabrook was sitting in full sun picking over some soft fruit when Arnulf rejoined her. She thought he had returned to bring her into the consultation and looked disconcerted when he told her that her husband was asleep. Also, that there was no consultation. Just a talk.

'But you've got to help him. I brought you here especially to get all this death stuff out of his head. You saw him. He eats well. He's full of life. It's the rector, putting ideas into his head.'

Arnulf crouched by her side and took her hand, forcing her eyes to hold his. 'It is cancer of the liver, the quickest kind – you know it is, don't you? Did you think that analysis would divert it for a year or so? Well, it might – until the winter. And then at the same time it is not 'cancer' but perfectly natural death, which he welcomes. He has told you that soon you can only possess him in your children. In that boy who is him all over again. That's what he said I have to tell you.'

Mrs Seabrook was neither comforted nor made reasonable by Arnulf's language because it was so antiquated. To have a distinguished psychologist in the house and have to listen to the kind of things which old Dr Bull down the road would have said had she let him! Nor did she like the perspiring Dr Moser touching her. She stood up, towering over him, and reminded him that she had *engaged* him to attend her husband in his capacity as a psychologist and that he had agreed to do so. She could show him his letter.

They quarrelled on in the hot afternoon. The young people played invisibly, their shouts flying over the hedge. Arnulf's long-disappeared professional interest had leaped back to protect him from what this powerful woman was saying, which at times was pretty dreadful. The adrenaline which had made him such a consummate listener in Vienna coursed through him. The more Mrs Seabrook abused him – rather as though he was a grocer who had delivered the wrong order, he thought – the more he heard. Trained and attuned, correctly readjusted by her revealing tirade, his ear picked up the good and the bad in her. The anti-semitism and parlour fascism, the longing in her to recreate an earthly paradise in which the body became spirit. He heard with this restored ear for such unsaid revelations, how she had had to marry a military hero and at the same time turn her back on the war. Her inconsistencies and her restless search all the time for something 'different' and 'better' would have in other circumstances made him like her, but liking or hating could have no role to play now. He was Sigmund's heir and an unrestricted channel for behaviour and outpourings. To put it in a nutshell, as these English said, it was Mrs Seabrook, of all people, who had unblocked the vacuous silence which had settled on him as part of the price for being a refugee, and who alone was responsible for letting the old fascination with everything 'human' race through him. A woman like her! A common casebook type! A woman who, once the first protective veil of manners fell in the first rage, had no other veils to hide her. What was making her so angry with him? It was his refusal to talk her husband back into the sun, if only for a year or two. To persuade him to postpone his heaven. Well, no one did this in the consulting rooms of the Berggasse. He eventually soothed her down by not putting up a fight. She apologised, wept. The young people reappeared, saw that this was no place for them, and slipped from sight. Arnulf saw the future – a start!

She went to make tea. He discovered a Houseman among her telltale books – *Mein Kampf,* Mrs Baker Eddy, *Pelmanism, Moral Rearmament, Naturism, Married Love* – and read:

> From the wash the laundress sends
> My collars home with ravelled ends;
> I must fit, now these are frayed,
> My neck with new ones London-made.
>
> Homespun collars, homespun hearts,
> Wear to rags in foreign parts.

She did not run him to the bus-stop as she promised. Instead she walked with him all the way, talking wildly but no longer accusingly. Now and then she would hold back briers with her brown grubby hands to let him pass. Waiting by the windmill, she said, 'I have talked too much. I haven't let you say a word. How did you escape?'

'I won't know until I've written up my notes,' he told her.

\* \* \* \* \*

**Bernardine Coverley** was born and brought up in London where she lived for many years before recently moving to Suffolk. She has has written features for national newspapers and magazines and runs creative writing sessions for MIND.

# Cyd's Place

## BERNARDINE COVERLEY

'Jesus, Jesus! wake up, you sloth.' God's voice reverberated through the Church of the Holy Thorn. Don't you know it's time to descend again, make your annual appearance to the massed crowds.'

His son's head moved, he groaned and his eyelids lifted. 'You don't have to shout, this isn't a mountain top. And there aren't any crowds.' Jesus inhaled the stale air, 'breathe in, hold, breathe out,' he told himself and after a few of these the arteries opened up and circulation started up. His skull prickled as oxygen reached the brain. It was painful, why couldn't God just let him stay here. A few drops of still thick blood dropped to the floor. He flexed fingers and prised his hands free from the nails.

'So where am I booked in this year? or has it got to be a 'miraculous appearance?' I hate those people, slobbering over my feet, touching the hem of my garment. It's a wonder I've any garment left and the number of miraculuous shreds of cloth in the world could make me a nice warm cloak like the sort Roman soldiers had. Can't you call in all the bits? Pretend it's the last day or something.'

'Stop whining, son, or I'll see you get another whipping.'

Jesus stepped down and rubbed his numb calf muscles, then opened the cupboard under the altar shrine. The communion bottle was nearly full, he raised it to his lips. The wine completed his recovery and brought a flush to his cheeks.

'Hurry, son, the girl is arrivng, I can hear her. She's asked for you to open the cafe for the homeless in Leiston High Street. Cyd's Place it's called. Don't let me down. Do a good job.'

Mags pushed the church door and walked down the aisle. For once, her hopes were fulfilled; there he was tall, with dreadlocks like hers, and dressed all in white, Indian style, a proper guru. He looked lovely, radiant, that was the word, the dust dancing around him in the sunlight from the chantry window.

'You did come when I called.' She breathed and reached out but dare not touch him, still afraid to believe. They stared at each other.

He saw the vague eyes, and the long shapeless garments that looked as though they needed a good tubbing. She caught the musty smell as he moved towards her. 'Let us go out into the world, sister,' and he put a hand on her shoulder. Mags smiled, fresh air, he must crave fresh air. It was just how she had imagined it, and the opening wasn't until 2 o'clock. He would be hungry, she would take him back to the hostel, smuggle him in and then they would break bread together and she had theived some figs from the Kurdish deli. The others would be impressed, they never believed her, said she was raving again but now it would be different. Respect, they'd give respect. Outside she saw how he hesitated. He isn't used to cars and noise she decided and when there was a gap in the traffic, she stepped out and waved him across, saw how he stretched out a hand, a sort of blessing. Yes, he was the Man, no problem. The girl led him through Valley Road and into the yard of the old foundry, now converted into a hostel. 'We'll go in the back, we're not supposed to have visitors.' And she slipped the catch of a window and opened it, beckoning to Jesus to climb in. He lifted his shirt and swung his legs over, Mags couldn't help noticing that he wasn't any different from ordinary men, but of course, he hadn't ever taken advantage of his female fans as far as she knew. Those that wrote down the Bible wouldn't put that in though, would they. I'm doubting again, she told herself, bad girl, she should be ashamed, and she dug her nails into the backs of her hands until she felt pain.

Jesus was waiting and she felt the glow again, it was like being under a sun lamp in his presence. Mags smiled at him, and ran up the stairs and threw open the door of her room. The bed was made, the cover neat, a daffodil brightened the table where she had put sesame bread, figs and a jug of water. She watched his face as he took in the setting, he looked pleased and she breathed again. Jesus sat on the bed and Mags settled herself on a floor cushion. 'Are you hungry? It's all fresh, I got it this morning.' Jesus tucked his feet up under his robe and tore the bread into into pieces eating like a man deprived of food for days. Which he was, of course thought Mags. You didn't think about food or need to eat when you were in the tomb or on the cross. When she was in one of her moods, she didn't think about food either. She rose above fleshly things, felt as if she was floating, levitating, like those holy pictures of saints. But Jesus needed a good meal before the opening and he'd want a wash and brush up.

'What shall I call you? I mean it's weird calling you Jesus, it feels blasphemous somehow, although I know in some countries it's a common name. You understand.' He leant back against the pillow, 'How about Jeez, or Jezza? That sounds good, Jezza. Yes, I like it. I baptise myself Jezza,' and he took out a bottle from a fold of cloth and half filled the two glasses.

'Let's drink to it, it's good for you homemade wine, bring some colour to those cheeks.' She took the glass and held it to her chest. Jezza raised his for a moment, and then drowned it in one go. Mags sipped. And he passed her the last piece of bread.

'Now what is it you want me to do exactly?' he asked twiddling his beard. He did look as if he'd been through the wars, Mags thought. The hand on the beard was scored and pitted with scars, she wanted to stroke it, smooth out the tightened tendons, wash his hands with the tears of joy that spilled on to her cheeks. He was here, her lord had come to her. He wasn't scornful of her offering, of a homeless girl that even the other hostel users jeered at. He was looking at her now, so patient.

'You've been very kind to me, I don't know your name.'

'Mary Mags, but everyone calls me Mags.'

'Mags,' he said, 'I think I'll call you Mary. Sounds better if you're going to be my helper at this event.'

The unaccustomed nourishment gave her a little rush of energy and she found she was enjoying telling Jezza about Cyd's Place and how it would help people to get their lives back, to believe in themselves again. 'It means Can You Do It, Cyd's Place, clever really. What do you think?'

'Well, can you, you know, do it?' he asked, those eyes, two blue sparks looking right into her. She held her breathe, her? she'd heard the big talk and thought for her it would be a warm place with cheap tea and people trying to make her learn about computers. Jezza brushed the crumbs from his lap and asked for the toilet. She jumped up and showed him the shower as well. 'Here, I've been saving it. We all got a present at Christmas.' And he took the fluffy white towel still folded and tied with ribbon.

'Isn't that lovely, thank you, sister.' She lowered her head and moved a step back, not wanting to shut the door, not wanting anything to keep him from her. But she better get ready too. She didn't want to disappoint him. His helper.

The mirror had gone; she didn't like mirrors, she was superstitious about mirrors, you could see things in them that weren't supposed to be there, shadows or things from bad dreams. They had tried to get out, to hurt her and she had cut her hands and her arms fighting them off. Ginny had a mirror in her room. Mags was frightened to look but it wasn't so bad. She moved closer, stroked the cheek reflected there, Jesus loves you, girl' she murmured.

Jezza wouldn't let her hang behind, 'Walk with me Mary, show me the way,' and her heart knocked against the stick ribs as she took the hand he held out. The woman in the newsagent's took a second look. 'There's that beggar girl takes them round the back of the White Hart on Saturdays. And who's he, he's a new one,' and she forgot to count her change. 'What's she on now. A ribbon in her hair and she's washed her face. Must be love,' and she and her customer laughed and went to the door to stare after them.

Cyd's Place was full. Most of the hostel occupants were there; the outreach workers looking as if they'd built it themselves, the skinny manager from Dixon's who had sponsored a PC talking to a couple of councillors from Suffolk District, and David, the vicar from the Church of the Holy Thorn in his favourite Hawaiian shirt and baseball cap back to front. The urn was boiling and plates of biscuits wer disappearing already. An aroma of roll ups pervaded the room and an atmosphere that could just about be termed excitement churned the smoke and steam of Cyd's Place Open Day.

Jezza and Mary paused at the entrance stunned at what they had let themselves in for. She turned in terror but Jezza gripped her and she remembered, she was his helper. Remembered all those lorry drivers cafes with the jukebox singing, Don't let me down. and Mary Mags stepped forward. 'Welcome, Jezza !' and she clapped as loud as she could, raising her hands above her head like the dancers on Top of the Pops. And they all fell silent and looked, not friendly those faces. Jezza was clearly the class of person Cyd's Place was designed to attract, a down and out, a rootless hippie sort. The blokes saw a rival, an outsider they'd have to put in his place, and the girls saw that slag Mags had attached herself like a leech already. Jezza stood there like in one of those cowboy films, tall, weathered, untamed, the blue eyes holding the crowd, He smiled and lifted a hand in acknowledgement. 'Blessings, friends.'

David was thrilled. He was sure he'd seen him before, so masterful, that posture and the tunic and sarong outfit; wonderful. The project workers added anotherr digit to their reportback on user numbers. Councillor Peters thought, better in here than out on the streets, a fiver he carried a knife.

'He's here, I told you he would be, but you doubted me,' and Mary Mags pushed a path through to the table set up with microphone and ribbon, took his hand again and placed him there before them all. Jezza looked at the faces around him, resentful faces, waiting for the wrong move and heard a voice whisper, 'Come on then, do the business, we want our free sandwiches.'

He grasped the microphone and surprised himself.

'So Can You Do It? Have you - and he pointed - got what it takes? Are you up for the big test? And I'm not talking about computer courses now, or are you feeble, will you turn away and stay in the alleyways of life? I am the message, I bring you true understanding, tread in my path and you will know how to live.'

There were a few cheeky remarks but the faces had changed, confusion replaced suspicion and one or two seemed to like it, a few whoops and claps concluded the ceremony. The vicar broke out into All you Need is Love, Jezza snipped the ribbon and the homeless fell upon the sandwiches as the project workers carried them through from the kitchen. 'I thought the mayor was . . . ' but Councillor Peters was swept aside. After a while clusters of men moved outside and hung around Little Adam. This one had been banned from attending Cyd's Place Open Day, was on remand for aggressive begging outside the church.

'Go on, see what he's got to offer, bet he's hiding something under that skirt.'

No one crossed Little Adam and gradually the homeless streamed back inside demanding more tea and jostling Jezza and Mary Mags so there was no escaping 'There's a bottle in there, I felt it. Come on fair shares, mate. We're all on the street.' Jezza held up his hands, 'OK, be patient. Bring water and you shall each have a taste.' and one brought over a jug of water and another placed the paper cups on trays and they crowded around him watching. The project workers were at the back of the room occupied with the councillors, happy that Cyd's Place was full, their worth proven. Jezza slipped a bottle from under his tunic and added a shot to each cup of clear water. They surged forward doubting, the water looked the same, someone raised a cup and tasted, he smiled and they cheered and grabbed one for themselves. They drank and asked for more, Mary Mags knew them too well and pulled at Jezza.

'Come away, they'll eat you. Come away, they'll be under the tables soon enough.' She pulled Jezza through to the door as the others reached for leftover cups and hastened him down the street. He put an arm round her shoulders.

'Mags, Mags, skinny slag, old bag,' they shouted as they burst from the doorway. Jezza looked back. There were a lot of them. Jezza and Mags ran round the corner. Mags stopped, lungs pumping, thin body trembling. Jezza wiped her face with the tail of his tunic pushing her head back to check her colour. 'Come on sister, don't give up. Trust in me. I am your friend, remember.' She could here the murmur of his voice, it was soft and warm and far away, a summer cloud of a voice filled with light. She had enough strenght to lift a hand to point. Jezza looked and saw the church down the road. Mags pushed at him. Jezza kissed her forehead and walked forward.

The running feet and shouts turned the corner, a howl went up. 'Get him.' A can flew by and a stain appeared on Jezza's white shoulder. The chunk of brick made him stumble and trip on the pavement edge even as he reached the Church and then Mags couldn't see any more as a pack of anoraks and straggly locks poured past her. She slid down and folded her arms over her head, 'God, please God, oh God.' Why did He let this happen, and she had tried to be so obedient, had listened to his will, had believed herself rewarded.

Did the vicar hear her beseeching or the noise of those he liked to regard as his special mission. Whatever, he had returned early to his parish house to set out the drinks for a post-opening celebration and now he looked out of the window and saw the crowd brawling in front of his church. An opportunity and he leapt at it.

'Stop, stop this disgraceful behaviour,' he shouted running between the sweating Jezza and his persecutors who stopped, deflected from their intention to beat the shit out of this poncy interloper by the little round figure of the Rev. David.

'If you want to be treated as valuable human beings then you must do the same for others less fortunate. Isn't that what Cyd's Place is about. Isn't that the message of our friend here,' and David turned to lift up the fallen hero. They all turned, the church forecourt was empty. A few passers by stood watching from the other side of the street waiting for a bit more action. The homeless felt embarrassed and then they scattered, that stuff had given them a headache anyway. David stood watching them go, just a bit disappointed. In theory he should have got them into the church and prayed with them. Still, he had prevented a sin, that was something. And he was looking forward to the visitors. They all deserved a pleasant evening of self congratulations. The girl was still there, squatting by the wall.

Inside the Church of the Holy Thorn, Jezza scooped water from the holy water stoop and drank and drank and washed the dust from his face. Close, he thought, thank God for the vicar fella. What a knackering day. He took David's surplice from a hook behind the vestry door, wiped his face on the sleeve and wrapped himself in its pleated folds. He stretched out on a bench, a kneeler under his head and slept the sleep of the dead.

David found it next morning, smeared with bloodstains, ripped, ruined. It was under the girl's head. He stared at her. Didn't he lock the door? She sat on a kneeler, her head leaning on the bench, clutching the surplice like a child with a security blanket. He waited, it was still, quiet, the cars outside slowing for the speed bumps might as well be miles away, here was peace. Why did it feel so much more spiritual, God's presence strong, without the congregation? Mags sat up and smiled.

'Did you sleep here all night?' He tried to sound concerned not critical, but he couldn't think of anything else to say.

'I didn't mean to but I slept really well. My prayers were answered,' she said. Folding the surplice and tucking it under her arm, she went out.

David saw her later, through the window of the new cafe, serving soup and teas; her apron said 'I Can.'

\* \* \* \* \*